PERSUASION OF DECEIT

ANTONIA KANE

For Sean, Asher, Jace, and James.
I love you bunches and oodles.

Pronunciation Guide

Archie - Ar-chee
Aster - As-ter
Chemari - Khem-ar-ee
Cora - Kor-uh
Dangiar - Dahn-jeer
Elarys - El-ar-us
Esrae - Ez-ray
Falstead - Fall-sted
Gio - Gee-o
Holden - Hol-dun
Jakanter - Jah-kan-ter
Kanan - Kay-nen
Kancar - Kan-car
Laurise DeKent - Luh-rees Duh-kent
Logan - Lo-gen
Luc - Luke
Maci - May-cee
Madeirah - Muh-deer-uh
Malakai - Mal-uh-ky
Mhanjar - Mon-zhar
Raven - Ray-ven
Sebastian - Se-bas-chun
Shanterac - Shon-ter-ahk
Shara - Shar-uh
Theodora - Theo-dor-uh
Torren - Tore-en

SHANTERAC
LANGRIDGE
SERENTES
CASOPRAN
KANKADRE
JAASE
VESIMAR
DANGIAR

GARASHAN
ARMAT
HUNTRIDGE
CHEMARI
JAKANTER DORONALL
RENOE
WHITEHALL
LYNMAR
CAROBA
KANGAR

PERSUASION OF DECEIT

ANTONIA KANE

PROLOGUE

There were only three short steps to the throne. He took them slowly, savoring the moment.

Blood dripped from the tip of his sword onto the marble floor, marking the trail of his ascension. He noticed, and his mouth quirked up at the edge, nearly imperceptibly.

Malakai turned, focusing his dark gaze on the bowed form of the man before him, the crown still sitting on his head, before he lifted his eyes and took in the opulent room. Deep green tapestries lined with gold thread hung on dark stone walls, torch light flickering off every surface. More men filled the space, bowing behind their disgraced king. Malakai's own soldiers made up the rest of the crowd standing, swords drawn, around the edges of the room. His gaze came to rest on his general and the man who stood beside him, and Malakai offered them a small nod of acknowledgment, which they returned.

Focusing his gaze back on the king at his feet, Malakai finally spoke. "Look what you've come to. You must have known you couldn't stand against me. After what you've done, how you rule. You must have known we would end up here."

The King lifted his head to meet Malakai's gaze. His face showed the signs of battle, cracked lips, a black eye swollen shut, a seeping gash across his cheek, but he did not cower. In fact, something like a smirk played on his broken face. "You will not remain in control. The people will not follow a monster."

Malakai's eyes widened slightly in amusement at the word *monster*. "I'm the monster? After all you've done? Slaves, torture... I've seen people after you were finished with them. I am not the monster here."

The King ignored him and spit a mouthful of blood on the floor at Malakai's feet, his green eyes flashing. "Enjoy your victory now. It will not last."

Malakai considered the man for a moment before stepping down in front of him. He bent over so that he could speak quietly into his ear. "You say they won't follow me? Who else will they follow?"

Before the King could answer, Malakai lifted the dripping sword, bringing it around in an arc. The motion was fast, the blade only a blur as it descended upon the neck of the conquered King.

ONE

"He smells like fish."

Esrae laughed, dropping her forehead onto the back of her hands where they rested on the wooden counter, her long golden curls creating a curtain as they fell around her. She looked back up at Raven, grinning. "He's a fisherman, and that was *one* time! He doesn't always smell like fish."

"Did he bring you flowers or just a bouquet of worms?" Raven teased, surprised by her friend's admission.

"Raven!" Esrae chided, though she was still smiling. "Alright, I'll admit Nevin can be a little ridiculous, but it's not like I have a Kanan." She punctuated her words with a small roll of her eyes.

Raven flashed her an exaggeratedly sweet smile, batting her lashes dreamily. She was definitely the only one with a Kanan.

"He's nice to me." Esrae shrugged, looking away as she picked at something invisible on her apron. "It was only dinner. I was just getting away for a little while. Honestly, I probably won't see him again."

"Because he smelled like fish?" Raven prodded, continuing her teasing.

Esrae opened her mouth to speak but whatever she was going to say died on her lips as the front door of the bakery crashed open, nearly ripping the tiny bell above the door from its perch. Raven and Esrae spun toward the sound, eyes wide, smiles gone.

Two of the King's guards stepped inside, their presence making the space feel very small. They were clad in black with the familiar maroon sash across their chests and large intimidating swords hanging at their hips.

The shorter of the two men spoke, his voice so rough he sounded like he had rocks for breakfast. "Good day, ladies. We're looking for Laurise DeKent. Do you know her? Have you seen her?"

Raven did know Laurise. She and her family lived in Chemari. She often took her three small children to splash at the edge of the Dangiar river that snaked its way along the outer edges of their small town. When she saw them, Raven always stopped to say hello. Laurise was kind, outgoing, and funny, and her children were happy and animated. The baby she kept close by her side smiled and cooed when Raven played with him.

"No, sir." Esrae'svoice was barely there, her eyes toward the floor. "She hasn't been in."

The men dipped their heads and turned to leave, but before she could stop herself, Raven called out to them. "What has she done?"

Esrae let out a disbelieving puff of air. It was a valid reaction. People didn't interfere with the King or his men. When they did, they ended up dead. Or worse.

People said when the current King, Malakai, overthrew the then King, Endryk, over twenty years prior, he'd been a different man. He'd liberated the country from many of Endryk's evils. But it wasn't long before Malakai was taking on some of the traits of his predecessor.

The guard who hadn't spoken turned and took a step toward Raven. She stood her ground, though inside her heart rate increased exponentially and she was sure Esrae flinched beside her. He had broad shoulders and was considerably taller than she was, and even though she could hold her own, his expression still sent a shiver creeping down her spine.

"She's been accused of spreading treasonous lies about the King." His voice was deeper than she had expected. "She's to be brought in for interrogation."

Raven's blood chilled. "She has children."

She could barely find breath. People who were taken for interrogation weren't usually seen again. Their king had no sympathy for those accused of speaking against him.

"And that exempts her from the law?" The guard's jaw worked as he slid his gaze once to his companion before returning it to her, appraising her.

"No," Esrae answered quickly, placing a hand on Raven's arm as she looked between her friend and the guard, fear glinting in her periwinkle eyes.

The guard's eyes flicked to Esrae but quickly found their way back to Raven. He took another step toward her, his blue eyes climbing up and down her body. His gaze narrowed and he repeated his question, slowly, speaking the words as though addressing a small child. "Have you seen her?"

Raven swallowed thickly and shook her head, her voice barely there. "I have not." She didn't add that even if she had seen Laurise, she would not have told him.

His eyes lingered on her long enough to make her uncomfortable, and she had to fight the urge to fidget beneath the weight of them. She drew in a short breath and held it, her nails digging into her palms.

Finally the other guard reached out, tapping him once on the arm. "Let's go."

Slowly she let out her breath. The knot in her stomach grew as she and Esrae watched the guards exit.

She had to do something. What could she do? Raven turned and met Esrae's alarmed expression. "Do you know where she is?"

She barely believed it was possible but Esrae's eyes widened further. "You think I lied to the King's men? However badly I want to get out of here, that is *not* how I wish to go. I have no idea where she is."

"I have to go."

Raven was already pulling open the door when Esrae called after her, "Raven, please be careful!"

Why was she even bothering? She couldn't help, couldn't stop what was about to happen.

Raven hurried down the dusty street, grateful she had chosen pants that morning and not a dress that she might trip over. Her eyes roved from side to side as she silently begged the Saints not to let the soldiers find Laurise. A few people called out greetings as she passed, but she didn't stop to talk. The guards had already disappeared, presumably down a side street. She continued on, ignoring the two kids racing across the street after a stray dog and the older man who called out to her to buy his small carvings.

But a moment later, someone caught her arm and spun her around to face them, halting her. Theodora was much larger than Raven and she was forced to come to a stop even as her heart continued its erratic thudding.

"Raven, good." Theodora's voice was deep and musical, and she spoke far too slowly for Raven's taste on a normal day.

"Theodora," Raven greeted as she tried to pull her arm from the other woman's grasp. It was no use; Theodora was nearly twice her size and held her firm.

Her instincts screamed at her to just make the woman release her. She could, but her upbringing and good business practices wouldn't allow it. She didn't want to hurt the woman, and even though the thought made her sick, she already knew she couldn't help Laurise.

"I need wine," Theodora continued, seemingly oblivious to Raven's meager attempts to escape. "I need a bottle of cabernet sauvignon. We're having prime rib, it's Archie's favorite, and your father's is the very best. Our anniversary is tomorrow, you know? I was hoping you could bring the wine by in the morning."

Raven was nodding, barely paying attention to Theodora, her eyes still scanning the streets around them. Then she heard it, the unmistakable sound of crying. Her stomach plummeted to her feet, her knees going weak, suddenly it was a good thing Theodora was holding her up.

"Oh my, what's this?" Theodora said, finally releasing Raven's arm.

Raven's blood had frozen her veins, all air gone from her lungs. The two soldiers from the bakery were now walking back up the street, a sobbing, straining woman held fast between them.

"Please, please, my children. My children." Laurise's cries were punctuated by sobs as tears poured down her face.

Raven clamped a hand over her mouth, fighting the bile that rose there. The guard she had exchanged words with in the bakery looked at her, his cold eyes pinning her. Her eyes stung as he held her gaze while they passed by, and a smile curved the corner of his mouth.

Anger quickly joined her horror as they continued up the dusty road. How did they have the right to steal a mother away from her children just because of something she said? They were only words, an opinion. It wasn't like Laurise was going to storm the palace. Though maybe somebody should—their king was a monster. But she knew there was nothing anyone could do about it.

TWO

S he squeezed her eyes closed as she concentrated on breathing and not giving into the panic that rose with every step she took. She'd found the wine Theodora requested and now held it clutched carefully to her chest, inhaling deeply.

She'd rushed home earlier in the afternoon to fill her father in on everything that had happened at the bakery and in town. Everything except Theodora's request for Archie's wine. Too many other things had crowded her mind, pushing that request in the recesses. Now she deeply regretted it.

Her father owned a small winery just on the outskirts of the town. Sometimes people came to them to get wine and sometimes they ordered it. Her father would retrieve the requested bottles from their cellars and leave them for Raven to deliver. Unfortunately this order never made it to her father, and now Raven was stuck. She hadn't told her father and he'd already gone to bed, leaving Raven with the task of collecting Theodora's wine. From the *cellar*.

As they always did when Raven was in the cellar, memories assaulted her. She'd been eight years old, and she'd become trapped there when the door handle broke. Panic had set in in seconds. Even at eight, she'd known that there were countless yards of earth pressing down on top of her. Her small mind worked until she was convinced the whole place would fall in, trapping and crushing her. She couldn't even get enough air into her lungs to call for help. Her father had found her what seemed like hours later, though was more likely only minutes. She'd been curled into a ball on the floor, gasping for air. He had to carry her outside before she could properly calm down. Ever since then, she couldn't go into the cellars without having to fight off a panic attack. She avoided the place as often as she could.

The torch she carried flickered and Raven held her breath for a moment, willing it to stay lit. She could not be stuck down here in the dark. Again she cursed her memory, navigating the halls of the cellar while still reminding herself to breathe.

Cool air filled her lungs, permeated with the scent of dirt and wood and wine. She counted to five silently before she released her breath. One more step, just one more step and then another. One step at a time and she would be upstairs in no time. She'd barely moved when the sound of voices met her.

She froze as her torch flickered again. As far as she'd known, she'd been alone in the cellar. She strained to make out the hushed words coming from the direction of the stairs. There was an urgency to their tone, and a sudden weight of fear settled in on her. Was something wrong?

She moved closer, careful to keep her torch back so they wouldn't see the light, until she recognized the voices. Her father and Logan. It wasn't unusual for Logan to be at her house. He'd had been around for her entire life. It had been he who'd taught Raven all she knew of hand-to-hand fighting and self-defense. And as the General of the King's army, his knowledge of such things was thorough and invaluable.

Thanks to countless hours of training, Raven could easily hold her own in a fight. His constant presence in her life made him like a second father to her. But she had no idea what he was doing in the wine cellar with her father, especially at such a late hour.

She moved as close as she dared and peered around one of the large casks of aging wine. She'd thought her father had gone to bed already. He'd *told* her he was going to bed. She was about to step out and make her presence known when the topic of their conversation caused her to pause and listen a moment longer.

"And you think now is the time?" Raven's father asked.

"I'm not sure of anything, Sebastian." Logan ran a hand through his short blonde hair. Exhaustion played on his face and seemed to weigh his shoulders down. "I just know that this has gone on far too long and I'm tired. He took Laurise De Kent today."

"Raven told me."

"Her father and I were friends."

Raven's chest tightened at the sadness in Logan's voice.

Her father's voice grew softer, "I know."

"I can't keep doing this. It's been too long. It's too hard."

"Do you have a plan?" her father asked. "An idea, a thought, as to how it can be done? Anything?"

Logan paused and crossed his arms in front of his chest. "It'll take time and it'll take others. We can't do it on our own. I mean, I suppose I could just run him through, but ideally, I'd like to live through this, if at all possible."

"Ideally," her father's gaze dropped to the ground. "But could you? Could you really do it? Just run him through? It's Malakai."

Raven froze.

There was a long pause before Logan spoke again, and when he did, his voice had taken on a quiet, deadly edge. "I could."

Her father met his eyes again and both men were silent for a while before Logan continued, "If we could make it appear to be an accident or an assassination... Maybe from outside Carashan. That would be best. Maybe we can pay someone from Shanterac."

Raven had completely forgotten she couldn't breathe. At that point, she wasn't actually breathing at all. She didn't dare to move as she allowed her mind to process their words. They were talking about the King. Her father and Logan, the General of the King's army, were in the wine cellar casually discussing assassinating the King of Carashan. Pride and terror swirled in her chest, making her stomach churn with them.

It was no secret that the King was ruthless. He terrorized his enemies. Even those he only perceived as such, whether or not he had proof. If the King suspected you were speaking against him in any way, that was the end for you. The incident that day with Laurise had been proof of that.

He'd ruled that way for as long as Raven could remember, her entire twenty-two years. No doubt many people wished for his death. But they wished it secretly. Rarely was anyone so brave as to admit their dislike for the King, you never knew who might be listening.

Hearing her father and Logan talking about taking a stand certainly brought a sense of pride, though, at the same time, if they were caught... Execution would be a kindness.

"Do you have others in mind?" her father's question pulled Raven's attention back to the men before her. Others—they needed help.

There was another pause before Logan spoke. "Finding help will be a challenge. There are few who would admit they're not loyal to Malakai."

Her father let out a bitter laugh.

She took them in, just the two of them, standing in the cellar, in the dark of night, making their plans to fight the corruption in their country. Alone. And they would do it alone if they had to. If she knew anyone, she knew her father and Logan. They would do what they could and win, or die trying. They were stubborn, no doubt where she got her stubbornness from. This was a crazy plan, but she couldn't let them do it alone. She couldn't allow them to give everything as she stood by and did nothing. They were her family and this was her country, as well. Even if they should fail she would give her all beside them.

She stepped out from the shadows of the wine casks. "I'll help."

The two men spun in her direction.

"Raven!" Shock was written across every line in her father's tanned face and wide chocolate eyes. "What are you doing down here?"

"What am *I* doing down here?" Raven repeated a bit sarcastically. "I'm getting wine. But I think a more interesting question would be: what are you two doing down here?"

"I thought you were in bed," her father countered, avoiding her question.

"Likewise," Raven replied, her gaze darting between the two men. "What's going on?"

Logan's face twisted in a grimace. "How much did you hear?"

"Everything?" her father asked.

Raven looked between them again. "Not everything, but enough. You're both out of your minds."

Logan's eyebrows rose and he looked like a man very much inclined to agree.

She looked at them again, just the two of them. They looked very alone. "I want to help."

"No," her father's answer came without hesitation. "Absolutely not."

She'd expected that response from her father. So, instead, she turned her gaze to Logan even as he looked away, avoiding meeting her eyes.

"I can help."

She knew Logan, she knew what his refusal to look at her meant. He believed she might actually be able to help, but he was hesitant to say it with her father there.

"No," her father spoke the word again, more adamant this time. "Raven, this is so dangerous. You think you know but you have no idea."

Raven turned her attention again to Logan, allowing her gaze to bore into him. She refused to be ignored. "You're quiet."

Her father shot a dangerous look at the other man. Logan opened his mouth as if to speak but then closed it again, shaking his head.

She nodded. They only wanted to protect her, but if it was so dangerous and if she could help, why not allow it? "I stood there and listened. I heard you say that you need help. You need people and it's too dangerous to go searching for allies, but I'm right here. I'm offering you my help. You already know you can trust me."

"Raven," her father's voice was quiet and pleading, desperation coating the word.

"I'm not a child," she stated, holding her father's gaze.

Sadness crept into his dark eyes and carried on his voice when he spoke. "You're *my* child."

It was only love and concern from her father, she knew that. But if he could just stop looking at her like she was nine and see that she was strong and capable and intelligent. He was blinded by parenthood. She turned to Logan and studied him for a moment. He loved her as well, but maybe he was far enough removed that he could see. He was logical, resourceful, and strategic.

"You know I can help."

"Raven," Logan began, but he was interrupted.

"No, Raven." She recognized the note of finality in her father's voice. She'd heard it often enough in her childhood.

"Fine." She glanced one more time at Logan before she turned and walked away.

She'd allow her father the victory in that moment, but she wouldn't rescind her offer. They needed her and she was pretty certain they all knew it.

Raven paced at the foot of her bed, replaying again and again the conversation she'd overheard. She needed to be a part of this. She needed to be there for her father and Logan, when possibly no one else would be or maybe even could be. She was tired of seeing what the King was doing to her country. It was becoming far too common to witness scenes like she had with Laurise. If left unchecked, who knew where the country would end up?

One day she might have children. What would be left for them? Worse, what if their life was more of the same? Would they grow up living in a place of fear where simply having opinions could get you executed?

But that was far in the future and this was now. And now she had a chance to be involved in something that could change things. At the very least, they would attempt to change things, and she intended to help.

She would sway them. If her father couldn't be turned, she was fairly certain, with a bit of conversation, Logan could be convinced. Logan cared about her, of course, but he was also logical. If there was something she could do to help, he would allow it. She only had to plead her case. She dropped onto the edge of her bed, releasing a sigh. How?

After staring at the floor for some time she stood, snatching her heavy knit blanket from the bottom of her bed and wrapping it around her shoulders.

When she entered the kitchen, she found her father seated at the table. In his hands was a drink that Raven was sure wasn't tea.

"Where are you going?" He asked, with barely a glance in her direction.

"Kanan's." She didn't want to speak to him. Yes, he only wanted her safe; but it just felt like he was shutting her out and ignoring facts.

"At this hour?" her father spoke into his cup.

"Believe it or not, I can take care of myself." The words sounded churlish even to her, but she was upset enough not to care. She'd regret them later.

Even in the dark Raven had no problem navigating the familiar, uneven stairs that clung to the outside of the smith shop. She knocked on the door before readjusting the blanket, pulling it closer around her shoulders, the wide weave doing little to keep out the cool night breeze. Normally she would just enter the small lodging, the two of them having done away with the formality of knocking long ago. But at such a late hour, she thought it best not to barge in on someone as familiar with swords as Kanan was.

"Closed." Kanan shouted, his voice slightly muffled by the door. "Come back tom—"

"Kanan?" Raven called, cutting him off.

Through the door she could hear the worn floorboards creaking and sighing under his weight as he moved across the room. The door opened and Kanan stood, towering over her. His black shirt hung open, his dark hair an unruly mess. His eyes narrowed in concern. "Raven? What's wrong?"

She moved past him into the small room, not stopping until she stood in front of the fire crackling softly in the hearth. She inhaled, letting the familiar scent of Kanan's home relax her. It was a mix of the blacksmith shop below and the fresh lemon and sage soap that Kanan's grandmother made and sold in their village. Agnes' soaps were very popular, and Raven loved the way Kanan always smelled faintly of lemons.

Kanan came up beside her and stopped, staring into the fire, waiting until she was ready to speak. She glanced up at him, noting the way the fire danced in his olive-green eyes. His brow rose, his head tilting in a question.

"I went into the cellars tonight and my father and Logan were down there." A log in the fire crumbled, sending a shower of sparks upward. That was about to be either her country or her family. Should she even tell Kanan? She trusted him implicitly, but telling him would put him in danger. But as she looked into his eyes, she knew she couldn't keep it from him. At the very least, he had a right to know what she had volunteered for.

Kanan still didn't speak, but now his brows drew together in confusion.

Raven bit down on her bottom lip.

Immediately Kanan's brow evened out, his shoulders straightening slightly as he turned his body to face her. "What happened?"

She turned as well, looking him fully in the eyes. Even though they were alone, she still felt the need to lower her voice. "They were talking about killing the King."

"What?"

A slight wave of panic flitted through her along with the absurd desire to giggle. Instead, she threw her hands out in front of her with a frenzied shrug. There were too many emotions and thoughts to try to process. "Right there in the cellar. Just casually discussing assassination."

"Why?"

Raven flailed her arms with another shrug. "They're fed up? They're insane? I don't know."

"Logan works for the King." Kanan spoke as though she wasn't aware of the fact.

"Yes," Raven blew out a breath, running both hands back through her hair.

"Logan is the General of the King's army."

"Yes," she repeated.

Kanan was silent for a few moments. His brow creased slightly as his eyes moved over her face. "Can it even be done?"

Raven returned her gaze to the fire, her shoulders slumping. Could it be done? Anything was possible, right? "He's a man, why not?"

"Raven, you and I both know he's not an average man." Kanan dropped into the cushioned chair next to the fireplace. "I just think that if someone tried to kill him, it wouldn't be difficult for him to stop them."

She looked at him as her chest seemed to cave in on itself. Logan and her father knew this and still they were ready to fight.

Kanan's look softened as he echoed her thoughts, "How?"

She backed up and dropped onto the bed that sat along the wall of the small room. She shook her head. "I don't know. I don't think they know."

Silence stretched between them as her fingers found a stray thread on the blanket and pulled at it until it broke free. She could feel Kanan's eyes on her, but she had nothing else to tell him. She didn't know how. When she finally spoke again, her voice was quiet. "They'll need help."

Kanan raised his head, his mouth falling open slightly. "No." It wasn't an order, it was a plea.

"You sound like them. Why not?"

He stood, his long strides covering the distance between them in seconds. The bed creaked under his weight as he sat beside her. "Raven, this is suicide. I'm sorry, but it is."

She met his gaze, biting down on her lip again before continuing, "They're set on this and they can't go ask for help. Look at me, who would suspect me? They can use me. I've never met the King, I can go places they can't. "

"I am looking at you, Raven. And I know you can take care of yourself, but what are you planning to do? Walk in and stab him? This is . . . 'dangerous' isn't even the right word for it," he said softly as he reached out and tucked a lock of hair behind her ear, letting his finger trail her jaw, before his hand came to rest on hers.

She inhaled deeply again. "I was at the bakery today talking to Esrae, and two soldiers came in looking for Laurise."

"I heard what happened. She's the one with all the kids." His voice was quiet. It wasn't a question.

"Yes," Raven answered. "They said she was spreading lies about the King. They were taking her for interrogation. Kanan, all those kids. The King just came in and took their mother because she had an opinion. And you know this isn't the first time this happened. It needs to end, and if I can help, I will."

Kanan sighed and dropped his gaze to his boots. "Why are you so good?"

She offered him a shrug and attempted to conjure a smile. It was small. "It's a curse."

He met her eyes again. "Well, I could remind you again how dangerous this all is, or I could tell you that this isn't the first time I've thought about it."

"What do you mean?" Fear gripped her for a second at the thought of Kanan trying something and ultimately being hauled away by guards.

"I mean, what he's done and doing to the people in this country is wrong." Absently he reached up and combed his fingers lightly through the ends of her hair. "I've thought about what it would be like to stop him, but that was it. Just thinking about it. I never knew any way that it could be done. Maybe this is it. Maybe the Saints put you and me together so we could do this."

It didn't surprise her hearing him say things like that. Kanan's grandmother was a firm believer in the Saints and the impact they had on the lives of common people.

"So," Kanan continued, "what can I do to help?"

She laced her fingers into his and leaned into him, resting her head on his shoulder, feeling so blessed to have him. "We're insane."

She felt his chuckle more than heard it. "I think we are."

"Thank you." Some part of her wished she could talk him out of it. Her father and Logan in danger was enough. But another part of her was grateful he had offered, and relieved to know that he would be there to offer his support.

He curled his arm around her and pulled her close. "I love you."

She twisted, wrapping her arms around him, burrowing further into his side. "I love you too."

He placed a kiss on the top of her head. "Come on, I'll walk you home."

He stood, and Raven allowed him to pull her to her feet. When he didn't move for a moment she looked up, meeting his gaze. He smiled, the corner of his eyes crinkling with the action.

Kanan's smile was warm and bright and infectious and she returned it easily.

He bent his head and brushed his lips softly against hers, sweet and chaste. Then he smiled again against her mouth before he buried a hand in her hair and slid his other arm around her back, pulling her to her toes and flush against his bare chest. His kiss turned fervent and she matched his eagerness with her own, sliding her hands over his abs and around his back, under his shirt.

He let out a quiet moan and pulled back, a mischievous glint shone in his eyes. "Maybe you should stay."

She giggled. "I would, but I have to make a delivery in the morning. And don't you have to work?"

"So you're good *and* reasonable," Kanan teased as his eyes danced over her face.

"Tomorrow is Friday. We'll see each other for dinner, with Torren and Esrae," Raven said.

"Yes." Kanan's eyes came to hers, narrowing. "And when will I see you alone?"

"We'll make time. I promise."

"Good." He kissed her again, softly. "Let's go."

THREE

W hen Raven was very young, her father built her a small playhouse directly in the center of their vineyard. From every angle she could see rows of grapes.

She used to play there for hours pretending she was the Queen of the land, or at least the vineyard. Occasionally she would drag Logan along and put him to work as her General.

As Raven became older, she outgrew the small playhouse and they removed it. But she kept her little space in the center of the vineyard. It was perfect for when she wanted to be alone, far away from prying eyes and listening ears. Sometimes she took a blanket and a book. Sometimes she took a blanket and Kanan. Sometimes, often on a Friday, she and her closest friends met there just to spend time and get away from everything else.

Currently the small group sat, surrounded by bright yellow and orange leaves, some on the ground, some still on the vines. The season had only just rolled over into autumn but already the ground was littered with leaves, swirling in the soft breeze.

Getting together outside with her friends was one of Raven's favorite things, but she was afraid before long the weather would turn cold and force them inside. She closed her eyes for a moment as the air flowed over her face. Esrae's voice dragged her back to the present.

"They were just down there talking about, talking about—"

"Es!" Raven said, cutting her friend off before she could continue speaking so loudly. Even though she knew no one was around, she still felt like the whole town was watching. Like the King's guards would jump out any second and haul them all away. "Really?"

The sky was bright and blue and the sun shone directly on them, like even it was out to expose their treasonous conversation. Maybe she shouldn't have told any of them, but she trusted them. She'd known these people for over half of her life. She knew how they felt about the King, knew that this was something they might like to have a part in, as well. And even if they didn't, they wouldn't sell her out.

"Sorry," the other girl said, averting her eyes as she continued pulling portions of her blonde curls into her hands, wrapping and rewrapping them around her fingers.

Raven inhaled deeply. "And yes. They were just down there talking about it."

"Do you think they'll really do it?" Torren sat cross-legged on the soft ground, the sun shining fully on his light brown skin and giving him a soft glow. He kept his fingers busy pulling blade after blade of grass out of the ground, tearing them to bits.

Raven's gaze reached across the space, past the rows of vines, toward where she knew the palace sat. "I don't know."

Nightmarish scenes assaulted her. Her father and Logan being hauled away through town. Her and her friends right behind them. Being tossed in the darkest dungeons to wait for who knows what would come next.

She didn't even notice Kanan had arrived until he was nearly in front of her, waving a hand in front of her face. "Raven?"

She shook her head, clearing her thoughts as she looked up, pulling herself back to the group. "Hey."

Kanan dropped to the ground beside Raven, tugging on her hair gently. "Where were you?"

She raised her brows with a slight shrug. "Dungeon."

He leaned back, resting on his elbows, stretching his long legs out in front of him and crossing them at the ankles. "I take it you told them?"

She took in each one of them as she nodded.

Kanan's brow creased, and he glanced around the group. "And what do you two think?"

Esrae turned her head toward him like she might say something, but then dropped her attention back to the ground.

"Hey," Torren spoke up as though a thought had only just occurred to him. "Isn't Logan the King's General? Why doesn't he just kill him and get it over with?" He brandished an invisible sword, stabbing the air in front of him in a quick strike.

"Tor, keep your voice down, please," Raven pleaded. "And because if Logan killed him, they would kill Logan."

"Have they said anything else about their plan?" Kanan asked.

Raven shook her head. "No. I haven't mentioned it since I heard them talking, and they haven't, either. At least, not around me. My father doesn't want me to help. But I think I can convince Logan."

Kanan faced her, moving his head until he caught her gaze. "And you're sure you really do want to help?"

She held his gaze, his olives eyes piercing into her. He was giving her the opportunity to back out, but she wouldn't. Did she want to put herself in this kind of danger? Of course not. No one in their right mind would want to do that. But she would do anything for her family. Anything to help keep them safe. And did she want to help free her country from a tyrannical ruler? Yes. She'd seen too many people hauled away and heard too many stories of others who'd disappeared to not want it to end. This was what she wanted. And she knew Kanan well enough to know that he loved his country and he loved her, and for both of them he would do whatever he could. At this point, even if she did rescind her offer, she didn't expect he would.

"They can't do it alone and they can't ask for help." She didn't want them to feel like they had no one. And She certainly didn't want them putting their lives on the line seeking out assistance. She was perfectly capable; more than capable, in some ways.

Kanan nodded slowly, reaching out to move her hair over her shoulder. "Well, you already know you have my support and my blade."

Raven smiled at his phrasing, her gallant knight. But before she could respond, Torren spoke up.

"I'm not sure volunteering to kill the King is such a great idea."

"No, but it's not like they can tack up posters and recruit volunteers," Raven said. "Even if they're subtle, if the wrong person overheard, they'd be dead."

"Can I also be the one to point out, our king is not your average ruler?" Torren raised a hand, wiggling his fingers in the air.

Silence fell on the group. They all knew the stories. Except they weren't just stories. That was the benefit of being so close to the King's General; you knew what was truth and what wasn't. And the stories about the King were not false. She tried to shrug it off. "It's not like he can read minds."

"No." Torren's eyes widened with an incredulous look. "Just control them."

"It doesn't matter," Kanan offered. "If he doesn't know what we're up to, he doesn't need to control us." He pulled in a deep breath, looking at the group. "We should do it. I'm going to, at least."

"If you're serious, really serious, I'll talk to Logan," Raven said. "It'll be easier to convince him, then he can convince my father."

"I want to help too."

Esrae's quiet voice drew everyone's attention. Raven was more than a little surprised to hear her offer. Esrae was serious and proper, and after the way she'd reacted to the King's guards, Raven hadn't expected her to volunteer so easily to defy them.

"Es, this is dangerous."

"You think I can't handle danger?" Incredulity dripped from Esrae's question. "Besides, who would miss me? I mean, if something happens to me, no one's going to lose any sleep. Anyway, you've been perfect long enough. I can't let you have all the glory in this too. If we change the country, I want them to remember my name."

"Esrae—"

"I'm helping." The finality in Esrae's tone cut Raven's comments off before she could speak further.

"All right," Torren sat forward, slapping both palms on the ground in front of him, dispelling a bit of the tension. "If everyone else is doing it, you might as well count me in. Someone has to watch Kanan's back."

"Yeah, that's why I have Raven." Kanan elbowed her playfully, his joke further lightening the mood. Though with his next breath, he was again serious. "I mean it, Raven, the King is vile. He doesn't have this country's best interest in mind, and certainly not it's people. If there's a chance this frees Carashan from him, I won't regret being a part of it."

Words left Raven as she nodded at him, grateful for his presence. She infused her next words with all the gravity she could. "Are you all sure? This isn't something we can come back from." She met each of their gazes, her dearest friends, these people she loved. "If it goes to plan, whatever that plan is, then maybe we can go back to our lives. Maybe. If it doesn't go according to plan . . ."

"Then we're dead and we won't have any worries anymore," Kanan offered in a lighter tone.

Raven turned her gaze on him. The very idea of Kanan's light being snuffed out, his presence taken from the world that he made better everyday . . . it left a pit in her stomach that churned like an angry sea.

"No more taxes!" Raven jumped, startled as Torren threw his hands up in a celebratory cheer, broken blades of grass raining down on top of him.

Raven let out a heavy breath. They were trying to lighten the mood, but she wished they would stop. She needed to see that they knew what they were getting into, and she couldn't tell when they were being so flippant. "I'm serious."

"Hey," Kanan reached over his hand closing around hers, squeezing gently. His gaze traveled around the group before coming back to her. "We get it. It's dangerous. I can only speak for myself, but if I can take part in a plan that could free this country, why wouldn't I? Not to mention, I already told you, I'm going where you go. I'm in."

Raven pulled in a long breath. "I'll talk to Logan."

Kanan pulled Raven closer to his side as they walked back to her house. She turned her face toward his chest, breathing him in, trying to push away the thoughts in her head that said this was going to end badly.

He placed a soft kiss on top of her head. "Alright?" His chest vibrated softly against her ear as he spoke.

She debated lying and saying she was fine, but this was Kanan. Instead of speaking she simply nodded.

Kanan stopped walking, bringing Raven to a stop as well. She looked up into his slightly narrowed green eyes, his lips in a line. "You don't have to do this, Raven."

"I know," she blinked as the cool breeze blew her hair into her face. Swiping at it, she brushed it out of her field of vision. "I know it sounds silly, but what if I was supposed to overhear them? What if this is what I'm supposed to do? But that doesn't mean it's what you're all supposed to do."

Kanan reached out and moved a last wayward strand of hair back into place. "Raven, there's one thing I know for sure." He pinned her with his olive green gaze. "It's that if you're supposed to do something, I'm supposed to be with you. Always, you and me." A tiny smirk turned up the corner of his mouth. "Anyway, don't be worried about me." He raised his arms, balling his hands into fists. "I can take care of myself." He tapped a knuckle lightly against her chin.

The action brought the smallest smile to her lips, and then she rolled her eyes, poking him in the stomach. "Oh, please. I could take you."

"Oh, is that so?" Amusement danced in Kanan's eyes as he raised his brow.

"It is and you know it." Raven threw a light, playful punch at his arm, "Without a sword in your hands, you're nothing."

Kanan's mouth turned up in a soft smile. They both knew it wasn't true. Of course Kanan could hold his own in a fistfight, but with a sword in his hand, his opponent wouldn't stand for long.

Kanan had started training as a swordsmith when he was only nine years old. By adulthood, he was a master of the craft and the art. He liked to practice with his wares as well as create them.

"Go easy on him, Raven."

They looked up to see a man walking toward them, two aged dogs trailing behind him, kicking up dust in their wake.

"Hello, Archie." Raven smiled and waved as the man approached.

"Good evening to you both." The man dipped his head slightly at them.

"Archie." Kanan returned the nod.

"The wine was delicious, by the way," Archie said as he passed by them.

"I'm glad you liked it," Raven responded, bending to scratch the dogs behind their floppy ears. "Happy anniversary!"

"Thank you very much. You kids take care." Archie slapped at his thigh and gave a short whistle and the dogs, who had stopped to greet Raven and Kanan, quickly returned to his side.

When Archie had passed out of earshot Kanan grew serious again, studying her. "Maybe a little self-defense training wouldn't hurt."

"You need training?" Raven teased.

He chuckled quietly. "Okay, I worded that wrong. What about, maybe a little self-defense refresh wouldn't hurt?"

Raven stepped into him, sliding her arms around his waist, letting her fingers dance over his hard muscles "Are you offering to let me beat you up?"

"Well, I wouldn't put it like that, but if you were looking for someone to wrestle with…" He reached behind him and his hands closed around her wrists. Before she could react he pulled them from behind him and wrapped them behind her, pinning her hands to her back and her chest to his. "Just to brush up."

She let out a surprised sound and he grinned at her, his eyes twinkling, before he released her.

She wrapped her arms around him again, looking up, resting her chin on his chest. "I mean, you know I learned all my fighting skills from Logan. I've been at this since I could walk. You don't stand a chance."

Raven punctuated her words by grabbing Kanan's waist, tickling him. He jerked in her grip with a sound of surprise, catching hold of her arms once again. He brought their hands up between them, holding them to his chest.

"We'll see." Then he dipped his head, nudging her with the tip of his nose until he could capture her mouth with his.

FOUR

Raven's breath swirled in front of her and she gripped her steaming mug tighter, bringing it close to her face, absorbing as much of the warmth as she could. Clouds swirled overhead, keeping the light of the sun at bay and making her wish for her bed. It was too early and too cold to be out. What had she been thinking?

A sound drew her attention and she looked up to see Kanan, clad in black pants and a black tunic, coming down the dusty path, flanked by grapevines. She smiled, sipping from her mug. *That's* what she'd been thinking.

She slid from her seat on the fallen log they dragged in there years before and picked up the other steaming mug waiting beside her.

Kanan's mouth split into a grin and he waved. "Hey, beautiful,"

Raven called her reply, "Hey, you."

"I brought you something." Kanan's smile widened as he finally stopped in front of her.

"Coincidence. Because I brought *you* something." Raven held out a mug to him. "Tea."

"Thanks." He accepted the mug, leaning in to brush his mouth over hers before he drank.

The tip of his nose brushed her cheek and she shivered at the chill it carried. "You're welcome."

"My turn." With his free hand, he pulled the leather strap that was slung across his chest over his head and handed it to her.

"What's the occasion?" Raven smiled accepting the belt and the sheathed sword attached to it. It was lighter than she expected. She placed her mug down behind her and pulled the sword from the sheath, holding it up, turning it over to examine it.

The blade shone even without sunlight, and the hilt... Raven held it closer, her mouth falling open slightly. It was beautiful. The hilt was a wine-colored swirl, the guard a shining silver with small crystal-like stones embedded in its surface, and the pommel held a single stone that matched the hilt.

"It's beautiful," she breathed, looking up at him.

Kanan was watching her, a soft smile on his lips. "I'm glad you like it."

"Like it?" Raven said. "It's amazing."

"It's yours." His smile widened.

"I can't." The time it must have taken him to create this sword...

He laughed. "Yes, you can. I made it for you."

"Kanan, you could sell this." She slid the blade back into the mahogany colored sheath and pushed it back in his direction. "It's beautiful. Someone would pay very well for this."

Kanan held up his hand and gently nudged the sword back toward her. "Raven, I didn't make it to sell. I made it for you."

Raven was about to protest again, but Kanan spoke first. "Want to try it out?"

"What if I break it?" Raven said, still holding the sword carefully out in front of her.

"Raven." Kanan's mouth fell open and he shot her an incredulous look. "Are you trying to insult me? It's not going to break."

Raven let out a short laugh. "I'm sorry. I know it won't break, I just don't want it to get scratched or anything."

"What are you going to do with it? Hang it on the wall?" Kanan teased, setting his mug down.

"I just might." She smiled up at him.

"You will not." Kanan slid his own sword from where it hung at his hip and pointed it in her direction, staring down the long blade at her. "Are you going to defend yourself?"

The way he looked at her, blade drawn, made her heart do funny things. She smirked as she finally pulled the sword from the sheath, crossing it with his, the metal of the blades scraping softly together.

"Are you sure you want to do this?" she asked, a teasing, warning tone in her voice.

"I think I can handle it. You might—*might*—have the edge in hand-to-hand combat, but when it comes to swords..." He brandished his own with a flourish before bringing the blade back to hers, and instead of speaking further he only cocked his head and gave her a playful shrug and a wink, a challenge lighting his olive green eyes.

She smiled, rolling her eyes. He knew exactly what that wink did to her. "You're humble." But it was true.

Coming from anyone else, the words might be hollow, but not from Kanan. Thanks to Logan and Sebastian, she was decent with a sword. But Kanan, he created swords and knew well how to wield them.

She moved first, a small strike that Kanan blocked easily. His mouth quirked up in an approving smile and mirrored her action himself. She blocked it and advanced on him. He sidestepped her next swing, like she knew he would, and she struck in the direction he moved. Still he jumped back easily, blocking her strike.

"Not bad," he laughed.

"Not bad?" She let the mock surprise fill her voice as she lunged toward him again. Again, he jumped back, catching her blade with the tip of his and flinging it away with a scraping sound.

Squaring off again, Raven brought her sword around hard in a swinging arc from her right shoulder. He easily knocked her sword away with his own. As she was paying attention to where her blade was traveling, Kanan wrapped his free hand around her wrist and pulled her into him.

The breath left her as he brought his sword down, stopping inches from her neck. A wicked, challenging grin spread across his face. Her eyes moved from him to the blade hovering over her head, and a smile pulled at the corner of her mouth. She'd been beaten. Just as quickly as he had captured her he leaned in, placed a quick kiss on the tip of her nose, and released her, stepping back.

She lunged again and Kanan brought his sword up as if to block her blow, but stopped short as her blade halted inches from his chest. Raven smiled triumphantly. Though, she was fairly certain he'd let her land that one. He bowed ever so slightly before taking a step back and once again holding his sword up in front of him.

They continued this way for a few more moments until Kanan jumped back out of striking range and held up his hands in surrender. He nodded toward the sword in her hands as he slid his own back into its sheath. "Do you like it?"

She turned the sword over in her hands, still marveling at its beauty. "I absolutely love it. It's perfect."

Kanan smiled, pleased. "I'm glad."

"Thank you, Kanan." She resheathed the sword and stepped up to him, stretching up on her toes to press her mouth to his.

He slipped an arm around her waist. "I'd bring you gifts more often if I knew this was how I'd be thanked."

She offered a flirtatious smile. "Don't be silly, I don't need gifts. You may have a kiss anytime you wish."

"In that case—" Kanan pulled her fully flush against his torso and dipped his head, pressing his lips to hers, teasing with his tongue until she opened to allow him in. Their mouths moved together until she was out of breath and wanting more than just a kiss.

When they broke apart, he held her gaze for a few moments before he spoke again. "So, I thought we were going to spar."

Was he kidding? "Spar?"

"That's why I'm here, isn't it?"

The smirk that accompanied his words told her he knew just how much of a tease he was being. He wanted her to beg? Fine, she could play that game too.

She schooled her face into innocence. "You mean being bested in a sword match wasn't enough for you?"

"Bested?" Kanan laughed, his smile lighting his face. "Yes, well, in that case, you owe me the chance to even the score."

Raven smiled, raising a brow. "Alright, then." She placed the sheathed sword back on the trunk before moving to a more open space. "Come on, then. Show me what you can do."

He grinned, pulling his own sword off and placing it beside hers. "Sparring?"

"Yes, sparring. What did you think I meant?"

Kanan winked. "You said 'show me what you can do.' I can do a lot of things."

"Maybe later." She returned his grin.

He gave her a one shoulder shrug, still smiling as he joined her.

Raven tilted her head to the side and raised one brow. "What are you waiting for?"

Kanan looked at her like her head wasn't on straight. "I'm not going to throw the first punch."

Raven rolled her eyes. "Come on, man, impress me."

The smirk returned. "I can impress you far better at home."

She leaned in, as though she had a secret, and whispered, "Later."

Kanan eyed her for a moment, a muscle in his jaw flexing, then he began to circle to his right. But only circle, not attack.

Tired of waiting, Raven dropped to the ground, sweeping her leg back behind her. Kanan jumped, easily avoiding the move.

She regained her feet, her hands already up, ready to fight. "Come on, Kanan. Do I have to do all the work?"

"Okay." He threw a right hook, and she dodged it with little effort.

Her mouth twisted, her head tilting. "You're holding back."

Kanan held his hands up in front of him with a sheepish grin. He didn't want to hurt her; it was sweet, but she wanted a challenge and she could handle herself.

"Come on?" she pleaded.

Kanan regarded her for a moment and sighed. He threw a punch straight at her face. But he was still being careful, and Raven caught his wrist easily with her left hand. She spun, trying to land her elbow into his ribs, but he broke free and jumped back, avoiding the jab. Instead, he caught both of her arms and pulled her backward into him.

Using his own momentum she backed into him and bent forward, tossing him over her shoulder. Kanan landed hard on his back with a grunt but recovered quickly, jumping up to face her.

"Nice." He sounded impressed.

"Yeah?" She smiled. "You're still holding back."

He sighed. "Guilty. But I think you are too."

Raven squared her shoulders and drew herself up to her full height, which was still significantly shorter than Kanan, and looked him in the eye. "Okay. I'll stop if you stop."

A slow smile lifted the corner of his mouth and his brow rose slightly, the effect making him look almost evil.

The look did things to her, deep in her middle, and Raven fought to keep her grin in check as she returned the expression.

When he responded his voice was low and quiet, his eyes never leaving hers. "Alright."

"Alright," Raven echoed, even as she fought the very real desire to call it a day and find somewhere to be alone.

Kanan's smile widened as he stepped back into a fighting stance.

Saints, this man. He knew exactly the effect he was having on her. No doubt doing it on purpose just to throw her off. Reluctantly, she took a step back, falling into her own fighting stance. They began to circle each other until finally Raven threw a punch at his arrogant smile, but Kanan blocked it easily.

She kicked and the sole of her foot connected with his ribs. The sound that left him was either a grunt or an amused laugh and he staggered back, moving to the side before he threw a punch of his own. Raven ducked out of the way, avoiding his jab, but just barely.

She kicked again, and Kanan took advantage of it, stepping out of range of her kick even as he knocked her other leg out from under her.

Raven landed hard on her back, air whooshing from her lungs as she cursed herself for being distracted. She moved to regain her feet but was stopped as Kanan climbed on top of her. She was spry but he was strong. She couldn't get away if he was already on her. She stopped fighting as he pinned her to the ground.

She looked up at him as she took in a mouthful of air. "That's more like it."

"You too." He smiled as he stood and offered her his hand.

Instead of accepting his help though, she placed her foot squarely in the center of his chest and tossed him over.

He landed with a groan and a chuckle. Raven moved quickly to climb on top of him, reversing their previous positions.

He laughed and held up his hands. "I concede."

"Wise," Raven said, smiling down at him.

Kanan's eyes roved over her face once and then his hands were on her thighs, sliding up to her waist and over her back until they were in her hair and he was pulling her mouth down to meet his.

The tension and adrenaline from their match seeped into the kiss as Kanan claimed her mouth and Raven found it hard to catch her breath.

Kanan sat up, not breaking the kiss, moving her back to where she straddled his lap, her thighs on either side of his. One hand stayed in her hair as the other slid around her back, pulling her flush against him. She wrapped her arms around his neck and pressed into him, losing herself, the world going quiet around her.

Kanan released her mouth, inhaling deeply, still holding her close. He looked into her eyes. "Productive morning."

"I think so," she said.

His eyes moved over her face to her lips and back again. "It could be more productive."

Her heart sped at his implication. "How do you think?"

He raised a brow before he bent his head, his lips finding the sensitive spot on her neck, just below her ear. "Like this." His breath sent shivers all over.

She exhaled, tilting her head back to give him better access. "Is that all you've got?"

He pulled back to meet her gaze again, a mischievous glint in his eye. "It's a little chilly, no?"

"She let her eyes drift away toward the sky before returning to his. "Have you never heard of body heat?"

He leaned close and nipped at her ear, his hands sliding to pull her shirt from where it was tucked into her fitted pants. "Is that a challenge?"

His hands slid under her shirt, his rough fingers settling on her back. She shivered as much from his touch as from the chill in his skin.

Slowly he slid his hands down, slipping beneath the waistband of her pants, pulling her against him.

Warmth pooled low inside her and her breath caught on his name.

He backed her up until her back hit the tall pole where the vines wrapped around. Covering her lips with his own, he slipped one hand out of the back of her pants and slid it slowly back down the front.

He caught her gasp in his mouth, deepening the kiss even as his fingers explored her.

Pressure built inside her and she began to squirm, but he held her steady, moving inside her, setting every nerve on fire in the best way.

Finally he removed his mouth from hers, but he still hovered there. His breaths tickled her cheek as she moved, desperate for that release the coiled her insides so tightly.

Her lips parted and she panted.

"Raven," his whisper tickled her cheek, swirling her hair. She barely knew what he was saying, so wrapped up was she in what she was feeling. "You're so beautiful."

And then the coil snapped and she cried out softly as the threads of pleasure wove through her. He removed his hand and her legs went limp. She was afraid she would fall, but Kanan's arms held her up. She opened her eyes to find him smiling at her.

"I love to watch you do that."

She breathed out a heavy sigh. "I think you did that."

He leaned in, brushing his nose against hers. "Either way."

"Saints," she said, still half panting. "I wish we could continue that."

"Nothing stopping us." He placed another kiss on her neck.

Reluctantly she rested her hand on his chest. "Yes, there is. I have things to do."

"Me too." He moved to the other side of her neck. "You."

She laughed and pushed lightly against him, silently cursing her responsibilities. "Other things. I have to go to the bakery."

"Esrae will understand if you don't stop by," Kanan said, dipping his head to kiss her.

"It's not Es," Raven laughed, finally able to stand steady on her feet. "I would like to have bread with dinner tonight. But I would not like to make it myself."

Kanan's lips moved over her neck. "Skip dinner. It's overrated."

"Dinner is overrated? Maybe sex is overrated," Raven teased, even as she leaned her head back, giving him better access. This was about to get out of hand again.

He pulled back, mock shock written across his features. "Bite your tongue, woman! Wait, you don't really think that, do you?"

She laughed again and gave him a sly smile. "I could never." She leaned in, kissing him lightly, determined to find her self-control. "But I do need bread."

"Fine." Kanan released her. "I'll come along. Get a turnover."

"Doubtful, they're the first thing to go," Raven said as she retrieved her new sword. "They never make enough."

"That's why they're a novelty," Kanan said, holding his arm out to her.

She smiled and slipped her arm into the crook of his elbow. "I just want to drop the sword off at home."

FIVE

Long before they reached the bakery the sounds of shouting met them, carried swiftly on the autumn breeze.

"What am I supposed to do with this? Who's going to buy this? You stupid girl!"

Raven's stomach turned as she and Kanan exchanged a glance. They picked up their pace, approaching the bakery.

"It's not burnt, Madam Falstead." Esrae's voice sounded small after Madam Falstead's shouting.

"Not burnt?" Madam Falstead scoffed, her words pitched high. "Come here, you stupid girl. Come here and look at this. It's brown on the bottom!"

Raven flinched every time Madam Falstead called Esrae stupid.

"Look, it's not burnt, it's just a bit darker. Actually, I prefer them that—"

The cracking sound of a slap followed by a yelp caused Raven to jump.

"Kanan."

Kanan's hold on Raven's hand tightened as he moved faster. "Come on."

When the small bell jingled announcing their arrival, Madame Falstead turned to them and her voice changed from disdain to what Raven imagined dripping honey would sound like, gooey and too sweet. "Kanan, Raven, good afternoon! What can we get you?"

Raven looked toward Esrae, but the other girl had turned away from them, cradling her cheek. The urge to lash out at Madame Falstead pressed on her, the words creeping up her throat. She took a breath and opened her mouth to release them but before she could get anything out, Kanan spoke.

"Madame Falstead." He shot a glance toward Esrae before he flashed the woman a smile. "I was wondering if you had any turnovers left."

Raven could see Madame Falstead's anger melt away under Kanan's handsome gaze and she was grateful for his interruption. Her words would not have soothed anyone's anger.

"Oh, no, Kanan, I'm so sorry. They sell out so quickly. Come in tomorrow, I'll set some aside for you. Is there anything else I can get you?"

"Raven is here for some bread. I mostly just came along for the company." Kanan shrugged. "And the turnovers,"

Madame Falstead offered him a very apologetic look. "Tomorrow." Her honey dripping voice changed in an instant as she turned. "Esrae! Get over here and get this couple some bread."

Slowly, Esrae turned, her throat bobbing, and moved toward the counter where Raven and Kanan stood.

Raven mouthed the words *I'm sorry* to Esrae, not daring to speak them aloud.

Esrae looked down and gave a quick shake of her head. "What can I get you?"

Esrae's left cheek was cherry red and Raven hated to make her do anything that awful woman told her to do. She spoke quietly, "I just need a loaf of sourdough for dinner. If you don't have any, that's fine."

"Nonsense," Madame Falstead cut in. "Of course we do. Esrae, don't just stand there, go get the lady her bread. Don't dawdle."

"Yes, Madame Falstead," Esrae said as she turned and disappeared into a back room.

"Ridiculous girl," Madame Falstead rolled her eyes. "I'm sorry. She won't be a minute."

Again Raven opened her mouth to speak, to defend her friend, but Kanan's hand landed softly on her shoulder, sliding down to the small of her back. "We're not in a hurry," he said.

Esrae returned shortly with a loaf of bread wrapped in brown parchment paper and tied with a length of twine. She handed it over the counter, not meeting his gaze as Kanan accepted it.

"Well, you young people have a good day. I'm back to work." Madame Falstead smiled at Kanan and Raven. When she turned to Esrae, her smile vanished. "You too, useless thing. Back to work."

After Madame Falstead left the room, the three stood in a silence that seemed to stretch for ages. Finally, Raven could stand it no longer. She intended to speak normally, but when she formed the word, it came out very quiet. "Esrae."

Esrae continued to look at the floor. "It's fine, Raven."

Raven stepped closer, placing her palm on the counter and sliding it toward her friend. "It's not, Esrae."

"Raven!" Esrae snapped, turning to look at the door that Madame Falstead had disappeared through before turning an icy gaze back on Raven. "I said, it's fine."

Raven shook her head, her next words out of her mouth before she could think. "Es, why do you stay here?"

Esrae shot Raven a withering look. "Are you joking? Where do you propose I go, Raven? I have no family. I would have no job. If I don't have a job, I wouldn't be able to afford a place to live." Some of the venom disappeared from Esrae's voice. "It's not that bad really, you get used to it. It's just words."

"Just words?" Her friend enduring those *words* day after day left a sour pit in Raven's stomach. "You could come stay with me. We have room."

Esrae shifted on her feet. "I don't need charity, Raven."

"It's not charity." Raven reached out to take the hand Esrae had resting on the counter, but Esrae snatched it away. "Es—"

"Is there anything else you need?" Esrae cut her off, glancing between them. "I really do need to get back to work."

Raven couldn't find her voice. She just stood there, her lips parted.

"Sorry to keep you, Es. We don't need anything else." Kanan dropped a handful of coins on the counter before steering Raven from the bakery. "See you later."

Esrae didn't respond as they exited the building to the soft jingling sound of the bell above the door.

"I—" Raven began but Kanan lifted a finger to stop her. He inclined his head and she followed him until they were out of earshot of the bakery.

Kanan removed his hand from Raven's back and slipped it into hers, their fingers interlocking. "What is it?"

Raven blinked, her eyes stinging. "I had no idea. I knew she wasn't happy, but she never told me it was so bad."

"Yeah, Madame Falstead isn't exactly the ray of sunshine she tries to convey, that's for sure," Kanan said.

"I wish she could get out of there," Raven sighed. "Why won't she just come stay with me?"

"Pride?" Kanan sighed heavily. "Maybe we can find her somewhere else to work. Anything to get her out of there."

Pressure built in Raven's chest. "She's been with the Falsteads since she was ten. She was ten, Kanan!"

Kanan's mouth pressed into a line, his grip on her hand tightening. "That's a long time to be told you're stupid."

Why hadn't Esrae ever told her this was happening? There had been times when they'd been younger that she'd found Esrae crying, but she was always quick to dry her tears. Even when she was little she was never one to share her emotions. Raven had always just assumed Esrae was sad because she didn't have any real family.

"Why didn't she tell me?"

Kanan released her hand, instead slipping his arm around her and pulling her close. "I don't know."

"She has to get out of there."

He kissed the top of her head. "We'll do what we can to help. Maybe our little adventure will get her out."

She slid her free arm around his waist and let him hold her. "I'm not sure that'll be better."

They fell into silence when moments later, it was shattered by a high-pitched wail and a woman's panicked voice calling out, "No! No! Please, please, no, don't take him!"

Raven's heart dropped and sped to a gallop as she looked in the direction of the shouting and back to Kanan. Alarm shone in his eyes, her own thoughts reflecting back to her as surely as if he'd spoken them aloud.

"Come on." Kanan took her hand and pulled her along back down the street toward the shrieking, following the crowd that was already moving in that direction.

They turned down a side street and the source of the commotion became apparent. A sobbing woman sat on the ground cradled between two friends. Every one of their gazes was focused on the soldiers.

Two soldiers stood surveying the gathered crowd. Raven recognized one of them as the man she'd spoken to at the bakery, the one who had come to get Laurise. She didn't know the one standing with him, she would have remembered his bright orange curls. Two more, one with close cropped dark hair, another shorter than most guards she'd seen, were walking up the street, a man held firmly in their grasp. Dust billowed up behind them from where his feet dragged on the ground as they hauled him toward waiting horses.

Terror twisted the man's features.

Kanan and Raven came to a stop as Kanan turned to the man beside them. Keeping his voice low, he asked, "What's going on?"

The man responded, voice also quiet, not taking his eyes off the scene before them, "They're taking him away. Said the King got word he was inciting disloyalty."

"Disloyalty?" Raven hissed.

"Keep your voice down. Don't know. Only heard him say the taxes were too high," the man responded, dropping his voice even lower so Raven had to strain to hear. "He might have said more. That might have been it. The King's definition of disloyalty is broad."

The guards had almost made it to their horses when the sobbing woman broke free of the hold the others had on her. She made a desperate sound that might have been her husband's name as she rushed toward the captive man. Her progress was halted as the shorter guard turned and backhanded her across her face. A cracking sound reverberated down the street and Raven flinched. The woman let out a sharp yelp as she was sent sprawling backward, crashing into the dirt.

A collective gasp sounded through the crowd and in the distraction the man wrenched free of the guards' hold. He didn't make it more than three feet as the bakery guard and orange-haired guard intercepted him. The bakery guard caught the prisoner easily by the upper arm and spun him back around. There was a gleeful expression on the orange-haired guard's face, as though he was glad the man tried to run, and he drove his fist into the man's stomach.

Raven clamped her hands over her mouth to stifle her cry of surprise.

The bakery guard stepped back from where the prisoner had crumpled to the ground. "Get him up!"

The man's wife was once again between her friends. She cradled her cheek, sobbing softly, the sound sending a stab to Raven's heart.

The familiar voice of the bakery guard boomed through the air: "Does anyone else have anything they'd like to say?" He turned slowly, taking in the crowd, challenge written on his face. And then his eyes found Raven and her blood turned to ice.

The blonde man's head cocked to the side, a sneer spreading across his features. He prowled toward her and Kanan took half a step, placing himself between them.

"Well, well," the guard took her in, ignoring Kanan. "We meet again."

"Can we help you with something?" Kanan's voice was much steadier than Raven could have managed.

The guard give Kanan a quick once over before returning his attention to Raven. "This your girl?"

"She doesn't belong to me," Kanan answered.

The guard's mouth turned up at the corner and a chill ran down Raven's spine. "Then you won't mind if I take her with me."

With another half a step, Kanan placed himself fully between Raven and the guard. "She doesn't belong to me, but she is with me."

Slowly the guard moved his eyes to meet Kanan's, a silent challenge forming in his stare. He opened his mouth to speak but was interrupted by the dark haired guard calling out in their direction: "Holden, let's go."

The guard closed his mouth and tilted his head to look around Kanan to Raven. He winked. "Next time."

"Time to go!" Raven jumped as the dark haired guard barked the command before he even turned around. "You all need to be on your way. And remember, the King does not appreciate treachery."

The guards mounted their horses, the prisoner with them, and dust billowed up from the road as they kicked their horses into a gallop.

The only sound was the woman in the dirt, wailing.

Raven slid her knife along the surface of the cutting board, scraping the mound of freshly diced carrots into the bubbling, steaming pot. The resulting splash sent a large drop of boiling water leaping from the pot and onto her hand. She let out a yelp as she snatched her hand back, trying shake off the pain.

Her father turned from where he stood, also chopping. "Alright?"

"Fine." She sucked on the wound for a moment before she continued what she had been telling her father. "Anyway, they just left her laying there. Potatoes?"

"Right here." He turned and handed her another cutting board piled high with freshly diced potatoes. "She should probably be grateful they didn't take her too. We all know how Malakai likes to make examples of people."

She stood as far from the pot as she could as she pushed the potatoes in. "Someone there told us he'd heard the man complain about the taxes. The taxes! And they hauled him away."

"Hello?"

Raven's head whipped around, her heart picking up slightly at the sound of Logan's voice. She was eager to speak with him. The thought of waiting all evening to get the chance brought on a feeling of butterflies in her stomach.

There was no way she could discuss anything with her father there. He would shut down any talk of her involvement quicker than he could slam a door. She would have to wait until Logan left and follow him out.

Logan came around the corner. "Raven," he greeted her with a slight incline of his head. "It smells amazing in here."

"Soup," Raven said. "Chicken, carrots, potatoes, etcetera."

"And wine," her father said with a snap of his fingers, already moving out of the room. "I almost forgot. Two minutes."

Raven remained still, listening for the sound of the cellar door clicking shut, then she spoke. "I need to talk with you later."

"Oh?" She could see that he was already wary about what the conversation might entail.

"When you leave," Raven said. "Not around my father."

Logan exhaled deeply, his shoulders drooping. "Raven, your father was very clear about this."

Raven feigned ignorance. "About what?"

He let his head fall to the side as he pinned her with a skeptical look. "I'm no fool, Raven."

She dropped the pretense, infusing her words with sincerity. "I know you're not a fool. That's why I need to speak with you. Obviously I'm not saying my father's a fool, but he's biased. He can't have a clear head about this."

Logan regarded her, something sad in his eyes. "And you think I can?"

"I don't mean it like that," Raven said. "I just know him and I know you. I know you'll see logic regardless of the package it's in."

Logan studied her. She knew he already knew what she was going to say to him, and he did look sad. Sadness most likely because he knew she was right and he didn't want her to be.

"Wine," her father declared, holding up a bottle as he reappeared in the kitchen.

"Red, I hope," Logan said, switching topics effortlessly.

Raven admired him for how easily he went from one subject to another. His entire demeanor changed in a blink.

"I do know a little something about wine, thank you." The bottle made a knocking sound as her father set it down on the heavy wooden table.

Raven retrieved three glasses and waited as her father popped the cork off the bottle and filled each one. She accepted the glass he handed to her. *Keep it coming,* she thought.

"I think I would like to make a toast," Logan said, holding his glass up, "if you don't mind."

Her father's brows rose as he picked up his glass. "What's the occasion?"

Logan raised his glass higher and looked at her father and then at Raven, his eyes lingering on her as he spoke. "To friends who became family."

She understood him. He was just as concerned with her joining in on their plans as her father. She held his gaze, but still felt like she could convince him. She knew Logan; she knew he would see the reason and the logic. She and Kanan, Esrae, and Torren—they could help, and Logan and her father needed all the help they could get.

"To family," her father echoed as he raised his glass higher.

"To family," Raven said, though her voice was quieter.

Raven hung the damp rag over the counter and absentmindedly wiped her hands on her pants. It felt as though there was a caged animal inside her prowling around, knocking into walls, trying to get out. More than once, it had taken someone calling her name multiple times before she realized anyone was speaking to her. She couldn't focus on anything as she waited for Logan to leave. She intended to follow him out to speak with him alone, but it was beginning to feel like he planned to stay forever. Would they never stop talking? Maybe Logan was doing it on purpose, wearing her down. Finally, she excused herself, kissing both her father's and Logan's cheeks, before going to her room. She had no intention of sleeping. She just wanted to be sure that she could get out to speak with Logan when he left without having to explain anything to her father.

She sat on her bed, a book in her hand, reading the same sentence a dozen times. With a grunt of frustration she tossed the book onto the bed beside her where it flopped closed with a muted snap. Unable to sit any longer, she stood and began pacing the length of her small room. She knew exactly how many steps were between her armoire and the wall on the opposite side of the room, and instead of watching the floor, she closed her eyes and focused her attention on the voices down the hall. Silently she counted the steps back and forth as she continued to wait for Logan to leave. She was confidant he would see the need for her help, but at the same time, she still anticipated a struggle.

When she finally heard Logan's deep, lilting voice bid her father goodnight and the subsequent click of the front door, she carefully and quietly slipped out her bedroom window, landing in a crouch on the hard-packed dirt. She moved swiftly down the path that ran along the vines, leading away from their house and toward the main road, making sure she was far enough away that they wouldn't be overheard. When she was satisfied, she leaned against a tree and waited, glad that Logan had taken his time riding up the road.

She remained still until he'd passed by and then she stepped out behind him. At the sound of her boots, he reined in his horse, turning the giant animal in her direction. His sword was already halfway out of its sheath before she spoke, hands raised in front of her. "It's just me."

His saddle creaked as he relaxed, sliding his sword back into the sheath with a hiss. "Sneaking up on a soldier in the dark, Raven. It's not your wisest moment."

"I'm sorry," Raven said. "I just wanted to be away from the house before we spoke."

Logan raised his hand, cutting her off. "I can't say I'm surprised, but if it's about what I think it is, we can't talk here." His eyes swept around them, even though it was far too dark to see much of anything.

Frustrated, Raven threw her hands in the air. "Then where? When?"

His shoulders drooped as he watched her. "How's nowhere and never?"

She rolled her eyes. "I can help you and you know I can."

"Not here, Raven." The tone in Logan's voice was that of a career military general, it held no room for argument.

"Fine," Raven conceded. "Where?"

"In the cellar." He inclined his head back toward the house. "Only in the cellar. It's the only place we can be certain we aren't being overheard."

"Except by me."

"Yes, well, you're not often in the cellar, are you?" He gave her a long-suffering look.

"Fine," Raven said. "Tell me when to meet you."

Logan was silent for a moment as he studied her, possibly trying to decide if she was serious. "You do realize if we're meeting in the cellar, your father will be there as well."

She shrugged, she'd assumed this. "As long as you point out reason to him. No shutting down because he says no."

"And what makes you think I'll do that?" Logan asked. "Why are you so certain I'll take your side in all of this?"

She straightened. "Because you're intelligent and logical. And desperate."

He regarded her for a long moment. "Goodnight, Raven."

She held his gaze. She knew him well enough to know that he would hear her out. "Goodnight, Logan."

SIX

Three nights later, Raven lay in her bed as the light from the candle danced on the ceiling. Her book lay abandoned on the bed beside her, having fallen victim yet again to her wandering thoughts and increasing inability to concentrate. She huffed a breath and leaned over to snuff out the candle when there was a soft knock on her bedroom door.

She propped herself up on an elbow, expecting her father. "Yes?"

"May I?"

Her heart rate kicked up at the sound of Logan's voice. She sat up, her bones humming. "Yes, come in."

The door opened, and Logan appeared on the other side. "You still want to talk?"

"You know I do." She was already standing, sliding her feet into her waiting slippers.

Logan inclined his head in an invitation. She slipped past him and down the hall, not needing to ask where they were going.

She followed the hall until it ended at the door to the cellars and froze. Logan stepped past her and pulled open the door.

Torches lined the wall along the descending wooden stairs. Her chest tightened stealing her breath as she stood there, looking down.

"Raven?" Logan asked, waiting.

"Yeah?" The whispered word was the only sound she could manage.

"It's alright." Logan reached out and placed a hand on her back. "Breathe, I'm right behind you."

She closed her eyes and inhaled a shaky breath, and then another. She would not let this ridiculous fear stand in her way. She stepped down onto the first step and a tremor wracked through her.

"Breathe," Logan repeated.

With another determined breath, Raven followed the stairs down as she tried not to think of all the earth pressing down on top of them.

At the bottom, Logan took the lead again, and she followed him down a long hall, passing two offshoots, until they finally turned the third corner to find her father waiting.

He took one look at Raven standing there and turned a sharp glare on Logan. Her father rarely got angry, but when he did, his eyes said it all. "What is this?"

Logan's voice remained neutral, the voice of a general. "She asked to speak with me and I told her I'd listen to what she had to say."

"You?" Her father's word dripped with accusation.

When Logan responded, his tone was careful, as though he was trying to avoid spooking an animal. "She's not a child."

After another moment of subjecting Logan to the full force of his gaze, her father turned to Raven. "Well?"

Raven barely registered their exchange, still trying to calm the wild horses feeling in her chest. She drew in as deep a breath as she could manage. Then she met her father's hard gaze. "You already know. I want to help."

"And you already know, I said no," her father responded, jaw set, dismissing her.

Arguing with her father was enough to get her mind off of the earth pressing in on her. "Are you really saying there's no place in your little, *very* little, band of rebels for me?" She turned to Logan. "Nothing I can do to help?"

Logan opened his mouth, and Raven waited, but he closed it again quickly as he glanced between her and her father. Finally, his gaze came to rest on the packed earth floor at his feet.

He hesitated, and then he was looking at her father again, and the look of warning in her father's eyes was clear. They were having an entire, silent conversation.

She couldn't take it any longer. "What?"

Logan's blue eyes met hers, and he didn't look at her father again. "Malakai does retain a number of young women in his service."

The implication stole Raven's breath even as her father swore.

"Have you lost your mind?" the words hissed out of him.

Logan ignored him, his focus remaining on Raven. "Their tasks range from kitchen work to maid service, reading, even dancing, and—" He hesitated. "Other things. They perform many different tasks. But they're always beautiful. And, more importantly, they have the potential to get much closer to Malakai than even I ever could."

Nausea tugged at her stomach and she suddenly felt very small as she met Logan's eyes. His meaning was clear, and she allowed herself the briefest moment to consider if she could go through with such things. Cleaning and dishes was one thing, but the prospect of more intimate obligations made her consider rescinding her offer. Of course, Logan was right. Who else could get that close to the King?

Then she saw children playing at the banks of the river, like Laurise's children had. But these were not Laurise's children. These children had thick, wild dark hair and Kanan's olive eyes. Raven's skin prickled, goosebumps rushing down her arms. For her children, for the future of her home, for her family—for these things she would do whatever needed to be done.

She was suprised at how steady her voice was when she spoke. "How do I get in?"

"Raven!" her father exclaimed, something like agony in his tone. "Do you have any idea what you're asking?"

Raven did her best to ignore her father, her gaze fixed on Logan. She knew he was just concerned, but she needed to focus. "How?"

Logan's brow furrowed deeply, his mouth set in a grim line. He glanced quickly at her father before he returned his attention to Raven.

"Raven," he began. There was hesitation and warning in his tone.

"Logan, how?" she pleaded, before she lost her nerve.

Logan exhaled a long breath before he spoke, steeling himself for his next words. "It would be best if Malakai chose you himself, not for you to volunteer. If he chooses you, there will be no question of ulterior motives." His expression turned sad. "It would only take one look at you, and he would be escorting you back to the palace."

"How?" Raven repeated. "How could I ever get close enough to him for that?"

She waited, watching the battle rage in Logan's eyes. "On occasion, Malakai rides. He likes to take his horse out. He takes a detail of men and goes riding in the forest for hours. If I know when he's going out..." He spoke as though every word caused him pain. "We could arrange for you to be on the road."

"Logan!" Raven jumped as her father's fist cracked off the top of a large wooden barrel beside him, the sound echoing through the chamber.

She ignored him. "And Esrae? She offered her help as well."

"Can you trust her?" Logan asked.

"Yes, of course. I mean, she can be a little moody sometimes, but she's in a bad situation where she is. She just wants out. Kanan and Torren want to help too. If you can find a way to get them in."

Logan huffed out a short breath, holding up a hand. "One thing at a time. First, you and Esrae. The next time I know that Malakai is going out, I'll get word to you." He paused, a crease formed in his brow as his eyes scanned her face. "Raven, make sure you talk to Esrae; she needs to know what she could be getting into. Everything."

Raven nodded once at Logan but didn't dare look at her father. She could feel him seething from where he stood.

Logan nodded as well. "It's late."

Logan turned to leave, but before he made it to the door, her father's hand shot out, wrapping around his arm. The look in his eyes would have scared any other man. His tone was deadly and held no hesitation. "We've been friends for a long time. I don't say this because I'm her father, I say it because it's true, and you know it. My daughter is very beautiful, like her mother. If Malakai takes her to his bed, I will never forgive you."

Logan's chin dipped once and her father released him, walking away and leaving Logan and Raven alone.

Raven had never seen her father like that, never seen that kind of rage in his eyes, never heard him sound so unforgiving. A chill cascaded over her, settling deep in her chest.

They were both silent as her father's footsteps grew further away. Finally, Logan turned his head toward her. "Goodnight, Raven."

There was a weariness in his voice and she moved swiftly, catching up with him. "Wait." Logan stopped and turned to her. "He still looks at me like I'm a child."

He smiled sadly. "Clearly, you're no longer a child."

"Clearly." Raven regretted putting the two friends at odds, but not her offer to help. "Look, I know this could go badly. I know what could happen. I just want you to know I'm still willing. I'll do whatever needs to be done."

Logan studied her for a long moment before responding. "Malakai... he's possessive and he likes young brunettes. I would love to tell you that you'll be fine, that you'll probably be sent to the kitchen, but I can't. I can only tell you to prepare." He paused, his eyes moving over her face. "Because Sebastian is probably right. You will most likely end up in Malakai's bed."

Her stomach bottomed out. She'd always appreciated Logan's candor, but these words nearly made her flinch as she fought to swallow the hard lump in her throat.

"When your father says he will never forgive me for this, it's the truth."

She couldn't meet his gaze. She didn't want to come between her father and Logan, but she had to be a part of this. Her heart cried out to help them, to help her country. "Please? Get me in. I'll bring Esrae."

Logan nodded slowly. "I'll see what I can do about the other two. Maybe I can get them in to train with the army."

Raven smiled at the picture that popped into her head. "Soldier Torren. That should be interesting."

"I'll be in touch." Logan reached out, gently touching her arm. "You should talk to Kanan."

Raven nodded, her focus on a knot in the wine barrel behind Logan. He was right. Kanan deserved to know what she was walking into, and he wouldn't like it. Of course, he wasn't dumb; no doubt already knew. "I will."

Logan nodded and gave her arm a small squeeze. "Goodnight, Raven."

"Goodnight."

For the first time in as long as she could remember, she didn't mind being in the cellar. She looked toward the stairs. As soon as she climbed them, all the secrets would become real. She would have to face these schemes and her choices. Face her father, speak to Esrae, reassure Kanan. A whole new weight would begin pressing down on her.

She pulled in a long breath, lingering a bit longer in the cellar.

SEVEN

Raven lay on the cool ground, head propped on her arms, staring at the clouds drifting across the sky. A twig snapped, and she whipped her head in the direction of the noise.

Kanan leaned against a pole at the end of one of the rows of vines, legs crossed casually at the ankles. He smiled, a broken branch held in his hands.

Raven sat up, narrowing her eyes at him. "How long have you been there?"

He smiled coyly. "A while."

She rolled her eyes, climbing to her feet. "Why don't you make noise when you walk?"

"That wouldn't be any fun." He tossed the branch aside and crossed to where she stood, pulling her into his arms. "Where is everyone?"

"It's just us so far. Esrae's busy at the bakery, so she'll be late." Raven shrugged. "And Torren is always late."

"So, what will we do to pass the time?"

She smiled up at him. "I don't know. Did you have something in mind?"

A smirk lifted the corner of his mouth and he tightened his hold, pulling her close. He bent his head just enough to brush his lips over hers.

Raven inhaled deeply, the scent of leather and lemon soap filling her senses. Kanan pulled his head back just enough to look her in the eye. "You could teach me more of your full contact combat skills."

"You really want me to throw you on the ground again?" Raven asked.

Kanan gave her a look of mild exasperation, then he smiled. "Anytime."

She laughed. Okay. Without warning him, she easily stepped out of his hold, spinning around. Stepping in front of him, she reached up and pulled his head down, flipping him over her back and onto the ground. She stradled him, smiling triumphantly.

Kanan laughed through his groan, grinning up at her. "A little warning would be nice."

She shrugged, smiling. "You said 'anytime'."

His eyes met hers. "I guess I did."

Kanan held her gaze until her heart ached at the emotion in his eyes. As he studied her face, his grin faded into something more serious. Reaching up he tucked a lock of her dark hair behind her ear, brushing his fingers lightly along her cheek as he did so.

"What?" Raven's voice died in her throat. She knew him well enough to know what he was thinking.

"You're beautiful." His voice held a sad, almost pained, quality.

She swallowed.

Kanan placed his hands on her hips, sliding her back enough so he could sit up. She moved off of him and he folded one leg underneath himself and brought his other knee up to his chest so he could rest an arm across it. "I saw Logan in town today. He said he saw you last night."

She folded her legs under her and wished for grass, if only to give her hands something to do. "He came by."

"Tell me." There was quiet urging in his voice and she knew what he meant, what he wanted. It was a conversation they had to have, but one that she was certainly not eager for.

His head tilted as his eyes ran over her face. "It's worse than I thought."

She studied her hands in her lap.

"Raven, look at me?" There was almost a plea in the words.

She dragged her eyes from the dusty ground to meet his.

"How are you getting in?" Kanan asked.

She didn't even want say the word. Would her relationship survive this? She swallowed. "Invitation."

Kanan's expression didn't change. "Invitation from whom?"

"The King."

Slowly his eyes slid down and back up. "He won't be inviting you to do his laundry, Raven."

The look in his eyes stole every word from her lips.

His voice grew quieter. "You know that though."

She blew out a long breath. "You want me to stay home." It wasn't a question, he didn't want her giving herself to the king.

"Yes, " he spoke quickly, but then continued, "I'm scared, Raven. I don't want you going in there. I want to keep you here with me where I know you're safe. I don't want you to offer yourself to a madman. I don't want to share you. I don't want to lose you."

"You won't lose me."

"You don't know that. You can't say that because there's no way to know what will happen here."

"Kanan—"

"Stop, Raven." He reached out, taking her hand. "I do want you to stay, but I know this is what you want to do. To help your father and Logan, to help the country. And I'm so proud of you for it. And I trust you completely. It's not a question of that. It's just a lot and dangerous, and I don't have to like it."

Her heart might as well have been cracking in half. The pain in his eyes and his voice squeezed her chest and she swallowed back the lump that was climbing up her throat. "I'm sorry."

His mouth ticked up ever so slightly in a sad smile. "I know you are."

"I am. I'm sorry there's no other way." She swallowed back a sob. "I'm sorry this hurts so much. But you don't know know how much I appreciate your support."

He slid closer and took her other hand, running his thumbs lightly over her knuckles. "Raven, you always have my support. Always."

"I don't know what I would do without you."

He dipped his head down to look her in the eye. "You would do the same thing without me as you would do with me. Because you're strong and you don't need me."

"That's not true. I do need you."

The sound of a cough drew their attention to the rows of vines.

"Are we interrupting something?" Torren asked from where he stood with Esrae.

Raven looked back to Kanan and smiled when his voice blended with hers as they answered in unison, "Yes."

"Too bad."

They approached, and Torren dropped onto the ground, sending a cloud of dust billowing. Esrae folded herself much more neatly, taking care to keep her dress as clean as she could.

Esrae reached over and brushed the dust off Raven's pants. "Been wrestling?" She smiled.

"Actually, I have." Raven shot her brows in the air and both women giggled

"Who's next?" Kanan asked, looking around.

"Next to get knocked on their back by Raven?" Torren said. "No thanks. Pass."

"I've spent worse afternoons." Kanan shrugged. "And it wouldn't kill you two to learn some basic self-defense. Es?" He toed Esrae's shoe with his boot.

"Do I look like I'm dressed for combat?" Esrae pulled her foot out of his range. "I came to talk."

"Ok, let's talk," Raven said.

"Did you get to talk to Logan and your father?" Torren stretched his long legs out in front of him and leaned back on his palms.

"Yes. My father was less than enthusiastic, but that's what I expected. He didn't really agree, he just sort of stopped talking. But Logan had an idea how to get us in. Well, *us*." She gestured to Esrae. "He thinks the best way is for the—" She paused, thinking maybe a code word would be better. Even though they had a clear view of the vineyard down the rows and would be able to see anyone coming, still, she edited her words. "The *Butcher* to invite us himself." Raven's eyes flicked to Kanan but found his eyes closed, a small crease between his brows.

"What do you mean? Why would the *Butcher* invite us? How?" Esrae's fingers were busy pulling at the fraying ends of a ribbon and she swallowed visibly when she met Raven's eyes. For a moment, Raven wondered if it was a good idea to take her along.

"Logan said he likes to go riding. Sometimes he takes some of his *friends* and rides for hours through the forest. He thinks that if we're on the road and he sees us he may just invite us back to *his place*."

"*Invite*," Torren repeated the word. "I don't think that word means what you think it means."

Raven could feel Kanan's eyes on her as she shrugged, acknowledging Torren's observation.

Raven looked back to Esrae who had gone very pale. "Es, you don't have to do this."

Esrae's eyes snapped to Raven's, cool resolve filling her irises. "I can do it. What else do I have? A backroom at a bakery where I work like a slave? I'd rather be anywhere else."

"And what about us?" Kanan's question broke the tension Esrae's comments had created. She'd talk to her later when they could be alone.

Torren turned to Kanan, a hand splayed over his own heart. "You don't think we're pretty enough to get an invitation?" He ran a hand over his short dark hair. "And I just cut my hair."

Raven appreciated Torren's ability to find humor in even the most dire of situations. "*Or*, Logan suggested getting you both in by way of the army."

Torren's hand dropped to his side, and he looked at her as though she'd grown another head. "Raven, I'm pretty sure I'd have a better chance of getting in on my looks."

"Sounds great." There was sadness and resignation in Kanan's voice and Raven studied him wishing she could divine his thoughts.

"That will never work for me. For Kanan maybe, but I'm not a soldier," Torren said. "I'll last five minutes."

She didn't disagree but she didn't say anything, only shrugged. "That's what Logan suggested. He is the General, I'm sure he has some say." She turned back to Esrae, who had gone quiet. "Es, are you sure you want to do this?"

"Raven, I said I'm fine!" Esrae snapped. "Anything is better than staying here. You're not the only one who can be a hero."

She almost flinched at the harsh words. She certainly wasn't trying to be a hero. "I didn't mean it like that, Es."

Esrae only shook her head. "Raven, I've had enough. I've had enough of that bakery, I've had enough of the Falstead's. If this is my way out and I can help the country, why is that even a question?"

Knowing what Esrae faced every day, Raven couldn't fault her for wanting a way out. Raven had no mother, but she practically had two fathers. Esrae really had no one. No one besides her, Kanan, and Torren. She offered Esrae a small nod. Of course she wanted out. If only there were a safer alternative than rushing into the arms of a mad king.

She wanted to beg Esrae to make sure this was what she wanted, but after Esrae had snapped at her, she thought better of it. "Okay. It's okay if you change your mind too."

"Right, Es. This is super dangerous." Esrae shot Torren a look, but he continued, "But, you know, not as dangerous as when we jumped off the cliff into the lake."

Raven rolled her eyes. But she noticed Esrae crack a small smile, rolling her eyes. Torren could always get to Es, even when no one else could.

"No, no. Nothing could ever be as dangerous as that." Though Kanan's words were light, his gaze on Raven remained serious.

There was silence among them for a long time. Raven took in her friends, and it was clear by their expressions that their thoughts also dwelled on what they were about to do and all the ways it could play out.

Raven finally broke the silence. "You're all still coming to dinner tomorrow, right?"

Esrae brushed the dust and dirt from her dress. "I'll be late. Someone placed a huge order and I have to bake."

Raven was relieved to hear that; she'd feared that the tension from earlier might make Esrae want to stay away.

"Food? I'm in," Torren said.

Rave turned to Kanan. "And you?"

"Of course I'll be there. I'll even let you manhandle me again." Kanan winked at her.

Raven smiled but then her eyes found Esrae where she sat on the ground. She took care to brush the dust away and smooth the creases of her dress every few moments. The other girl had been quiet for much of their conversation, but Raven didn't miss the way she picked at her nails, her hands constantly moving. It was a nervous habit that Esrae had had since they were young. Though she was careful, she would never tear or break them on purpose; she liked to keep them well groomed.

"I need to go." Esrae stood and once again brushed at her light blue dress. "I have to get up early."

Raven turned to Kanan to tell him that she wanted to walk with Esrae, to talk to her, but she found she didn't need to speak. Kanan knew her well.

He pulled her hand to his lips and brushed a kiss across her knuckles. "I'll see you later."

She smiled and stood, brushing at her own fitted, tan pants. "Hey, Es, do you mind if I walk with you?"

Esrae seemed a bit surprised. "Sure. Isn't it a little out of your way?"

Raven shrugged, and Esrae returned her attention to the road. Raven waved a hand at Torren and Kanan and joined Esrae.

They walked in silence for some time as Raven ran through ten different ways to start a conversation in her head. She couldn't come up with one sentence that wouldn't end in misunderstanding. Being direct, it seemed, was the best option. She huffed out a small breath and spoke, "Es, I did want to talk to you."

"Hmm?"

"About this whole thing with the *Butcher*." Raven dropped her voice low, even though they were alone. The path that led from their spot in the vineyard to the road into Chemari was used by almost no one but the four friends.

Esrae blew out an annoyed breath. "I told you, I'll be fine. Honestly, it's like you don't want my help. Why? If I'm there, will I steal some of the glory?"

"Esrae." Raven flinched. She didn't really think that was the case, did she?

Another long sigh. "I'm sorry. It's just a little stressful. A week ago, my future looked pretty bleak. Now it's potentially bleak for another reason. But at least this is my choice."

What could she say to that? Esrae's life was so different from her own, and she could never understand what it was like.

Esrae spared Raven the need to speak when she stopped walking and turned to face her. She was silent for a few moments, and Raven waited. Esrae swallowed. "You saw what it's like with the Falsteads. Raven, I would do anything to get out of there." Esrae's eyes shone as she reached out and grabbed Raven's arm. "Anything."

Raven swallowed down her own tears and nodded. "It's dangerous. I mean, you know why he invites women back to the palace. It's not for tea."

Esrae held her gaze, her lips pressed into a thin line. "Anything," she repeated the word.

"I'm sorry, Esrae," Raven breathed because she didn't know what else to say.

Esrae pulled her arm back and straightened her spine, holding her chin a bit higher. "Don't be. We're going to the palace, we're going to meet the *Butcher*, and we're going to save the country. Who wouldn't want to be part of that?"

Raven rolled her eyes and let out a small laugh as she linked arm through Esrae's. They walked the rest of the way to Esrae's room in the back of the bakery in silence.

EIGHT

Raven placed the kettle on the small stove as Kanan pulled out a chair at the table. He'd stayed the night with her, both of them unwilling to give up any of their time together when they had no idea what the future held.

"What are you reading?"

She turned around to him to find him holding a small book, flipping through the pages. She must have forgotten to put it away the previous day.

"It's a book of poetry. Logan gave it to me years ago. I have most of it memorized." She stepped up to him and flipped to the first page holding it out for him to see the note Logan had inscribed there.

Kanan accepted the book from her and read the words aloud. "'*Little Bird, I have no doubt you are meant to soar in this life. I look forward to seeing where you land. Logan.*'" He handed it back. "Thats sweet."

She accepted the book with a small shrug and a smile. "He loves me."

Kanan's gaze softened, his mouth turning up at the corner as his eyes ran over her face. He reached out, taking her by the waist and pulling her down so she perched on his lap. "How could he not?" He ran a finger over her jawline before sliding his hand into her hair and pulling her face to his, moving his mouth over hers.

The tea kettle began to whistle loudly and Kanan broke the kiss, giving the pot an annoyed look. "You needed tea."

"Hey!" Raven pulled back. "You wanted tea too."

His eyes found hers again. "But at what cost?"

Raven laughed, rolling her eyes as she pushed off his lap and turned to remove the screaming kettle from the heat. She prepared them each a cup and when she turned to hand one to Kanan, his eyes held a look that made it seem as though he was far away from her small kitchen.

"You look like you're thinking."

"Thank you." Kanan accepted the cup and blew softly over the rim, sending the steam curling into the air. "I am. How did Logan end up the King's General if he doesn't even like the King?"

Raven cupped her hands around her mug, savoring the warmth as it crept into her skin. "Logan's been the King's General for a long time. I think he thought Malakai would improve things after Endryk. I've heard terrible things about him."

"So have I, from my Grandmother. He was king when I was born. But not for long, Malakai overthrew him a few years later."

Raven nodded. "They expected him to be better. I don't think he was always the way he is now. "

"You ever ask?" Kanan sipped his tea.

Raven shook her head. "No. There's always been sort of an unspoken rule that we don't talk about that stuff when Logan's here. Like, this is where he comes to leave it behind. He doesn't even wear his sword or insignia inside the house. Takes it off at the door."

"But your father was in the army. He left and Logan stayed," Kanan said.

"My father left because he met my mother and they had me, not because he wasn't happy with the ruler," Raven said. "Logan didn't have any of that, so he stayed. Also, Logan was the General and my father was just another random soldier. It was easy for him to leave and not be missed."

"So, why now? What changed for Logan?" Kanan shrugged.

"I don't know. Like I said, he doesn't talk about it," Raven answered. "Not while I'm around anyway."

Kanan's eyes met hers and he smiled slightly. "Did you ever ask Logan to show you the palace?"

She laughed. "What do you think? I used to beg him when I was young. My father would get so upset."

"He didn't want you going?" Kanan swirled his cup in a circle on the table.

"No, at first it was that I was too young to go be away from him." Raven sipped her drink. "But honestly, when I got older, 17, 18... I think he was afraid that what we're hoping will happen now would've happened then."

A shadow crept into Kanan's eyes and she suddenly felt guilty for bringing it up. "You mean that Malakai would take one look at you and keep you?"

A heavy sigh pushed from Raven's lips and she looked away. She knew that was a distinct possibility and it was something that bothered Kanan greatly, but on the other hand, why did they believe that? "I don't know why everyone assumes that he'll just snatch me up. I'm just me."

A sad, barely there smile touched Kanan's face. "You're not serious."

"I am." Raven waved a hand in his direction. "You all seem to think he won't be able to help himself. It's a little ridiculous, really."

The tiny smile dissolved into something much more grim. "Raven, you're beautiful." He wasn't offering her a compliment. He was stating a fact.

Raven felt the warmth as it crept into her cheecks.

"You know your looks aren't average. You can be modest, but you can't deny the truth. He's a man like the rest of us. He'll notice." He narrowed his eyes slightly, as though willing her to grasp the seriousness of it all.

As if he or any of them thought she hadn't thought through all the possibilities. As if they thought she didn't lay awake at night, dwelling solely on the seriousness of it all; on all the things that could happen and all the ways this could end. She knew. Saints, she knew.

She didn't respond, didn't know what to say. She'd been told all her life how beautiful her mother was and how Raven resembled her.

Her father had been instantly taken with Serene's beauty. Raven had heard again and again the story of how her parents had met.

Her mother's parents owned an inn and her father and Logan had stopped there for the night. Her mother, Serene, had been working there, and the moment her parent's had seen each other they'd fallen hard.

Both her father and Logan had mentioned her sharing beauty with her mother. But still, Raven couldn't help but feel like it was a bit presumptuous and vain to assume the King would be unable to resist her.

Kanan's voice interupted her thoughts. "You know how dangerous this is." It was not a question.

She forced a smile that she didn't feel. "Well, you don't have to play." Yet despite her best effort at nonchalance, she couldn't keep the small tremor from her voice.

His eyes met hers, his gaze solid and unwavering. "I'm serious. I heard what you just said. But you aren't ignorant. You have to know that Malakai will take one look at you and have you delivered to his bedroom."

A lump formed in her throat at the way his words caught, even as a chill chased down her spine and over her arms. She could no longer meet his eyes.

But she couldn't sit back and do nothing while Logan and her father died trying to do everything on their own. Still, when she spoke, she herself could barely hear the words. "I'll do what I have to do."

Kanan's chair creaked as he leaned forward. "He could hurt you." Pain laced his words, causing her vision to blur.

"I'll be fine," she said the words with much more conviction than she felt. "Besides, you'll be there too."

He reached across the table and wrapped his large, warm, work calloused hand around hers. "You know I would do anything I could to keep you safe. But you also know I won't be around. Not at all at first, and not really later, either.

Being a part of the army, if we can get in, is not the same as living in the palace. You'll be on your own."

He was right, of course. There was little chance they would get to interact at all. She sent a silent pleading prayer to the Saints that their plan, getting into the palace and whatever came next, would work and work quickly. She was already ready to be back home with Kanan.

Kanan opened his mouth to speak again when movement at the kitchen door drew their attention.

Torren stopped, his eyes taking them both in. "Who died?"

Kanan gave Torren a pointed look and then offered the same look to Raven.

"No one," Raven said.

The legs of a chair scraped against the wooden floor as Torren pulled it out and seated himself beside Raven. "So what's going on?"

She swept a thumb under her eye, clearing away the moisture there. "Kanan was just talking about all the bad feelings he has about our plan,"

"Then I'm here just in time." Torren slapped the table and leaned back in his chair. "Because I have some of those feelings myself."

Raven raised her eyebrows as she looked at the two of them. "Dinner tonight. We can discuss all the bad feelings."

NINE

Something thudded against the front door and Raven automatically called out, "Come in!" But when the sound repeated, she finally registered the cadence. It wasn't knocking, it was kicking.

"We can't. Help?" Esrae's muffled voice called from the opposite side of the door.

Raven set the stack of plates she was carrying down on the table and hurried to the door. When she pulled it open, she found Esrae and Kanan on the threshold, their arms layden with multiple baskets of baked goods.

"What—" Words evaporated, replaced by a groan of pleasure when the scent hit her. She pulled in a long slow breath. Bread. "You smell so good." She stepped aside and allowed them to enter. "What is all of this?"

As they stepped across the threshold, Kanan paused to lean down and kiss her lightly. "You make that sound for bread too? And I thought I was special."

She laughed, slapping him playfully. "Get in the house."

She followed them to the table where they dropped the baskets as carefully as they could.

"We made too much." Esrae gestured to the assortment of bread and rolls that now littered the surface of the large table. "I thought I'd bring it here. I'm sure someone will eat it."

Kanan moved to Raven's side and he slipped an arm around her. "I found her trying to carry it all. She was drowning in dough."

Raven laughed.

"Wow," her father said as he entered the room and stopped in front of the table.

Raven inclined her head to the piles of food. "Es brought snacks."

"That I can see," he said. "Had we known this was coming, we wouldn't have had to cook."

"It's not that much, really," Esrae said.

Kanan met Raven's look and rolled his eyes.

"Es, you needed two people to carry it all!" Raven gaped. "It is that much."

"I was doing fine carrying it on my own," Esrae said.

"Right." Kanan didn't sound at all convinced.

Esrae surveyed the room. "Is Torren here yet?"

"Yes." Raven began rearranging the baskets, creating more space on the table. "He's been sent to the cellars for wine."

"It's been some time." Her father glanced in the direction of the cellar door. "Maybe he's gotten lost."

"Not lost!" Torren emerged from the hallway, a bottle of wine in each hand. "I just didn't know which one to get so I . . . Holy bread baskets!"

Raven laughed, spreading her arms out over the table. "Yes, Saint Esrae brought us her holy bread baskets. Now, we feast."

Torren wasted no time, moving past Raven and barely stopping as he set the bottles on the sideboard. He continued around the table, placing his hands on Esrae's shoulders and turning her to face him, his expression serious. "Knots?"

Esrae laughed and rolled her eyes, pointing to one of the baskets. "There."

Torren moved to the opposite side of the table and pulled the towel off the top of the basket that Esrae had indicated. He leaned down and pulled in a deep inhale before plucking up one of the knotted balls of dough. "These are the best things I have ever eaten." He popped it in his mouth, making a very pleased sound.

"You need a girl, mate," Kanan mumbled the words low enough that only Raven heard.

She turned to him, mouth hanging open, a scandalized smile on her face. She slapped him lightly once again, and the intense look he turned on her heated her through to her core.

"What?" he whispered.

She only shook her head slightly, still smiling, and returned her attention to her friends.

Her father placed a stack of dishes beside where Torren had left the wine. "Eat." He stepped back allowing the others to form a line and fill their plates.

"Go ahead" Raven stopped and gestured for her father to choose a plate.

Kanan's breath at her ear sent goosebumps racing down her arm. "I hid a chocolate cake for you."

She turned her head toward him, looking up into his olive eyes. "A whole cake?"

His low smooth chuckle vibrated through her. "Well, a small one. Don't tell."

"I promise." She turned her head a fraction more and his lips met hers.

The center of the long table was completely covered with flakey crescent rolls, pinwheels of dough and cheese sprinkled with parsley, various loaves of bread, and other items, some of which looked to have fruit or chocolate seeping from the creases. They filled their plates and found places at the table. The conversation was light, flowing easily, centered mostly around baked goods. Raven looked around at her friends, seated at the long table, and noted the smiles, their voices blending in a pleasant hum, the clinking of silverware on china. She sent yet another silent prayer to the Saints, begging for aid in carrying out their plans.

Her wish was that they would succeed quickly and find themselves back here, just like this.

As if everyone's thoughts traveled similar paths, the conversation ebbed, the room growing quiet. Her father finally broke the silence, and it was not of bread which he spoke.

He kept his eyes on his plate, his food barely touched. "I wish I could convey to you all how dangerous this is."

Her father was always a more serious person, and any other time Raven might have made a joke to tease him, to lighten the mood, but this was not the time for jokes. Even Torren said nothing. Kanan caught her eye with a look of concern, and she knew that if he were to speak, he would say, *"It's too dangerous."*

She blew out a breath and looked around the table. "We know. We know it's dangerous. I can't speak for anyone else here, but for me, this is what I want to do. I need to help change things. And I don't feel like you and Logan have other options." She glanced around the table at her friends. "But I don't want any of you to feel like you have to do this. I want you to be sure. It is dangerous... extremely."

"Hey." Kanan's voice was soft, and when she looked at him, every other person in the room seemed to fade away. His hand wrapped around hers, squeezing gently. "I'm going with you. You just try to stop me."

The intensity in his words robbed her of all thought as her breath caught in her chest. "Thank you," she breathed.

The moment was interrupted when her father spoke again. "If it were up to me, I would shut it down right now. I don't feel like it's worth it. But Raven is right." His eyes rested on her for a moment, sadness swirling in their dark depths. "And none of you are children. You're each free to make your own choices. Even if I believe those choices to be very poor, indeed. However, Logan seems to think this could work. I've known him a very long time, and I've learned not to question his instincts. So my suggestion is that you wait to make any plans until he's here. Have your conversations with him. He'll be able to offer more insight. He'll know what you should expect and what you should be working toward."

Kanan's hand flexed on hers. "Let's wait for Logan then, and leave this for tonight."

Across the table, Esrae stretched in her seat. "If we're waiting for Logan, then I'm going home. I've had a long day." She gestured to the baskets of baked items that still littered the table.

Torren reached across the table and grabbed another bread knot. He popped it into his mouth and brushed the crumbs from his hands as he rose from the table. "I'll walk you home."

"My hero." Esrae stood and nodded toward the table. "Keep the food."

Torren scooped up the basket containing the knots. "I'm taking these."

Raven smiled. "Are there even any left?"

Torren glanced into the basket and then gave Raven a wary look. "Wouldn't you like to know?"

She laughed, grateful for his sense of humor. "Goodnight to you both. Be safe."

"Goodnight," Esrae waved as she moved to the front door

"Goodnight," Kanan echoed.

"Night," Torren said, following Esrae out.

Her father, who had followed them to the door, pushed it closed behind them. When he returned to the kitchen he stopped, leaning on the back of a chair, studying Raven and Kanan still seated at the table, and sighed deeply. "You know, you two will have to carry this fiasco."

"Papa..." Raven began.

He held up a hand, cutting her off. "You already know what I think. This should be stopped, it's too dangerous." He paused and studied her, and she tried not to shrink under his gaze. His shoulders rose and fell on another weary sigh. "But if anyone can do it, Raven, I know you and Logan, stubborn as stones the both of you, can. And I have no doubt Kanan will stay close. You're each strong and persistent and unwilling to fail. If this plan is to succeed, you'll need all those things.

"Torren and Esrae, I don't doubt their sincerity or their desire to help. But I don't see in them the same fortitude I see in you. Though, maybe they'll surprise me. So, go and do what you must, but please, please, Raven—be careful?"

She had never heard her father speak like this before. A painful lump formed in her throat at his pleading tone and she swallowed it down, even as tears began to sting her eyes. She was grateful when Kanan spoke because she could find no words.

"We will," Kanan said quietly. "I promise."

Her father nodded, his eyes traveling between the two of them, his expression sad. "I'm going to bed. Goodnight."

He stood, moving slowly, as though he carried a heavy weight. If only she could take that burden from him and assure him everything would turn out fine. But she couldn't summon the confidence to make the words sound sincere. Instead she only said, "Goodnight."

"Goodnight," Kanan's voice was a twin to her own, quiet and sad.

"Are you alright?" Kanan rested his hand on her back, his thumb caressing her neck gently.

She wanted to say yes, she was fine, but she could only picture her father's look of trepidation. Instead of speaking, she closed her eyes and blew out a long breath.

Kanan stood and held a hand out to her. She accepted it, allowing him to pull her to her feet.

He tucked her close, wreathing his arms around her as she breathed in his scent, relaxing into his embrace. "What do you think will happen?"

His steady breaths faltered for a beat before he spoke. "I don't know. But whatever happens, we'll deal with it together."

They stood there for a few moments, and Raven tried to forget about everything happening, tried to concentrate only on the feeling of being in his arms, to commit every sensation to memory.

"Let's go for a walk." Kanan's chest vibrated softly with the words.

She pulled back to look him in the eye. "It's dark."

He narrowed his eyes, mischief dancing there. "Are you afraid to be alone in the dark with me?"

"Should I be?" she taunted, brows raised slightly.

He leaned down, his nose brushing the sensitive skin just behind her ear, his breath skating across her skin. "Definitely."

She closed her eyes, air passing over her parted lips as goosebumps rose along her flesh.

"Fine. I promise to be a perfect gentlemen." Kanan brushed her hair behind her neck, allowing his lips to gain better access. "Unless you ask me otherwise."

She smiled.

"Come on, we won't go far." He pulled back, holding his hand out to her. "Let's just get out."

She nodded, but instead of taking his hand to hold it she clasped it with her other hand and wrapped it around her shoulders, tucking herself back into his side. He held her tightly as they stepped outside.

They walked in silence for some time, the only sounds coming from the chorus of night insects calling to each other in the darkness, and Raven was content to continue that way. Just his presence was a comfort, and she intended to take full advantage of it while she was still able. Things would change soon enough.

Kanan broke the silence. "You'll never guess who came into my shop the other day."

"Someone who wanted a sword?" Raven mused.

"No." Kanan's voice was laced with mystery, and Raven smiled. "Someone who wanted a knife."

She jabbed him in the ribs and he jumped, causing her to stumble along with him. "Are you going to explain?"

"Yes!" His laugh rumbled through her from her place tucked beneath his arm. "Isak. Apparently he has *eyes* for Maise."

"Oh, yes!" Raven turned her wide eyes on him. "Esrae told me he followed her into the bakery and bought her a turnover!"

"Well, he's buying her more than that." In the moonlight, Raven could just make out the conspiratorial smile on his face. "He told me he heard that in Shanterac—you know that's where she's from, right? Well, when a man likes a woman, he gifts her a knife, and if she accepts, he's free to pursue her."

"Will she accept, do you think?" Raven half-whispered the words.

"I hope so!" Kanan turned an exaggerated look of dismay on her. "It's a nice knife!"

She laughed, rolling her eyes, an expression that quickly turned to accusation. "Hey, you never gave me a knife!"

He stopped walking, pulling her to stop as well. "I gave you a sword!"

"Not a knife," Raven amended. "I don't know what a sword means."

He turned, looking into her eyes. The playfulness was gone as the moonlight cast a blue glow across his features. "I'll tell you what a sword means." He brushed her hair back over her shoulders. "A sword means I have pledged myself to you forever. And I'll always be there, to the best of my ability, whenever need me."

He ran his hands down her arms, taking both of her hands in his. "You should also know that every moment spent forging that sword, you were on my mind. When I say it's made with love, you can be sure I speak true."

She stared into his eyes, bright with the moon's reflection and, not for the first time, wondered how and why he'd chosen her. "I love you."

"Not as much as I love you," he replied.

"Thank you for distracting me tonight." Because that's what he'd been doing and she was glad to have had this time to think about anything other than what was coming.

He slid his arms around her waist, pulling her against him. "I'd be happy to distract you any time." He bent and kissed her forehead softly. "But we should get you home now. Sebastian will start to worry."

She sighed, rolling her eyes. "Fine."

He smiled and kissed her again before taking her hand and walking back toward her house.

TEN

The next week seemed to fly by. The days were the same as always, all things pertaining to grapes and wine. Often in the late afternoons, their small meeting place within the vines became a training and planning ground. Kanan and Raven spent a few hours with Esrae and Torren working on basic self-defense. Raven hoped they wouldn't need to draw on these newfound skills, but she also didn't want the need to arise and have them ill-equipped to defend themselves.

The hand-to-hand techniques Raven handled. Kanan offered tips on wielding a sword. Raven had the advantage of having had Logan's training for essentially all of her life. Even her father added to her technique. But when it came to swordplay, there were few people better than Kanan. As a swordsmith, Kanan learned the weight and nuances of the blades he crafted. He lived and breathed swords. It was difficult, even for those skilled, to best either of them in their respective skills. It was impossible for Esrae or Torren. But that wouldn't stop them from trying.

And always in the back of her mind loomed the knowledge that one day it would be their last day to prepare and it would be time for action.

Raven yawned, pushing a chunk of potato across the plate with her fork. She was glad for the end of the week and looked forward to some extra sleep. Across from her, her father sat in silence, staring at his own plate. Their eyes met when the soft creak of the front door signaled it had been opened.

"Good evening," Logan appeared from around the corner. He'd stopped knocking a long time ago. Family didn't knock.

Raven sat up in her chair, the rhythm of her heart kicking up, as she took in his somber features. Logan showing up was normally a pleasant surprise. Recently, however, his presence only brought more tension.

Her father's fork made a soft clinking sound as he placed it on the edge of his plate and faced Logan. "What is it?"

Logan turned his attention to Raven, his brow knit in contemplation as though debating sharing whatever information he had.

She tried not to fidget under his gaze and failed. "What?" she demanded.

"Can you get everyone here tomorrow evening?" His voice was quiet but still held the tone of the General.

She didn't trust her own voice to reply, only nodded as her heart sped even faster. *Tomorrow.* Tomorrow was soon.

He nodded back. "Tomorrow, in the cellar."

Raven inhaled deeply and blew it out slowly, willing her heart into a steadier rhythm. "Would you like something to eat?" Her voice trembled in spite of her best efforts to control it.

An obviously forced smile appeared at the corner of his mouth. "No, thank you. I need to go. I just needed to let you know about tomorrow." He moved back toward the door, glancing between her and where her father sat in silence. "Good evening."

"Goodnight," Raven managed.

Her father said nothing.

Raven sat on the plush couch, her legs drawn up under her, clutching a pillow. In front of her the fire cracked and popped softly, sending sparks escaping up the chimney. The room should have been warm enough, yet she still shivered. The others had arrived earlier, each already in the cellars. Raven, in an effort to stay out of the cellar for as long as possible, remained upstairs waiting for Logan. Logan who was on his way to change their lives. Was she prepared to leave her home? To give herself over completely to the whims of a tyrant? It was suddenly so real, and for a moment, she wondered if she could go through with it. Was she that brave? Then she remembered everything that was at stake. She could do this. It wouldn't be easy, but she could do it. She shivered again and was about to get up to stoke the fire when the door in the entryway opened.

She glanced over her shoulder. Logan stood on the threshold, pulling his maroon sash over his head as he always did, and hanging it carefully on a hook outside the door. He stepped further inside and glanced once around the room. "Alone?"

She uncurled herself from where she was seated and dropped the pillow on the sofa. "Everyone else is already downstairs."

He nodded and glanced between her and the hallway that would lead them to the cellar. "Ready?" It was only one word but the look in his eyes held a much deeper question.

She looked down the hallway. "For the cellar, or to hear what you came to say?"

His reply was barely audible. "Both."

She exhaled long and slow, steeling herself, before finally looking back at him, waiting. He said nothing for a long moment, only studied her.

"What?"

"I remember you standing there, you must have been four or five, wearing a crown you made, telling me I was to be *your* General." His voice was laced with the awe of nostalgia and the quiet of sadness.

She knew he must have been experiencing many of the same emotions as her father was, but he tended to keep his thoughts to himself, a trait Raven had tried to learn from. He had the same feelings and thoughts as others, he just chose more carefully when to share them. She waited. After another moment, he gestured for her to go ahead.

She paused when she reached the door. The small handle seemed to loom in front of her, promising terror on the other side. She silently cursed the irrational feelings swirling inside her, telling herself there was nothing to fear. Yet, as she reached for the handle, her hands still trembled.

Logan's large hand, callused from years of wielding a sword, covered hers. "It's alright." His words were quiet and steady and held no judgement. She lowered her hand and allowed him to reach past and open the latch.

Logan pulled the door open, and the stairs were a gaping chasm waiting to claim her. Air, she couldn't get enough air as an irrational sense of dread enveloped her.

"Breathe." Logan placed a hand on her shoulder and turned her toward him as he bent his knees to look her in the eye. A thick lock of her dark hair tumbled into her face, and Logan brushed it back. The action made her feel like a small child again. Instead of looking at her like she was insufferable or telling her to get over it, he only held her gaze. "Breathe with me."

He took long, exaggerated breaths, and Raven held his gaze, mirroring his actions. She was no less anxious, but the spots that had begun dancing along the edges of her vision subsided.

"You can do this." He took half a step back.

Raven's eyes moved from the stairs back to him. Her shoulders rose and fell as she breathed deeply, once, twice, telling herself that she was safe. She was not in danger. She was okay. She nodded.

A small smile tugged at the corner of his mouth and he gestured for her to go ahead.

The first step was always the hardest and she willed herself to lift her foot and place it on the step. She was okay, she was safe. She continued to descend the slatted wooden stairs. Logan kept a hand on her back, and she unabashedly leached strength from the contact.

At the bottom of the stairs, Logan stepped in front of her, leading the way down a stone walled hallway. She could hear the others speaking as they rounded a corner and found the waiting group.

Raven stopped beside Kanan, leaning into him as Logan continued further into the space.

Kanan's arm slid around Raven's shoulders. "Are you alright?"

She settled into his side. "It's just the cellar."

Kanan's only response was to pull her a little closer. From there it was easier for her to concentrate on his breathing and she matched her own breaths to his.

Logan's voice drew her from her concentration. He stood in front of the group, an arm resting on one of the barrels that lined the small space. "I want to give you each the chance to leave right now." His eyes scanned over them, meeting each of their gazes, though he avoided her father's eyes.

Her father had looked at no one since she'd arrived, his attention fixed solely on the ground as he rolled a cork between his fingers.

Logan paused, giving them a chance to back out.

When no one made a move to leave, Logan looked at Esrae before allowing his gaze to rest on Raven. "Malakai is going riding tomorrow."

Beside her, Kanan went completely still; the breaths that she had been concentrating on ceased. The cork that her father had been holding made no sound as it dropped to the floor and his hand clenched into a fist so tight his knuckles turned white. As for her, her heart sped so quickly she wondered if she might pass out.

"He'll take just a few soldiers, myself included, and ride for a few hours. He likes to take the roads through the woods." Logan paused as though steeling himself for his next words. "If you can make it to the north road three or so hours after daybreak . . . If you're there, he's sure to see you."

Tomorrow. Tomorrow. Tomorrow. The word bounced around in Raven's head like a cricket in a jar. Tomorrow was incredibly soon. Esrae came alongside her and slid her hand into Raven's, and when Raven looked at Esrae, her friend's eyes were wide.

"You don't have to do this, Es."

"No. I can do it." Esrae's voice sounded so small, the words barely a breath. "It's just...tomorrow."

"I know," Raven breathed, grasping Esrae's hand a little tighter.

Logan shook his head slowly. "Dress like you may meet a King."

If Raven didn't know him so well she might not have noticed it, but she did know him well, and there was a hesitation, the slightest catch, like he didn't want to speak these words.

Her father pushed hard off the barrel he'd been leaning on and it swayed wildly, threatening to spill its contents. He didn't say a word to any of them as he turned and left the room, knocking into Torren in his rush to be gone.

Silence stretched out among them for many moments.

Beside her, Kanan, who had not loosened his hold on her, nodded toward Torren. "What about us?" Raven had never heard Kanan's voice sound so icy.

"We recruit soldiers occasionally. I'll see to it that you're brought in." Logan glanced sidelong at him, pulling his eyes from where they had been fixed on the floor. "I can't know how long it'll take though."

"And until then?" Kanan's jaw clenched and his grip on her tightened, tension lining his words. "Raven and Esrae are just supposed to endure whatever's waiting for them?"

Logan met Raven's gaze, distress flickering in his crystal blue eyes. "I don't know how long you'll be there before I can get the others in." Esrae's grip on Raven's hand became painful. "Days. Weeks. I don't know."

"It's okay." Raven nodded.

Beside her, she thought she felt a tremble run through Kanan. His breathing gave away his emotions, as well. He wasn't happy with this arrangement. But really, were any of them?

Torren finally spoke up. "What happens when we finally get in? When we're all there?"

"I have a plan." Logan's words came out staggered, and he paused before he continued. "Right now, just get inside and wait for word. I will do my very best to make sure things move quickly, I give you my word. And I know it's enigmatic, but I think the less you know the better."

"In case they catch us and torture us." Every head turned toward Esrae. The girl's voice had been so quiet, and Raven wondered if she'd even meant to speak the words aloud.

Raven met Logan's pinched gaze. Hesitation seemed to flicker behind his eyes.

"I trust you." She spoke the words with as much sincerity as she could because she did trust him. Fully and completely, she trusted him with her life.

On her other side, Kanan exhaled sharply, another shudder rushed through him as his fingers clenched tighter on her.

Raven stared into the darkness, the sounds of the crickets and frogs filling the air around her. A breeze tousled her hair and she wrapped her arms tighter around herself. Even she didn't know if the resulting shiver was from the chill or from the anxiety that was burrowing into her chest.

"You don't have to do this."

She didn't turn. "I know." A breath of a whisper was the only volume she could muster.

Logan lowered himself onto the wooden step beside her, his size making her feel small. His voice was also quiet, though it still possessed the note of authority that came with so many years of being the General. "I mean it. One word from you and we call it off. All of it. It's alright to change your mind, it's alright to be scared. I'm scared."

Raven pulled her focus from the blackness of the path before her and turned her head to face him. In all her life she'd never heard him say he was afraid of anything.

He shook his head as though he'd read her thoughts. "Raven, I've never been so scared. I can't imagine what your father must be feeling. Sometimes when I think about it, I can't breathe."

Raven returned her gaze to the dark. "If we let fear stop us, nothing would ever be accomplished."

There was a note of amusement in his voice when he spoke, "Where did you hear such nonsense?"

She looked back at him. Indeed, there was amusement, and sadness, in his eyes. "You."

"Do you have to listen so well?" His eyes ran over her face, studying her.

She rolled her eyes and smiled. "Not always."

He huffed a quiet laugh. But when he spoke, the amusement had vanished. "Raven, I am so proud of you. Of who you've become. Strong and sure. Stubborn."

"That's the part I learned from you," she cut in.

Undeterred by her joke, he went on, "I would be honored if any part of you rubbed off from me."

"Logan..." She met his eyes. She'd grown up learning from him. Not just how to fight, but how to exist. How to deal with problems rationally, how to be kind but not let others walk on her. How to live in the world and be a decent person. Her eyes burned. "You know, so much of who I am came from you." Tears formed in his eyes and she quickly changed the tone of the conversation. If Logan cried, there would be no hope of her holding it together. "I mean, thanks to you, I have a better round kick than any girl I know."

Logan's laugh was genuine. "You have a better round kick than most men I know, and I command an army."

Raven laughed as well. "It's certainly better than Kanan's."

"You found a good man in him," Logan said. "Anyone can see how much you love each other."

Warmth spread through her at his words.

"Tell him."

"I always tell him." She smiled.

"Tell him again."

She turned to him, eyebrows raised.

He exhaled a small breath, lowering his voice further. "Raven, you're about to offer yourself to a king. As a man, I can tell you, I'm sure Kanan's feeling more than a little uncertain." She opened her mouth to speak, but Logan continued on, "Possibly he's afraid you'll be taken as a slave, or found out and tortured. Maybe he thinks you'll prefer the King. Either way, tell him again how you feel. Make sure he knows."

She knew he was right. Kanan had been supportive of her choices because even he wanted to stop the King, but he was never very enthusiastic about the idea. Of course he didn't want Raven to run off with the King. No doubt he was also wondering what would happen tomorrow, just like the rest of them. Though maybe for different reasons. Kanan was protective; not controlling, but he always wanted to keep her safe. To be suddenly helpless must be making him extra anxious

She blew out a long breath. The reality of what the morning would bring loomed over them. "I suppose we could all be dead tomorrow."

"We could always all be dead tomorrow, Raven. That's why what we do right now is so important."

She looked up at him. "You should write a book with your wisdom."

He huffed a laugh, rolling his eyes. Then he grew silent for some time as if weighing his next words. "I think it would be best if we kept our relationship a secret when you're at the palace. I think it would be safer."

Raven nodded. Definitely safer should any of them get caught. A shiver ran over her again as the enormity of what they were about to take on settled further on her.

Logan stood and offered Raven a hand. He studied her for a moment, and when he spoke, his tone was deadly serious—the General's tone that was so rare when he was with them. "Raven, if you decide you don't want to go through with this, for *any* reason, stay home. Don't be on that road tomorrow. No one will think less of you, I promise."

She knew he meant it too. He would probably never mention it again if that's what she chose. Raven worked to swallow the lump in her throat and nodded.

Logan's brow knit deeply and he blinked a few times, and Raven wondered if he was working to control his own tears. "Goodnight, Raven." There was a catch in his voice that went straight to her heart.

"Goodnight." Her voice sounded so small, even to her own ears.

Instead of turning to leave, Logan took a step toward her and pulled her into his arms. Sensations of childhood pressed in as she settled into his chest and wrapped her arms around his waist. She breathed deeply, the comforting scent of birch and oakmoss that always followed him wrapping around her.

Logan placed a kiss on the top of her head before he released her and turned to leave.

Raven stared into the thick darkness for some time after the sounds of Logan's horse's hooves on the dirt had disappeared.

Were they even doing the right thing? Did they stand any chance at all? When it was all over, would it have been worth it? Or would she be wishing she was back on this step, making a different decision? Neither the blackness nor the crickets offered any answers.

She stood and brushed off her pants before entering her house. Kanan, who had been sitting on her sofa, waiting, stood and turned toward her. Their eyes locked and Kanan seemed to examine her. "Are you alright?"

She gave him a shallow nod before she looked around the room. No sounds came from the kitchen, and her father wasn't in the living room.

"I haven't seen him at all." Kanan answered her unspoken thoughts. "Not since he left the cellar."

She hadn't really expected him to be waiting for her, but it might have been nice to spend some time with him.

"I imagine he's working through quite a lot, Raven." Kanan's gaze had leveled on her and she could feel it's weight. She looked up at him. His shoulders rose and fell with deep intakes of breath and his brow furrowed slightly. It was like he was trying to make a decision. Finally, as though a taught band snapped, he moved. "So am I."

He was around the sofa and in front of her in two heartbeats. His hands grasped either side of her head, fingers buried in her hair, as he pulled her mouth to his. It was a different kiss than what they usually shared, fraught with desire and despair all at once, and it stole her breath.

He lifted her off her feet and she wrapped her arms around his neck and her legs around his waist and held on as he carried her down the hall to her bedroom, never breaking the kiss.

She held onto him, afraid to let go, afraid to relinquish the solid feeling of him in her arms. If things went well, she expected it would still be some time before they were together again like this. If things went poorly... She pulled him closer, pressing her mouth more desperately to his. He laid her down on the bed beneath him, breaking his hold on her only long enough to pull both their shirts off. Then he was on her again, as though he, like she, was unwilling to have any space between them.

His hands slid down her sides, down to the band of her pants, and he pushed them over her hips as his kiss moved from her mouth to her neck.

She arched her neck, giving him all the access he needed as she lifted her hips, allowing him to free her legs. His mouth traveled down her chest, nipping and kissing, and she buried her hands in his hair, needing to touch him.

His lips moved to her hip, then lower until she let out a gasp as his mouth closed around her most sensitive spot. Her hips bucked off the bed and Kanan wrapped his arms around her legs, holding her in place as he worked.

Raven reached behind her, grasping the headboard of her bed, holding on as her body wound into ever tightening coils. Her breaths escaped in staccato pants until all at once everything unraveled. She cried out, but in a heartbeat Kanan's mouth was on hers, stifling the sound.

She wrapped her bare legs around his waist, feeling his pants. She pulled her mouth away long enough to beg him to remove them. He laughed lightly against her lips as he moved a hand to his belt, working it until, with her help, he pushed them down, kicking them off.

"Kanan, I need you closer." She didn't want any space between them, not while they had this chance.

Kanan pulled back, his eyes meeting hers as he brushed her hair out of her face with one hand. "I know."

He moved his hand, slipping it under her knee, lifting her leg until he could slide into her. He held her gaze the entire time and a fire seemed to rage in his olive eyes.

He moved his hips and her lips parted as she breathed out at the perfect feeling of the two of them joined together.

"I love you, Raven." He punctuated his words with his exquisitely slow movements. "Forever, you'll be in my heart, mine. And I'll be yours."

A tear escaped from her eye as she nodded, unable to form words around his movements. Then she reached up, wrapping her hands around his head and pulling his lips to hers as he continued to move slow and deliberate, drawing out every sensation until there was nothing else but him and her. She never wanted this to end.

His finger traced lines and swirls down her arm as she lay with her head resting on his chest, running her own hand softly over the hard lines there. Her legs still twined around his. She stilled her own breaths as she listened to the quiet thumping of his heart.

He placed a soft kiss on her hair. "What are you thinking?"

She turned her head slightly until her lips brushed his chest. "That I'm glad you're in my bed." She smiled at the soft rumbling chuckle that vibrated in his chest.

"So am I." The chuckle was gone, replaced by something like resignation.

"What are you thinking?" It was the echo to his own question, though she was sure the answer would be much different. For a moment she thought he might have stopped breathing. Even his hand stilled on her arm.

"Tomorrow." His fingers resumed their slow trek across her skin.

Tomorrow. Tomorrow. Tomorrow. There was that word again, invading her moment. She said the only thing that came to mind and hoped she put enough feeling into it so it sounded like she believed it. "It's going to be alright, Kanan."

Another low laugh, though this one held no humor. "I told that guard in town that you're not mine. But when we're like this, it feels like you're mine. And tomorrow you're going to offer yourself up to a king who's not exactly known for his kindness. You'll have to forgive me if I'm a bit apprehensive."

She swallowed the lump his words had caused and splayed her hand on his chest, over his heart, to allow the soft thumping to seep into her. "I don't mind being yours. I like it. And I'm not offering myself to him."

His hand came up, wrapping around her wrist, as he lifted his head to look at her. "Yes, you are. You know that, right?" His breath sent strands of her hair waving. "Of course you know that. Why aren't you more concerned?"

She was concerned. She was so concerned it kept her up at night and drew tears sometimes when she was alone. But she didn't want to admit it to him because it would only make him feel worse. Instead, she said another word, and regretted it almost instantly. "Jealous?"

Nothing. He said nothing for a moment. For two. Then he pulled his arm out from underneath her so he could lean up on his elbow. His frame hovered over her as his green eyes bored into hers. "I'm not jealous, Raven. I'm terrified. Not that you'll choose the King, but that something will go very wrong and we'll never have *this* back again." His hand tightened around her wrist.

Tears ran down her face as she reached up and placed her hand on his cheek, rough with stubble, the way he always kept it. She wanted to assure him that she wouldn't let that happen, but she couldn't. She had no idea what would happen. He was right, something could go very wrong. But she couldn't dwell on that and she didn't want him to dwell on it.

"I could never choose him and I could never give this up. I will do everything in my power to make sure we're back here again. I promise." She stretched up even as she pulled his face to hers in a desperate kiss. When they broke apart, she noticed his face was wet as well, though she didn't know if it was her tears or his own.

"I love you, Raven." He pulled her to him for another kiss. It was fierce and claiming.

She felt like *his* and that was fine, she never wanted to be anyone else's.

"I love you too." She rose up, moving into his lap, so they were nose to nose and repeated the words as she looked him in the eye. "I love you too."

ELEVEN

When Raven opened her eyes, the room was still dark, the only light from the lone candle that had burned down quite a bit. Kanan lay beside her, one arm behind his head, the other draped across his bare abdomen. She watched the steady rise and fall of his chest as he slept, studied the line of his jaw, covered in dark stubble, examined the planes of his chest, the well defined muscles in his arms. She lingered on each feature, committing every part of him to memory.

Finally, she turned to the still dark window. They couldn't have slept long, but she was surprised they'd slept at all.

Outside her door the sound of a cup tumbling onto the counter startled her and she jumped. Kanan was immediately awake, his arm curling protectively around her.

She rested her hand gently on his arm, his muscles tensing beneath her palm. "It's okay. I think my father's making tea."

He relaxed and slumped back against the pillow. "What time is it?"

"I don't know. Early." She inclined her chin to the small table beside the bed where a pocket watch rested.

He picked up the watch and squinted at the clock face in the dim light. His eyes closed for a moment as he exhaled.

"How long until dawn?" Even she could barely hear her voice.

There was a hitch in his steady breathing but he met her eyes. "Two hours or so."

Her heart stumbled. *Hours. Tomorrow* had turned into *hours*.

His head tilted as he scanned her face. He knew her so well. "You don't have to do this."

He was saying she didn't have to, but everything about him was pleading with her not to.

She pulled her gaze from him. If she looked into his eyes much longer, she might have been convinced to abandon their plan. She inhaled what she hoped was a fortifying breath. "Come on."

She stood and chose a plain dress from her wardrobe, pulling it on, before she retrieved his pants from the floor beside the bed and tossed them at him. He caught them in one hand, his eyes going wide. "Come on? Isn't it a little early to leave?"

"It's not too early for tea." She pulled a brush through her thick hair.

Kanan stood and she paused her brushing to watch him dress, once again committing every move to memory. All while a small voice scratched at the back of her mind. *Don't go. Don't go.*

"What?"

She blinked, meeting his eyes. "Nothing," she lied as she took the door handle. "I just need tea. Come on."

Kanan hesitated, looking from her to the door as though he could see beyond it. "Are you sure you don't want some time alone with your father?"

She bit her lip. "I don't know that he wants time alone with me."

She held out a hand, grateful when he took it. Not necessarily for holding her hand, but for the strength he offered. Facing her father was something she both wanted and was apprehensive about. After yesterday, she wasn't sure if he'd even wanted to speak with her. Was he that upset with her? Or was it just hard for him to face her knowing what she was about to do? She wasn't upset at him, she knew this must be hard, but she did wish he would talk to her; share this little bit of time together until she had to leave.

They stepped around the corner into the kitchen. Her father sat at the table, both hands clutching a mug. He looked up with barely a glance before he stood. "I'll get more cups."

Raven glanced at Kanan and he gave her hand a small squeeze before they found seats at the table, opposite her father.

He placed steaming cups in front of each of them and returned to his seat. A heavy silence settled on the room and Raven fought the urge to fidget. She wanted to have a conversation with him. Something, anything. The fact that this was their last chance to speak before she left weighed on her. She opened her mouth and then closed it again. What would she say, anyway? Her father had returned his attention to his mug.

Kanan squeezed her hand again and she looked at him. His eyes darted to her father and then back to her. "*Do you want me to go?*" he mouthed the words, and Raven was quick to shake her head. She didn't want him to go, not at all. But then he aimed another pointed look at her father, encouraging Raven to speak. So she did.

"I know you think this is a bad idea."

He didn't look up, but she heard the breath of air he blew out, saw his eyes close, his lips purse.

"I am nervous, if it helps," she all but mumbled the words.

His head drooped further, as his brow furrowed. "Raven, you ought to be terrified. There are things you don't . . ." His voice trailed off.

She hadn't wanted to admit terror to her father, or Kanan, or herself, for that matter. But she was. "I am. I am terrified." Kanan's hand closed tighter around hers. Whether it was to comfort or to acknowledge he shared the feeling, she didn't know.

Her father's dark eyes met hers, so unlike her own, and he held her gaze for a long time, wetness shining around the edges, a crease that seemed almost permanent on his brow. He opened his mouth to speak but was interrupted by a knock at the door.

Raven looked toward the door and back to Kanan. "Esrae."

Her stomach tightened into a knot. Had it been that long that they'd been sitting here? Was it really almost time? Esrae's knock was like a call to action. They had planned so much the night before, but now that it was time, her lungs seemed to want to betray her.

"I'll go." Kanan released her hand and his chair scraped softly across the floor as he pushed it away from the table. She and her father sat in silence and she wished she could fill it with something, but couldn't think of any words that would make anything better. Thankfully it didn't last long as Kanan reappeared, his brows raised with a *wait til you see this* expression. Raven didn't have long to wonder though as Esrae stepped into the room behind him, and Raven's mouth fell open.

Esrae's long, blonde locks fell down her back in soft curls, cascading over one of the most beautiful silver-blue dresses that Raven had ever seen. Slate blue flowers and twisting green vine embroidery covered the dress, and Esrae looked every bit the part of some sort of winter princess.

"Esrae..." The name left Raven's mouth in a breath.

Esrae's uneasy smile quickly vanished when she took in Raven's appearance. "Raven, your dress! You can't meet the King like that!"

Raven looked down at the simple dress she had thrown on. Surely Esrae didn't think this was what she was planning to wear. "I haven't dressed yet, Es. We were up early."

Esrae brushed past Kanan to where Raven sat. In a fluid motion of swishing skirts, Esrae pulled her from her seat and toward her room. "Come on, time to make you beautiful."

Raven could do nothing but allow herself to be swept away.

Raven examined herself in the mirror but, standing next to Esrae, her own sapphire dress paled in comparison. Both dresses were nice, while still being something that well off young ladies might wear every day, but there was just something about Esrae's that set it apart. Raven couldn't take her eyes off the other girl in the mirror.

"Es, you look amazing."

Esrae looked at her own reflection, and Raven noticed a slight blush creep into Esrae's cheeks. "I didn't know what to wear. What do you wear for this?" She shrugged.

Raven offered the best smile she could manage. "I think you got it right. Where did you get it? The dress, I mean."

Another shrug. "I had some money saved."

Raven pulled her gaze from the mirror to instead look her friend in the eyes. "You used your savings to buy a dress for this?"

"Why not?" Esrae met her stare with no regret. "We're meeting the King, Raven. I can't do that in a work dress. Besides," Esrae returned her gaze to the mirror and held her chin a bit higher as she took in her own dress, smoothing away nonexistent wrinkles, "what else would I use the money for?"

Raven's eyes drifted to the window, and her heart stumbled again when she noticed the dim rays of light peeking into the room. Dawn.

"We should go," Esrae spoke, her attention also on the sun lighting the room through the window. The look in Esrae's eyes was so different than even the day before, like the dress was supplying her with confidence. As she watched Esrae leave the room, Raven found herself wishing she had found her own magic dress.

With a last look in the mirror and a deep breath, Raven followed Esrae into the kitchen. Kanan looked up, his lips parting slightly.

She made a half-hearted attempt at a smile as she swished her skirts. "You like?"

His shoulders drooped ever so slightly as he exhaled. "You're beautiful." There was a pained edge to his voice, a small, sad smile turning up his mouth. Raven couldn't help but think he looked defeated.

She tried to offer an encouraging smile. She tried. But when her eyes drifted to her father and the look on his face could only have been described as devastation, her stomach clenched. She turned a pointed look on Kanan and was grateful when he understood.

Kanan moved to Esrae and placed a hand softly on her back. "We'll be outside."

Esrae offered a small smile and allowed Kanan to usher her from the kitchen. Raven watched, waiting for the sound of the door closing behind them.

She turned to her father, who still hadn't looked up. "I'll be careful, I promise." She'd tried to be louder but could only manage a whisper.

His head rose slowly, his eyes shining when they met hers. He looked at her for a long time like he wanted to speak, but he said nothing. A tear trailed slowly down his cheek and she had to swallow back the sob in her throat. She crossed the space between them and dropped to her knees, wrapping her arms tightly around him. His hand came to her head and began to smooth her hair and she could no longer keep her tears at bay. It was something he used to do when she was small, but it had been a long time.

He took a deep, shuddering breath, and when he spoke, his words were barely audible, even though she was right beside him. "Stay safe, Raven. When you get to the palace, don't draw any more attention to yourself than you need to. The King... he's not like other people . . ." His voice trailed off.

"I'll see you soon." She managed to imbue more confidence than she felt into the words.

"I love you." He bent, placing a kiss on her head, his hold tightening around her.

"I love you too." He did not say he would see her soon, and she could only assume it was because he perhaps didn't believe it.

Outside Esrae stood, shifting from one foot to the other, her hands drifting absently over the embroidery of her dress. Raven couldn't tell if it was nerves or impatience that caused Esrae to fidget. Kanan leaned against one of the porch's support beams, his eyes fixed intently on his boots. He didn't move when they came out, though his eyes lifted to meet Raven's.

Esrae started when Raven appeared. "Are you ready? We need to go."

Raven marveled at her friend's newfound confidence. If only some of it would rub off on Raven.

She gave Esrae a nod and then turned back to face her father. He looked so hopeless and lost, a lump formed in her throat. She'd never seen him like this, not once in her life. She hated that she was the cause, and also that, to have a look like that, he must've held no hope for their success.

She stepped up to him and took his hand in hers, squeezing gently. "Please don't hate Logan. We'll be careful, I promise."

He didn't answer, and she stretched up on her toes and placed a kiss on his cheek before releasing his hand and joining Kanan at the bottom of the porch stairs.

He looked down at her, somber and serious as he studied her face. With a small puff of air, he held his arm out and she stepped close to him, snuggling into his side.

Esrae looked back at them, seeing they were ready, and began walking. Raven ventured another look over her shoulder at her father, but he stood, head hung low and eyes closed. She pressed closer to Kanan.

"We can take horses for a bit if you want," Kanan said.

"I'd rather walk, if that's alright." Maybe walking for a while would work out some of the nervous energy that had been building up inside her. She craned her neck to look up at him. "Thank you for coming along." He couldn't go the entire way with them, but Raven was grateful for his support and presence for as long as he could be there.

He leaned to kiss the top of her head. "Where else would I be?"

Silence settled between them as they walked, the only sounds the occasional chirping bird and the steady crunching of their boots on the path. Raven's mind, on the other hand, buzzed with every *what if* scenario it could conjure. She wanted to put her hands over her ears, for all the good it would do. She could only assume it was the same for the others since they hadn't spoken either. Kanan's arm was still a comforting weight over her shoulder, and she stayed tucked into his side, unwilling to let him go. She committed every breath and sigh, every heartbeat, to the deepest confines of her memory. Locking them away so she could pull them out when things became hard.

After a long time, Esrae spoke. "What do you think it'll be like?"

Raven turned her head toward her friend. "What? The palace or the King?"

Esrae stopped, her head whipping in Raven and Kanan's direction, her eyes widening as though she'd just thought of something. "I was talking about the palace. What do you think the King will be like?"

Raven had wondered herself what it would be like to meet the King. The rumors about him were everywhere, the effects of his reign seen in the towns every day. But what was he, the man, really like? Would he be instantly cruel? Steal them off the side of the road and drag them back to the palace? Would he be commanding, as she would expect a king to be? Demanding obeisance? "I have no idea."

Kanan's hold tightened on her again as they resumed their steady pace. "Maybe he didn't even go out today. Maybe he's sick." Kanan's voice was light, giving off a joking quality, but Raven knew him well enough to pick out that underlying edge. That tone lining his words that clearly gave away that it was more than just a joke, it was a wish.

"Maybe." It was the only thing she could think to say because she certainly didn't expect it to be true.

They continued to walk as the sun crawled across the sky, warming the air. Birds chirped in the trees and squirrels darted about, and it seemed odd to Raven that these forest dwellers all acted as though everything was normal when her life was about to change in ways she couldn't begin to imagine.

She was pulled from her thoughts when Kanan stopped, bringing her to a stop beside him. She looked at him and his eyes were trained far down the road in front of them, as though he could see what was coming.

"What?" Raven's voice cracked.

He inhaled deeply and so slowly that Raven thought he might not respond. But then he did look at her, and the pain and sadness in his olive eyes made her heart clench. "This is probably as far as I should go."

Raven's legs went weak and she clutched him tighter as he pulled her into him, wrapping her tightly in his hold.

"I wish you could go all the way." Her voice was muffled by his shirt.

"You don't have to go." His words vibrated in his chest.

She craned her neck to look at him and tried to smile, though she feared it was more of a grimace. In his expression she only found frustration and fear. Kanan looked at Esrae and silent words seemed to pass between them.

"I'll just be up here." Esrae moved further up the road, stopping to examine some wildflowers along the path.

Kanan ran his fingers over Raven's long braid where it fell over her shoulder, giving a small tug. "You are beautiful." Raven could barely stand the sadness in his voice. The small catch to his words.

"Thank you." She was unable to speak above a whisper as she swallowed the painful lump in her throat.

He moved his hand from her braid to her arms, sliding them down until he could take her hands in his. "This is so dangerous." His lips pursed together, his eyes darting back and forth across her face as he exhaled deeply through his nose.

"I know. I promise I'll—"

"Can you just let me talk?" His smile of exasperation was small, but it was there.

"Sorry." Her eyes dropped to his chest but then found his gaze again.

"I've been thinking about something," Kanan continued, "and I don't want the idea of what might happen to keep me from saying it." He looked down at their joined hands and then back up at her. "I love you, Raven, and when this is over—" She didn't miss the emphasis on *when*. "—I want you to marry me."

She was speechless, blinking at his words.

"Marry me, Raven," he repeated the words, his eyes never leaving hers. "I've been thinking about it for a long time, and I don't want to wait anymore. Marry me." He hadn't really spoken the words like a question, but his brows rose, waiting.

A warmth bloomed in her chest, spreading through her body and heating her cheeks. Her grin reached to the corners of her eyes, nearly making her face ache. "Of course." Happy tears sprang to her eyes, falling down to her chin.

Kanan huffed out a relieved laugh as he wiped the tears from her face, his own grin flashing in the morning sun. He slid his hands around the back of her neck and pulled her to him. The kiss was deep, desperate. It felt like a victory and a goodbye and a promise of things to come, and it was something she would hold on to fiercely when they were parted.

Kanan broke off the kiss but still held her head gently in his hands as he looked her in the eyes. "Raven, don't waste time. I need you to come home because I'm making plans, and I need you."

"I promise." She smiled.

He kissed her again, kissed her like he was a dying man and her lips held the promise of life. "I love you," he said quietly, his head resting on hers.

"I love you." Her voice cracked on the words and she held him tighter, breathing in his scent one final time.

When he released her and stepped back, his absence stretched out like an abyss between them. The cool morning air seeping into every place where he had been moments before.

She closed her eyes and tried to take a steadying breath, though it shuddered through her. When she opened her eyes she gave him a small nod. He returned it and ran a thumb softly down the side of her face, a sad smile playing on his lips.

She dropped her gaze to the ground and forced her body to turn. The walk to where Esrae was waiting seemed longer than what it was. She didn't look back, afraid that if she looked at him, she wouldn't be able to continue.

When she made it to Esrae's side she turned back to where he'd been, but no one stood there. A coldness washed over her. Not just physical, but a sense of foreboding she hadn't had before. She shivered and wrapped her arms around herself.

Esrae straightened, smoothing her skirts, and looked to where Kanan had been and back to Raven, giving her a sympathetic look. "I'm sorry." She brushed a hand along Raven's arm.

The ache in her chest was deep but she found herself offering Esrae a small smile anyway as she blinked back the tears stinging her eyes.

"Are you alright?" Esrae asked.

"Yes. No. I don't know." The tears escaped then, and Raven swiped at her cheeks.

Esrae's head tilted slightly and she ran a hand over her sleeve, picking at and smoothing a piece of thread. "Are we doing the right thing?"

Raven looked up the road in the direction they were heading and pulled in a deep breath, trying to muster the confidence to answer Esrae's question. "Yes," she said the word with more conviction than she felt.

Raven tried not to think about the empty place beside her as they resumed walking. Was Kanan still with them? Watching from the woods? She expected so, and her eyes drifted to the forest along the path more than once, though no sounds indicated his presence, no crunching leaves, or snapping twigs. But Kanan had always had an unnerving ability to remain silent. She shook her head and instead focused her attention on the sun's slow progress as she tried to calculate how long they'd been traveling.

"What do you think it'll be like with the King?" Esrae's question pulled Raven from her thoughts.

Raven looked at her. "You mean, *with* with the King, I'm assuming."

"Yes." Esrae nodded as a blush crept into her cheeks. "I mean, I know you've been with Kanan, so it won't be new. But, do you think he'll be cruel?"

Raven bit her lip as her chest tightened at the words. She'd had the same thought, mostly at night when she was trying to sleep. All the possibilities and what-ifs of the situation played out in her mind, usually culminating with her in the kitchen making tea and not getting any sleep. But they had just been possibilities. Now, on the road heading straight toward it . . .

She swallowed, forcing the fear back down inside her. "I don't know."

"Maybe they're all just stories and rumors." Esrae's forced smile held no encouragement. "Maybe he won't want to sleep with you at all."

A chill ran over Raven's skin, raising her flesh. "Maybe." Esrae's words did nothing to comfort her, as not one of them rang true.

Silence settled around them again, though Raven's mind had not quieted. She was still forming plans. They needed a way to keep in contact once they arrived at the palace. Perhaps at meals they would be able to speak to each other. She opened her mouth to speak, but beside her Esrae had stopped, still as a statue, clutching Raven's hand to the point of pain. All the color had drained from Esrae's face as she stared, her eyes wide and unblinking.

Dread washed over Raven, settling deep in her chest. "Es? What?"

"Don't you hear it?" Esrae's voice trembled, the words no louder than a breath.

Raven's heart stumbled as she looked in the direction Esrae was staring. "Es, I don't hear any—"

But then the sound reached her, quiet at first, a whisper on the breeze. As the seconds ticked by the sound became clearer, louder. Hoofbeats. Raven's legs went weak, all the air leaving her lungs, and she couldn't remember how to fill them again.

The rhythmic thumping as the horses' hooves pounded the ground, grew louder. There was no mistake: riders were approaching, at least four of them.

It took two tries for Raven to swallow the lump that had formed in her throat. "Yeah."

TWELVE

The reality of their situation seemed to crash down on Raven. She latched onto Esrae's arm. "We have to get it together. We're not supposed to know he's coming. Keep walking."

She pulled on the other girl and Esrae blinked and nodded as they resumed their walk. Raven slowed her pace, Esrae falling into step beside her. Calm, they had to calm down. She closed her eyes and pulled in a long breath, even as her heart thundered right along with the approaching hoofbeats.

In moments, the horses were in view. Logan rode at the front atop his deep grey mount, the white patch over the horse's left eye standing out in the sunlight. He looked so out of place in that setting. She was used to seeing him at her table or training with her in her yard, not wearing the King's insignia and maroon sash, leading a contingent of men.

Raven's heart thundered, and pain lanced through her hand where Esrae gripped her fingers. The sting pulled her back to the present and she scrambled out of the middle of the road, dragging Esrae with her to avoid both of them being trampled.

For a moment it looked like all their careful planning would fail. The riders were coming fast and they didn't appear to be slowing. Should she be relieved or disappointed? She didn't have the chance to decide as one of the men called out to the others and every one of the riders reined in their horses, pulling them to a stop mere feet in front of Raven and Esrae.

She was staring, her mouth hanging open, and she knew she must look ridiculous. Still, she couldn't make herself move. Then Logan's voice rang out a barking order. "Show some respect to your King!"

Raven and Esrae both jumped as the command split the air but quickly regained their composure, dropping into low curtsies.

When they stood, Raven's eyes met the King's, and for that second she forgot how to breathe. They were here, they'd done it. Saints, what had they done?

As he watched her it seemed, for a moment, something passed behind his dark gaze. A shadow, a spark, sadness? Something. None of those things made sense, but when she blinked, whatever she'd thought she'd seen was gone.

Raven had seen the King twice before, both at large gatherings from very far away. Up close, his face was different than she had imagined. She'd expected him to look older and more severe. But he wasn't that old at all; Logan's age, perhaps. His dark hair was short and curling, speckled through with grey, and a shadowy scruff covered his jaw. But it was his eyes that caught her off guard. Where she had expected cruelty, there was only a thoughtful, but not unkind, look in their deep hazel-green irises.

"Good morning, ladies," the King greeted them, his voice deep and scratchy and not at all unattractive.

"Good morning, Your Majesty." Raven tried hard to keep the shakiness from her voice. Though, she suspected the King was used to people being nervous when they met him.

The leather of his saddle groaned as the King shifted, leaning in a bit closer to them. He looked around, taking in the trees and sky. "It's a lovely morning for a walk."

"Very, Your Majesty."

Raven didn't know where to look. She vaguely recalled something about not looking the King in his eye, but was that real, or from a book? If she didn't look him in the eye, would that be disrespectful? She silently cursed herself for not asking Logan these questions when she had the chance. And she silently cursed Logan for not volunteering the information.

"Or a ride."

At the sound of her voice, Raven whipped her head toward Esrae to find the girl unabashedly watching the King.

"Yes." The King's eyes roved over Esrae, and Raven shoved down an absurd desire to step in front of her friend and shield her.

"Your horse is beautiful." Esrae nodded at the giant black beast the King sat astride.

The King reached out and stroked the horse's long neck. "He certainly is. His name is Mhanjar."

"That's a word in the old language from Shanterac," Esrae observed.

Esrae seemed to have no issue conversing with the King.

He looked at Esrae, clearly impressed with her knowledge of the old language. "Yes. Do you know what it means?"

"I do not, Your Majesty," Esrae answered, her cheeks blushing pink.

"'Conqueror of the mind'."

Raven's blood chilled.

"Magnificent," Esrae breathed the word as she reached out to touch the horse's nose. Had she realized what he'd said? Or did she not care?

"Yes." The King watched her for a long moment before turning his attention to Raven. "You're very quiet."

Her breath caught in her throat. "I'm afraid I'm not very well versed in horses, Your Majesty."

"No?" His eyebrows rose with the word. "What is it that interests you?"

Raven swallowed the lump that had formed in her throat with the King's attention. She hadn't expected the question and fumbled around in her mind for a hobby. Anything. "I enjoy reading, Your Majesty."

"As do I," he said, and he sounded completely genuine. "Do you enjoy poetry?"

She did enjoy poetry and was thankful he had questioned her on something she could talk about easily. "I do, yes, Your Majesty."

The saddle creaked again as the King leaned back slightly, tilting his head, studying her. His voice softened slightly when he spoke.

"I looked on her, so fair, with her raven black hair.
She pierced me in turn with her obsidian stare.
In her touch was a fire that made me feel lighter,
As I kissed her lips and she burned ever brighter."

Her cheeks heated, her breath catching at his words, at her name, as he unknowingly spoke it.

"Have you heard that one?" His tone returned to something more casual, but his eyes were still intense upon her.

A chill ran over her, raising the hairs on her neck and limbs and she did her best not to shiver. "I have not, Your Majesty."

"It could almost have been written about you," he mused. "Though you hardly have an obsidian stare. What's your name?"

She swallowed hard. "Raven, Your Majesty."

She had expected more of a reaction from him, an acknowledgment of the coincidence. Instead, he only said, "Interesting." Then he turned his attention back to Esrae. "And your name?"

"Esrae, Your Majesty," she said, blinking. It was clear that she had not missed the parallel.

"Esrae and Raven." The King's piercing gaze settled on Raven, and she fought the urge to shift under the attention. "I have enjoyed our interaction this morning, it was a welcome distraction to the monotony of our ride." His eyes took them in once again. "I would like to extend an invitation to you both. Have you ever been to the palace?"

Raven's heart kicked up and she sent a silent plea to the Saints that she wouldn't pass out, but it was Esrae who answered. "We have not, Your Majesty."

"I would be honored if you would join me." His eyes held Esrae's for a moment and then came to rest on Raven.

Raven's legs went weak and she put all her concentration into holding herself up. She couldn't tell if it was relief or terror that washed over her. Something about the King's poem had left a pit in her stomach, though this very invitation was what they had been planning toward. Every one of those present understood that though the King had worded it as a polite invitation, they had little choice. They dared not say no. Fortunately, this had been their plan.

Raven dropped into another curtsey, Esrae following. "Thank you, Your Majesty, but we have no horses with us."

The King smiled, the action causing his eyes to crinkle at the corners. "I'm sure we can find a place for you. Logan?"

Logan turned his horse to face the king, his eyes briefly meeting Raven's. "Yes, Your Majesty?"

"This young lady," he gestured to Esrae, "will ride with you."

Raven's heart sank. She had hoped to ride with Logan. But then the King turned, extending a hand toward her. "I would be honored if you would join me."

Raven's lips parted on a sharp inhale. She'd expected to ride with a guard, not with the King himself. She dipped her head and reached out to take his hand. "Thank you, Your Majesty."

The King grasped her hand and lifted her easily into the saddle in front of him. Further up, Logan pulled Esrae onto his horse.

"Come," the King spoke softly, his breath coasting over her ear. Then he clicked his tongue, and the horse began moving. The rest of the riders fell into step around them.

There was little room on the back of a horse, and even though Raven sat up as straight as she could, she was still able to concentrate on nothing save for the King's breath in her ear.

"Raven." His voice was quiet, as though he was aware of the proximity of his mouth to her ear and didn't want to be too loud. "A beautiful name for a beautiful woman."

His breath sent tendrils of her hair fluttering against her neck, and goose-bumps prickled on her arms.

"I'm flattered, Your Majesty." A pathetic reply, but she had no idea how to respond to his words.

"I don't say it to flatter you." His arm around her waist tightened ever so slightly, and she fought the urge to stiffen. "You're trembling. You have nothing to fear with me."

It felt like something was skittering around in her stomach, and she didn't trust her voice to reply. She could barely pull in a full breath. She only nodded.

"Your friend says you've never been to the palace."

It wasn't a question, though he paused as though waiting for a response.

With effort she was able to dredge up her voice. "I have not, Your Majesty. I've only seen it from a distance. It's lovely."

"Wait until you see the inside." There was pride in the words. After a moment, he changed the subject. "Your friend, what is her name again?"

"Esrae, Your Majesty."

"Esrae," he repeated, sounding contemplative. "The two of you were out walking rather early today,"

"Yes, Your Majesty." Though he hadn't actually asked a question, it felt, again, like he was waiting for a reply. "We enjoy walking. We hadn't been on a walk for some time. It was so nice this morning, we decided to go out before the weather grew too cold."

"Did you imagine how your life might change when you left your home this morning?" he asked.

Raven was infinitely glad that he could not read her mind in that moment. "Not at all, Your Majesty," she lied.

"Don't be concerned about your families. We'll have messages sent to them as soon as we get back to the palace, informing them where you are and that you are safe. Do you have siblings?"

"No, Your Majesty," Raven answered. "It's just myself and my father."

"And your mother?" he asked.

"No, Your Majesty." Raven hadn't expected the King to be interested in her family, though she expected he was simply making conversation. "My mother died when I was very young. Still a baby. I never knew her."

Behind her, the King had gone still and silent, and Raven dared to hope that he'd had enough small talk. He had not.

"I'm sorry about your mother," his voice was soft and sincere, though Raven had little time to contemplate his tone before he spoke again. "You don't even know what she looked like?"

She stumbled over her words at first, finding the question odd. "No, Your Majesty, not for myself. Though, I'm told I resemble her. So, I suppose I can have some idea of what she looked like."

There was something different in his voice when he spoke, nothing big, but she noticed the change. "Indeed. Well, my dear, if you look like your mother, I think it's safe to say she must have been very beautiful."

Again, the sincerity in his voice made her uncomfortable. The way he spoke contradicted the things she knew about him. Were they wrong about him, or was he just that good at masking his vileness? She was glad for the silence that followed, leaving her alone with her thoughts.

THIRTEEN

T he wall was the first thing she saw, a massive stone barrier separating the outside world from the palace within. Above it, grey stone towers rose high enough to brush the clouds. She counted eight from where she sat, all covered in uniform crenellations. A few had vines climbing all the way up the tower. She couldn't contain the small gasp that escaped her throat.

"It is quite beautiful," the King said with unmistakable pride.

As the riders drew closer, the looming granite wall that encircled the palace grounds took on a more defined shape, growing larger with each step they took toward it. Then they were passing through an archway in the stone, an enormous iron gate suspended above their heads. They emerged into a bustling courtyard, and Raven had the sense that they had just entered through the back door.

Countless servants and grooms swarmed the small party as the King brought his horse to a stop and dismounted, handing the reins to an olive skinned woman with dark eyes and darker hair. Raven's eyes met the woman's and she gave Raven a small smile. She was beautiful, and Raven had the fleeting thought that she must be very good with horses to be a groom and not on the King's arm.

"Thank you, Madeirah."

She only had a moment to register the King thanking the woman by name before a hand on her waist turned her attention back to where he waited.

"Allow me."

It was not a request as his other hand settled on her opposite side. A chill raced down her spine as he lifted her off the horse and placed her gently on the ground.

Raven glanced toward where Logan was helping Esrae down from his horse; she hadn't been able to see them during the ride, but now they both looked grim.

Logan spoke, but Raven wasn't sure to whom. "Send for Elarys."

"I'm here, Milord."

Raven turned toward where the voice had come from as a short, round woman with a mass of unruly red curls pinned to her head rushed toward them. She stopped and dropped into a curtsey before the King. "Your Majesty."

The King waved a hand in their direction. "Please, show my guests our hospitality." He turned toward Raven, and her heart thudded wildly against her ribs. "This one will be my personal servant." His attention turned to Esrae, his eyes moving from her shoes to her hair. "Bring that one to my rooms."

Raven's thudding heart stopped before quickly resuming again at twice the speed. Her stomach rolled and she breathed hard, attempting to swallow down whatever was rising there. Esrae had gone pale, though something else seemed to play in her eyes. Awe. She looked like she might be sick, but at the same time wonder and terror lit her face.

Instinctively, Raven began to turn toward Logan, to find that moral support that he always offered. But she wasn't supposed to know him here, that was their agreement. No one was to know they knew each other. She stopped short and instead fixed her attention on dirt under her shoes as her panic rose and a feeling of isolation settled.

"Come, my dears." The woman Logan had called Elarys stepped behind them and placed a soft hand on each of their backs, steering them toward what looked to be a servant's entrance in the stone wall. When Raven looked around, the King was already gone. "Let's get you both cleaned up. Those horses make everything so dusty."

Elarys led them up a flight of stone stairs and down a hallway covered in a maroon runner and lit with torches. More stairs and halls followed, giving Raven the feeling of being lost in a labyrinth. She'd never have been able to find her way out had she tried. The walls were lined with intricately woven tapestries depicting landscapes and battle scenes, the torches giving off just enough light to make them appear eerie. The King had not been lying about the beauty of the palace. She was distracted by the scenes as she walked and could have spent hours studying the intricacies of the displays. That was if the circumstances were different and she could concentrate on anything besides the King's last words as they echoed over and over in her head.

"—tub to get you all cleaned up."

Elarys had been speaking and she hadn't heard a word.

"I'm sorry?" She didn't even recognize the pitch of her own voice.

"I was saying, child, that we'll get you both rooms with a tub so you can get cleaned up," Elarys repeated.

She didn't even seem fazed that Raven hadn't been listening. The woman was probably used to it. How often had she done this same thing with other girls the King had taken a fancy to?

Elarys stopped and pushed a door open. "You both wait right here while we prepare the baths. We won't be long." They stepped inside and she gave them a warm smile as she pulled the door closed behind her.

Raven whirled to face her friend. "Esrae!"

Esrae dropped onto a grey velvet covered, overstuffed ottoman. A parade of emotions crossed her friend's pale face. Shock, fear, wonder.

Raven knelt in front of her. "Es? Are you okay?"

"He chose me." Esrae spoke the words as though she couldn't believe them, but also as though they weren't wholly awful. As though she liked the way those three words tasted on her tongue.

Raven sat back on her heels, concerned that Esrae didn't seem more worried.

Esrae's eyes rose to meet hers and clarity shone there. "I'm okay. He is a king. I could do worse."

Could she do worse? Fear settled on Raven. Was this shock? There was no way Esrae was grasping the full ramifications of what was happening. "Esrae."

"He picked me." Esrae's voice rose an octave as she returned her gaze to nothing in particular. A slightly crazed laugh issued from her lips. "He had you in his arms and he picked me."

Raven scrubbed at her face, frustration building inside her. "Es, I don't know that this a good thing."

Esrae's eyes snapped up to meet hers. "Because you're jealous?"

Raven rocked back. "What?"

"You're jealous," Esrae repeated, "because he chose me instead of you? Isn't Kanan enough for you? Or is it because you want the recognition? Or you don't think I can handle it?"

"Esrae, no." Raven scowled, she couldn't believe the words that were coming from her friend. "I just don't want you to get hurt." She reached out, grasping Esrae's hand in her own. "Please promise me you'll be careful?"

"I'll be fine, Raven." Esrae pulled her hand free from Raven's grasp. "I can handle it."

"I know you can." Sadness overtook Raven. She didn't want to offend Esrae further, but she knew Esrae. So few people had been kind to her. And now Malakai was taking her and what would he do? "I'm sorry."

Raven stood and placed her hands on her hips, defeat pressing in on her as she surveyed the room's wood-paneled walls. She'd expected larger rooms in the palace, though there was no bed, only two cushioned sofas, a chair, and an ottoman, all arranged around a low table. Clearly a parlor of some kind. A room meant for waiting. They didn't have to wait long, however. Moments later, the door opened and Elarys reappeared.

"Come on then." She beckoned them to follow as she led them farther down the wood-paneled hallway. Finally, Elarys stopped outside a door. Pushing it open, she turned to Raven. "This is you, child. Bathe. There are clothes for you. Just wait when you're through; someone will be along to show you where to go next."

Raven took a tentative step into the room. Before the door closed, she heard Elarys telling Esrae she wouldn't have to dress herself because someone would be along to help. Then the door clicked shut, and Raven was alone with her thoughts.

A large copper-colored tub sat in front of the fireplace, steam rising off the still surface of the water. It certainly looked inviting. She stepped further into the room. Beside the tub sat a plush armchair, over the back of which was draped a long tan dress with a small folded pile of what Raven assumed was underclothes sitting beside it. Beside the chair, on a peg on the wall, hung a deep maroon-colored sash.

Raven made a pass around the room, checking behind furniture and curtains, until she was satisfied she was alone. She stripped off her dress and sunk into the hot water. The tub was large enough that if she pulled her knees to her chest, the water covered her to her neck. She sighed as the warmth seeped into her. She could have stayed there for hours, though the thought of Elarys returning and finding her naked in a tub was enough to encourage her to finish. She washed quickly before reluctantly standing and stepping out of the comforting warmth. She dried with a towel that had been left for her, slipped on the underclothes and pulled the plain dress over her head. She eyed the maroon sash and decided to leave it on the peg and wait.

She perched on the edge of the chair, hands on her lap, hair dripping down her back, and waited. When the door opened Raven jumped, spinning to face whoever had entered.

Not Elarys, but a different woman. She seemed to be about Raven's age. She wore the same style dress that Raven had been given, though her sash, which she wore as a belt, was a burnt orange color. It almost matched the girl's hair, so red it was nearly orange, which was piled on top of her head, though unruly tendrils escaped around the edge of her face.

"It's a belt, goes around your waist."

"I know how to wear a belt," Raven snapped at the girl, though she was ignored.

The other girl held her hand out to Raven, a silver buckle resting in her palm. "Secure it with this."

When Raven didn't move, the girl walked over and reached past her, snatching the maroon sash from where it hung. She gave Raven a pointed look as she reached around Raven's waist, looping the sash around her.

"I'm Aster," the girl said as she secured the sash with the buckle. Raven could see now that the buckles were actually the king's crest, a large, ornate letter M pierced through with a sword. "What's your name?"

"Raven."

"Raven," Aster spoke her name as though she were testing it. "Raven, are you sure you're in the right room?"

Raven furrowed her brow. "This is where Elarys brought me."

Aster stepped back, hands on her hips, eyeing Raven from head to toe. "It's just, everyone knows the King prefers brunettes, and it's not as though you're plain. So, why is the blonde on her way to his room and you're on the way to the kitchen?"

Raven swallowed. Esrae, on her way to the King's room, like a piece of meat. "I don't know."

Aster shrugged. "Doesn't matter either way to me. Alright, pay attention. The belt. Always wear your belt. The belts, or sashes on the guys, show others where we belong in the palace, where we work. They come in especially handy when someone is looking for help to weed a garden or wash a chamber pot."

Raven's confusion must have shown on her face because Aster sighed. "If you're wearing a green sash, indicating you're an outdoor servant, then they can't pull you away to mop a floor. And you can't be taken to help with dinner unless you're wearing blue. Get it?"

Raven nodded. "What's orange?" She indicated Aster's belt.

"Orange is for those of us who do more than one thing," Aster explained. "Like a catch-all. Maroon is for—"

"The King," Raven cut in, catching on.

"The King." Aster nodded approvingly. "That's right. Now, your hair." She tilted her head to the side and pointed at the knot of orange-red hair on her head secured with two sticks. "Always up. You can use the sticks to keep it in place."

Aster moved behind Raven and began to gather Raven's long, thick waves together, twisting and piling the hair on top of her head. She continued speaking as she worked, "Even on your day off, you wear your hair up. It's just the way."

"Day off?" The words were a surprise to Raven. She hadn't expected days off.

Aster craned her head around to look at Raven. "We're not slaves, Raven. We get a break every now and then. Of course, we can't leave the palace grounds."

So different than what she had expected. "Do you like working here?"

Aster shrugged. "It's a place to sleep and meals to eat. Honestly, it's not like it's difficult work."

"What about the King?" Raven asked.

"What about him?" Aster wound the sticks into Raven's massive pile of hair.

"What's he like?" Raven grimaced as one of the sticks stabbed her scalp.

Aster moved back to where she could face Raven. She shrugged. "He's fine. Honestly, I don't know much about him. I serve him very rarely."

"Have you ever—" Raven couldn't even bring herself to finish the sentence and instead swallowed.

"Have I ever been in his bed?" Aster's brows rose in emphasis on the last word.

Raven raised her own brows in silent question.

"I haven't," Aster answered. "But if he asked, I wouldn't need convincing."

"Really?" Raven had expected more fear of the King.

"Have you seen him?" Aster's brows rose toward her hairline before crashing back down in scrutiny. "It doesn't matter. He wouldn't ask. Like I said, he prefers brunettes. Well, at least we thought he did, until today. Your friend must be very special."

Raven blew out a long breath. Special.

Aster clapped her hands together and stepped back to take in Raven's appearance. "Alright, it's time to get to work. So far, so good. You're to go to the kitchen and get a tray for the King and his lady. Wine, strawberries..." She rolled her eyes. "You know."

Raven's stomach flipped.

FOURTEEN

Aster led Raven to the kitchen and the moment she approached the door she was hit with a cloud of warmth. The kitchen was abuzz with activity. Blue sashed servants conversed loudly, fires crackled in the hearths, knives knocked steadily into cutting boards as they sliced through vegetables, all blending together in a low din.

Aster moved expertly through the bustle. Raven, on the other hand, seemed to run into nearly every servant, and when she did manage to move out of the way, inevitably, there was a table or workbench behind her that she didn't miss.

"Hot water!"

She spun in time to avoid the young man carrying a pot that appeared to be nearly half his size. "Sorry."

"Raven."

She turned to find Aster watching her, arms crossed, looking highly amused. Raven moved quickly to her side, thankfully avoiding any more servants or objects. "It's busy."

"Yeah." Aster appeared entertained. "It's a palace kitchen. It's busy."

Raven blew out a breath to steady herself as she waited for Aster to continue.

"Here, Aster." A girl with a messy blonde bun placed a tray on the workbench in front of them. A bottle of wine and two glasses stood next to a large covered plate.

Aster pulled the lid off and peered underneath. A bowl of strawberries sat beside another bowl heaping with white cream. She plucked up one of the strawberries and dipped the end slightly into the cream. Raven frowned as Aster bit the end of the berry. She closed her eyes and a wholly pleased expression spread over her face.

Aster released a low sound before she opened her eyes and offered the last of the strawberry to Raven. Raven shook her head, still surprised at the other girl eating the King's food. Aster swallowed.

"Taste test. Someone always tastes the King's food in your presence." She shrugged. "I just beat them to it this time." Aster brushed her hands together and picked up the tray, shoving it toward Raven. "Okay, here you go."

Raven accepted the tray and listened carefully as Aster gave her directions to the King's rooms. "If you get lost, just ask someone in a sash. They'll help."

There were so many stairs. She took them carefully, afraid to trip on the hem of her dress and send the King's food clattering to the floor below. This was her life now: climbing hundreds of stairs to deliver meals. She would be exhausted by the end of the day. The few servants she met along the way offered greetings, which she returned. It was, to her, an oddly pleasant environment; so far from what she had expected.

Raven arrived at the King's chambers to find two young guards standing outside the door. She was asked her name and one of them disappeared into the room, announcing her presence. When he returned he said nothing else, only pulled open the door to allow her to enter. The door closed behind her and she stood alone in a large room. A maroon rug with silver threads covered the floor and a crackling fire in the hearth to her left made the room warm and inviting. To her right sat a round wooden table with two chairs.

She was alone, but built into the far wall, almost camouflaged in the paneling, was another door she suspected led to the King's bedroom. He was probably there, on the other side of that door. Esrae too. Her heart tripped and then sped and then a familiar tightening squeezed her chest. She took two deep breaths as she balanced the tray on one hand and raised the other, knocking softly.

She barely had enough time to step back before the door opened. "Raven!"

"Esrae!" Raven nearly dropped the tray. She spun to the small table behind her and set the tray down, careful not to topple the wine or glasses. She turned back to pull Esrae into a hug. "Are you alright, are you okay? Where's the King?"

"I'm fine. I told you I'd be fine." Esrae stepped back and smoothed nonexistent wrinkles from the deep purple silk gown she wore. "The King will be back any minute."

"I'm so sorry, Es." Raven shook her head. "This wasn't supposed to happen."

"It's okay, Raven, really." Esrae placed a hand on her arm.

"Your first time shouldn't be like this. Not with him." Tears began to well in Raven's eyes, but when she met Esrae's eyes she found her blushing. "What is it?"

Esrae's eyes darted away. "I slept with Nevin."

"What?" She was confused for a moment before the words sank in. Raven let out a long breath. "Nevin?"

Esrae shrugged, a shy smile lining the edge of her mouth. "He's not so bad, really."

"Of course not. I'm glad." Raven smiled too. A half sob, half laugh escaped her. "Did he smell like fish?"

"Raven!" Esrae's smile widened almost to a grin. "I didn't expect you to say you were glad."

Raven laughed as well, a nervous sound. "I'm just glad that—"

"I know." Esrae's opened her mouth to speak again, but was cut off when the door across the room opened and they both jumped. Quickly they regained their composures, dropping into low curtsies before the King.

Malakai entered the room and stopped by the table where Raven had left the tray. He pulled his gloves off his hands and dropped them onto the surface before turning to take in the two women. His gaze lingered on Raven as her heart took up a staccato sort of rhythm, skipping beats.

He glanced once at Esrae and then stepped past her toward Raven. "This will not do."

Raven and Esrae shared a confused glance. She'd already made a mistake? Fear gripped her. She couldn't think what she might have done wrong. Malakai stepped closer, close enough to touch her. She held her breath and when he raised his arms, Raven fought the urge to flinch away. He reached out and took hold of the sticks Aster had so expertly used to weave her hair into place. He pulled and all her hair tumbled free, unwinding and falling down her back.

"That's better. Wear it like that." Malakai handed the two sticks back to her and her hands shook as she accepted them. She knew the King noticed and her cheeks heated but there was no amount of will that would stop them trembling.

"Of course, Your Majesty." Raven bobbed another curtsey, too shocked to say anything else.

Without another glance at her, he moved back to the table to continue removing what little embellishments he wore. "Come back later for the tray."

It sounded like a dismissal, and Raven gladly took it as such. "Yes, Your Majesty." She shot Esrae one last apologetic glance before she dropped into yet another curtsey and left the room.

Raven stepped out of the room and stopped. She couldn't even remember which way she'd come, and her mind wouldn't quiet enough to figure it out.

"Right, to the stairs," one of the guards spoke, startling her.

"Thank you," she murmured and he nodded once in answer.

At the bottom of the steps she had to ask again for directions. A small part of her tension released when she finally made it back to the kitchen where Aster waited.

"Looks like you survived your first—" Aster turned to face her and stopped mid-sentence. "Your hair! Didn't I tell you, always in a knot?"

"I'm sorry." Raven raised her hand, touching her hair. "He told me to take it down."

"Who?" Aster demanded.

"The King," she answered. "He took it down when I delivered the tray. He just walked over to me and pulled it down."

Aster's disbelief was clear. "He did?"

"Yes," Raven repeated. "He told me to wear it down."

Aster looked at Raven as though she were a puzzle she couldn't piece together. "And you're not in his bed. You're a servant."

Raven shrugged. She was certainly relieved to not be in his bed. But knowing that was exactly where Esrae was left a guilty knot in her stomach. The room seemed to tilt and she swayed.

Aster's hand shot toward her. "Are you alright? You don't look so well."

Raven grasped for the nearest chair. "I just need to sit for a minute."

"Do you need some water or food or something?" Aster asked, eyeing her warily.

"No, I'm fine, really." Raven didn't think she'd be able to eat if she wanted to.

"Okay." Aster didn't look convinced. She moved to the kettle. "I'm going to make some tea anyway. What were your instructions?"

"From the King?"

"Of course," Aster sighed. "Are you sure you're alright?"

"I'm fine," Raven repeated. "He only said to come back later for the tray. When do I go back?"

Aster shrugged. "Two or three hours. Not that long. How long could it possibly take them to do what they're doing?"

Raven's stomach rolled at the thought.

Aster continued, "Unless he calls you back sooner. There's a bell here; if it rings, it's for you."

Aster indicated the wall behind her where an entire bank of bells hung. "How do I know which one is for me?"

Aster moved closer and flicked one of the bells on the wall with her finger and a high-pitched tinkling sound filled the air. A maroon ribbon was tied to the top of the bell. "This one is directly from the King's chambers. If it rings, you're up."

"Do I need to be announced every time I go there?" Raven asked, still looking at all the bells.

"*You* don't." Aster emphasized the word 'you'. "As the King's personal servant, you may come and go, within reason, of course. As long as you have a task. You can't just wander into his chambers in the middle of the night or anything. Though, with you, he might appreciate that."

She couldn't tell if Aster was joking or being serious.

"Really, why are you a servant again?" Aster's face was a mask of confusion. Then she shook her head as if to clear it. "Anyway, I hope you're an early riser because we get up early around here. Maci will wake you before she goes to light the fires. At least you don't have to do *that*. But the King does take his breakfast in his chambers, and he is an early riser. Sometimes he's up before Maci. But he never calls for his breakfast before the fires are lit. Sometimes he even lights his own fire."

"He does it himself?"

Aster shrugged as the kettle began to whistle, and Aster quickly set about preparing two cups as she continued speaking, "If he's cold. He doesn't call a servant to come if they're not up yet. He's considerate in that way."

Raven's brow knit together. She hadn't expected anyone to refer to the King as considerate. "What does he have for breakfast?

"Bread. Toasted with cream and some type of fruit." Aster shrugged. "He's not particular. Whatever fruit is in season he'll eat. But you have a maroon sash, which means you don't have to worry about any of that. Someone else will prepare the King's meal, and another person is there to taste it while you watch. Remember, it's very important that you witness the taster sampling the meal. Your duty is then to deliver it to the King. Sugar?"

Raven nodded as she tried to absorb all the details. "Two."

"Sometimes after he eats, he goes riding, though not often," Aster continued as she dropped sugar into the mugs in front of her. "If he doesn't go riding, he still leaves his rooms. That's when you go in and clean. But while he's not particular about his food, he is very particular about his things. Don't move anything, or, if you do, put it back where it was. Milk?"

Again, Raven nodded. She was lost in her own thoughts when she realized Aster had stopped talking. She looked up to find Aster watching her. "What is it?"

"You know about him, right?" Aster asked as she placed a steaming mug of tea in front of Raven.

"About the King?"

"No, about the General." Aster rolled her eyes. "Yes, about the King. Has anyone told you of his unique abilities?"

Realization dawned. "Oh. Yes."

Aster nodded and inhaled deeply. "So you know?"

Raven gave her a quick nod, not trusting her voice.

Aster tilted her head quizzically. "How do you know?"

"Uh, rumors." Raven looked down into her mug and sipped.

"Well, they're true," Aster assured her.

"He's not able to know your thoughts though, right?" Logan had already made it clear that the King couldn't read minds, but she would gladly hear it confirmed.

"No, that he can't do. Thank the Saints. I imagine that if he could, there would be a few more executions around here. But he can bend anyone to his will."

A chill raced down her spine. Hearing someone besides Logan confirm this fact about the King was even more unsettling, as though it somehow made it more real.

Raven's thoughts wandered to Esrae. Would the King use his abilities on her? And what might he make her do? Raven placed a hand over her still churning stomach.

"Has he done this to you?" Raven asked, too late wondering if it might have been too personal a question, considering the things the King could make a person do.

Aster laughed. "Of course not. I'm not nearly important enough for something like that."

"Have you seen it done?" Raven asked.

Some of the color drained from Aster's cheeks, her eyes finding the table. "Yes."

Raven waited, but when Aster didn't continue, she prompted, "And?"

"It wasn't pretty, okay?" Aster said.

Raven's chest tightened as she tried to speak, causing her words to hitch. "What happened?"

Aster opened her mouth as though she were going to answer, but then she closed it again. A moment later she did respond. "You don't want to know."

Raven blew out a frustrated breath. "How can I be prepared if no one will tell me anything?"

Aster's attention snapped to her. "Fine. A man was brought to the palace. He'd been accused of attempting to steal a horse. The King's horse. And the King is very attached to his horse. So they brought him before the King and he lied. He said he hadn't been trying to steal the horse, said he'd merely been grooming it. The King didn't believe him. He got into his head and forced the man to tell the truth. The man confessed. So, the King made him take one of the guards' swords and—"

Aster stopped, that last word hanging in the air as a shadow passed over her face like she was witnessing it again. Raven needed to know what happened next.

"And? What?"

Aster looked Raven in the eye. "He cut off his own hand. Are you happy now? Are you glad I told you?"

Icy coldness seeped into Raven's bones, and she looked away, focusing instead on a knot in the wood of the table. She inhaled a shaky breath. Was that what the King was doing to Esrae now? Was he controlling her? Making her do unspeakable things to please him?

The bell with the maroon ribbon jingled softly, and Raven jumped so hard she nearly knocked her chair over. Her hand flew to her heart, her breaths heaving wildly.

"You're up," Aster said as she sipped her tea.

FIFTEEN

Raven pulled in a fortifying breath and stood, praying to all the Saints that the dizziness would pass. It took effort to make her feet move.

The King had made a man cut off his own hand. She couldn't decide if she was glad Logan hadn't shared more details or if she was angry with him for holding back.

Raven had to talk herself into every step on the way to the King's rooms, and before she realized it, certainly before she was ready, she stood outside his door.

The same two guards still stood on either side of the door, looking serious and sturdy. She nodded once to the guard on the left, the one that had given her directions to the stairs earlier, and he turned and pulled the door open, allowing her to enter.

She stopped just inside the door, surveying the space. There was no one else in the room and the only sounds came from the softly crackling fire. On the table sat the tray, picked mostly clean. She picked it up with a glance at the bedroom door, praying it didn't open.

She turned and reached for the door handle, but stopped when she heard the soft thunk of metal on wood as the latch on the bedroom door was moved. Her breath caught and she gripped tightly to the tray with both hands to hide their shaking.

He was behind her. She turned and froze in her place. Malakai stood just on the outside of the door. He wore no shirt and it was clear that even though he was a king, he had not let himself go. He had a solid physique with tanned skin and well-defined muscles. She was staring. She looked away quickly, dropping into a curtsey.

"I was just collecting the tray, Your Majesty." She did not meet his eyes, though she felt his attention on her.

He seemed to study her for a moment, and when she glanced up she found his gaze weighty, pressing on her.

"Thank you." He waved a hand toward the door and Raven took it as permission to leave.

"Thank you, Your Majesty."

She needed to go, needed to be out of his presence. Would he control her? Would she be aware of it if he was? The thought of not being in control squeezed her chest and stilted her breathing. She dropped into another curtsy and quickly exited the room.

As soon as Raven was out of the King's rooms and away from the guards, she quickly found the nearest staircase. Her legs trembled as she dropped onto the step, setting the tray down beside her. She pressed a hand on the cold stone wall beside her to steady herself. The other hand she placed on her chest as her heart raced, her breaths coming shallow and quick. In seconds her hands began to tingle, growing cold and clammy, and the familiar black spots swam in her vision, closing in, pushing the world out.

She tried to take a breath but it was as though it had nowhere to go. As if there was no room for it in her lungs even though she felt there was no air there to start. Panic grew and she knew she was about to pass out on these steps, only to be found by a servant or a guard. She tried again to take a breath, but it was ragged. Her hands began to shake. She was spiraling further out of control. Tears formed, blurring her vision further.

"Raven?"

She jumped at the sound of the voice behind her, leaping up from where she sat and nearly toppling backwards down the stairs. She caught the rail and looked up, her heart stuttering further.

"Your— Your Majesty." *Bow, you stupid girl,* she thought it, but before she could act on it, the ground tilted and the walls spun dangerously.

Malakai stepped closer, extending his hand. "Are you alright?"

Her breaths had become too erratic to form a response. Was he concerned? Was he there to take advantage of her in her tenuous state? He took another step, and without thinking she recoiled. She might have gone toppling down the stairs had the King not had quick reflexes. He reached out and caught hold of her arm, steadying her.

"You need to slow your breaths," he said, making sure she was solidly on her feet. He moved his head until he captured her line of sight. He spoke slowly and steady, as though he could calm her with his tone. "Breathe slower. Do this— count backward, starting at fifty."

Fifty? She couldn't count forward to ten right then; she certainly couldn't concentrate enough to find fifty in the sea of numbers.

"Fifty," Malakai began, still holding her gaze, his eyes intense. "Forty-nine, forty-eight, forty-seven—count with me. Forty-six..."

"Forty-five," she forced the words out, though they were barely more than a breath on her lips.

"Good." Malakai tugged her forward slightly, turning her so she could sit. He lowered himself beside her, not breaking his count. "Forty-four... keep counting. Forty-three..."

"Forty-two..." Raven joined him as he counted.

When they were at thirty-eight, Malakai paused. "Good. Now, go make yourself a cup of peppermint tea. Inhale the steam slowly and continue to count, slowly. Slow is what you want. You need to tell your body to slow down." He nodded at her. "The peppermint will help with the anxiety and the counting will help take your mind off of it."

Malakai glanced to where his hand still rested on her arm, as if he didn't realize he was still touching her. He released her and moved back. Raven's breathing had already become easier, even though she was still alone with the King. The thought was hazy at the edge of her mind and then it solidified. She was alone with the King. She needed to be anywhere else. She stood and managed a careful curtsey.

"Thank you, Your Majesty."

The King also stood, turning to leave, but paused to speak over his shoulder. "We'll have dinner in the Great Hall, but bring breakfast for two in the morning."

"Yes, Your Majesty," Raven said and quickly left.

In the kitchen, Raven dodged cooks and servants preparing the evening meal as she went through a number of different cabinets, searching for the peppermint tea. She did her best not to draw attention to herself as she filled a mug from an already warmed kettle and waited for the tea to steep. A basket of bright red apples sat on the counter by where she stood. With a glance around the busy kitchen, she surreptitiously pulled two of the fruit from the basket and pocketed them. The cup warmed her hands as she slipped out of the kitchen and found a seat on the currently empty servants' staircase. She held the cup to her face and inhaled the warm, minty, steam that rose from the surface of the tea. Immediately she could feel her tension ease. She needed to remember this trick. Her heartbeat returned to normal and she was able to pull in full deep breaths. She no longer needed the counting trick, as other thoughts filled her mind. Not only did he stop to help her, but the King's advice actually did what he said it would.

When Raven had finished her tea and was again breathing normally, she climbed the stairs to her room. The directions had been straightforward, and for that she was grateful. As the King's personal servant, she was required to be available at all times. So as not to disturb anyone else, she had her own room. It was at least one thing she could find to be grateful for. It wasn't big or beautiful; in fact, it was smaller than her room at home. Simply a bed, a small table, a basin, a mirror, and, of course, the bells above her bed.

Raven kicked off her shoes and lay back on the bed, blowing out a long, slow breath as her body relaxed into the mattress, adjusting to no longer being on her feet. She closed her eyes and immediately an image of Esrae in the King's bed formed in her mind. She snapped her eyes open and groaned.

"Definitely going to have to get over that."

She sighed aloud as she sat back up. A yawn pushed its way out. It was still early. In a little while, the palace would be sitting down to the evening meal in the Great Hall. No doubt Esrae would be there by the King's side. And no doubt the palace inhabitants would whisper about the new girl warming the King's bed. She groaned louder and rubbed her eyes as if she could wipe away the thoughts and images.

She didn't expect the King to need her anymore that night and was just about to pull her dress off when a knock on her door nearly caused her to jump out of her skin. The knock repeated softly as she caught her breath. She crossed the room to the door.

"Who's there?"

"Raven?"

She quickly unhooked the lock and pulled the door open. "Logan?"

He stepped past her into the small room, his size filling up much of the space. When he turned to face her there was a deep crease in his brow. "Are you alright?"

"I'm fine." She closed the door. "What are you doing here?"

"I came to check on you. Make sure you're well." Logan's eyes ran over her, taking in her appearance as if checking her for injuries.

"I'm fine," Raven repeated, attempting to reassure him and possibly herself.

Logan scanned the small space. "This room certainly makes it convenient to speak with you,"

"I can't believe I'm alone in here." Another thought struck her. "Won't you get in trouble for being here? Or won't I get in trouble?"

Logan's head cocked to the side and he raised one brow. "Raven, if you think the soldiers don't cavort with the servants, you're more naive than I thought."

"Cavort?" Raven repeated as she realized what Logan was saying. Her face scrunched up. "Disgusting."

Logan chuckled. "I'm only explaining that it's a reason I might be in here and no one would question it."

"And I'm just saying, yuck." Raven wrinkled her nose.

Logan nodded. "Thank you for that. Have you seen Esrae?

Raven took a deep breath and bit her lip. "Yes, she's fine. At least, she said she was fine. I don't know. This isn't what I thought was going to happen. This isn't what was supposed to happen. It's not supposed to be her. She didn't agree to this." By the time she was done speaking, the words were spilling off her tongue and her voice had risen to a high-pitched squeak.

"Raven." Logan's voice was calm as he captured her gaze, placing a hand on her shoulder. "I know."

She exhaled, feeling helpless.

Logan pursed his lips. "I don't think she's in danger. I don't think he'll hurt her."

"How do you know?" Her voice was still coming out shrilly.

Logan tilted his head to the side, concern filling his features. "Sit down, please?"

The bed creaked as she dropped heavily on the mattress. She wanted to do something but she didn't know what, and even if she did, she knew she wouldn't be able to.

She sighed. "Now what?"

"Now you continue to do what you're doing," Logan said. "And Esrae will continue to..."

"Do what she's doing?" Raven finished his sentence.

He frowned. "I'll be taking a patrol out in the next couple weeks to find new recruits for the army. I'll be sure to find Kanan and Torren."

Kanan. Something inside her uncoiled at just the mention of him. She needed him here with her. Or at least under the same roof. "This week?"

"This one, or the next." Logan nodded.

"Good." Some of her tension eased at his words.

She and Kanan had never spent this much time apart, not since they were children. Not having him around left a void inside her.

He folded his arms in front of his chest. "How do you find Malakai?"

His question brought Aster's story back to her mind and reminded her she had an issue to bring up with him. "How? I find him confusing. Kind, even? But still a little creepy. Aster told me some stories about his little trick, which you failed to mention."

Logan's brow rose. "Would it have helped?"

She looked away, annoyed that he was right. Of course it wouldn't have helped. It would only have been one more thing for her to worry about. Then she remembered.

"He told me what to do for my anxiety."

"What do you mean?"

"He found me panicking on the stairs and suggested some things, like tea and counting," Raven explained. "It helped."

"Interesting,"

"Yes. Actually, he's been quite pleasant," Raven mused. "Hardly the monster I've heard of."

"Yes." Logan's expression was grim. "He does put on a good show."

What did that mean? Before she could ask, he spoke again. "I'll keep you up to date on the army."

"Thank you."

"Be careful, Raven." Logan's tone was sober.

"I will."

Logan opened the door and did a quick scan of the hallway before he stepped out. And with a nod, he was gone.

The sudden ringing of the bell above her bed jarred Raven awake. It peeled continuously as she jumped up and pulled on her dress, urged on by the insistent sound. She was fully awake and dressed before she noted which bell was ringing. It wasn't the bell with the maroon ribbon. It was the general alarm bell. Where before she had been awake, now her skin buzzed with alertness. She stepped out her door and was nearly trampled by other palace servants as they streamed into the hall, some only barely awake.

"Come on!" Aster rushed past Raven, catching her by the arm as she went.

"What's going on?" Raven struggled to keep up with Aster's long strides. "What happened?"

"I don't know," Aster answered. "We're to gather in the throne room and we'll find out then."

"Is it bad?" Raven asked.

Aster glanced at her. "It's the middle of the night, so it's not good."

Chills slid over Raven and dread settled in her stomach. She didn't even know how to get to the throne room, so she allowed Aster to drag her along. Though it wouldn't have been hard to figure out—she would only need to follow the crowd.

When they finally came to the large room, it was already filling with people. Four large stone columns ran down each side of the room, leaving a larger space in the center. Torches hung from the columns, and on the walls were tapestries and weapons. Some of the weapons Raven didn't even recognize. Raven and

Aster stopped near the second pillar back from the dais where the throne sat. She had expected something a bit more ostentatious. There was a throne, but it wasn't overly pretentious or showy, and it sat on a platform that was only raised above the rest of the room by three short steps. The floor was made up of stone squares alternating in color between dark grey and darker grey.

The dais sat empty and tension was palpable in the air as everyone stood waiting. Low whispers spread through the room, but it was as though no one dared to speak too loudly.

"Now what?" Raven added her voice to the low din.

"Now we wait."

Aster lifted onto the tips of toes, her eyes running over the gathered crowd. She caught the eye of a young man with a green sash standing on the opposite side of the room. '*What's up?*' she mouthed the words to him, adding a palms-up gesture. He shrugged back, mouthing his own reply of, '*I don't know.*'

They didn't have long to wait. A door to the right of the dais opened and silence fell on the room as Logan entered, looking grim, along with five other soldiers. Behind them, Esrae appeared, followed by a servant with a yellow sash. Esrae looked tired and nervous. Raven hoped she was okay. She stared hard at Esrae, as though she could will the other girl to look in her direction, but she never did.

Moments later, the King entered and, as one, the occupants of the room bowed low. When they rose, the silence continued as they waited.

Finally, he spoke, his voice carrying past her all the way to the back of the room, "Each and every person within these walls should feel safe. You should all be able to rest easy within the palace. No one should have to fear for their safety. Not you and not I. I strive for that assurance for each of us. But tonight, that was not the case. Tonight, our walls were breached by an enemy. Someone with ill intent found their way inside. Someone came to do harm."

The King paused and Raven held her breath, trying not to tremble. She was about to see, first hand, what Malakai did to traitors.

"Bring him in," he called.

Logan moved to the door and pushed it open. He stepped to the side as two more soldiers entered the room. Between them, they dragged another man. Both his arms and legs were in shackles. His face was bloody and bruised, his lip split. A gash ran along his cheek and his left eye was almost completely swollen shut. She took a shaky breath.

The soldiers pulled the man to a spot in front of the King, where he stood on unsteady legs.

Malakai stepped to the edge of the dais. "You don't bow before your King?"

To Raven's great surprise, the man pulled his head back and spit on the ground at the King's feet. He raised his chin, looking up to meet Malakai's eyes. "You are not my King."

A collective gasp permeated the otherwise silent room.

The King stepped down once, though he still stood above the man. When he spoke, his voice was quieter and infinitely colder. This was not the man who had sat beside her on a step and counted with her. "I said, *bow*."

The man dropped heavily onto both knees, his head hung low. It might have appeared to be an act of submission if it weren't for the look of pure hatred on the prisoner's face. This was not his doing.

A chill crawled over Raven as she realized what she was witnessing. The King using his power.

"You cannot force submission," the man growled through gritted teeth from his place on the ground.

Malakai's brow rose. "No, but I can do this."

For a moment, nothing happened. But then the man began to groan, a low sound emerging from deep inside him. His teeth were clamped together and Raven's breath caught in her throat as his still chained hands flew to his head and his groans turned to full-fledged cries of agony. The sound echoed off the high ceilings of the throne room and reverberated in her chest.

She squinted against the desire to look away and reached out to clutch Aster's arm as she swayed. Finally, she looked from the screaming man to the King. He hadn't moved, not one finger. The only thing she noticed that was different about him was the slightest uptick to the corner of his mouth.

The prisoner dropped fully to the floor, chains ringing as he writhed, still screaming.

Terror raced up and down her spine. This wasn't just mind control, this was something else. This man was being tortured from the insdie. Raven glanced at Logan. He stood deathly still, his mouth set in a grim line, his eyes trained on something on the far end of the room. What was it like for Logan to work for Malakai and witness things like this for all these years? Her heart ached.

A sudden silence fell on the room as the prisoner's cries stopped. And through the crowd Raven could just make out his still form; could just barely see his eyes wide, staring at nothing. He was dead. Ice filled her veins.

"I hate this."

Raven nearly jumped out of her skin at the sound of Aster's whispered voice in her ear.

She turned to her, her voice shaking. "How often does this happen?"

"Occasionally." Aster's voice held no inflection as she half shrugged one shoulder, like she had become numb to such things during her time at the palace. "I mean, not someone breaking into the palace. That almost never happens. But the King does take opportunities to show his power fairly often. Come on."

Aster nudged Raven's arm and pointed her chin in the direction of the dais. Malakai was disappearing out of the door. Those that arrived with him, including Esrae and Logan, followed him out. Everyone else in the room began to disperse as well.

"What do we do now?" Raven asked.

"We go back to bed. It's barely three in the morning." Aster let out a heavy sigh. "Maci will wake us when she goes around to light the fires."

"How am I supposed to sleep after that? How can anyone sleep after that?" She would never get the face of the dead man, or his screams, out of her head.

Aster's head cocked to the side and a sadness swirled in her eyes as she blew a long breath out her nose. "You learn to deal with it."

Goosebumps crawled over Raven's arms. "Great."

SIXTEEN

"Excuse me, miss?"

She groaned as she rolled over, not ready to be awake. Beside her bed stood a girl she had never seen before. Her confusion was short lived as she remember Aster saying someone would come to light the fires. Maci.

Raven acknowledged the girl, her voice muffled by sleep. "Fire girl."

Maci giggled. "That's me. I'm just here to make sure you get up so you can get the King and his latest conquest some breakfast."

Raven frowned. She didn't like people speaking of Esrae like that. Again, she wished she could switch places with her. Not because she was jealous, but because she was truly concerned.

Raven dragged herself out of the bed, shivering when her feet hit the cold floor. She decided she wasn't a fan of being awake before the fire. In a wave, the events of the early morning hours flooded her memories. She glanced at the rumpled bed. How had she even slept at all after what she'd witnessed in the throne room? She inhaled deeply, the smoky scent of the newly lit fire filled the room as she blinked against the memories.

"Maci?"

"Yes?" the girl replied from where she knelt on the floor, gathering up her supplies.

"How do I get to the kitchen again?"

Maci gave her a sympathetic look and offered simple instructions for the quickest route to the kitchen, and then she was gone, leaving Raven alone as the day loomed in front of her like a sentence for a crime. Raven pulled on her dress and fastened the maroon sash around her waist, and then she stood in the middle of the room, staring at the door. Being late wouldn't help anything. She blew out a quick breath and shook her head at her own silliness.

She stepped into the hallway and immediately forgot what Maci had told her. She was pretty sure she was supposed to go left, so she turned that direction. At the end of the hallway a man with a blue sash across his chest hurried around a corner. Perfect, kitchen staff. With luck, he was heading to work. She followed him.

The large kitchen was already humming with activity when she entered, and she was suddenly grateful she wasn't wearing blue. They had to be up far earlier than the fire. The scent of baking bread already hung in the air as blue-sashed servants skittered around, carrying trays, and bowls, and slabs covered in more bread dough. Steaming pots hung over fires and savory aromas wafted from inside. Another servant pushed past Raven and it was all Raven could do to keep out of the way.

"Oi there, you, girl!"

Raven didn't know if the person speaking was addressing her or not, but she turned anyway. Her eyes fell on a round woman, her face bright red from work, waving her over. Carefully, Raven maneuvered through the busy kitchen to the woman. When she was barely close enough, the woman shoved a tray into her hands and threw a thumb over her shoulder. "You're late. He's waiting."

Raven looked at the tray in her hands. Toast, a bowl of cream, and a bowl of fruit. "Excuse me?"

The woman, who had already returned to her work, turned back to Raven, looking annoyed. "What is it?"

"I need two meals," Raven said.

"Oi, right." The woman rolled her eyes, throwing her hands in the air. "There's a trollop this morning."

"Hey." Raven's eyes narrowed. "She's not a trollop."

The woman turned a look on her that clearly conveyed she didn't care what Raven thought of the King's companion. With another roll of her eyes, the woman snatched the tray from her hands and set to work piling on more food.

Raven stepped out of the way of the bustle to wait.

"Cora!" A grinning guard stood at the entrance to the kitchen, arms thrown wide as to announce his arrival.

Raven's breath left her in a whoosh and she pressed herself further into the wall, wishing she could become invisible. It was the guard she had encountered at the bakery and later in town. Two more guards followed him in.

The round, red-faced woman, Cora, who was preparing Esrae's tray, looked up and huffed. "Oh, no, you don't. Not today. Take your friends and leave."

"I'm hurt." He clutched his chest in mock pain. "We've only come for a snack, a morsel."

"That's what breakfast is for," Cora waved her knife in the direction of the door. "Out. All of you."

His shoulders dropped and he surveyed the room. "Well, if you won't give us a snack, we'll just have to find—" His words ceased as his eyes came to rest on where Raven stood along the edge of the room. "Our own."

His head tilted to the side as the playful look in his eyes was replaced by a more menacing glint. He stepped up to her, and she forced herself to hold her ground and not flinch away from him. It was a daunting task. He stopped in front of her and she had to tilt her head far back to look him in the eye. Saints, he was taller than Kanan.

"Well, well. We meet again." His shoulders were broader than Kanan's, as well, and Raven felt very small next to him. "I had no idea you'd joined us at the palace."

Raven set her jaw, clenching her teeth together.

The guard's eyes traveled the length of her body before coming to rest on the maroon belt at her waist. He reached out and hooked his fingers into the belt. She was unprepared when he gave a swift tug, and she stumbled forward into him. Without thinking, she reached up, bracing herself on his chest. There was a wicked glint in his smile, and she quickly pulled back her hands.

"Maroon. You serve the King," he mused, not releasing her. He bent slightly and lowered his voice. "That means you have your own room."

"Oi!" Cora's voice cut through the room. "Holden, leave her alone. Get your food and get out. She has work to do."

With a dangerous smile and a wink, Holden disentangled himself from her belt and took a step back. "I'll see you later."

Then he turned and he and his friends strode toward the door. He pulled an apple from a barrel on the way out of the room. When he was gone, Raven released the breath she'd been holding. Her shoulders sagged and she swallowed. When she looked up, Cora was watching her, shaking her head.

"You'll do well to stay away from that one," Cora said as she shoved the precariously piled tray into Raven's hands and motioned toward a young man, who stood at a counter chopping carrots. "Henri, taste this."

The young man laid his knife down and turned to where Raven stood, balancing the tray Cora had given her. He broke off a few small bites and popped them into his mouth, smiling and waggling his eyebrows at her, before he returned to his chopping.

"Henri tastes everything before you leave the kitchen. No exceptions. Now go, you're really late now." Cora shooed Raven from the kitchen.

Raven did her best to balance the tray, praying to all the Saints that Holden and his friends were gone. Though with every step she took bringing her closer to the King's chambers, she found a whole new reason to be anxious. She wished she was back in the kitchen rather than about to enter the rooms of a man who was capable of killing with only a thought. A shiver ran down Raven's spine as the cries of the dying man echoed in her head.

Outside the King's chambers, the guard opened the door and allowed her entrance. No one else was around, thank the Saints. Breathing a sigh of relief, she placed the tray on the table and exited the room.

Raven had been at the palace for a week and had fallen into a routine that almost never changed. She would deliver meals in the morning, and when the King was out for the day, she would return to clean his rooms. She never had much to straighten. Malakai seemed to take care of his room mostly on his own, something that surprised Raven. There was also barely any evidence that Esrae was even there. In fact, the only time Raven saw her was at the evening meal. Malakai often took his dinner in the Great Hall and Esrae was always by his side. Of course, Raven did not have an opportunity to speak with her. She did observe her carefully, though, looking for any signs that Esrae was being mistreated. There were none. Esrae seemed the picture of health, even appearing happy.

There was no word from Logan. Raven longed for him to come to her, desperate for news of Kanan and Torren. But there was silence from the General.

She lay on her bed, staring at her ceiling. The words on the page blurred together as her thoughts were elsewhere, wrapped up in Kanan. She missed him so much it left an aching knot in her chest. She closed her eyes and imagined him there, beside her, running his fingers through her hair, listening to her talk about her day, or listening to him talk about his latest sword commission. Often the details bored her, but the sound of his voice and the touch of his hands made up for it. And just then, staring at the wooden cross beams on the ceiling, she might have given just about anything to hear the specifics of fire temperatures and the weight of a blade.

The knock, breaking into the silence, sent her heart into her throat. She sat up in bed and was about to call out when the door opened. Aster stood on the other side, both her smile and eyes holding mischief. "Come on."

Raven swung her feet off the side of the bed. "Where are we going?"

Aster shrugged playfully. "You've been here long enough, it's time you learn some secrets."

With her interest piqued, she stood and followed Aster from the room. "Secrets?"

"Shh, no questions. Just follow me." Aster led the way down the hallway, but when they came to the end, instead of turning toward the stairs, Aster turned the opposite direction and stopped.

Raven studied the wall in front of them. Aster had said secrets. She ran her gaze over the dark grey stone, looking for something etched into the surface, like words or a picture. There was nothing and nowhere else for them to go.

Aster glanced down at Raven, a spark dancing in her eyes. "Now."

"Now?"

Aster placed her hand on the wall, and when she applied some pressure, the spot compressed. Stone ground against stone and Raven stood stunned as the wall slid to the side, revealing a descending stone staircase.

"Come on." Aster stepped toward the stairs. She stopped and turned when Raven didn't follow.

"Uh..." Raven stared down the staircase as the darkness seemed to grow in front of her and familiar anxiety began creeping up her spine.

"What's wrong?" Aster asked.

"Where does it go?" She failed to keep her voice from shaking.

"I can't tell you, it's a surprise," Aster answered. "Just follow me."

Raven couldn't pull her eyes from the blackness of the staircase. "I'm not going down there unless you tell me where it goes."

Aster rolled her eyes and her whole head. "Fine. It goes to a room just off the kitchen. The servants know all kinds of these secret passages. There's always something going on down there because it's so close to the kitchen. No shortage of food. Now, will you come?"

"It doesn't go underground?" Raven needed to clarify that she wasn't about to find herself below the weight of the stone palace.

"No, just to the kitchen." Aster's exasperated expression softened as her brow crinkled further. "Are you okay?"

Just to the kitchen, Raven. She let out a breath. "Yeah, fine. Okay, let's go."

"Great." Aster smiled and stepped aside, allowing Raven past her so she could push the door back into place.

Raven followed Aster as she descended the staircase.

"So what do you have against stairs?" Aster asked over her shoulder.

"Not stairs. Cellars." Raven kept one hand on the stone wall, paying close attention to her feet on the steps.

"Okay, what do you have against cellars?"

"My father's a Vintner," Raven explained as the memories played in her mind. "We have a decent sized wine cellar. When I was eight, I went down alone and the handle on the door broke. I was trapped. It left an impression. I can barely go down there at all now."

"That sounds awful," Aster said "Well, I promise this doesn't go underground. In fact, we're here."

In front of them loomed yet another grey stone wall, giving the impression that the stairs they had just taken led to nowhere. At least Aster knew where they were.

Aster slid her hand down the wall until she found the spot she was looking for. She pushed, and the wall emitted the same grinding sound, moving just as it had at the top of the stairs.

As soon as the door opened, the smell of fresh bread and tea wafted into the stairwell, along with the soft warm glow of firelight.

Aster looked back over her shoulder and smiled. "Welcome."

She unfurled her arm and allowed Raven to step past her through the doorway. The room wasn't overly large. Big enough for two tables with a few chairs. The tables had been pushed to the side and the chairs were arranged in a semi-circle around a small fireplace. Besides the fireplace, a few torches hung on the wall, giving the room an inviting orange glow.

There were only three other people in the room, and Raven assumed it was due to the late hour.

Aster lifted a pot off one of the tables where it sat next to several small loaves of bread and a few cubes of cheese. She plucked the lid off and peered inside. "Save me some tea?"

"It's there; don't know if it's still hot, though," a young man who appeared to be a year or two younger than Raven answered from where he sat on the floor by the fire.

He wore a green sash across his chest and Raven recognized him from the throne room the night she had seen the King kill the intruder.

"You took forever to get here," another man about Raven's age said over his shoulder.

He wore an orange sash tied around his head and sat backward in his chair, facing the fireplace.

"Who's your friend?" the only other girl in the room asked.

Her thick, dark curls were piled on her head in a knot, though clearly she'd been working hard, as ringlets were escaping all over her head. The light from the fire made her rich copper skin glow. She also had a blue belt, and Raven briefly wondered how someone with such classic beauty had been hidden away in the kitchen. The girl popped a bite of bread into her mouth as she studied Raven.

"This is Raven." Aster gestured toward Raven. "This is Shara, Gio, and Luc." She poured herself a cup of tea and turned to look at Raven. "Tea?"

Raven nodded. "Thank you."

"Maroon, huh?" the one with the orange sash on his head, Luc, said. He turned sideways in his chair so he could face the others in the room, his hair fell in dark waves around his slim, handsome face. "Malakai's new pet?"

She'd never heard anyone at the palace refer to the King by his first name.

"No. That's the blonde," Aster spoke up as she handed Raven a cup of tea. It was barely warm. "She's just the new servant."

"Lucky," Gio said.

"Lucky? Which one?" Shara laughed.

"I meant Raven." Gio gestured toward her with a dark, tanned hand. "You think the blonde is lucky? She has to share the King's bed."

Raven tried not to flinch at the words. No one noticed.

"Has too?" Shara winked at Aster.

Aster raised her eyebrows and held her cup high in a salute to Shara.

"Gross." Luc's tone was clipped and thoroughly unimpressed.

"You're just jealous," Shara said.

"Of what?" Luc scoffed in Shara's direction.

"That you're not as attractive as the King, Luc," Aster answered.

"I'll learn to live with it," Luc deadpanned.

"What about you, Raven?" Gio asked. "Anyone special?"

Raven had just taken a sip of her tea and before she could swallow and answer, Aster laughed. "Yes! The General."

It was all Raven could do to keep the tea in her mouth and not spit it everywhere.

Shara's curls bounced around her face as she sat forward in her seat, her eyes growing to the size saucers. "I have never seen eyes so blue! You really have something going with the General?"

"I saw him leaving her room." Aster winked.

Raven shot a glance at Aster. She hadn't thought anyone had seen Logan leave.

Luc held a hand up in front of Aster. He addressed Raven, eyes narrowed, brow furrowed. "Do you speak?"

"Yes," Raven replied.

"I was just checking because Aster's been speaking for you since you came down," he said.

"I speak." Raven smiled as Aster scowled and batted away the hand that Luc still held in front of her.

"So, what's it like working for the King?" he asked, hooking his feet around the legs of his chair and leaning back.

Raven shrugged. So far it hadn't been either bad or good. Besides the scene in the throne room, and that wasn't directly related to her.

"It's okay."

"Okay?" Gio repeated. "Not terrifying?"

Shara rolled her eyes. "Please."

"Not everyone is quite so taken with him as you, Shar," Luc said.

"It's really fine," Raven said again. "I don't see him that often, actually. When I do, he's always been nice to me."

"See?" Shara stuck her tongue out at Luc.

"You're really not scared of him?" Luc's brow rose. "Like, maybe you put too much sugar in his tea and he makes you stab yourself?"

"I wasn't worried about that until now." Raven scrunched her face as she peered into her own cup.

"Ignore them," Shara said, tearing off another piece of bread and passing it to Raven.

Raven accepted the bread. "You don't like the King?" she asked Luc.

All signs of relaxation vanished as Luc sat up straight in his chair. His eyes widened as they darted from her to Gio and back to her. "I didn't say that. I didn't mean that. Don't tell anyone that." An edge of panic laced his words.

Realization hit Raven. Luc was afraid that as the King's servant she might inform on him for being disloyal.

She shook her head. "I won't. I would never."

He released a breath and his shoulders relaxed a touch. "Good. I was just asking." Luc's eyes widened in emphasis. "That's all."

"Don't worry. Really, I won't say anything." She pushed as much assurance into her voice as she could. "I promise."

"Well," Aster stood and brushed her hands together, sending a shower of bread crumbs to the floor, "I hate to break up the party, but I need to get to bed."

"You just got here." Gio gave her a disbelieving expression.

"I just wanted to show Raven around. But now I need sleep. Raven?"

Raven stood. "Yes. Me too."

"Come back anytime," Gio said with a wave.

"Yes, bring stories. Preferably of the King or the blue-eyed General." Shara smiled.

Raven's mouth quirked up at the edges. She wondered what Logan would think of her admiration. "I'll tell him you said 'hi'. The General, not the King."

Shara grinned, sitting up straighter. "Please do! Tell him if he's ever bored or lonely, he can find me above the gardens. I have a roommate, but I'll lock her out."

Raven laughed. "I will. I promise." And she would, if only to see Logan's reaction.

The next day followed a similar pattern to those of the previous week.

By the end of the night exhaustion was weighing heavily on Raven. She pushed her door closed and sighed. Another day done. A yawn forced its way out as she kicked off her shoes, leaning on the door behind her. Her bed was so close, and she eyed the pillow that seemed to beckon her. She had only taken one step when there was a knock on the door behind her. She could ignore it...

just lay down for the night. But it could also be important. She cast a wistful look at her bed.

"Yes?"

"Raven."

She nearly tripped over her recently discarded shoes in her rush to pull the door open. Stepping to the side, she allowed Logan to enter before she latched the door and turned back to face him.

"They're here."

Her breath whooshed from her as relief settled over her shoulders like a blanket. "Are they okay?"

"They're fine." Logan dropped his voice, though no one could hear them. "And we have a plan."

Her heart stuttered in her chest. A plan. This was why they were there, but that didn't stop the trepidation that crept over her arms and down her spine.

She gestured to the only chair in the room. "Sit."

The small chair creaked in protest as Logan settled his large frame into it. He didn't seem to notice. Raven perched on the edge of the bed, leaning forward, waiting.

When Logan spoke again, his voice had dropped even lower, and she had to strain to hear him even though he was only feet away from her. "We're going to poison Malakai."

She sat back, considering his words, letting them sink in. *How could that be done?*

She shook her head. "You can't poison his food. He has a taster."

Logan's eyebrows raised as he shrugged one shoulder. "Actually, we're going to poison his taster."

That seemed to be taking things a bit far. She thought of the smiling young man, Henri, who tasted the King's meals. She always enjoyed interacting with him. "You're going to kill the King's taster?"

Logan's look turned incredulous. "Give me some credit, Raven. Of course not. There will be just enough poison to sicken him. Then Malakai will need a new taster."

Understanding dawned on her and tugged at the corner of her mouth. Perfect. "Torren."

Logan's eyebrows rose, confirming her assumption. Kanan would have no problem fitting into a position in the army. But Torren, he wasn't even remotely a soldier. He was much better suited to kitchen work. Taster would be a perfect place for him. With him in the position, it would be an easy task to slip poison into the King's drink. Torren simply wouldn't drink it.

"Kanan I can use. Torren . . ." Logan said with a tilt of his head. Raven nodded. "We should be able to get each of us close by, and if Esrae is with him when he drinks the poison, she can delay calling for help. We'll plan to have Kanan stationed outside his door on that night. Myself, as well, though that will be harder. Kanan may need to deal with the other guard if Malakai calls for help."

Deal with him. She couldn't even imagine Kanan hurting someone. She had no doubt he was capable of it physically, but the thought of him actually injuring someone on purpose was something she couldn't picture.

It was real. Suddenly, all the talking was an actual plan. Her stomach tightened and an absurd urge to laugh filled her when she looked around the small room where they sat, planning the assassination of the King under his very roof. She took a deep breath in an attempt to settle her stomach.

"Are you alright?"

She shrugged. "I'm just great." What could she say? That she was extremely anxious and terrified about the whole thing and just wanted to go home? "I knew what we were working toward when I offered to help. It's just a bit more real now, that's all."

"Yes," the word left Logan on an exhale

"And it's not like I can bow out now." She smiled weakly. There was no turning back from here. They were in far too deep.

She swallowed. The image of the prisoner, dead and bloody on the floor of the throne room, reemerged. "Please be careful. If you or any of us get caught . . ."

Logan did not break her gaze, and the look in his eyes sent a shiver down her spine. "We're going to try to do this as soon as we can. We have a plan to have Torren appointed taster in two days. Be at dinner then."

"I will."

Logan stood and Raven followed. "Goodnight, Raven."

She blew out a breath. "Goodnight."

There was a pause and Logan reached out, placing a large hand on her shoulder and pulling her into an embrace. She rested her head on his chest, sliding her arms around his waist. The action immediately left her feeling better. He placed a kiss on the top of her head, and when he spoke, his words were soft. "I love you."

"I love you too," she said into his shirt. "Be careful."

"I'm always careful." He released her and there was a small smile on his lips.

"Clearly." She smiled back at him as she stepped back.

He pulled the door open, but instead of leaving, he took a step back into the room. "Excuse me."

"No, excuse me, sir." Raven heard Aster's voice outside her door.

Logan offered her one last smile before he exited the room. If only he knew the conversation she was about to have.

Aster stepped into the spot he had vacated, though her gaze lingered on Logan as he walked down the hall.

When Aster returned her attention to Raven, she wiggled her eyebrows, shaking her head. "Why is it never me? Share?"

Aster's presence and personality brought a change to the atmosphere of her room that she was grateful for. She managed a smile as she stepped back into the room. "You're welcome to try. I don't own him."

Aster winked. "I just might. Is he any good?"

Raven schooled her features so as not to betray how unappealing and gross she found the implication. *Play the part*, she reminded herself.

"What do you think?"

"I think he certainly looks like he has experience," Aster remarked. She shook her head. "And strong. He must be quite the tumble."

She pushed aside the thought of poisoning the King and the fact that Kanan was here, somewhere on the grounds, as she searched for a reply to satisfy Aster.

"It's not boring." She hoped she had successfully turned her grimace into a smile.

Aster made a noise that was something between a sigh and a squeak. "It's been too long, let me tell you. The options around here are way too limited."

At that, Raven's smile turned genuine. "Did you need something?"

"Not really, I was just coming for a chat, but it's late, I'll let you sleep." She winked again. "You must be exhausted."

"Very," Raven confirmed, though it was not for the reasons Aster suspected.

SEVENTEEN

The disappointment Raven had been feeling all day established it's hold firmly when she entered her room the next evening. She had gone about her daily tasks, even taking time to loiter in certain areas of the palace and grounds, and not once did she see Kanan. It made sense that he would be getting acquainted with his new surroundings, most likely training with the other men, but that hadn't stopped her from hoping. At one point she did see a group of soldiers carrying armfuls of what looked like staves back toward the barracks, but none of them were Kanan. A veil of sadness settled on her as she lit the candles and sat on her bed.

One more day. One more day, then their plan would be in action. An odd comingling of dread and relief curled inside her. She was ready for this all to be over; ready to be back at home where her biggest problem was the blasted cellar. Instead, she sat on a bed in the palace, thinking about the day they would poison the King. What had she gotten herself into, and would it even work?

When she realized she'd been staring at the floor, she shook her head and blew out an exaggerated breath through her almost pursed lips, causing her cheeks to puff out. She stood and washed at the water basin that sat on the small table in her room. When she was finished, she eyed the bowl. It took seconds to decide to empty it in the morning instead of leaving her room again tonight. Instead, she pulled on a short gown, the hem reaching just above the knee, and dropped onto her bed.

She laid back and threw an arm over her eyes. Sleep seemed very unlikely, even though fatigue weighed on her. Someone knocked gently on her door and she let out a frustrated groan. Why did Aster always show up so late? Didn't that girl get tired? As much as she wanted to call through the door and tell whoever it was to go away, she didn't want to be rude. With a frustrated, weary growl that she made sure was quiet enough not to be heard on the opposite side of the door, Raven stood and crossed the room.

She pulled the door open, but it was not Aster who greeted her.

"Kanan!"

He pushed into the room and immediately, his arm was around her waist, a hand in her hair, and his lips on hers. She wanted to melt into him. She slipped her arms around his waist and was acutely aware of the familiar feel of his muscled back under his rough shirt. She flexed her fingers slightly to assure herself he was real. The kiss was long, intense, and when it was over, he didn't pull away. He simply rested his forehead on hers.

"Kanan, I—"

"Shhhh," he cut her off, his words just above a whisper. "I just want to hold you for a minute."

She closed her eyes and relaxed into his arms, breathing him in, smiling at the lemon scent.

Moments passed before he spoke, though he didn't move. "Are you alright?"

"Yes."

He slid his thumb over her jaw as he spoke. "I wanted to come sooner, but I couldn't get away."

She leaned her head into his palm. "I'm glad you're here now."

He pulled his head back just enough to see her face. His eyes roamed over her features as though he was taking inventory. "You're sure you're alright?"

"I really am," she assured him.

"I've spent every day worried about you," he said. "When we heard from Logan that the King hadn't chosen you . . ." He exhaled deeply. "Maybe I shouldn't have been, but I was so relieved. That's not fair to Esrae, I know, but I was." His hands gripped her tighter as he spoke the words.

"She's fine too." Maybe if he knew Esrae was well he wouldn't be so hard on himself. "Honestly? I think she was excited." Kanan pulled back, his brows climbing. She shrugged. "I mean that she was chosen over me. I think she was jealous." Raven hated saying it because she thought it made her sound conceited, but it was the truth.

"I hope she gets over that." Kanan raised his brows. "Have you seen Logan? Has he told you the plan?"

She nodded, feeling like some sort of creeping crawling insect had taken up residence inside her chest.

"It's almost over." His gaze pierced hers. "We're almost home."

She wanted to believe that too, but she'd had a niggling sense of dread for weeks that would not leave her alone. Kanan must have sensed it. "I mean it, Raven. Days. In days, we'll be back home and we can plan our wedding."

Plans. Plans took too long. She shook her head. "No, no plans, I don't want to wait. I just want to find a cleric and marry you in the vineyard."

Kanan's mouth split into a grin. "That's the best thing I've heard since the day you said you'd marry me. It shouldn't have taken me so long to ask. What was I thinking?"

"I don't know, but I'm glad you did." She smiled up at him.

He kissed her forehead. "My intended."

The words sounded like a prayer, and Raven's heart clenched a bit. Then his mouth was on hers again, as his hands moved in slow perusal over her form.

He walked her backward until her legs hit the bed and she was lowered carefully to its surface.

She closed her eyes, allowing herself this moment of letting everything else fall away and focusing only on the way Kanan's hands slid over her body. The way they found the hem of her gown and slipped beneath; concentrating on the way his fingers moved expertly, wringing pleasure from her until her back was arching off the bed and she was biting her pillow to keep quiet.

The scent of rosemary and roasted chicken hung in the air and a low hum filled the room as those sitting down to dinner shared conversation. Dinner in the Great Hall was not an elaborate affair; no one changed for the evening meal, and the atmosphere was very relaxed. Though not for Raven. Everything inside her curled and buzzed and coiled as she stood along the wall with a few of the other servants. The room glowed a soft orange as the light from countless candles and torches reflected off the wooden surfaces of tables and beams. The King's banner hung along the wall at intervals down both sides of the room, interspersed with an array of shields, each showing a different crest. Silverware clinked against plates and Raven almost wanted to laugh at how oblivious everyone was to what was about to happen.

Two days had seemed to fly by, and now here they were. Across the room Logan was seated with a few other officers. She wondered if anyone else noticed the tense way he held his shoulders or if it was just because she was so familiar with him. Another table over Kanan and Torren sat with half a dozen others from the batch of new recruits Logan had brought in. Someone beside Torren laughed, and she couldn't help but smile. Leave it to Torren to lighten the mood.

Her attention drifted back to Kanan, and as though he sensed her, he glanced up and met her eye. He threw a wink at her before returning his attention to where it had been half-focused on those around him, half-focused on the King.

The King sat in his usual spot at the large table at the front of the hall, Esrae beside him. There were others that sat with them, Lords or Knights; Raven actually had no idea who they were and she didn't care. She did notice, though, that the King also seemed not to care, his attention focused on Esrae. He picked up an almost empty decanter of deep red wine and poured the remaining liquid into Esrae's cup as he spoke something into her ear. Esrae's face lit up and she looked at the King, her smile almost scandalous. Raven scowled. This whole situation needed to be over.

Movement to the side of the King's table caught Raven's attention. Henri, the taster, approached the King. He carried a tray with a fresh decanter and wine goblet perched atop it. The King ignored him as Henri raised the goblet to his lips. Her stomach clenched to the point of pain and she held her breath. The moment seemed to stretch on and on.

Henri placed the goblet back on the tray. He stepped toward the King but then hesitated before stopping where he stood, bending forward. The color drained from his face, and he doubled over completely as the tray tumbled from his hand, the decanter and goblet crashing against the stone floor. A pool of wine spread across the tiles, turning them from grey to black. Henri fell to his knees, clutching his stomach.

Every eye in the room went to the commotion at the King's table and the cheerful atmosphere evaporated instantly.

There was silence for half a second and then someone screamed, and it was as though the sound released a damper. The room erupted in shouts and more screams and Kanan's voice rang out above the din. "Someone tried to poison the King!"

"Get the King to safety!" Logan jumped from his seat, sending it crashing backward to the floor as he rushed toward the King.

In seconds, a group of soldiers descended on where the King stood, Esrae clutching his arm, her face scrunched in terror. The men surrounded them, herding them from the room.

"Get this man to a physician." Logan gestured to where Henri lay curled in a ball on the floor, clutching his stomach and groaning.

Two servants rushed to the side of the young man and picked him up. He released another loud sound of protest as they carried him away.

The voices in the room had risen to a clamor. Wooden chairs scraped against the stone floor as people either moved to get a better look or made swift exits from the room.

"Silence!" Logan's voice filled the room and the rumble quieted. "I think it's time for everyone to leave. Do not go far. We will be questioning each person present."

There was an authority in his tone that no one dared question. The people that still remained in the hall began to move toward the exits.

Raven tried to move closer to where Logan stood.

"Excuse me, General?" A middle-aged servant wearing a blue sash approached Logan.

"What is it?" Logan bit out.

"Sir, the King has yet to eat and we have no taster," she said.

Raven nearly laughed, amazed at how smoothly Logan's plan had fallen into place.

Logan rolled his eyes, huffing out an annoyed sound. He turned to where a group of recruits had gathered." You." Logan pointed toward them. A man, obviously assuming Logan had pointed at him, stepped forward. "Not you." Logan gestured behind the man. "You."

Torren stepped out from the shadow of the man in front of him. "Yes, sir?"

"You're a rubbish soldier. But I can't imagine you can fail at tasting food," Logan said. "Go with this woman. You've been transferred."

Torren put on a decent show of looking stricken as he sulked off after the woman. Raven couldn't stop her mouth from falling open slightly.

"You, girl!" Raven turned as another blue sashed servant called to her. "The King still needs dinner."

"Of course." Raven exited through the servants' door at the front of the room and took the staircase to the kitchen to get the King's dinner tray.

The kitchen's were even louder than normal as the servants gossiped about the poisoning. Who was responsible? Someone in the palace? Someone from outside? Was the food safe now?

Across the room, Torren stood with his back to her, receiving instructions. As though his job was hard—all he had to do was taste food.

A tray piled with two meals was shoved into her hands. "Here, off with you. He's waited long enough."

"It needs to be tasted."

She didn't dare leave the room without someone tasting the food, not after what everyone had seen upstairs. She didn't want to forget to have the meal tasted and be accused of trying to poison the King.

"I prepared this myself," the woman who had shoved the tray into her hands snapped. She lifted a few bites and chewed them demonstratively in front of Raven. "Satisfied? Go, now!"

Raven turned and left the room. Speaking to Torren would have to wait for another time. She carried the tray carefully up the stairs to where the guards waited outside the King's door. The guards opened the door and she entered the room. Her breath caught as she found herself standing in the room with both the King and Esrae.

Esrae paced the room, wringing her hands, looking far more anxious than the King. He stood, leaning on the mantle, running a thumb over his bottom lip, his eyes tracking the young blonde.

When the door clicked closed, Esrae's attention shot to Raven. "Raven!"

She barely had time to place the tray on the table before she was being crushed in her friend's arms. Raven slid her arms around the other girl.

"It's okay, Es. Everything is fine now. You're safe."

The King's attention lingered on the two young women, his mouth set in a thin line. He pushed off the mantle and approached the table. "And what of this food?"

Raven disentangled herself from Esrae and dropped into a curtsey. "Your Majesty, this food has been tasted and a new taster has been appointed."

The King's eyes narrowed. "By whom?"

"By your General, Your Majesty."

She forced herself to meet his intense gaze, though she found it extremely difficult. His attention didn't waver and she wanted to seep into the ground. From the look alone she began to wonder if he could actually read minds. She said the first thing she could think to redirect his attention.

"Would you like me to taste the food again?"

His jaw worked. "That won't be necessary. You may go."

She dipped into a quick curtsey. "Thank you, Your Majesty." She reached out and squeezed Esrae's hand, offering her one more reassuring look before she exited the room.

As she traversed the torch-lit halls back to the kitchen, she thought of Esrae. She clearly hadn't been aware of their plan. That made sense to Raven; she was always with the King. How would they have told her? Though what really bothered Raven was Esrae's attitude. What had her so nervous? Was it that she had almost been poisoned, or had she been concerned for the King? Raven's stomach tied into a knot, Esrae seemed to be becoming far too attached to Malakai. She wished she could talk to her, if only to see where her head really was in all of this.

Raven stepped into the kitchen where servants still worked, cleaning or preparing for the morning. She hadn't taken two steps inside when Shara appeared in front of her.

"Did you see it? Were you there?"

Raven stopped short. "See what?"

"Someone tried to poison the King!" Shara said. "You were there, right? What happened? Who do you think did it?"

"Shara, I don't know. I didn't see much. Just Henri pass out." She realized she hadn't heard anything about the young man. "Do you know how he's doing?"

Shara shrugged. "As far as I know, he's doing okay. Just feeling sick. But he's not dead."

Raven lifted a brow. "Well, that's good."

"I heard the General appointed a new taster from his recruits." Shara chuckled. "He must have been a really bad soldier."

Raven allowed a small smile. "Is he here?" She had hoped to speak to Torren.

Shara shook her head. "Aster took him away to show him to his room and fill him in on all the details."

Raven nodded.

"Well, I have to get back to work. The dishes don't wash themselves." Shara rolled her eyes. "Though, I wish they did."

"Have fun."

After Shara had gone back to her work, Raven grabbed a bit of bread and cheese and an apple from the barrel by the door and climbed the stairs back to her room. It was too early to return for the King's tray and she didn't want to stay in the kitchen and have to answer more questions.

Raven lay on her bed, staring at the fine lines and cracks in the wooden beams that ran across her ceiling. She went over the conversations and actions that had brought them to this point. When her memories caught up to the present, her thoughts began to take on a life of their own, filling in what might still happen with the worst possible outcomes.

How long had it been since she'd been home in her own bed? Not very long—weeks. How long would it be before they really set their plan in motion? How long before the King was gone? Days? Then what? They hadn't discussed what would happen after that. She rubbed her temple, her head beginning to pound. She honestly wasn't concerned with what happened after they were through. Logan could be king for all she cared, as long as it was over and she could go home. She had a future to plan and it did not include kings or palaces.

Noise above her bed woke Raven and panic gripped her as she bolted up, twisting to see which bell was ringing. The little bell with the maroon ribbon danced wildly on it's hook and Raven let out a breath as she swung her feet off the bed.

Relief that the King was summoning her, that was a first. Of course, the alternative was most likely an execution. And right then she and her friends were far too close to the block for her liking.

She'd been even more relieved when she arrived at the King's rooms and found them empty. She was able to collect the tray and return it to the kitchen without any further interactions with the man.

Exhaustion seeped into her bones as she slowly took the stairs back to her room. She paused on the landing before the last set of stairs, staring up at the final hurdle between her and her bed. It wasn't that many steps, but they seemed to loom in front of her, almost growing longer. Bed was her goal, and these stairs were the only thing between her and that goal. With a heavy sigh, she placed her foot on the first step when she felt the presence of someone behind her.

Her heart kicked up as a chill raced over her, certain it was that guard, Holden, finally come to make good on his threat. Raven spun, prepared to fight, to send him tumbling back down the steps, but stopped when she saw who stood behind her. Fear gave way to relief as she slumped against the wall, covering her pounding heart with a palm.

"Es!"

"Raven!"

Esrae ascended the few steps that separated them and fell into Raven's arms, holding her tightly. When she stepped back, Raven noticed that Esrae had changed from the dress she had been wearing at dinner into a simple, pale blue frock. Her hair, which had been up, now fell in blonde waves down her back.

"Es, are you alright? You scared me. Is everything okay?" Raven still held the other girl's hands.

"I'm fine, really." Esrae smiled, though it looked a bit forced.

"He's not hurting you, right?" Raven's brow pinched together.

Esrae stiffened, pulling her hands from Raven's grasp and taking a step back. She smoothed her already smooth skirt. "Not at all, Raven. He's not unkind to me at all. He's not like that."

Raven didn't know how to respond to that; Esrae seemed annoyed at her question. She glanced around. She didn't like talking like this on the landing where anyone could overhear.

"Come to my room? It's just up these stairs. We can talk."

"Of course." Esrae nodded.

Raven climbed the last of the stairs and led Esrae down the long hallway to her room. When they stepped inside, Raven turned to Esrae.

"Where does he think you are now?"

The look Esrae gave her made Raven wonder if she'd suddenly sprouted a horn. "I told him I was coming to see you."

Of course. Raven didn't know why she was surprised. The King knew they were friends. They'd been together when they met him and he had no reason to mistrust Raven.

She nodded once and gestured for Esrae to sit. "We have a plan."

Esrae perched on the end of Raven's bed, her eyes widening at Raven's words.

Raven sympathized. She knew Esrae was feeling the weight of action. It was easy to speak of assassinating a king, but to put it into action was something else entirely.

"What's the plan?" There was a tremor in her friend's voice.

Raven inhaled deeply. "Poison." It felt strange to say the word aloud.

A small gasp whooshed from Esrae as her eyes went wide. "How?" The word was barely a squeak.

"The wine," Raven answered.

Esrae's head turned up quickly toward Raven, her eyes growing even wider, if that were possible. "Earlier, the taster. Did you do that?"

Raven's mouth turned up at the edge. "That was us. We didn't hurt him. It was just enough to make him sick so we could put another taster in place."

"Who?" Esrae's voice shook.

"Torren, Es." Raven smiled.

Esrae shifted in her seat as her gaze moved around the room and back to Raven. "When?" Esrae's voice seemed much steadier.

"I don't know, and I don't know how to let you know when we decide to act. Just be ready."

"What will I need to do?" All tremors were gone from Esrae's voice.

Raven shrugged. "Nothing, really. And I mean *nothing*. It'll be in his wine in his rooms, not at dinner. So, just don't do anything. Let the poison run its course. And, don't drink the wine until he does."

Again, Esrae's eyes tracked around the room before she nodded.

Raven moved to sit beside her friend. "Are you sure you're alright, Es? You can tell me if he's being unkind to you. Maybe we can get you out of there or move quicker with this."

"No." Esrae's head turned to Raven with a heavy sigh. "I mean, no, he's not unkind. I promise." Esrae placed her hand on Raven's and offered a small, encouraging smile. "I'm fine."

Raven nodded. "This'll be over soon. I promise. Then we can go home."

"Right." Esrae smiled, but it didn't seem to reach her eyes. "I should probably go. He'll wonder what's happened to me."

"Of course." Raven's chest tightened at the thought of Esrae returning to the King. *Days. Only days*, she told herself. "It was nice to see you. I'm glad we could talk."

Esrae stood and smoothed her dress. "Me too."

Raven pulled her friend into a hug. "Be careful, Es."

Esrae pulled back out of Raven's grasp. "I will."

Raven opened the door and Esrae exited the room. When Raven closed the door again she released a long breath, thankful she'd had the chance to speak with Esrae. It was a comfort to see that she was well. And now they all knew what was going to happen. Another knot began to form in Raven's stomach, but she tried to ignore it. Worry wouldn't do anyone any good.

She was about to change for bed when there was a knock on her door. She jumped up, pulling open the door, hoping to find Kanan on the other side.

"Sorry, no handsome generals tonight. Just me." Aster smiled and stepped into Raven's room. "I'm just here to let you know you can take the day off tomorrow."

"Really?"

Aster's smile was amused. "Yes, really. You've been here a while. It's time you take a day for yourself. You should have had one already, I'm sorry about that."

"Thanks." Raven smiled. "Who will serve the King?"

Aster held up the end of her sash. "I will. Orange. I do everything, wherever I'm needed." Aster's voice dropped as she pinned Raven with a look. "And you make sure to tell your general that I do *everything*. *Wherever* I'm needed." She raised her eyebrows on the last word for emphasis.

Raven laughed. "I'll tell him."

Aster cocked her head to the side and gave a quick waggle of her brows. "Have a good day tomorrow. Goodnight."

"Thanks. Goodnight, Aster." Raven was still smiling when Aster left the room.

EIGHTEEN

Raven rolled over and stretched, burying her face in the pillow. The angle of the sun told her that it was already late morning. The temptation to stay in bed all day was real, but she didn't want to waste an opportunity to explore. With a groan she finally sat up. For as long as she'd been at the palace she had seen very little of it. It would be a shame to have spent so much time here and not even really look around before she left. It was a beautiful place.

She dressed in her servant's frock but left the maroon belt and silver buckle hanging on the hook. She stepped into the hall and nearly collided with Aster.

"Well, look who finally regained consciousness." Instead of Aster's usual orange belt, today she wore maroon. "I'm off to collect some trays. Did you sleep well?"

"Very well." Raven smiled.

Aster looked behind Raven toward her door. "Alone?"

Raven's smile grew and she rolled her eyes. "Yes, alone."

Aster's return smile dripped incredulity. "What? First, if I didn't have to get up in the morning and I had someone who looked like that just waiting for a tumble, you better believe I'd take advantage of that. Second? I was just hoping for a glimpse of those blue eyes."

Raven chuckled. "Don't you have trays to get?"

Aster sighed heavily with a glance at the ceiling. "I do. Anyway, since he's not with you, if you wanted to see him, you should check the training yard. He has all those new recruits. I'm sure he's drilling them mercilessly. Something you could have had last night, but passed up."

A laugh escaped Raven at Aster's words.

"Anyway, if you need me, I'll be around." Aster shot Raven a wink that dripped with innuendo before she continued down the hall.

When she'd stepped into the hallway, she hadn't had any destination in mind. But thanks to Aster's suggestion, she decided the training grounds would be a fine place to start her exploring. The possibility of seeing Kanan fueled her steps as she made her way down hallways and stairs and out onto the palace grounds. She wouldn't mind seeing some of the training either; even if she could only watch, she could still glean.

The sun shone brightly, making the cool Autumn day feel warmer than it probably was. She drew in a long breath of crisp air as she began walking down the gently sloping grass-covered hill that led away from the palace. She did have to stop and ask a servant for directions, but when she drew close enough, the sound of clanging steel and Logan's voice barking orders led her the rest of the way.

When she was finally close enough to see, it became clear that watching the soldiers train must have been a common pastime of the palace staff. A group of servants, both men and women, mostly sans belts and sashes, stood off to the side, well away from the soldiers training.

There were about twenty of the newly recruited soldiers standing in two rows, facing each other in a large dusty circle, the grass having been trampled away by many years of soldiers training on it.

Logan stood at the end of the rows, issuing simple commands to men who clearly had no blade training whatsoever. At least most of them. Raven could pick out four in the rows who seemed to know how to hold a sword. One of them was Kanan, and she smiled as he easily knocked the sword from the hands of the man opposite him.

Raven moved to join the observers.

"That one will never last." A girl with short black hair pointed toward the man that Kanan had disarmed.

Someone beside her laughed. "No, but that one he's fighting will."

Raven smiled again, pride blooming inside her.

"What now?" A young man, tanned dark from working outside, pointed with his chin to the gathered trainees.

Logan had called the four men Raven had noticed out from the lines and paired them off. "Fight to disarm. The last man fights me."

Beside her, two servants placed bets, gambling weed-pulling duties. Neither of them bet on Kanan. A mistake.

"Him." Another young man pointed at Kanan, eyebrows raised. "He fights the General."

Raven had no doubt Kanan would best the other men, though she wasn't sure if he could win against Logan. On the other hand, Kanan and swords were nearly one. Surely Logan already knew he would be matched against Kanan.

"Why?" a girl beside her asked. She was bent over tying a knot on the bottom of her skirts to make them shorter.

"Look at him," the man who'd bet on Kanan said. "That sword is part of his arm. I don't know where he came from, but he's not new to this."

A girl who had seated herself on the ground murmured quietly, "I bet he's not new to a lot of stuff."

The memory of Kanan's hand gliding up the skin of her back was so strong, she could almost feel it, and she clamped a tooth down on her lip to fight off the smile that tugged at her mouth.

In the training circle, Kanan had already nicked his opponent's elbow, causing him to drop his sword. He stood to the side, arms crossed over his chest, watching the match between the other two. Raven could tell by the way his eyes tracked their movements that he was learning. Learning the way they fought so when it was his turn again, he had an advantage.

It took longer, but finally, a sword clattered to the ground. A short, stockily built young man with mousy blonde hair moved back to the center of the circle. Kanan joined him, retrieving the fallen sword from the dirt.

Logan indicated they begin, and in five moves, the blonde man was left weaponless and gaping at Kanan. He laughed and shook his head, stepping forward to shake Kanan's hand. Kanan accepted the man's hand, an easy smile lighting his face. Then he turned to where Logan stood behind him, eyebrows raised.

Logan moved to the center of the circle to join Kanan.

A girl standing further down the row of spectators called out, "Hey, soldier! If you win, you get a kiss." She punctuated her words with a wink.

Kanan grinned, shaking his head. His eyes wandered along the line of people gathered and stopped, widening slightly, when they met Raven's. She smiled as even now her heart fluttered. His grin softened and he held her gaze for a moment before his attention drifted back to the girl.

"Sounds like great incentive."

Logan watched the exchange, his smile holding mischief. "You have to win first."

The duel lasted far longer than the previous ones, the opponents now equally matched. Voices called out, some whistling in favor of Logan, others in favor of Kanan. The voice of the girl who had offered the kiss could often be heard above the others. Raven didn't blame her, she knew what kissing Kanan was like. Who wouldn't want that?

The clang of metal striking metal rang out as the two blocked blow after blow, dancing expertly around the circle. Then Kanan moved as though to attack from the left, but instead, spun to the right. Logan's blade came up a second too late as the tip of Kanan's sword caught on his pommel. With a considerable heave skyward, Kanan wrenched Logan's sword from his grip, sending it clattering to the packed dirt.

A cheer sounded through the gathered crowd, mixed with disappointed groans and Raven squared her shoulders, grinning, as she applauded with those beside her. Kanan inclined his head in a small bow to Logan, and the General returned it.

Raven didn't miss the wink Logan offered Kanan when he said, "Go get your kiss,"

Kanan grinned as he handed his sword to Logan. He turned to the group, eyeing the beaming girl who had offered her favor.

Kanan took one step toward the crowd, before he turned and moved with a determined stride to where Raven stood. He didn't slow down as he slid his hand into her hair and pulled her flush against him. The kiss made her knees weak and she leaned into him, allowing him to support her weight. He was showing off and she didn't care one bit. She slid her hands behind his back, feeling the dampness of his shirt as she was swept away by the kiss, vaguely aware of shouts and whistles from the crowd around them.

"Hey! That's my kiss!" the girl called out, and there were laughs at her expense. Raven couldn't bring herself to care.

It was over too quickly when Logan called the men back to the ring. Kanan released her with a wink and a quick squeeze of her hand before he moved back to fall in line, leaving her breathless.

She could feel the other girl's glare but didn't turn to look. The girl spat a curse at her just before someone else in the crowd offered to kiss the girl to appease her.

"Shut up, Clayse," the girl bit out, adding another curse.

Raven's mouth turned up at the corner and she forced it back down.

With effort, Raven pulled herself away from the training ring. If she didn't leave, she might spend all day there, and there was more she wanted to explore.

As she turned to leave, her stomach growled, reminding her she'd not only missed breakfast but lunch as well.

She made her way back to the palace where the kitchen were in that short lull between lunch and dinner prep. She found a small loaf of bread, a chunk of cheese, and a few olives, then plucked an apple from the barrel and pushed it into her pocket on her way out of the kitchen.

The palace contained a servant's library. She'd been there once before but had since forgotten the way. But she was determined, and after some searching and one stop for directions, she found it again. It wasn't overly large like one might expect a library in a palace to be, though it was just for servants. Four small shelves were built into the back wall. There was a small fireplace and a few of what looked like enormous, overstuffed pillows lying on a deep green rug.

She scanned the shelves, her head tilted at an angle to better read the spines. The small selection made her wonder if there was a larger trove of books hiding somewhere else within the walls of the vast palace.

She selected a book of poems, wishing she had the book Logan had given her. Balancing her food and the book, she climbed the stairs to her room.

With a relieved groan she dropped onto her bed, her feet and legs letting her know that she had done much more walking than she was used to. Propping her pillow against the wall and swinging her legs onto the bed, she pulled out her apple and opened the book.

The bell clanged and clanged above her bed, and she sat up with a gasp. Had she slept through mealtime and forgotten to bring the King his dinner? Wait, no, it was her day off. She wasn't responsible for that today. Finally, her mind cleared. The bell was still ringing, and there were voices outside her door. Dread coiled in her stomach as she turned to look at the bells above her bed. The King's bell, with its tiny maroon ribbon, sat still and silent. Instead, the general alarm bell rang on and on. She stood and slipped her feet into her shoes as she stepped into the hall and joined the growing number of people moving in the direction of the throne room.

She saw a flash of orange-red hair, and she elbowed past a number of palace servants to get to Aster. "What now?"

Aster turned to glance at her and shook her head, her mouth set in a grim line. "I don't know."

They entered the throne room where a crowd had already gathered and more were still filing in.

Raven's heart pounded out an irregular rhythm. When that bell rang, her first thought was her friends. Had they been found out? Was this the end?

"I can't see."

Raven craned up on the tips of her toes, but there were too many heads, many with piles of knotted hair on top, to see. Frustrated, she pushed through until she was closer to the front and could see the large throne with its maroon upholstery and golden edges. Aster followed, stopping beside her.

They didn't have long to wait before the door to the right of the dais opened, and Logan emerged, followed by a group of soldiers, Kanan among them. Raven sighed with relief. There was no reason to expect the King knew anything about their plans or who was involved, but seeing them still filled her with some form of comfort.

The soldiers took up positions around the throne. When the door opened again, the King emerged, Esrae behind him. Raven scowled. Did he take her everywhere? Wasn't it about time for him to move on to the next girl?

The King wore black pants and a black doublet inlaid with silver threads and buttons. His long maroon cloak brushed the floor behind him. He wore no traditional crown. Raven had never seen him in a traditional crown, only a thin silver circlet resting on his dark curls. He needed no crown at all. Even when Raven had seen him in his rooms, he looked like a king. And Esrae, behind him, in her finely embroidered grey dress that seemed to shine as she walked, was beginning to look like she belonged. Raven hated it. It wasn't jealousy; she was angry that the King thought he could dress Esrae up and use her for whatever purpose he wished.

The King stopped in front of the throne and the room went silent. Waiting.

"Yesterday, I was the target of an assassination attempt." The walls of the room seemed to amplify the King's words. "By now, you are all aware that my taster was taken ill after drinking wine that was meant for me. It is a mercy that he will recover. That, and possibly due to the fact that he only consumed a small amount, where I would have consumed the entire cup.

"Since that evening, I have had my men searching for the perpetrator of this crime, and I am proud to report that they have come through. My would-be assassin has been found."

Raven's heart stalled, but then she remembered that Logan still stood with his men, as well as Kanan. She looked at Logan, and his eyes locked with hers for a moment, though his expression betrayed nothing. Logan, Kanan, and Esrae were all here, but she had yet to see Torren. Again her heart missed as she looked around, her movements nearly panicked.

"What are you doing?" Aster hissed beside her, and Raven stopped her frantic searching. She couldn't find Torren in the crowd.

"Bring him in," the King commanded.

Her throat threatened to close up completely as the door opened and two more soldiers entered, dragging a limp body between them. His head hung with his chin to his chest. Raven exhaled in relief when she saw the waves of thick, dark hair and tan but not dark skin. Not Torren. Guilt pressed on her. Even though it wasn't Torren, it was still someone. Blood flecked the front of the man's tunic. Beside her, Aster's hand flew to her mouth, stifling a gasp. When one of the guards grabbed a handful of the dark curls and pulled his head up to face the King, Raven saw why. Luc. Raven had met him the night Aster had shown her the secret passageway.

Aster's body went rigid beside her as the King stepped up in front of the young man. "What is your name?"

The man let out a groan that sounded a bit like *"Luc."*

He looked terrible. His slim, handsome face was bruised and swollen.

"Luc," the King's head cocked slightly to the side, the action giving off a disturbingly conversational aire, "did you conspire with others to poison my wine?"

"No." The word emerged from Luc in a fit of coughs.

"Did you poison it of your own accord, without outside help?" The King's tone remained conversational, as though he was asking Luc where he had purchased his horse.

Raven didn't dare to breathe, wasn't actually sure she could have if she'd wanted to. He couldn't admit to this. She, at least, knew he was completely innocent of these charges. She waited.

Luc coughed again, and it was clear speaking was an effort.

"Yes," he rasped out.

"What?" Aster squeaked the word.

Raven covered her mouth as all the air left her lungs and the room seemed to tilt with his admission. She threw another glance at Logan as her stomach twisted, but he continued to stare straight ahead. What was happening?

The King's expression took on an almost sympathetic look. "You must have known you couldn't succeed. Look around you. These people are here to serve me, to protect me. You had to know that any plan like this would fail, that you would be caught." His voice turned deadly. "You must have known you would be the one who would not survive."

Raven's breath hitched, and beside her, Aster breathed out, "No."

The King raised a finger at the guards and they shoved Luc to the floor. He let out a pained sound as his knees cracked off the marble surface. Raven flinched and swallowed hard, trying not to be sick.

The King turned his attention from Luc to survey the gathered crowd. His eyes moved, starting at Logan and his guard, from person to person. Raven had to fight the urge to recoil when his eyes found hers, but they didn't linger as he continued to take in the crowd.

"Now see what happens to anyone who would dare to make an attempt on the life of the King."

She tried to inhale, tried to steel herself against what she knew would come next, though it seemed like any air she breathed was gone in the same moment. It was like there was no air to breathe. The memory of meeting Luc pushed into her head; the look of fear on his face when he thought she might tell the King that he didn't like him. She fought back a sob as she wondered if Luc thought she had turned him in. She clasped her hands together to hide the way they had begun to shake.

The King took half a step forward and looked down at where Luc knelt. A small puddle of blood was beginning to form in front of him from where it dripped off his face.

Luc began to scream. Wild, groaning cries reverberated around the room as he clutched at his head. Wave after wave of agonized wails crested and crashed around them. Raven squeezed her eyes shut, wishing she could cover her ears. Then it stopped. Silence rushed back into the room, filling the places where it had been pushed out.

"Take him away," the King said, and Raven looked up in time to see two guards drag Luc's limp body from the room, his feet sliding through the blood on the floor, leaving a sickening trail.

She jumped when the King began speaking again. "Let this be an example of what happens to the man or woman who dares to threaten the life of the King. This will be their fate."

With those words, the King turned, offered his arm to Esrae, who took it, and exited the room, followed by Logan and the rest of the soldiers.

Raven barely had time to take a breath before Aster's hand clamped tightly around her arm. "Come with me." Aster dragged her off to a far corner of the swiftly emptying room.

Aster released her and Raven rubbed at her arm. But her breathing was too erratic for her to form words.

"Did you say something?" Aster hissed, her face streaked with tears. It was more accusation than question.

Raven shook her head wildly again and again. "No! Of course not! I would never. Saints, Aster, never."

Aster let out a silent sob as she brushed the hair back from her face, as though she could brush away the memory of what they'd witnessed.

"What do you think happened?" Raven's vision swam with unshed tears.

"I don't know." Aster swallowed hard. "I've known him for so long. He had opinions, but I never would have thought he'd actually try to kill the King."

"Maybe he hated the King more than you thought." The words made her feel sick and she hated herself for speaking them.

"I don't know." Aster's eyes darted wildly around the large room. "I mean, he confessed, didn't he?"

She wanted to respond, but she couldn't find words; couldn't think. The only thing in her head were the echoes of Luc's screams.

Aster blew out a long breath and swiped at the tears on her face. "I have to get back to work. Saints! I have to serve the King."

Raven felt awful for Aster, but she was infinitely grateful that she'd been given that day, of all days, off. The very thought of being in the presence of the King made her chest tighten to the point of lightheadedness.

"I'm so sorry."

Aster shook her head and gave a weak shrug. "I have to go."

They exited the now nearly-empty throne room together, Aster heading in the direction of the kitchen and Raven heading straight to her room.

She dropped onto her bed, snatching up her pillow to bury her face in its downy softness. She was desperately relieved to know she didn't have to leave her room again for the rest of the night. Missing dinner wouldn't be a problem—she couldn't eat after what she'd just witnessed. How could she even begin to process what had happened? The King's words played over and over in her mind: *"Let this be an example of what will happen to the man or woman who dares to threaten the life of the King. This will be their fate."*

She couldn't stop picturing Luc's lifeless form and then soon his face was replaced with the faces of her friends. She barely had time to lunge for the basin before she brought up her measly lunch. Theirs was a very bad plan.

She lay on her bed for hours, staring at nothing, but seeing her friends die over and over in that throne room, suffering. She tried smothering the thoughts with the pillow over her face, but the images still came. She wanted to scream at them to chase them away.

When the knock came, she bolted from the bed, sure it was the King's men coming to take her. It took a moment to realize the soldiers most likely wouldn't knock. She composed herself as best she could and opened the door, expecting to see Aster.

Logan stood on the other side of the door, his brows knit deeply. His eyes went immediately to the basin. She'd emptied it but her room must have still held the lingering scent of sickness. She was too upset to care.

Logan's head tilted slightly, concern lining his features. She stepped aside and he entered, pushing the door closed behind him. "Are you alright?"

"No, I'm not alright," she bit at him. She knew it was unfair, what else could he say? "What happened?"

"He was searching for his would-be assassin. We knew he would," Logan said. "Then, before I knew what was happening, he'd found that man. I didn't even know who he was, not really. I'd seen him around working, but I didn't know him. Malakai had me question him, but he maintained that he was innocent. And why wouldn't he? He *was* innocent!"

Logan ran a hand through his short blonde hair, and something like panic tightened Raven's chest. Nothing rattled Logan, or so she'd thought.

"I knew he was innocent. I tried to tell Malakai that, but then he ordered everyone to leave the room so he could be alone with him. Five minutes later, Malakai was leaving and the man was confessing to everything!"

"Why?" Raven's voice shook.

"Malakai," Logan answered.

"What do you mean?"

"Malakai did something to his head," Logan explained. "By the time he was done, that man probably thought he was guilty himself."

"He can do that?" Fear churned inside her.

Logan offered a sobering look. "He can. Whatever that power he has is, it's like he can rewrite a man's mind if he wishes. Make him into something different."

Raven shivered at the implication. "Now what?"

Logan leveled his gaze on her and did not blink. "Now, we need to be very careful. Because what Malakai did was a show of power to the people and a threat to the assassin. I don't know if he knows who poisoned the wine or not, but I do know that you and I know that man was innocent, and Malakai knows it too."

Raven's blood ran cold. She hadn't considered that the King might already know who was trying to kill him. She was going to be sick again.

"Raven, I need to ask you a question." Logan's tone implied that perhaps this was something he was reluctant to address.

Her mouth went dry. She tried to swallow, but there was nothing there. "What is it?"

"Have you spoken to Esrae?"

"Hardly. I barely see her."

"And when you have, how did she seem?" Logan's brow lowered with the inquiry. "Because I do see her, and she seems quite comfortable in her new position."

A shiver raced up Raven's spine at what she thought he was implying. "Do you think she told him?"

Logan pressed his lips together and blew a slow breath out his nose, a look of concern crossing his features. "I hope not, Raven. Being in the position she is, she knows first hand what would happen to you and the others if she told Malakai anything. Surely your friendship is worth more than that. I hope."

Raven swallowed. Surely, of course. There was no way Esrae would turn them over to the King knowing what would happen to them.

Raven shook her head. "She wouldn't."

But even she could hear the question there. Would she?

She wouldn't.

Logan drew in a deep breath and nodded. "We need to put our plan into action as soon as possible," Logan said. "Before Malakai becomes more suspicious or decides to act on knowledge he may already possess. Days, Raven. We need to be done with all of this in days."

She couldn't speak, so she nodded.

"Until then, you be very careful." Logan emphasized the last words.

She nodded, attempting to swallow again. "I will." The words came out in a whisper.

NINETEEN

Raven was functioning on almost no sleep. After Logan had left her room, it had taken a long time for her to fall asleep, and when she did, her dreams were plagued by all the ways their plan would fail and they would die. Dreams in which she watched, unable to help, as her friends were killed, one by one, by the King.

She dragged herself to the kitchen. The very idea of seeing the King caused her stomach to clench. She'd even considered feigning illness to remain in bed, though it wouldn't have been much of a lie.

The kitchen were already hot from the ovens, the scent of baking bread heavy in the air. The King's tray was waiting for her and beside it stood Torren, having an animated conversation with Aster. She wanted to launch herself into his arms and make sure he was real. It had been real terror she'd felt when she thought he might have been captured. Seeing him nearly made her cry with relief.

"Raven." Aster waved her over, smiling. "This is Torren. Your General fired him as a soldier and brought him up here to taste the poison."

Torren's brow rose. "The poison? Wait—" He turned his attention from Aster to Raven. "*Your* General?"

"Oh yeah, Raven here has a special arrangement with the General." Aster lifted her brow with salacious emphasis.

Torren's mouth fell open.

"No!" Raven directed the statement directly at Torren, rolling her eyes. But then, what other reason would Logan have to be in her room? "Well . . ."

Torren's eyes grew to the size of saucers.

Raven huffed out a breath. "Aster!"

Aster threw her hands out in a demonstrative shrug, a grin forming on her face. "I've seen him come from her room myself."

Raven noticed the look that flashed across Torren's face as the pieces fell into place, and he understood why Logan was in her room. But that didn't stop him from joining in on the teasing. Nothing ever stopped Torren from joining in on the teasing.

His face lit up. "Wait! Didn't I see you kissing that other soldier the other day?"

Aster's eyes and mouth both went wide. "What? And I thought you were so innocent. Which soldier?"

Her cheeks warmed. She couldn't deny either of them. What that must make her look like... But even as the thought passed through her mind, the memory of seeing Kanan at the training yard pushed it away.

"Oh, Saints." Aster grinned. "And you're proud of it."

Again she rolled her eyes. "I need to take this tray to the King. It was nice meeting you, Torren. Now if you wouldn't mind tasting this so I can go?"

Torren smirked at her as he lifted a piece of toasted bread to his mouth.

"Better watch out for poison there, eh?" The words came from a very young boy as he stumbled by, carrying a tub of something that looked as though it weighed nearly as much as he himself.

"Shut your yap, boy, and get that lard over here now," Cora ordered from across the room, her cheeks already red from exertion.

The three of them exchanged a glance as Torren bit into the bread, chewing carefully. When they were all satisfied he wasn't going to keel over, Raven lifted the tray from the table and turned to leave.

"First task done, and you're not dead," Aster said to Torren.

"Good, because I have plans for *other* tasks."

Torren was flirting with Aster. Flirting in the face of peril—only Torren.

"Is that so?" Raven could hear the smile in Aster's voice, and as much as she wanted to know what the girl would say next, she had moved too far out of the room.

She glanced once back at where her friends stood, Torren's attention fully focused on Aster. Leave it to Torren to maintain a positive attitude in such dangerous circumstances.

As she climbed the stairs, her smile faded, replaced by a knot of dread that coiled tighter with every step. She had to force herself to take the necessary steps to the King's door, unprepared to come face to face with the man again. One of the guards reached out and rapped once on the heavy wooden door before he pushed it open and allowed her to step inside. The hair on the back of her neck and her arms stood on end, and she had to remind herself to breathe. The feeling that something was off lingered. But of course things weren't right. They were conspiring to assassinate the King. If she wasn't apprehensive, that would be a concern.

"Raven."

The contents of the tray nearly crashed to the floor as it wobbled in her hands. The King stood by the far wall, arms crossed over his chest. Had he been waiting for her? She shook off the thought. Of course he'd been waiting for her, she had his breakfast. She stepped further into the room, quickly placing the tray on the table. Her curtsey was unstable, and when she rose she clasped her hands together, praying to all the Saints that the King wouldn't notice how fiercely they shook.

"Your Majesty, good morning. I hope you are well."

"I am well." He uncrossed his arms and moved to lean against the back of one of the two overstuffed maroon chairs situated in front of the fire. His gaze was intense and heavy on her and she desperately wanted to be out from beneath it. "Are you?"

"I am, thank you, Your Majesty." She silently begged for dismissal as she focused on keeping her breathing steady.

He regarded her for several seconds that seemed to stretch on for hours. "Are you enjoying working here, at the palace?"

"Yes, Your Majesty. I am." It wasn't completely a lie— it wasn't hard work. Her room was nice, and she had made friends. But she certainly was ready to put it behind her.

"Were you told we received a letter from your father?" The King's gaze remained steady on her. "He thanked us for seeing to your well-being and safety while you're here."

Unlikely. It didn't seem like something her father would say, though if he were trying to avoid suspicion, he might have sent the note. "I hadn't been told, Your Majesty. I'm pleased he isn't worried."

"Why might he be worried?"

"I meant no offense, Your Majesty." She dipped her chin and the urge to wriggle, to squirm under his gaze was nearly overpowering as she fought to tamp it down. Saints, did the man never blink? What had she been saying? "I only say that because I went for a walk one morning and never returned home. I'm not a parent, but I think that might be cause for concern."

There was a long pause and Raven allowed her gaze to fall to the floor.

"Yes. Though I am also not a parent, I believe you speak the truth."

Everything inside her had gone taut like a bowstring. She resisted adjusting her weight to her other foot, resisted toying with her maroon belt, resisted any movement—afraid anything would give her away. It was an absurd thought, as though if she shrank under his gaze he would know her thoughts. Would he never let her leave?

The King, instead of dismissing her, took a step toward her. Her breath caught in her chest and she knew he heard it. It didn't matter, she was sure she'd gone pale as well. No one looking at her would question her fear.

"You don't need to be afraid of me, Raven." He stopped mere feet in front of her.

He was well built and tall, and she had to tilt her head back to see his face. "Your Majesty?" Her vision swam and her voice faltered.

He reached out and took her hand. His touch was light, his fingers warm against her cold skin. "You're trembling." His eyes narrowed slightly. Not in accusation, but as though he was trying to make her understand. "I only deliver justice to those who would seek to do me harm. Not those who are loyal."

"Of course." She gave up any false sense of bravado; he had presented her with a real reason why she might be so anxious. "Forgive me, Your Majesty, I'm just not used to seeing those things."

He still held her hand, and it trembled more with every moment he refused to release her. His gaze remained on her.

"You are very beautiful."

"I—" What? The change in topic was so wholly unexpected that it took her a moment to respond. "Thank you."

"Your eyes are very blue. Did you get them from your father?"

Why was he asking her these things? "N-no, Your Majesty. My father's eyes are brown."

A soft, barely-there smile curved his lips. "Your mother, then?"

She blinked, shaking her head. "No, my mother also had brown eyes. Though I'm often told I look like her; that is the one feature I didn't inherit."

"Yes." The word was a whisper of breath from his lips. Finally, he released her and stepped away, moving to the tray and picking up the mug of tea that Raven was sure was now cold. "You may go, Raven."

Thank the Saints!

"Thank you, Your Majesty. Have a good day." She wanted to run from the room but managed to keep her steps steady.

She had the door handle in her grasp when the King once again called her name.

She exhaled, turning back to face him. "Yes, Your Majesty?"

He peered into the mug as though answers lay in the dregs. "Take care. It seems there is treachery afoot in the palace." Without looking at her, he raised the mug to his lips and drank.

"Of course."

She threw the door latch and flinched at the desperate sound it made. She all but ran from the room, sparing a passing thought as to what it must look like to the guards. She didn't care, only wanted to be far from the King with his piercing stare and unsettling tone.

Raven didn't see the King for the rest of the day. He wasn't in his room when she'd brought lunch or dinner, which he'd requested be delivered instead of coming to the Great Hall.

She had one final chance to run into him when she retrieved the dinner tray at the end of the evening, but he wasn't there. Relief washed over her like a bucket of water. She'd had enough interaction with the King that morning and was not eager for a repeat. She picked up the tray, feeling lighter, and was almost to the door when she heard a laugh, deep and genuine, coming from beyond the closed bedroom door. Had she ever heard him laugh? She couldn't recall once.

The laugh was soon followed by a female giggle, one she recognized. Her stomach bottomed out. Apprehension trickled though her as she recalled Logan's words while listening to the easy way with which Esrae interacted with the King. Or maybe it was that Esrae was a much better actor than anyone had given her credit for. Their low muffled voices continued, followed by a louder laugh from Esrae. Raven blinked, pulling the door open and moving from the room as quickly as her feet would carry her.

She left the tray in the kitchen and climbed the stairs to her room. Her mind was a chaotic swirl of thoughts and fears that seemed to sap her energy. She stifled a yawn as she passed two servants in blue sashes.

She stepped into her dark room, locking the door behind her. Not even the moon lit the space as she crossed the room and lit the candle on the bedside table. The flame flared to life before settling into a soft dance. She was turning to remove her shoes and lay down when a large hand landed solidly over her mouth. She let out a muffled squeak as panic exploded in her chest.

"Shhh!" Kanan hissed as she stepped back. "You'll draw the guards."

She spun around, slapping his arm as relief poured into her. "You scared me to death! And if there are guards up here, they have other things on their minds."

"I'm sorry." His sheepish smile quickly turned serious. "I had to see you. After…" He ran a hand through his hair, dropping onto her bed with a heavy sigh. "I thought it was you."

She took his hand, sitting beside him on the bed.

His gaze roamed over her face, his hold tightening on her hand. "The King sent for us. Specifically for Logan and his new recruits. I heard the messenger tell another servant that they'd caught the person responsible for poisoning the wine." He paused. "I've never been so scared, Raven. I was sure it was you. I wanted to crawl out of my skin and find you. I couldn't talk to Logan. I couldn't breathe."

He drew in a ragged breath. "By the time we got to where they were keeping the prisoner, I thought I was going to pass out. Then we walked into the room and I saw him." His voice cracked and he dropped his head. "Saints, I was so relieved."

She slid closer and ran a hand over his arm. She understood, knew exactly how he'd felt. She'd felt the same way.

"*Relieved.*" He made a disgusted sound.

"Then you felt guilty because you were relieved." When he looked at her, she could see the truth of it reflected in his eyes. "I know. I thought it was Torren. The King came out and said they found the person. You were there and Logan and Esrae. Everyone was there but Torren. I thought I'd be sick. But when they brought him out and it wasn't him—I *knew* him."

Kanan turned his head to her. She nodded. "Not well, but I knew him. Aster, another servant, a friend... she introduced us."

She pictured Luc, sitting in front of the fire, his orange sash tied around his head. "He'd said things. He sounded like he didn't have very positive thoughts toward the King. I mentioned it, and he got scared. The look in his eyes, he thought I might say something to the King. I promised him I never would, but—"

Kanan's head cocked to the side, sympathy in his eyes. Raven met his gaze. "All I could think was that he must have thought I turned him in. What else could he have thought happened?

A tear slipped from the corner of her eye and Kanan's arm slid around her, drawing her in to his side. "You don't know that."

She breathed in his familiar scent, burrowing closer, soaking in his comfort. "I'm glad you came."

His hold tightened and he kissed the top of her head. "It's almost over."

Her chest tightened. She should be relieved, but she couldn't shake that feeling of dread from earlier. "I feel like something bad is going to happen."

"Why?"

She pulled away to look him in the eye. "Logan said he might already know."

"Who? The King? How could he know?"

"I don't know."

She didn't mention hearing Esrae laughing with the King or Logan's questions. She wanted to trust her friend and certainly didn't want anyone else to think poorly of her. But now there was that feeling.

They sat in silence for a long moment. Raven savored every spot where their bodies touched, aware the moment would be over too soon.

He pulled in a breath and she closed her eyes, not wanting to hear what he would say.

"I should go."

He couldn't go. Not yet, she needed him. "Stay? Please?"

His lips pressed softly to the top of her head. "Are you sure?"

She looked up, meeting his eyes. "Why wouldn't I be sure?"

He lifted a hand, brushing the hair off her forehead. "I wasn't sure, with all that's going on… It might draw extra attention that you don't want. A man in your room, I mean."

She settled back into him. "I always want you here. Anyway, they all think there's something going on with me and Logan, so what's the difference?"

He pulled back. "Okay, first, if you can't tell the *difference* between me and Logan, we have a bigger problem." She smiled. "Second, *why* do they think there's something going on with you and Logan?"

She couldn't help the small laugh. "Because he's been seen leaving my room, and you soldiers have a reputation of being rather frisky with the servants."

She felt his low laugh as a wicked glint entered his eyes. "In that case—"

She let out a surprised yelp as in one swift motion, he disentangled her from his side and pinned her to the bed, capturing her hands above her head.

His brow raised with playful intent. "I can't betray the reputation."

"Perish the thought." She grinned.

His hand found her chin, sliding to her neck as he kissed her grin away. His mouth wandered down her jaw line, to her neck.

"I love you," Kanan's whispered words tickled the sensitive skin at her collarbone.

She brought her hands down to weave her fingers into his soft hair. "I love you. I missed you."

Kanan slid back until he was kneeling before her. His hands wrapped around her ankles, sliding up, pushing her dress up until she grabbed it and pulled it over her head.

His gaze on her was so intense she could almost feel every place his eyes touched. "I miss you too."

His mouth found the inside of her knee, moving upward to her thigh and then higher still until his lips closed around her and her back arched off the bed.

Kanan's hand splayed across her stomach, holding her in place as he worked his mouth over her. The air left her in small gasps through her parted lips as her body moved involuntary of her wishes.

Everything in side her coiled tighter and tighter until everything released at once as Kanan's name ripped from her lips.

He chuckled softly against her sending more, nearly overwhelming vibrations through her.

He raised up, a wicked smile on his face. "Yes?"

She reached out, grasping his shirt, dragging him closer. "I need you." She barely got the words out before his lips were on hers.

She could feel him working at his pants and then he was sliding into her, rocking gently as his hand tangled in her hair and he never broke the kiss. She was home.

Home. She was home. Not in her physical home, but not in a palace either. Her home was with Kanan. She'd missed him so much, there'd been an actual ache inside her. But he was here now and she intended to savor every last second. She blinked back tears, closing her eyes and focusing on every place their bodies met.

TWENTY

Things were quiet over the next two days. Neither Logan nor Kanan had come to her room, but there had also been no public executions. She would take that as a mark in the win column.

Torren seemed to be adapting well to life in the kitchen. He wore a blue sash and when he wasn't tasting the King's food, he was helping to prepare meals or clean dishes. Raven hadn't missed the number of times she saw Aster by his side, sleeves pushed up her arm, elbow deep in suds, her hip resting comfortably against Torren.

It was that sight that greeted her when she entered the kitchen, leaving the King's dinner tray on the long table next to the rest of the dishes waiting to be washed. Her chest warmed at the sight, bringing a smile to her face. She silently wished them happiness as she slipped from the kitchen, not wanting to interrupt.

There was no way to know what the next few days would bring. She wanted them to have their happiness before . . . before what? She didn't know. Only that the constant dread that left her just on the edge of panic never went away.

Quietly she exited the kitchen, climbing the stairs to her room. How many more times would she make this trip? How long before she was home?

Inside her room she lit the candle and stretched out on her bed, sliding her hands under her pillow. Her fingers brushed the edges of something. Paper. She pulled the small folded slip out from beneath the pillow and opened it. Her breath caught and that panicked feeling edged in a little closer. The paper trembled in her grip as she read the one word message: *Tomorrow.*

Her breath caught as her heart began to speed. She clutched the note to her chest, the paper wadding up in her fist. Air, she needed air. She tried to pull in a deep breath, but where was the air? No matter how much air she took in, it seemed to disappear.

The King's words came back to her: *count.* She began at fifty, counting backward. Tears sprang to her eyes and she tried to blink them away, continuing her count.

Tea, the tea had helped the last time, but Torren and Aster were still in the kitchen. She couldn't let them see her like this, they'd expect her to explain. Torren would understand, but not Aster. Instead, she continued to count.

She picked up the glass of water beside her bed and brought it to her lips with a trembling hand. In her other hand she still clutched the note. If anyone saw that note... It was only one word, but if it was found later... She slid closer to the bedside table and held the slip of paper out above the flickering candle. The flame quickly caught on the edge, and within seconds there was nothing left but a small bit of ash. She could almost believe she had imagined it, if it weren't for her still hammering heart.

Tomorrow. Tomorrow. Tomorrow. The word pounded in her head over and over like the clanging of a gong, or a too eager death knell. She lay back on her bed and pulled the pillow over her head, trying to drown out the constant repetition of the word.

The grey dawn had only just given way to a soft yellow glow, but Raven was already awake, staring at her ceiling. She was surprised she'd gotten any sleep, though it had certainly not been restful. The dread in her gut seemed to have taken on a life of its own and was slowly attempting to crawl up her throat. She tried to swallow it down but to no avail. Today. This was the day they had worked and waited for, and now that it had arrived, she found herself uncertain if she was glad it was all about to be over or terrified at the possible outcome.

If the dampness of her skin or the slight tremble of her hands were any indication, it was the latter. She bit down on her lip before forcing a long breath into her lungs and standing. Lying in bed and dwelling on the possibilities would only make her feel worse.

Her feet felt heavy as she trudged up the stairs carrying the King's breakfast. Unless they failed, this would be the last time she would deliver breakfast to the King. By the end of the day, he would be dead.

Dead. Her stomach rolled as a wave of nausea hit her. Was she really a part of a plot to murder a man? How had she ended up here?

The guard opened the door to the King's rooms and she entered. The room held touches that she suspected were unique to the King. Pillows, rugs, tapestries with pops of maroon—which Raven had come to learn was his favorite color—dotted the space. A pair of his gloves sat discarded on the table near where she'd left the tray. A book lay on the table next to one of the chairs by the fire, a gold ribbon marking a page.

Why was she only noticing these things now? As though her conscience was trying to remind her that the King was still a person and she was going to kill him. With a final look at the book, she clamped down on her lower lip and drew up the memory of Luc, screaming in the throne room, and then fled from the rooms as quickly as she could without appearing suspicious.

The day moved with a momentum Raven wasn't prepared for. Once when she was very young she'd been on a horse that had been spooked. It had raced headlong across an open field and it took all her ten year old strength to stay on its back. That was what the day reminded her of. A headlong race toward a final glass of wine.

"Raven!"

She jumped, the tray in her hands shaking with the movement. A bowl that had once held sweet cream crashed to the floor and shattered. The sound ringing around the room.

"Oi, girl! Watch yourself," Cora yelled from across the room. "We don't have an unlimited supply."

"I'm sorry." She quickly placed the tray on the long work bench beside her, trading it for a towel. She crouched to the floor and began mopping the edges of the mess.

Another body knelt beside her and Raven noted the shock of red hair out of the corner of her eye.

"I didn't mean to scare you." Aster began gathering the larger pieces of the broken crock into the folds of her apron. "You seem extra jumpy today."

If only Aster knew.

"I didn't sleep well."

It wasn't a lie. She carefully lifted the towel and the bits of cream and smashed crockery off the floor, moving to the rubbish barrel and dropping it all in.

Behind her, Aster did the same.

"Thank you. Did you need something?"

Aster shook her head, wiping her hands against each other over the barrel. "No, I was just going to ask if you wanted to meet us in the gathering room by the kitchen? Tonight, after you collect the last tray and dinner clean up is over. We're just getting together to eat the leftover fruit tarts."

After. Would there be an after for her? Would she be long gone by then? Would anyone know the king was dead while they enjoyed their tarts?

"Raven?"

She'd been staring at Aster but hadn't even really seen the other girl.

"Are you alright?" Aster's eyes scanned her face.

They wouldn't have to worry about getting caught if Raven's behavior gave them away first. She closed her eyes and gave a swift shake of her head. "I'm fine, really, just tired."

"So, tonight?"

Raven forced a smile onto her lips. "Yes, tonight. I'll see you there."

"Great." Aster's grin didn't last. "Now I'm off to clean stables." She held up the end of her orange sash and offered it to Raven. "Want to trade?"

It was almost tempting. "No thanks, but tell the horses I said 'hi'."

Aster puffed a breath out of the side of her mouth, blowing away a wisp of hair that had already escaped her bun. "Whatever. At least the Stable Master is nice. She always helps."

Raven's return smile was genuine, though as soon as Aster left and the distraction was gone, the weight of the day crept back in.

She didn't see the King during any of the times she delivered his meals. For that, she was grateful. She didn't trust herself to look him in the eye and not give everything away.

When she returned with the King's empty lunch tray, there was a note for her. The King would be having dinner in his rooms. She balled the note in her fist and dropped it in a rubbish barrel. It was Friday, the King always had his meal in his rooms on Friday.

"Love letters?"

She looked up and stopped short. If Torren hadn't spoken she would have walked right into him.

She stared at him, in his tan shirt and blue sash, and again wondered how they'd come to this place.

A deep crease formed in Torren's brow as his head cocked to the side. "Raven?"

She wanted to speak with him, talk about how mad they all were, but the kitchen were not the place for that. She looked up as another servant brushed by. "Sorry. I'm just distracted today."

His mouth closed into a line and it was odd to her to see such a serious expression on a face that was normally smiling and animated.

He nodded at her. "Tomorrow's a new day."

To anyone else it would have meant, *"perk up, start again tomorrow."* But there was a much deeper meaning to Torren's words. Tomorrow would be a new day; not just for her, but for the country. A chill raced down her spine and settled in her stomach. If she didn't calm down she was going to be sick.

Torren's warm hand rested on her shoulder, bringing with it the scent of carrots. "It's okay, Raven. Why don't you go rest, I'll see you at dinner."

The word "dinner" caused her heart to riot again and she nodded even as a wave of dizziness hit her.

Torren's eyes widened. "Hey, why don't you sit?" He led her to a bench and helped her sit. "I'll get you some tea."

"Peppermint, please?" She managed to push the words out between erratic breaths.

Fifty, forty-nine, forty-eight... she counted down in her head.

Torren slid onto the bench beside her and pressed a warm mug into her hands. "The water was already hot."

She brought the mug up and inhaled. The strong scent of the peppermint leaves took the immediate edge off the panicked feeling. She almost laughed. She was using techniques the King had taught her to calm herself from the panic attack that was brought on from thinking about the plan to assassinate the King.

"Feeling better?"

She nodded, a lie, but she didn't want to keep him any longer. "I'm fine, you can get back to work before you get in trouble."

"You sure?"

She forced what she hoped was a reassuring smile. "Really."

Torren gave her wrist a gentle squeeze. "I'll see you at dinner."

"See you at dinner."

She finished her tea and, when she was feeling steady, decided to go for a walk. She needed to be moving, doing something. If she went to her room with nothing to keep her mind occupied, she would most likely end up panicking again. She pulled a heavy blanket off a hook by the door and wrapped it around herself.

She pulled the blanket tighter as a gust of wind swept by and threatened to pull it from her grasp. It was certainly starting to feel more like autumn.

The wind bit through the blanket and she shivered. Going outside was a mistake. Instead, she made her way to the servants' library.

She skimmed the shelves, reading every title four times before she gave up and went back to her room. She wouldn't need a book anyway.

She'd wandered around for long enough that it was almost time to return to the kitchen. She took a few moments to run her fingers through her long, thick hair, picking out the tangles left by the wind. If only she could stay there, playing with her hair for the rest of the night. Dinner time had come far too quickly. She'd occupied her time too well and it seemed to have moved even more swiftly.

When she pulled open her door, she once again had that runaway horse feeling. She clamped her teeth together until her jaw ached. There was no longer time to fall apart. Instead, she began the long count backward from one hundred as she made her final trek to the kitchen.

The sounds of commotion greeted her before she stepped into the kitchen.

"It was 'ere, who ran off with it?" Cora's sharp accented voice rose over the normal din of meal preparations.

"I have it!" There was no mistaking Torren's voice and Raven looked up to see him rushing to where Cora stood, hovering over the King's meal, a wine decanter cradled in his hands.

Her heart started a wild staccato pounding as her breath hitched. She needed to pull herself together.

Cora's gaze narrowed on Torren. "What are you doing with it?"

"It hadn't been put out yet." Torren picked up two glasses and joined Cora at the tray at the same time as Raven.

"Everything alright?" Raven did her best to make her voice sound casual. She suspected she failed, but the others didn't seem to notice.

"All good." Torren placed the glasses on the tray and carefully poured the wine. The deep red liquid sloshed against the sides of the glasses and Raven studied it, wondering what poison looked like.

"Well, then." Cora gave him a wary look before her gaze shifted to Raven. "Get on, go."

"Yes, ma'am." Raven nodded at Torren to taste the food.

He took a few bites of the meal and then lifted the wine glass to his lips. He met Raven's eyes over the rim of the glass and gave her a subtle lift of his brow. When he set the glass down he dragged a sleeve across his mouth.

"All good."

She swallowed, sure everyone in the kitchen had heard it. No words would form so she simply gave him a nod, lifted the tray, and made her way up the stairs to the King's rooms.

Logan and Kanan stood outside the King's door. Her breath hitched and she gripped the tray tighter, trying to keep it from tumbling to the floor as her hands began to tremble.

Logan gave her a solemn, encouraging nod as Kanan knocked once before reaching out and pushing the door open.

Raven stepped inside and let out the breath she'd been holding when she realized no one was in the room. She set the tray down and exited the chambers as swiftly as she could. She spared a glance at Kanan and Logan before moving so fast she was nearly running from the King's chambers. She made it to her own room in record time, slipping inside and bolting the door behind her. She dropped onto her bed and pulled the pillow over her head, trying to smother away the images that played in her mind: the King drinking the wine and falling to the floor, spurting and choking before he finally died.

How long, she wondered, before she would start to hear the shouts? Before the news would spread?

It wasn't long. Less than an hour later she heard the sounds, but they weren't the sounds she'd been expecting.

Booted feet thudded on the floor and startled cries rose from servants in the hall outside her room. She sat up, trying to hear what was happening.

Her door burst open, the little iron lock that secured it tearing from the frame with a splintering crack, pieces flying across the room, scattering to the floor. Raven yelped in surprise as two guards stepped into her room.

"There she is. Grab her."

She scrambled back from the two large figures. "What's going on?"

One of the men clamped a large hand around her arm, his grip so tight it hurt. He hauled her from the bed as the other guard drew his sword. Terror burst in her chest at the sight of the gleaming blade. She stumbled as she was ripped forward toward the second guard who stepped closer and brought the pommel of his sword down on her head.

TWENTY-ONE

"She's waking up."

The voice was familiar but it sounded far away. She groaned when she tried to open her eyes and pain lanced through her head.

"Is she alright?" *Kanan?*

"I think so. I don't know. I can't tell." The words were edged in panic and in the haze she wondered where she was. He shouldn't be there. "Raven, darling?"

It was him. She forced her eyes open. "Papa?"

Her father smoothed the hair back from her forehead, his brows furrowed deeply. "Yes, it's me,"

Raven was suddenly much more alert in spite of the pain in her head. The room spun as she pushed up to a sitting position. Why was her father here? What had happened?

"What—"

"Slow down. I think you must have been hit very hard," he said.

"Where are we?"

Fog clouded her head as she looked around. The walls were still the stone walls of the palace but it was colder, and the smell . . .

"In the dungeon," her father answered.

She turned to her father. "Dungeon?" It wasn't a leap to know why she was in the dungeon, but her father? "Why are you here?"

He shook his head. "I don't know."

She glanced around the small space. Moss grew on the stone walls, dark stained straw littered the floor, and she didn't even want to think about what caused that smell, but they were alone.

"Is anyone else here?"

"We're here." Raven's heart leapt in response to Kanan's voice coming from somewhere beyond her cell door.

"Kanan? Where's Logan and Torren?"

"They're both here with me, but Logan . . ." Kanan's voice trailed off.

Raven stood, her head throbbing as she moved to the door of the small cell. She squinted out between the two bars set in the very small window.

"What? Logan what?" Fear squeezed her heart.

"He's rough, Raven." His words were laced with a concern and unease that he didn't often possess, and the sound made her nauseous. "They beat him pretty hard before they brought him down here."

She swallowed down the sob in her throat. "Is he awake?"

"No."

Tears filled her eyes and she squeezed them closed, wanting to be with him. A thought struck her and she opened her eyes, looking around. "Is Esrae with you?"

Kanan's voice grew more serious. "No. She's not here. I haven't seen her."

Raven slid back to the cold ground. Logan unconscious, no Esrae, her father in the cell with her... A tear fell down her cheek. "What happened?"

"I don't know." It was Kanan who answered. "After you left we waited, but nothing happened. Then about ten minutes later, more guards showed up and started beating on us. Mostly Logan. Then they hauled us down here."

"And Torren?" Raven asked.

"Same for me. They came and pulled me from the kitchen. I didn't know what was going on." The edge in Torren's voice made him sound foreign.

"But not Esrae."

Something turned in her stomach. What happened to Esrae? How had this fallen apart so quickly, what had given them away? She looked to where her father sat on the floor.

"Why are you here? When did you get here?"

He gave her a sad look. "I've been here since yesterday."

"What?" Her voice didn't sound like her own. "How?"

"Raven?"

Raven whipped her attention toward the door, the motion causing the room to spin and her head to throb. "Es?"

Straw scraped along the stone floor as Raven scrambled to her feet, relief flooding her at the sound of her friend's voice. She sounded okay, but where had she been? In another cell, unconscious?

"Es, are you okay?"

"I'm fine." Esrae's voice shook, making her sound anything but fine. "Raven, it's going to be okay."

Raven grasped the bars on the door, peering through the space. "Are you sure you're alright? Are you hurt?"

"I'm fine, I'm not hurt," Esrae repeated. "I just wanted to come tell you it's going to be okay."

She turned her head from side to side, trying to find the cell that held Esrae. "I don't know, Es." Her voice quivered.

Nothing about their circumstances was okay. She wanted to encourage Esrae's optimism, but it was too hard for her to dredge up false hope. Their situation was bad and she was all too familiar with how the King handled these things. She couldn't see a way they would be walking out alive.

"This is bad."

"No, I'm telling you." Esrae stepped closer to the cell door and Raven's brow furrowed as it took far longer than it should have for her mind to process what she seeing. Esrae stood with her hands folded in front of her, resting on the full skirts of her gown, in the hallway that separated the cells.

"It's going to be okay." Her voice pitched high with an unnatural squeak. "He promised he wouldn't hurt you."

Esrae's words finally sank in, stealing the air from her lungs. *'He promised he wouldn't hurt you.'* Esrae had said she wanted to *come* tell them it would be okay. Raven shook her head, backing away from the door. No. She couldn't have. She was their friend, they had known each other for years.

"Es?" Her voice was so quiet, had she even spoken aloud?

When Kanan spoke from his cell, his voice was much louder. "Esrae, what did you do?"

TWENTY-TWO

E srae could have walked into Raven's cell and punched her in the stomach and it would have felt the same.

Her father had been there since the previous day.

"That's how they knew." Her voice was barely above a whisper.

She was going to be sick. Esrae. It had been Esrae who'd told the King of their plan. That's how he knew to get her father. Esrae had told him and he'd known for days. How many days? Since he'd talked to her about treachery? Had he known then? Her vision swam. If she'd only known how much danger she'd been in that day, alone with the King.

Her blood pounded in her ears until she couldn't think around it, couldn't think of anything beyond Esrae.

She tore at the bars of the door and they rattled with the force. "How could you?"

Esrae stepped back with a sharp intake of breath, shaking her head, surprise on her face.

How did she have the right to be shocked?

"He's not what you think," Esrae said quickly.

"Not what I think?" Esrae was defending the King. Salty tears fell down Raven's face. "Where were you when he was torturing and killing those men?"

"They tried to kill him first!" Esrae's pitch rose.

"No!" Raven shouted back. "One of them, maybe. The other was innocent and you knew it! You *know* it! He knew it!"

Esrae's high pitched voice took on a note of desperation. "He had to do something. Someone had to be made an example of or people would just keep trying to kill him."

Raven opened her mouth and then closed it again, trying to fight her sob. Was this really her friend? "Esrae, do you hear yourself? He's a monster, and you're standing up for him. Worse! You turned us in. He's going to kill us all." The fire had gone out of Raven's voice as the reality of her words sunk in.

They were all about to die at the King's hand. All those nightmares that she'd had were about to come true.

"No, he promised he wouldn't hurt you."

Esrae's tone was so insistent, as though she really believed what she was saying. How stupid.

"He lied, Esrae!" Raven jumped at the shout that tore from Kanan. She'd never hear him sound so angry. "Logan's half-dead already."

"He promised," Esrae squeaked the words, her curls flying around her face as she shook hear head from side to side.

"Es." Torren sounded like he was about to appeal to her. "I think he's done something to your head. I know you couldn't have done this, not on your own."

"My head is fine." Esrae's squeaky tone had become sure.

Torren continued, sounding like he was trying to coax a wild animal, "On your own, you gave your friends up? Es, he's using you."

"You were going to kill him. How would that make you better than him? My head is fine, Torren," she snapped at him. "Yours needs help. He promised he wouldn't hurt you if you surrendered. It's your choice now."

Raven sank back onto the damp stone floor. "Go away."

"Raven—" Esrae began.

"Get out, Esrae." Kanan's angry voice rang off the walls before Raven could repeat herself.

"You don't understand." Esrae's tone was rising again. "He's not what you think. He's not evil. But he has to protect himself. He's the King, he can't just let assassination attempts go unchecked."

"He wouldn't have even known if you hadn't told him, Esrae." There was fury in Kanan's words.

Silence followed for a moment before Esrae began again. "Raven, I—"

The bars in the door across the hall rattled. "Get. Out." There was no question in Kanan's voice, and even though he was behind bars and she was safe, Esrae still yelped.

Numbness crept over Raven as Esrae's steps retreated. "We're dead."

"Darling—" her father began.

"He's waking up!" Torren called.

Raven jumped up, running to the door. "Logan? Logan!"

She couldn't actually see anything but a small stone hallway lit only by torches, but that didn't stop her from craning her head to try.

A low groan came from somewhere close by and the sound made her chest ache.

"I'm fine." The words were nearly unintelligible, drowned out by a sudden coughing fit.

She threw a helpless glance at her father, who had joined her at the door. He rested a hand on her shoulder and she leaned into him.

"Easy, easy," Kanan soothed. "Don't try to move. You really took a beating."

"I know." More coughing. "I was there."

Raven released a breath. At least Logan's personality was still intact.

"What happened?" Logan's voice was so rough, like he'd been eating stones.

"Esrae sold us out." Bitterness dripped from Kanan's words.

Torren was quick to speak up, "The King is in her head, she wouldn't do this."

"What?" Logan half-choked the word out.

"Either way, she gave us up," Kanan confirmed. "Even Sebastian's here. She must have told the King everything."

"Seb?" It sounded like it caused Logan pain to say the word.

"Together again," Sebastian called back, sounding bitter.

"Not the reunion I planned." More coughing sounded from the cell. "Are you going to say 'I told you so'?"

"I'll skip it," her father responded. "Besides, it could be worse."

Raven turned a disbelieving gaze on him as Logan's voice echoed her thoughts, "You think so?"

"I don't know. I was just looking for something to say,"

"Be quiet, then," Logan responded.

Raven was so thankful Logan was coherent enough for their banter she didn't even care this wasn't the time or place for it.

Her relief was short lived as helplessness took it's place. "What do we do now?"

"I think, now, we are at Malakai's mercy." It was clear from his tone that her father felt the same helplessness.

"I don't think 'mercy' is what he has in mind." Kanan's words echoed her own thoughts.

"No..." was all her father said in response.

There was silence for a long time after that. What else was there to say? Raven's mind, however, was anything but silent. Her imagination put on a gruesome show in which each of her friends died screaming before the throne.

She didn't know how long they'd sat in silence waiting. Minutes? Hours? It felt like days. But when the door to the block of cells banged open, then it felt like it had only been seconds. Raven leapt to her feet, her heart pounding in her chest. It hadn't been long enough. The thudding of several pairs of boots invaded the dank space and the door rattled violently as a fist pounded on the outside. Raven scrambled backward at the sudden noise as the voice of a guard rang out, "The King wants to see you."

TWENTY-THREE

Hedged in by maroon sashed guards, Raven followed Torren and Kanan as they supported Logan, her father walking behind them. It was no mystery what awaited them at the end of this trek. The King on the dais and a room full of palace inhabitants, summoned to witness their executions. She fought to even her breaths. She refused to breakdown in front of the King.

They followed the guards through a door of the throne room. But instead of being met by a room full of people, there was no one. No one save for the King, his guards, and Esrae.

Raven glared at Esrae standing beside the King, one of her closest friends. How could she? But Torren's words swam in the back of her mind. Was the King really to blame for this? Was he controlling Esrae?

They were herded to the front of the dais where the King stood, waiting.

The room felt infinitely larger with so few people in it. The light from the torches caused the shadows to dance, giving Raven the eerie sensation that they were gleeful to witness their demise.

"I chose not to call everyone here for this," the King spoke and Raven looked up to find his eyes on her, "considering the intimacy of our group and how close we all are."

The King threw a pointed glance at Logan, but then he turned his attention on her father as well. "Sebastian. It's been a long time, my friend."

Sebastian glared back at him, his nearly black eyes filled with rage. "Malakai."

Raven straightened, glancing between the King and her father. "What?"

Her father knew the King? He had been in the army, but a lot of people who were in the army never met the King. Their exchange was personal.

The King chuckled and she looked up to find him watching her. "I can't believe they never told you, not in all the time you were plotting. They didn't tell you that we know each other? That we grew up together? That they were sending you in to kill their childhood friend? Pertinent information, don't you think?"

Raven clenched her fist, her fingernails digging into her palms, blindsided by the King's words. Was that tang in the back of her throat what betrayal tasted like? How could they let her come here and not tell her these things? Grew up together? Her mouth parted at the looks on their faces. Clearly the King spoke the truth.

"And you, Raven." Trembling, she dragged her attention back to the King whose voice had softened a bit as he addressed her. "You really do look just like your mother."

The air pushed out of her lungs in a whoosh. Her mother?

"Oh, yes," the King said, as though he'd read her mind. "I knew your mother, as well. She truly was the most beautiful woman I've ever known."

Out of the corner of her eye, Raven saw Esrae stiffen at the comment.

"I knew who you were the moment I saw you on the road," the King continued. "That poem? I wrote it for her. She was the kindest woman, she saw the good in everyone. I mourned her death. There was a point when your mother and I were very close."

Raven's head swam.

"Shut your mouth, Malakai!" her father hissed.

Terror gripped Raven. No one spoke to the King like that. But when she looked at Malakai, he was only smiling bitterly.

Malakai addressed Sebastian. "No need to be like that. She chose you in the end, did she not?"

She couldn't process the things she was hearing. Chose him? She'd had to choose? Had her mother been in a relationship with Malakai?

Malakai turned his attention back to Raven. "Your mother and father and Logan and I, we were friends."

She had no words. Her mother had been friends with them, as well. The story of how her parents met—if the King spoke the truth—the things she had known to be true, had been lies.

The softness in Malakai's countenance was gone when he turned to speak to Logan and her father. He regarded them for a moment before his mouth turned up in a small smile. "Do you remember the party? The one that lasted for days? I do. I'll never forget it."

"Make your point, Malakai." Annoyance coated her father's words.

Malakai continued as though he hadn't spoken, "Of course, you may remember it differently than I. I seem to recall Serene being very free with her affections that evening."

Her father lunged in the King's direction, only to be quickly restrained by the guards. He growled. "You are a liar."

"Am I?" Malakai looked amused. "I recall a young woman, free from inhibitions. Joyful, smiling, dancing, loving."

Repulsion crossed her father's face. "Lies."

Malakai's smile didn't waver. "Loving me, loving Logan, loving you. Everyone too *drunk* to care whose body ended up where."

Raven heard Logan cough and glanced at him to see he was also scowling. At least, she thought he was scowling; his face was so bruised from the beating he'd suffered, it was hard to tell.

"And by the next day, everyone had forgotten," Malakai said with a flourish of his hand.

The implications of the King's words settled on her like a stone. He'd either made them think they were drunk or had actually gotten them drunk, and her mother had slept with all of them. Bile rose to her throat at the reality of such a violation, at the realization of the extent of the King's power.

"Of course, nine months later, a surprise arrived," Malakai continued with a pointed look at Raven. She gagged, fighting down the vomit. "You, Raven, who look exactly like your mother but nothing like your father."

Raven covered her mouth with a shaking hand as her stomach revolted and a sob punched from her. Her father turned his full attention on her, though she couldn't tear her eyes away from where the King stood looking pleased with himself.

"Don't listen to him, darling. He is lying."

"Lying?" Malakai said and laughed again. He addressed Raven. "Didn't you wonder why I didn't take you to my bed? Your beauty is unquestionable and yet you serve. It's because I had no way of knowing whether you were my daughter or not. But now that I've gotten to know you, heard so much about you, I know better."

A tear escaped down Raven's face as the horror of the King's words settled on her.

"I remember none of this." Logan choked on a cough.

Malakai turned his attention on Logan and studied him for a long minute, his attention straying once to Raven before returning again to Logan. "You could be her father. It's just as likely as the rest of us. Maybe more so."

"These are lies," Logan echoed her father's earlier words.

"Are they?" Malakai's eyes moved between Raven and Logan yet again before he stood straighter, inhaling deeply. With a raise of his eyebrows and a soft, "Hmm. Would you like to see what you've forgotten?" Malakai raised his arm and swept it in front of him as though he was brushing away a fly.

Raven's father stumbled beside her and her breath caught in her throat at the look on his face. He doubled over as though he'd been punched in the stomach and vomited on the floor at her feet. His expression held devastation. Her chest clenched painfully.

She turned to look at Logan whose attention was fixed on her and not her father. He stared, looking at her as though it was the first time he'd ever seen her. His bloodied mouth hung open, pure shock lining every feature.

Raven's jaw trembled as her jumbled mind began sorting through the words of the King and the reactions of her father and Logan. Sorting each piece like a puzzle. Insignificant memories joining in, crowding her mind.

Her father speaking to Logan, laughter in his voice. *"She reminds me of you."* Another memory, her father's voice again, less amused. *"She is just like you. Spends too much time out there fighting."*

Tears streamed down Raven's face as her expression mirrored Logan's. Actually mirrored it, as she looked into his face, her own eyes staring back at her.

Malakai turned to Logan. "Well, she does have your eyes."

TWENTY-FOUR

"And now here we all are again. Reunited. But by betrayal." Malakai glanced between her father and Logan, his gaze lingering on Logan. "You. I never would have expected this from you. You've been by my side for so long."

"You're a monster, Malakai." Logan sounded sad. "You needed to be stopped."

"And you were the person to do that?" Malakai flicked his chin toward Raven. "You and your daughter and her friends."

The word "*daughter*" bounced around inside Raven's head.

Logan's eyes flicked quickly to her, as though he was having the same reaction, before returning to the king. "If not me, who?"

"Well, that is a good question. One that will now need to be answered." Malakai stepped toward Logan. "Because you won't be around much longer."

"No! Please!" Raven recognized the movement. She lunged at Logan but was brought up short as Kanan's arms came around her and held her as she fought him. "Please?"

"Your father betrayed me." Malakai's attention remained on Logan even as he spoke to Raven.

Father. The word made this so much worse. She'd never known. Her whole life she'd loved him as though he was a second father, and now to find out he actually *was* and to lose him—

"Please?" she sobbed again, her fist clenched in Kanan's shirt.

Malakai ignored Raven. "Any last words?".

"Please!" she screamed the word, desperate for Malakai to stop. Her chest heaved, spots dancing at the edge of her vision. Her legs shook as Kanan held her, wrapping her in his arms.

"Raven," Logan coughed her name, looking at her and ignoring Malakai. "I would have been proud to call you my daughter."

Sobs shook her and she clutched Kanan's shirt in her fist, her tears soaking through the material.

Logan offered her a weak smile. "Knowing wouldn't have changed the way I feel about you. I couldn't love you more or be more proud of you than I am."

Raven's chin slumped to her chest, tears pouring down her face, dropping to the stone floor.

"Enough," Malakai said, taking another step toward Logan.

She didn't even have time to register what was happening before Logan had dropped to the floor. His hands gripped his head and the sound—Raven had never heard him make such a sound. His cries echoed off the stone walls of the empty chamber while the shadows danced.

"Malakai!" her father's shout lifted over Logan's cries.

"Please, stop? Please?" Her throat felt raw as she screamed and begged, dropping to her knees, Kanan still holding her. She would do anything, anything he wanted, anything to make this stop. She pulled, desperate to free herself from Kanan, but he held her fast. "Please, stop!"

"Very well," Malakai said, his eyes on Logan.

The silence that fell in the chamber was louder than any of Logan's screams.

"Saints," Kanan breathed.

His grip on her loosened and she wrenched free from his grasp, scrambling to Logan's side.

"Logan, Logan." She shook him. She could wake him, she just needed him to hear her. "Logan, wake up," she pleaded, pulling at his body, rolling him to his back. Blood trickled from his nose but he did not move. "Wake up."

"Kanan's hands were on her arms again, gentle but firm. "Raven," he spoke softly. "Raven, he's gone."

She shook her head wildly, her hair flying into her field of vision. He wasn't gone, he couldn't be. It was Logan. Logan was always there, he would never leave her. "No. No."

"Come on." Kanan pulled her up and away from Logan. "Let him go."

On her feet, she looked down at where Logan lay as the truth crashed into her, crushing her chest. Gone. Gone, just like that. The sensation of someone dumping a bucket of cold water on her head washed over her and before she could breathe, it was replaced with nothing. Her limbs went slack, her mouth open as she stared.

There had been so many emotions all at once, it was as though her body turned them off to give her a chance.

But then Malakai turned to her father. "And you..."

She battled the fog in her mind to turn to look at them.

Her father stood in front of the King, his brows drawn together, shoulders back, his gaze moved from where Logan lay on the floor to the King and his jaw clenched. "Do your worst."

Malakai smiled.

Her body was reacting before she could think, wrenching out of Kanan's hold for a moment before he recaptured her. "Papa..."

Malakai moved to stand in front of her father and Raven could only think that her dreams were becoming reality as the King executed them one by one in front of her.

Her father's knees buckled and he dropped onto the stone floor, his face contorting in pain.

Then Raven was screaming again, begging for Malakai to stop.

Through her cries she thought she heard Kanan's voice in her ear. "I love you."

He spoke the words quickly, and then he released her, Torren's arms closing around her instead.

It happened so quickly, she didn't have time to react or to be confused.

"Stop." Kanan had moved to stand in front of Malakai, placing himself between her father and the King. His voice did not waver.

"Stop?" There was no question that Malakai was amused at this new development.

On the floor her father went slack, falling forward and catching himself on his hands. He pulled in a great breath and turned his head. "Kanan, go back to Raven."

Kanan ignored him. "Take me."

Raven froze. She'd heard him wrong. He hadn't spoken the words she thought she'd heard. He couldn't have. He wouldn't.

The King raised one eyebrow, as though he too questioned Kanan's words.

"Raven's lost enough." She thought she heard a tremble in his voice when he spoke her name, but then it was gone and his words were sure. "Take me instead of Sebastian."

"Instead?" The King's tone left little for interpretation. There would be no '*instead*.' Only first and last.

Kanan stood his ground.

The expression on Malakai's face changed as he observed the group before him. "She is special to you."

Kanan turned his head to look at Raven and a small smile lifted the corner of his mouth.

"Kanan." Terror robbed her of her breath as she shook her head wildly, desperate for him to take back his stupid bargain. She struggled in Torren's hold, "Don't! Please? Please!?"

His eyes softened. Soundlessly his lips formed the words *"I love you"* before he closed his mouth and blew a breath out his nose. His shoulders squared and he returned his attention to the King.

"No!" She pulled every way she could but Torren's hold was solid. She shook her head, wrestling to free herself, shoving at Torren's arms where they held her waist. "Let me go! Let me go! Let me go?" The words came out in cries and pleas as she watched her worst nightmare take shape in front of her.

"Raven, stop," Torren pleaded quietly in her ear.

"She is," Kanan answered the King's question.

A sob tore through her. She was going to have to watch them all die.

Malakai glanced at Raven and then back to Kanan. "How will taking you instead of him teach him anything?"

Kanan didn't respond. She desperately wanted him to come back to her, to tell the King he changed his mind. But he didn't, he stood there, holding Malakai's gaze.

Malakai ran a thumb over his bottom lip, considering them for another moment, his gaze running from her father to Kanan to Raven, before settling back on Kanan. A smile lifted the corner of his mouth. Raven's already erratic heart stuttered at the sight. Whatever he was thinking, it wouldn't be good. Terror stole her breath as tears rolled down her face.

Malakai stepped toward Kanan, his head cocking slightly to the side, and immediately Kanan's body went stiff. His hands went to his head as his legs buckled, the sound of his knees cracking on the marble floor echoing around the room. But the sound was nothing in comparison to the agonized scream that broke from Kanan's lips.

"No!"

Sobbing, she broke free, launching herself toward Kanan. Torren's hands flailed to regain a hold on her, but she was out of his grasp. She gained no ground, though, as her father caught her. He pulled her back to where Torren stood, and they both held her as she wrestled desperately to free herself, her own cries blending with Kanan's.

She was vaguely aware of Esrae's voice calling out to Malakai, "You promised! You promised!" Raven had almost forgotten the other girl was there. As though Esrae had the right to be appalled—this was all her fault!

Esrae latched on to the King's arm, pleading, but he ignored her. She raised her voice louder above the din, begging, "Please, end this?"

"Very well."

As quickly as Kanan's screams had started, they stopped. He lay, still and silent, just as Logan had.

An agonized scream tore from Raven's throat, her sobs coming so hard she couldn't breath around them. She ripped herself free from the grasp of Torren and her father and rushed to where Kanan lay, hitting her knees and sliding to his side.

"Wake up! Please—" The word was long and desperate.

He had to wake up, had to, he had to. He couldn't leave her. She needed him.

"Get up." Tears drenched his shirt as she fell across his prone form. Her cries and pleas were the only sound in the room.

Then, beneath her, as though he had heard her, Kanan's chest rose as he pulled in a deep breath. She gasped, lifting her head to look at him. His hand landed on her back, resting lightly before sliding up her spine to rest at the nape of her neck.

"Kanan?" she whispered the word, irrationally afraid that if she spoke too loudly he'd be gone again.

He gave her neck a light squeeze as he blinked his eyes open.

She risked a glance at Malakai. Had something gone wrong? Had he intended to kill Kanan and failed? That didn't seem possible. The King didn't seem surprised; he only stood quietly, watching.

She lifted herself a bit more to meet Kanan's gaze. "Kanan?"

A half smile turned up the corner of Kanan's mouth. A hysterical sobbing laugh burst from her. He was alive. He was okay.

"Raven." She had never heard anything so beautiful as the sound of her name on Kanan's lips.

Her smile grew and she nodded. "Are you okay? Do you want to sit up?"

His hand moved again up her neck into her hair, and pain lanced through her skull as his fist tightened and he pulled, snapping her head back. She squeaked more from shock than pain. What was happening?

He moved to a sitting position, his fist still clenched in her hair. His hand closed tighter, pulling painfully at her scalp.

"Kanan, you're hurting me." Tears trailed her face. She couldn't understand.

Kanan's eyes met hers but they were different. The softness was gone.

"Kanan?" her voice shook, the words only a breath as the panic in her chest rose.

His gaze held hers but it was so cold. "Sorry." The word held no sincerity, no emotion at all.

Kanan gave a swift tug on her hair, bringing her head down to crack off the floor. She yelped, stars dancing in her vision as she reached up slowly to find a large knot already blooming.

Beside her Kanan stood, paying no attention to her as he reached down to brush off his clothes. She blinked several times, trying to clear her vision. Her father and Torren appeared beside her, pulling her away, every eye fixed on Kanan.

Blood pounded in Raven's ears as Kanan sank to one knee, lowering his head before the King. Malakai smiled.

"Saints," Torren hissed.

"What's wrong with you?" The pounding in her ears was replaced by the sound of her heart splintering.

The King spoke, "I don't care what you do now." He indicated Raven, her father, and Torren. "As long as they're taught a lesson. As long as they suffer a bit."

Kanan turned to face them, his eyes finding Torren and then her father, before coming to rest on Raven. A smile she had never seen before played on his lips. Despair poured into her as her body began to tremble. The look he leveled on her could only be described as malicious, and it did not belong on Kanan's usually kind face.

He curled a finger at her. "Raven, come here."

Blind terror crushed her chest, cutting off her air. She was moving, moving toward Kanan, and she couldn't stop herself. Her mind screamed, mental fists slamming against the inside of her skull, pleading with her body to stop, but she had no control over her legs. No control. It was her body and she couldn't fight him.

When she was young, a horse-and-wagon theater stopped in her town. She sat through at least a dozen shows before they finally pulled out and headed somewhere else. She remembered the way the puppeteers held the cross sticks with string attached to them, and made the puppets walk and dance. She felt like one of those puppets. Like someone else was holding her strings, making her move against her will.

Torren released her and tears slipped down her face as she moved to Kanan, unable to stop until she stood in front of him.

"What's happening?" Fear made her voice small.

"Hey, Rae." Menace coated the words. It was not a term of endearment. He leaned in slightly, his voice lowering so only she could hear him. "Kneel."

She was powerless against the compulsion as she dropped to her knees. She swallowed. "This isn't you. Please fight this?" She pleaded but her cries seemed to fall on deaf ears as Kanan completely ignored her.

He had to be in there somewhere. She wanted to shout at him not to give in to the King, but no words would come. Only silent tears. They had failed and it had cost too much.

Malakai laughed quietly. "This should be very interesting."

TWENTY-FIVE

Kanan turned toward the King, brow raised in question. Malakai answered with a raised hand, inviting Kanan to continue.

When Kanan turned back to Raven, there was no kindness in his eyes, no warmth in his tone. "Get up."

She struggled to her feet, head still pounding as Kanan took a step closer. He bent slightly, towering over her, his height and frame making her feel small. She'd always enjoyed his large presence, but now... Her body and emotions were confused. Confused by his intimidating stance and his calculating, cruel gaze. She didn't recognize this man in front of her.

"I'll make a deal with you, Rae. Fight me. If you win, you can go."

Go? She blinked, attempting to process his words. "What?"

He leaned close enough that his breath sent her hair fluttering around her face, and goosebumps erupted over her entire frame. "I said: fight me."

Tears pooled in her eyes as she searched his gaze. How could this be happening? Kanan stood in front of her, but also not. It was as though an entirely different person inhabited his body.

"I don't—I don't want to fight you."

His brows rose. "You would rather stay?"

Her gaze strayed to where Logan lay, eyes closed, covered in blood and bruises. She looked to Torren and her father to find Torren shaking his head.

"Don't," he pleaded. "It's not a fair fight. They can control you."

Kanan glanced at Torren and then back to Raven, giving her a shrug. "Fair fight, I promise."

She shook her head, her mind swimming as she tried to process this version of Kanan. Logan had told her that the King could rewrite a man's mind but she hadn't fully believed him, or certainly hadn't understood what he'd meant. Now, with the man she loved, the man who loved her, standing before her, threatening her, she still had difficulty believing it was real. He wanted her to fight him? How could she?

Her head began to shake from side to side. "I can't."

Kanan rolled his eyes, sighing loudly. His head swiveled to the side, eyes landing on Torren.

Raven's heart stuttered.

Kanan look back at her. "Fine."

Terror clawed at her chest as he moved like a flash to Torren, pulling back an arm and punching the other man in the face. Torren's head whipped to the side as he lost his balance and hit the floor, clutching his bleeding nose.

Raven yelped, trying to rush to Torren but finding she couldn't move, her feet rooted firmly to the spot. Kanan glanced over his shoulder, a malevolent smile on his handsome face. Then his attention was back on Torren.

Bile rose into the back of her throat at the scene in front of her. Kanan—her Kanan, her intended—with that look on his face. She couldn't make it make sense, couldn't reconcile these two things. A sob broke free as she tried again to move to no avail.

Kanan pulled back a foot and sent it flying. Torren cried out, rolling into a ball when Kanan's foot connected with his stomach.

Raven began hyperventilating, her head swinging from side to side, her whole body shaking. No air would fill her lungs. She had to do something.

Kanan pulled back again and Raven screamed, "No! Stop! Stop, please. I'll fight you. Just stop, leave him alone." Tears spilled down her cheeks as she begged the man she loved to stop hurting their friend.

Kanan dropped into a crouch beside Torren, and Torren flinched, groaning in pain when Kanan flicked his nose. "Looks like it's your lucky day."

Kanan moved back to where Raven stood. Rubbing his fingers together, he studied them as Torren's blood smeared across his skin. He raised his hand, presenting the sight to Raven. "My favorite color."

Disgust bloomed in her chest along with pain. Red was Kanan's favorite color, but this was not Kanan. She took him in, same clothes, same hair, same face, but so different. Had she really been in his arms only moments ago? Hadn't he only just whispered in her ear that he loved her? She could still hear his voice, feel the breath on her ear.

"Kanan, please?" She searched his olive green gaze, desperate to find a trace of the Kanan she knew was in there somewhere. Had to be in there.

He bent slightly, meeting her gaze fully. "Don't bother, you're not going to find what you're looking for."

Cold, detached words. She glanced at the King who had silently taken his seat, Esrae standing beside him, his arm laced around her waist.

Raven's despair morphed into anger. They had to get out of this place, and then they could figure out their next move. Figure out how to fix Kanan and rescue Esrae. How to end the King. She didn't want to fight Kanan. How could she? This would not be playful sparring. This would be a fight to win. She wasn't sure if she could, but she had to try.

She faced him, doing her best to square her shoulders though she couldn't make her voice remain steady. "If I win, you let us leave."

He considered her for a moment before his gaze tracked around the room, amusement flickering in his eyes. "Well, how about this? If you win..." His eyes landed on her, the amusement vanishing, turning to something deadly. "I'll give you a head start."

Of course he wouldn't just allow them to leave. She would have to run from him. Her breath stuttered out of her and she bit down on her lip briefly before closing her eyes, steadying herself. When she opened her eyes, she inhaled deeply, staring into the nothingness that sat in Kanan's, her heart cracking even further.

His mouth quirked into a smirk as he waited. He would not pull his punches this time. He looked eager to hurt her.

She let out a slow breath and Kanan seemed to take that as a signal. She didn't taker her eyes off of him as he began to circle to his right. So much lean muscle and sure footing. She shook her head, trying to recall all the times they'd sparred, dredging up his tells, his tendency to go for the feet first.

She waited for his move. She'd beat him in the past, but he'd never actually been trying to do her real harm. And she'd had a clear head. Neither of those things were a factor here. They were each playing to win.

She didn't want to hurt him, she only wanted to gain a chance to get her father and Torren and run.

He continued to circle, she could kick him, but he was still too far away, so she waited. And then he moved.

Kanan lunged at her feet, the move she'd been waiting for. She spun out of the way, turning just enough to latch onto his back. She wrapped her arms around his neck, and his hands flew to her arms, gripping her painfully.

She was the better fighter, but Kanan was bigger and stronger and had the benefit of a clear head. He broke her grip easily and in one swift movement wrenched her off of him, tossing her forward. Pain shot down her spine as her back hit the stone floor, and she let out a loud groan.

She quickly regained her footing as Kanan stalked toward her. Not willing to give him a chance to make another move, she swept her feet around, catching his ankle. He flailed his arms as he fell backward, hitting the ground with a grunt.

When he tried to stand she was waiting. She brought her knee up hard and cringed as it connected with the soft flesh of his stomach. He folded in half, and a sob punched out of her as she brought her other knee up into his jaw.

A completely unsatisfying crack sounded, and he sailed backward, landing on the ground with a thud. Before he could pull himself together, she moved to his side.

He smiled at her, blood streamed from his nose and coated his teeth, giving him the look of a feral monster. Another sob escaped her lips as she brought her fist down into his face.

He groaned again and rolled onto his stomach, holding his face. "I concede," Kanan coughed, or laughed, spitting a mouthful of blood onto the marble floor.

Tears streamed down her face as adrenaline coursed through her, making her entire body tremble. He still knelt on the floor, on his hands and knees, catching his breath.

He shot her a look over his shoulder. "Go," he said, coughing again.

Raven stared at him coughing and bleeding on the floor, and couldn't bring herself to move. Her instincts warred inside her: help him, run, comfort him, or get away.

Neither Torren nor her father, however, needed to be told twice. Torren rushed at her, latching onto her arm, dragging her away from where Kanan was beginning to pick himself up from the floor. She didn't want to leave him and that was completely mad, but it *was* Kanan, and she didn't want to leave him here.

"Come on!" Torren pulled at her again, hauling her toward the door.

They were almost there when her eyes fell on Logan's body. She froze, her limbs locking, refusing to carry her further. She shook her head. How could she leave them here?

Torren pulled on her arm but she remained rooted to the spot. "I can't."

"Yes, you can." Torren readjusted his grip. "Raven, we have to get out of here." His next tug was stronger, and Raven stumbled, a sob shaking her as she allowed herself to be led away.

"I'm sorry, Raven," Torren was saying as he tugged her firmly along behind him. "I'm sorry."

She was coming apart. Pieces of her heart were scattered through the room and she was powerless to gather them back together.

As Torren pulled Raven through the servant's entrance, her eyes met Kanan's. A vicious pit of cold darkness. And the wicked smile that spread across his handsome features held chilling promises of things to come.

They slipped through the door into a hallway, the light from the few torches dancing off the stone walls casting long shadows, causing their trio to appear much larger than they were.

They'd made it halfway down the hallway when someone stepped out in front of them.

"Aster!" Raven exclaimed.

"Come with me." Aster's eyes bounced wildly between them and the door they'd just come through.

"What?" Raven fought to understand already moving.

"Come with me," Aster repeated. "I can help get you out of here."

Torren released Raven, instead latching onto Aster's arm, pulling her to a stop. "Aster, if you get caught helping us, they'll kill you,"

"Then let's not get caught." Aster pulled free. "Come on, please. Follow me."

Aster began moving, leaving them with no choice but to follow. They followed her closely down the hall, passing through another door and down a set of stairs, then through a door that looked like a wall.

"Why are you helping us?" Raven was still shaking with adrenaline that would not ebb.

"I was listening," Aster spoke over her shoulder. "It's easier to dismiss the King's actions when he's not hurting people I know. Luc was the beginning and, Raven, I'm so sorry about the General. I thought you two were—I didn't know he was—"

Raven only nodded. If she spoke, she would start to cry and not be able to stop.

Aster knew her way around the hidden areas of the palace, and soon they were emerging into the woods behind the structure.

"Aster." Torren caught her arm again, forcing her to stop and turn to him. "You can't go with us."

"Why not?" Aster said. "I can't stay here, Torren. I can't keep serving him after that. And I want to go with you."

He stepped closer, placing a palm on the side of her face. "If we're caught, we're done for. You'll be killed with us. Please?"

Aster rested her hand on his, curling her fingers in. "Better than to stay here. I'm going with you. You can't stop me."

The look in Torren's eyes was admiration mingled with annoyance and a lot of affection. Something stabbed at Raven's already broken heart as the crack grew further. Kanan should be there with her. They should be leaving together. They did everything together—and she left him behind. His absence mingled with her guilt was like a beast in itself, threatening to either tear her apart or crush her.

"I don't care who's coming and who's staying, but we have to keep moving," her father spoke through gritted teeth as he moved further into the trees, pulling Raven along after him.

"Moving to where?" Raven asked as nothing but dark forest spread out before them.

Her father looked ahead as though he could see through the trees to some far off destination. "There's a cabin. Logan—" He cleared his throat. "Logan and I used it for hunting some years ago."

"And Malakai?" Raven's question fell more like an accusation.

Her father glanced at her, guilt behind his eyes. "Not with Malakai. After."

"And you know how to get there from here?" Torren asked.

Her father nodded. "It might be slower in the dark, but there's a moon."

A chill skittered down Raven's spine. She was grateful for the cover of darkness, but that meant that the soldiers also had the advantage.

Torren's hand was still closed firmly around Aster's. "Let's go."

The group moved as silently as possible through the darkness of the forest. The only light came from the places where the moon filtered through the trees, but it was enough.

A cold breeze blew and Raven hugged her arms tightly around herself. Every time she closed her eyes she saw the look in Kanan's eyes as they left the throne room. She fought to swallow down the sobs that threatened to consume her.

It was Kanan's face, his tanned skin and olive green eyes, but nothing about the look he had given her was reminiscent of her Kanan. She'd rarely even seen him angry. He was so good at keeping his emotions in check. He and Logan had shared that quality.

Logan.

He had been there her whole life and now he was gone. Everything ached as another hole opened inside her.

She felt like she wasn't even in her own body, just floating, watching what was happening in complete disbelief. Finally, they came upon the cabin. They'd walked for hours and she'd barely noticed.

Her father pushed on the door and it creaked, sticking against the warped wooden frame. It was obvious no one had been here in some time. Thank the Saints.

He threw his shoulder at the door and it moved another foot, scraping against the dusty floor. One more shove and there was enough room for them to push inside. "Come on."

Thick dust plumed around them and Raven choked on it, coughing into her sleeve. The others were having similar reactions to the dank interior.

Wordlessly, Aster and Raven moved to opposite sides of the small cabin to the windows. The windows screeched loudly as they pushed them open, and Raven flinched, holding her breath.

"Now what?" Torren asked.

"Now we take turns watching and resting," her father said. "Not long, but we can't keep going like this."

Raven slumped against the wall. "I wish I had my sword."

"Yeah." Torren massaged his temples. "Any weapon would be nice."

Aster patted her thigh. "I have a knife. Don't leave home without it."

Torren slid an arm around her, pulling her close. "Sexy. Also, you go first from now on."

Raven couldn't even work up the slightest smile for Torren's joke, but Aster managed to roll her eyes.

Aster, still tucked to Torren's side, turned to Raven. "You have a sword?"

"Yeah," Torren answered for her. "Kanan made it for her."

I've pledged myself to you. Raven's breath caught the memory.

Aster twisted to look at Torren. "The guy chasing us?"

As far as Raven knew Aster had never met Kanan, but listening at the door, she would have picked up names. She couldn't stand any longer, there was no strength left. She slumped to the floor where she stood.

"Yes."

Aster was quiet for a moment before sadness painted her fair features. "How long were you together?"

Raven closed her eyes as deep pain settled inside her. "Forever."

"I'm sorry," Aster whispered as she brought her arm up to wrap it around Torren's thin frame.

There was silence for some time before her father spoke. "Why don't you three get some rest. I'll keep watch first."

"I can watch too," Aster said. "I had the day off today, slept in."

Her father nodded. "I'm Sebastian, by the way. I haven't thanked you yet for your help. We're in your debt."

"Aster," she answered quietly as she looked around, taking in the dark space. "And maybe you shouldn't thank me yet."

"Alright, you two." Her father indicated Raven and Torren. "There's some beds in the back room."

The thought of closing her eyes, of taking anytime at all to rest, terrified her. Apprehension gnawed at her, but her father was right. They couldn't just keep going, they needed a break.

Reluctantly, she moved to the single door at the back of the small room, another dust plume greeting her as she pushed it open. A single bed with a dust covered mattress sat along the wall. She swiped at the surface a few times, holding her breath as the dust billowed around her. It was no use, there was no way to get rid of it. She lay down, moving to the side, leaving room for Torren, or anyone, who decided to join her.

Her body ached as she stretched out, and exhaustion rolled over her, mental and physical. But she knew as she lay there, staring at the ceiling, she wouldn't sleep. Closing her eyes only invited images of Kanan's sneering face and Logan's broken body. She lay there for a long time until she couldn't stand it any longer. She blew out a long breath, pushing hair back away from her face, and sat up. Might as well keep her father company as he watched, or maybe relieve him so at least one of them could get some rest.

In the main room of the cabin, her father sat in a chair in front of the dark fireplace, the knife that must have been Aster's, gripped in his hand, resting on his lap.

Across the room, Torren and Aster sat on the floor, curled together in each other's arms, both of them asleep. Jealousy and anger hit her and she closed her eyes, shaking off the feeling. This wasn't their fault.

"Couldn't sleep?" her father asked quietly.

She shook her head, moving to where he sat and lowering herself to the floor beside his chair. For a long time she sat silently, staring into the place where a fire should burn, pulling at a loose string in her sleeve.

"Why didn't you tell me?"

There was no movement from her father when he replied. "I didn't know about Logan. Malakai took the memory from us."

"No." She shook her head. "Why didn't you tell me you knew Malakai?"

There was a long moment of silence, in which she wondered if he would answer her at all, before he spoke. "It was bad enough you knew I served in his army. I didn't want you to know I had anything to do with him, much less that we were friends. I was ashamed of even that."

She could almost understand that, but to keep this information from her... "Even going into this?"

"He liked your mother."

It wasn't what she had expected him to say. She waited for something more. Waited as he appeared to struggle.

"He liked her very much, and she liked him."

Malakai had said as much, but Raven hadn't known what was true and what he'd been saying just to get under their skin. Hearing her father confirm it was like a punch to her gut.

"Malakai and your mother were together for a short time," he continued. "But when we met, your mother and I, the attraction... I'd never felt anything like it, and she felt it too."

Her father's gaze grew distant, as though he were looking into the past and seeing Serene again for the first time.

"She soon told Malakai and he seemed to take it well. We were friends and he claimed to be happy for us. But it hurt him more than we'd realized. For a while he was quiet, acting like everything was fine. But then he threw that party. He hid his feelings so well. None of us realized the effect it was having on him."

She looked away, swallowing the lump in her throat. The party. The party where she was conceived between her mother and Logan.

"He may have taken most of our memories of that night, but I still remember plenty. He tried to lure her back. I suppose when she told him 'no' that's when he decided he would have what he wanted either way. I suppose it's a small mercy that, while it was against all of our wills, it was not unpleasant for anyone. He made sure a good time was had by all."

Raven's stomach churned. A good time or not, it was a violation of everyone. She fought to get her next words out. "Could he be, I mean, Malakai— could he be my—"

"No." His response was so quiet, an edge of sadness to his words. "You're Logan's. If I had known it was even a possibility, I would have seen it from the beginning. You're so much like him, Raven. I thought it was just because of all the time you spent together. Turns out, it something more."

There was nothing for her to feel guilty about, but that didn't stop the feeling from crawling down her spine. This was hard for her, but she couldn't imagine how difficult it was for her father. The things that Malakai had revealed were awful.

"I'm sorry."

Her father's attention fixed on her. "You have nothing to be sorry about. Absolutely nothing. This is not your fault. You are a victim like the rest of us."

"I know but, it's all just so much. You know nothing can change what we have. You'll always be my father."

"Always, my darling." His head tilted ever so slightly, his brow furrowing. "I'm sorry too."

"Why would you be sorry?"

"I'm sorry about Logan. To have that revealed only to lose him."

"You lost him too." Logan and her father had been so close her entire life, and now he was just gone.

"I'm sorry for the time that was stolen. I'm not angry at Logan, this was certainly not his fault. But I know you must have questions that now you can never have answers to."

She didn't know what to say to that. He was right, but she still felt guilty.

"You really should try again to get some rest. In a few hours we'll need to decide what to do. Certainly we'll need to move on from here."

"What about you?"

"I'm not tired."

She knew that couldn't be true, his thoughts must have been more chaotic than even hers. But he'd always been quiet. He needed time to process, to grieve. He wouldn't want an audience.

She glanced to where Torren and Aster slept before standing.

"Goodnight." She wrapped her arms around her father's shoulders, taking a moment. An arm came up, resting on hers, hugging tightly. "I love you, Papa."

"I love you too, my darling." He released her, patting her arm gently. "Get some rest."

As she passed the window she stopped to look out the dark glass. Nothing was visible past the line of trees that surrounded the small cabin. A perfect blank canvas for her mind to replay the day. She squeezed her eyes closed, rubbing them. When she opened them, the darkness seemed even more vast. What lurked out there? How much of a head start would they get? Was Kanan already there, waiting? Watching from the darkness?

Only nights ago they had been in her bed, their bodies curled together, his mouth trailing kisses down her body. She gasped in a quiet breath, shaking her head, banishing the memory. It was too much right then.

It took only moments for her thoughts to turn from Kanan to Logan. Gone. She hadn't realized how much she counted on his presence in her life. He'd always been there, steadfast and constant. Her trainer, her confidant, her second father, even when she had no idea of their actual relationship.

Now that she knew, she could feel it, feel it as though she had always known. Of course they were blood; the connection should have been obvious. Their bond had been unique and strong and today it had been snapped.

Bone deep exhaustion washed over her as she lay down on the dusty mattress, curling in on herself as all the events of the day crashed in on her like a tidal wave. She held her stomach as the sobs came, wracking through her body, an endless torrent of grief like she had never known.

TWENTY-SIX

Raven opened her eyes, groaning at the dull ache that seemed to be in every part of her body. Voices filtered in from the other room, but a glance at the window told her it wasn't yet dawn.

She stood with a heavy sigh as her body protested. She'd actually slept. Apparently exhaustion won out over despair.

She exited the room, joining the others where they were gathered around a small table in the corner of the room.

"Raven!" Torren greeted, holding a wrapped package in each hand. "We raided the cupboards and discovered that for breakfast, we have salt jerky or salt jerky."

She moved to the table. "I guess salt jerky." She accepted one of the small packets of dried meat. "Thank you."

"Anyway, I think she thought she was special," Aster finished whatever she had been saying before Raven had joined them and bit down on a piece of the jerky. The dry meat made a tearing sound as she pulled it away.

Her father nodded a chin toward Aster. "Raven, you should hear this."

She bit into the meat, brows raised toward Aster.

When Aster finished, chewing she continued, "I was just saying, when I was a kid, my grandmother used to tell me that she once knew someone with power like the King's. I think my grandmother thought she was special because she knew someone like that." Aster scoffed. "I guess that makes us special too."

"And was this person evil as well?" Torren deadpanned before popping a bit of jerky in his mouth.

Raven's insides twisted at his words. Kanan was not evil.

Aster went on, "I don't know. My grandmother said the woman didn't enjoy having the ability so she blocked it by drinking some sort of tea."

"Tea?" Torren's brows dipped.

Aster shrugged and tore off another bite. "That's what she said."

"So if we invite Kanan for a tea party, that'll fix him?"

Annoyance rose in Aster's voice. "I didn't make the story up, Torren. I'm just telling you what she told me."

Torren pinched the bridge of his nose and squeezed his eyes closed, looking tired. "I know, I'm sorry."

Her father ran a hand over the scruff on his face and then rested his chin on his hands, looking at her.

"Now what?" She had meant to speak louder, but the words emerged as a squeak.

"Now what?" Aster's brows shot toward her hairline. "Now we run. We go as far away from here as we can. We disappear, probably change our names."

Raven straightened, looking from Aster to her father "We can't just leave him . . ."

"Leave who?" Aster looked from Raven to Torren.

"Kanan." She nearly choked on his name.

Aster's raised brows crashed together, forming a deep crease. "Aren't we running from him?"

"What about Esrae?" her father asked.

"Esrae? The King's whore?" Aster rocked back, clearly shocked. "You people need to get your priorities straight. I really don't think she wants to be rescued."

The words burrowed into Raven, ringing painfully true. She'd spoken to Esrae herself and she hadn't spoken like someone under any sort of thrall. She'd spoken like Esrae, self-absorbed and jealous. And Raven didn't feel bad thinking those things either. Esrae had betrayed them.

"What if Esrae's under the King's control, like Kanan?" There was an almost hopeful sound in Torren's voice.

"I think she's just *under* the King, Torren." But when Aster looked at Torren, her expression softened to something more sympathetic. "Look, I've been around the palace for a while now. I've seen people under the King's control. I'm sorry, Torren, she's not one of them."

"How can you even tell?" Raven asked.

Aster blew out a deep breath. "First of all, she's not cowering or ruthless. When the King has you in his grasp, you're almost always one of those things. Like your friend."

Kanan's awful expression, his dark eyes staring down at her, forcing her to kneel before him. Ruthless was obviously the category into which he fell. "And what about Kanan?"

Apology coated Aster's tone. "I don't know how to save him."

"Whatever we do, we can't stay here," her father's voice broke in. "We have to keep moving. They'll find this place soon enough."

Despair weighed on Raven. She couldn't just forget about Kanan. She needed him. They had to find a way to save him. But right now, they needed to leave. "Where do we go?"

"My home town isn't very far." Aster shrugged. "A day's walk."

"We'll need supplies," Torren said.

Aster reached into the folds of her skirts and drew out a small pouch. "I have money. Maybe enough for horses, I don't know. Certainly enough for some food and clothes."

Raven looked down at her own dress. She'd long since abandoned the maroon sash, but anyone who'd been to the palace would know that both she and Aster were servants there. And probably Torren too. "We definitely need other clothes."

"Then let's go," her father said. "Gather what you can carry from the stores in the cupboards here and we'll leave right away."

They pulled a thin threadbare blanket from the foot of the bed and divided it into quarters, each taking a piece and filling it with food, emptying the stores in the small cabin.

Outside the air held the scent of dawn, leaves damp with dew warming in the rising sun. They pressed on, walking hard, stopping only when necessary, hoping to reach the next town by nightfall.

Torren elbowed Aster as they walked. "Where'd you get the money?"

Aster shrugged. "I stole it."

"Just like that?" The smile in Torren's voice was evident, even holding a note of pride at Aster's actions.

"A little at a time, no one missed it. I thought it might come in handy one day."

"Good for us," Raven's father said. "Clothes and horses will definitely be helpful."

Raven moved to his side. "Then what?"

"I don't know." He glanced at the sky. "My instincts say to keep going. Get as far away as possible and disappear."

"But—" Her heart ached. "Kanan…"

Her father glanced down at her and his eyes held infinite sadness. "I know you don't want to hear this, but I don't think there's anything to be done for him."

"Nothing?" Raven choked on the word.

"I've seen Malakai use this trick many times," he said. "If he chooses to end it, then it ends. But there's no other way I know to break his hold. Possibly killing him, but I honestly can't say if that would even work."

She swallowed the painful knot in her throat, willing herself not to cry. She refused to give up on Kanan. She didn't know what she could do, but she would not abandon him. Her throat closed as a thought pressed in. There might not be a way to save him without . . . She squeezed her eyes shut, shaking her head. She couldn't think of that, if she did she would crumble.

The sky grew darker and she looked up at the gathering clouds. It would rain. It wasn't a surprise. Any luck they'd had had run out long ago.

Her thoughts returned to Kanan and the King. "We have to kill him, the King."

"Raven." Her father's head tilted as his expression softened. "We tried that, it didn't work."

She was saved responding by Torren. "But this time we have no one to turn us in."

She shifted her gaze to where he walked with Aster. "What do you think?"

Torren's glance moved between the three of them. "I think they're our friends and we should try to save them if we can.

"I'm telling you," Aster looked to the sky as the first drops of rain started to fall, "that girl does not want to be saved."

"And Kanan?" The wind whipped her hair into her face and she ripped it away, wishing she could rip away the hopelessness she felt. She would get Kanan back, she would go herself if she had to. She refused to believe he was beyond help. But she couldn't fault Aster, she had no connection to Kanan, she didn't know him at all.

Aster nodded. "He's under the King's control. I'm sure if you could save him, he'd be grateful."

Raven spoke quietly, "We have to get him."

Her father nodded. "I agree." Lightning streaked across the sky, followed moment later by a crack of thunder booming overhead. "But first, clothes, horses, and a dry bed and fire."

The rain grew steadier as the sky grew darker, lit only by massive bolts of lightning, but they pushed on. Raven shivered, cold to the bone, squinting against the water droplets pelting her face. She wondered if the others were as miserable and exhausted as she was.

"There!" Aster pointed through the trees.

Torren let out a groan that turned into a yawn. "Finally, I'm so tired."

The group trudged through the muddied streets, past a large sign where an unlit lantern swayed in the wind. As they passed, Raven could just make out the words, "Welcome to—" but nothing else.

"Welcome to Kancar." Aster didn't even look at the sign as her pace increased.

They stopped at the first inn they passed. A three-level building with a creaking sign above the door that read *Kancar Kanteen.*

They stood huddled at the door, trying not to drip all over everything, waiting for Raven's father to rent a room.

There were tables around but few patrons, most likely due to the hour. Those that were there gave them odd looks but returned quickly to their drinks.

When her father returned to them, it was with a stack of clothes and a key. She didn't know if the clothes would fit, but as long as they were dry, she didn't care.

They chose to get only one room to take advantage of safety in numbers. Or, "So Aster can keep us safe with her knife," Torren had said.

Raven's father changed first and left the others to do the same as he headed downstairs to find some stew. After eating, they collapsed into the nearest beds, two each, and allowed themselves unguarded rest. Either no one would bother them in an inn, or the King's guard would burst in, demanding prisoners. Either way, there wasn't much they could do about it.

Raven stared at the ceiling, listening to the rain drops pelting against the roof and windows. Closing her eyes brought images of Logan's body or Kanan's cold gaze. She was afraid of what might find her in her dreams, and terrified of what she was sure would find them, eventually, in the real world.

The others seemed to think they could get away, but some feeling down in her gut told her they wouldn't escape. It was the same feeling she'd had the last few days at the palace—a deep sense of certainty something was going to go wrong.

Finally, Raven couldn't stave off the weariness any longer, and sleep crowded into the edges of her mind, spreading through her thoughts and fears. Even her dreams were held at bay by the exhaustion.

The sun filtered through the small window, casting a beam directly across Raven's face. She opened her eyes and blinked at the brightness. For a moment she had to reacclimate herself to her surroundings. Then it all came rushing back. She closed her eyes at the memories, but that just left the image of Logan on the floor.

She stood and stretched her arms first toward the ceiling and then to the floor. Her whole body held that dull ache that came from too much exercise. Her new dress was wrinkled and a little snug, but it was dry and she no longer looked like a palace servant.

Carefully, she opened the door and tiptoed out of the room onto the loft that overlooked the dining area and bar below. She peered down and realized it must be very early, if the lack of patrons was any indication. Two older men sat at a far table holding a friendly conversation over two mugs, and on the other side of the room a lone man sat, bent intently over a book. But beyond that the room was empty, though she could smell coffee and the savory scent of some sort of meat cooking.

She wanted fresh air, but if she went outside, would the King's men be waiting for her? If it was early enough, maybe they wouldn't be around yet and she could have a short walk. She just needed some time alone to try to sort through her thoughts and everything that was happening. She wouldn't go far. If the others woke up and she was gone, they would certainly panic. Just a short walk down the street and back was all she would take.

At some point in the night it had stopped raining, and wet leaves and mud squished under her shoes as she walked along the mostly empty streets. A cool breeze raised goosebumps on her arms, whipping her hair into her face. She shivered, wrapping her arms around herself.

"Cold?"

Her stomach dropped to nowhere, dread filling the space. The voice. His voice. Icy tendrils, colder than any wind, rushed down her spine. She could barely make her feet obey as she turned to face him.

He stood in a recessed doorway, casually leaning against the frame, arms and legs crossed, head tilted at an angle.

"Kanan." Her heart was thudding erratically, making it hard to breathe

"Hey, Rae," he said, detangling himself, standing to his full height. He lifted his chin in her direction. "Come here."

She couldn't have moved if she'd wanted to; her feet seemed frozen to the cold street.

He smiled at her, but it wasn't Kanan's warm, inviting, contagious smile. This smile was icy, with menace lurking at its edges. "I said: *come here.*"

Her throat closed up as claws seemed to wrap around her mind and she began moving, unable to stop herself. She cast a wild look around. Someone had to see. But if they did, what were they seeing? He wasn't touching her; she was going to him on her own.

Slowly Kanan mirrored her action, his head sweeping from side to side as he extended his hand. "It's just us, Rae."

Against her will she reached out, her hand shaking as she slipped her fingers into his palm. Gently he lifted her hand to his lips and kissed it softly.

Kanan reached behind him and opened the door, his hand still holding hers as he backed up. When they were fully inside, he reached past her, his sleeve brushing against her temple as he pushed the door closed. The sound of the latch falling into place was like the sound of a coffin lid slamming closed, trapping her inside.

Kanan's breath blew out of him in a huge sigh. His shoulders sagged as his eyes darted around the small dark space. When he spoke, his voice was quiet and there was something like panic in his tone. "Raven, I've been looking everywhere for you. I was hoping he would just let you go, but he could never."

She twisted her brow, shaking her head once. "What?"

Then his arms were around her as he pulled her close, enveloping her with his lemon scent. "I was so worried."

She froze at first, but as he stroked a hand over her hair, it was easy to let her guard down. A sob pushed out of her as she realized the King's hold had been broken, and her Kanan was back.

He pulled back, studying her face, conflict raging in his eyes. He brushed his knuckles softly against her cheek, wiping away her tears before he slid his hand into her hair and gently brought her face to his.

The kiss was tender, familiar, Kanan. It stole her breath and she closed her eyes and kissed him back.

Pain lanced her lip and she squeaked, pulling away, her hand flying to her mouth. When she pulled it away there was blood. She could feel the place where her lip was already swelling. When she looked at Kanan, the cold, amused smile he'd worn earlier was back.

He wiped a thumb across his lip and then examined the blood that coated his finger as well. "Tasty."

She backed away, her breaths coming in fits as she hit the door behind her. Anger flared inside her—at him for being so cruel, at herself for falling for his act.

He chuckled, taking a step toward her and resting a palm on the surface beside her temple. "Honestly, I can't believe you fell for that."

He leaned in, pressing his body against hers, pushing her flush against the wall. She pressed her back into the door, turning her head away from him.

His other hand landed on her hip and the contact stole the air from her lungs. She froze with no where to go. "Isn't it fascinating to know that I could make you do anything?"

She gasped as his knee slid between her legs, her heart hammering wildly behind her ribcage. He brushed her hair behind her ears and she shivered at the contact.

"Anything I wanted."

She'd experienced his persuasion, or compulsion, or whatever it was; that absolute control he held over her mind. Whatever it was, it was real and it terrified her to lose that control of herself. Tears began to slide down her face as her entire body began to tremble.

Somewhere in the back of her mind she knew she could take him. She could fight him and maybe even win. But nothing inside her would move to attack. It was as though that part of her had broken when Kanan had hurt her.

"Kanan..."

His head cocked to the side, his breath skating along the bridge of her nose. "Are you going to beg?" His words were soft, like a lover's, his eyes roaming over her face, pausing briefly on her lips. "You should."

She couldn't look away from his cold eyes as the horror of her situation burrowed deeper into her. He would do whatever he wanted with her, and no one would find her because they had no idea she'd gone. She couldn't even protest. Like her fighting skills, her language skills seemed to have disappeared as well.

In a breath he moved, clamping his hands so tightly around her upper arms she was sure to have bruises. She cried out as he pulled her off the ground, her face inches from his.

"I think you should beg." His hands closed tighter and her breath caught. He was hurting her. "Beg for yourself and for your friends. Beg for Sebastian, your *father.*"

A surprised chuckle shook his chest. "I couldn't believe that. The King was right, though. We should have known. You really are just like Logan. Too bad you won't be able to bond as father and daughter."

Tears streamed down her face, her chest tightening to the point of not being able to pull in any air. He was enjoying being cruel to her. Malakai had taken the kindest, sweetest man she had ever known and turned him into a monster.

As suddenly as Kanan had latched onto her, he released her. "I could bring you back to the King now, but I'm enjoying myself. It's like..." He appeared to be searching for a word. "...Hunting. I'm going to let you go. Tell your friends to watch their backs. And you—" she flinched when he reached out to run a finger along her jaw, his skin warm in spite of the cold air "—well, I'll be watching you."

Kanan stepped past her and pushed open the door, disappearing into the light.

Raven crumbled to the floor as her legs refused to hold her up any longer. She buried her head in her hands as her body shook with sobs.

After what seemed like an eternity, she finally composed herself. The others would be awake by now, probably panicking over her disappearance.

She pushed open the door and looked out into the street. There were more people out now, the sun higher in the blue, nearly cloudless sky. Kanan was nowhere to be seen. Raven turned back the way she had come and walked as fast as she could without running back to the hotel. She could feel him watching her the whole way.

"Raven!"

Raven jumped at the sound of her name, spinning to see who was calling her. Torren was coming down the street toward the hotel.

"Raven, we've been looking all over for you!" Torren said, coming to a stop in front of her. "Are you al—?"

He paused speaking, taking in her appearance further. When his eyes came to rest on her lip still marred by dried blood, his face fell. His gaze met hers again. "What happened?"

She shook her head, not trusting her voice just then. Also, she had no desire to repeat the story more than once. She turned and entered the hotel, Torren on her heels.

Immediately upon stepping into the room she was crushed in her father's arms. "Raven! Where have you been? Are you alright?"

When he finally released her and took in her appearance, the color drained from his face. "What happened? Raven?"

Exhaustion seemed to overtake her and she dropped heavily to the bed, her body resuming its trembling. She closed her eyes, heaving out a heavy sigh. "He's here."

Aster spoke, "Who?"

"Kanan." Her voice broke on the name.

"What?" Even with only one word, it was clear that Aster was panicked at the thought.

Torren moved to the window, sliding the curtain to the side to peer out.

Her father settled on the bed beside her, running a comforting hand over her shoulder. "Are you alright?"

"No. I mean, yes." She shook her head. "I mean, he grabbed me, but that's all. He just talked."

Aster slumped onto the opposite bed. "What did he say?"

She shook her head, not wanting to think about—not wanting to remember—the cruel words. But they had to know. "He said he was watching us and to watch our backs."

"Great."

"He's here now, he's been following us. He'll follow us wherever we go." Her father ran a hand through his dark hair.

Raven jumped as Torren slammed a hand down on top of the small wooden table that sat beneath the window. "Why doesn't he just kill us and get it over with?"

Raven stared at the floor, blackness creeping into her vision. "He has to bring us back to the King. That's what he said."

Her father leaned back, nodding. "Malakai would want to take care of us himself, in the end. He's only allowing this to torment and toy with us."

"It's working." Torren nodded absently. "From now on, no one goes anywhere alone."

"Yes," her father agreed, looking at Raven.

"Don't worry. I'm done being alone."

TWENTY-SEVEN

"Now what?" Defeat sat in Torren's gaze.

"Now nothing. We're done." Aster shared a look with Torren. "We've been done. He's just been toying with us. He's probably been following us sine we left the palace."

Raven stared at the dark floorboards, not seeing them. A chasm had opened inside her and she was being sucked in. "I want to go home."

She could feel their gazes on her as she looked up. "What does it matter? He knows where we are, he'll know where we go. We can't run. If he's going to kill us anyway, I want to die at home, in my own clothes."

"She's right."

She looked up, surprised to hear Torren agree with her.

Aster flung her arms out, frustration rippling off of her. "So what, we just go back to your house and wait for him to show up at the door?"

Raven stood. "You don't have to go. You've already done more than you should have. Go, run the other way. He's not after you. He'll chase us and leave you alone. I'm so sorry, Aster."

Aster turned pleading eyes on Torren. "Please, Tor, if you let him take you back to the King, he'll kill you."

Torren held her gaze. "I don't know what else to do. I'm sorry."

Aster blew out a long breath as she slumped back, swiping quickly at something on her face.

"I'm leaving." Raven turned to collect her small bag.

Her father picked up his own pack. "Not alone."

Raven watched her father, remembering times he'd held her when she was scared or hurt. At that time that small gesture had seemed to make all the pain go away. She longed for that feeling now.

Torren moved to Aster's side, placing a hand softly on her shoulder. "I'm going too. You can come if you want, but you don't have to." He moved his hand to the side of her face, his dark eyes locking with hers. "Saints, I hope you don't. Go somewhere else, please."

Aster stood, covering his hand with her own, holding his gaze. "You're stuck with me. I was gone the moment you played drums on the pots with the carrots."

Torren's smile was sad and Raven turned away as he lowered his head and placed a soft kiss on Aster's lips.

When they stepped out onto the street, Raven could feel Kanan's eyes on them. The hairs on her arms stood as they walked. She was sure if she turned around she would see him. She didn't turn. Instead, she shook her shoulders out, wishing the feeling would pass.

Whatever. Let him follow. He was going to kill her anyway, and then it would all be over. But something whispered in the back of her mind, telling her not to be ridiculous. Kanan wouldn't kill them, he would take them back to the King. Death would be kind.

Before leaving town they purchased two horses, choosing to ride together. Sitting on a horse with her father, her home already felt closer.

After hours of riding, Raven was beyond relieved when they came across a small stream crossing the path. They dismounted to allow both horses and riders a much needed rest and drink.

Aster stretched her arms into the air, pivoting from side to side. "I'm going to be in pain for a week after this."

Torren mirrored her actions. "I haven't ridden so much in . . . ever."

"Don't go far," Raven's father reminded them. As though they needed reminding.

After meeting Kanan, she had no plans to be alone for any reason. She would relieve herself within sight of someone. She expected the others felt the same.

Raven's stomach growled as they sat, opening their packs and pulling out some of the food they had refilled before leaving Kancar.

Torren held up a piece of jerky, examining it from all angles. "What I wouldn't give for some bread knots."

Raven glanced at him as her appetite evaporated at the mention of bread knots and the reminder of Esrae.

A twig snapped to their left and they all turned toward the sound.

"Did you save me any?" Kanan stood less than ten feet away, a broken branch in his hands.

They scrambled to their feet, food scattering on the ground. Aster pulled her dagger from where it had been strapped to her thigh.

How did he always move so silently? It used to be charming, now it was terrifying.

Kanan tossed the sticks to the side, eyes scanning the group. His attention came to rest on Aster and the dagger in her hands. He narrowed his eyes, pointing a finger at her. "I remember you. Didn't you work for the King?" He rubbed at his chin. "And you gave all that up to die with them?"

If it was possible, Raven's heart broke a little further at the casual way he spoke of their deaths.

Kanan's expression became one of amusement as he chuckled. "And is that really your only weapon?" He turned a suprised look on Torren. "You're going to let her defend you with that little dagger? Then again, I've seen you fight. You probably do have a better chance if she's the one in charge."

His gaze shifted back to Aster, amusement gone. He took a step toward her and they all backed up once. "What are you going to do when I kill her? Who will protect you then?"

Raven's heart hammered faster as Torren moved in front of Aster, chin raised. "Over my dead body."

"Yeah." The smile was back. "That's the idea."

Her chest was cracking open, tears welling in her eyes.

Kanan turned and she recoiled, taking a step backward under the force of his gaze. She tried to swallow but the lump in her throat would not allow it.

He smiled and it was awful. It was Kanan's smile and yet nothing like his smile. "Hey, Rae. You know, for someone who's been on the run for days, you still look nice."

The more she tried to keep her lip from trembling the harder it was.

He noticed, his smile growing crueler. "Oh!" His brows rose as though he had just remembered some news. "I almost forgot. I wanted to let you know that your sword is safe."

He patted the sword at his hip, drawing her attention. Her sword, with the twisted wine-colored pommel and sparkling silver guard, hung off his belt.

He drew it from the sheath with a soft hiss, turning it from side to side, allowing the sun to glint off the diamond-like stones.

Nausea twisted in her gut as her mind drifted back to the morning he gave it to her. To the smile on his face when she saw it for the first time, the sword that he had crafted especially for her because he loved her.

He would probably kill them all with it eventually.

She looked up to find his gaze intent upon her. He winked and she looked away.

Raven jumped as the silence that had settled was shattered as Kanan clapped his hands together loudly. "Well, I think we've rested long enough. Time to go."

The blood in Raven's veins turned to ice.

"I've let you all have your fun, but I'm done now. It's time to get back. The King is waiting."

"And you think we're just going to go with you? I really thought Kanan was smarter than that," Torren said.

Kanan turned a look on Torren, dripping with incredulity. "I am Kanan."

Raven's chest tightened. He only looked like Kanan. There was nothing left of the man she loved.

He continued, "And yes, I do think you're just going to come with me."

Torren scoffed.

"Clearly you don't agree." Kanan crossed his arms in front of his chest. "So, how will you stop me? Fight me? You can barely defend yourself against pretend attacks."

Torren took a step toward Kanan, and Raven's heart missed.

"Torren." She barely recognized her own voice. The single word carried warning and pleading.

Kanan glanced at Raven and back to Torren. "You should listen to her. You can't fight me."

"We can find out," Torren challenged.

The edge of Kanan's mouth quirked up. "Okay. Let's."

Torren whirled toward Aster, pulling the knife from her hands. But instead of turning back to Kanan, he leveled the blade at Aster's face.

Aster gasped, jumping away from the blade, eyes wide.

"Torren!" Raven called, everything inside her seizing.

Torren spun, and Raven jumped back as he leveled the knife at her.

Torren's eyes were wide as pure terror showed in their brown irises. He watched his own hand moving the knife, clearly not under his control. He turned again, pointing it at her father.

Her father ignored Torren, his gaze fixed on Kanan.

"Kanan, please?" Raven called as Torren continued to move the blade from person to person, fear etched into every corner of his face.

Amusement lit Kanan's expression.

Finally, Torren stopped flailing the knife around their group. Instead, he raised his other arm and moved the knife until it was poised, trembling, over his forearm.

Torren's expression vacillated between terror and helplessness as the knife drew closer to his arm.

"Kanan!" Raven screamed his name, desperate, pleading for him to stop.

Kanan's brows rose in challenge as Torren brought the knife down on his arm, the blade drawing a thin line of red across his skin. "You were saying?"

The world around Raven seemed to go silent as panic clawed at her, tearing at her chest. Beside her, her father held Aster. The other girl looked like she was screaming, but Raven heard no sound beyond the pounding of her own blood through her veins.

She dropped to her knees and the sound returned, crashing in on her. Aster screaming, Torren grunting in pain as the shaking knife dug into his flesh, and her own voice shrill and loud.

Raven's face was wet with tears, and she realized she was in front of Kanan, clutching at his clothes, pleading, "Stop, Kanan! Please stop! We'll go with you, just please stop."

All at once, everything stopped. The knife clattered to the packed dirt in front of Torren as he dropped to his knees, slapping his other hand over his wound. Aster pulled her orange sash from her pack and rushed to Torren's side, dropping into the dirt beside him and wrapping the cloth around his arm.

"Good." Kanan looked down at her, cold and unaffected. "Now that we understand each other, mount up. We have a long ride."

Raven stayed on her knees, palms on the ground, her breaths coming in gasps as she tried to wrestle back control of herself.

Kanan disappeared into the trees, returning a moment later with his horse. He mounted and waited, shifting with impatience.

Silence hung thick in the air as the others gathered their small packs together. With difficulty, Torren mounted his horse, cradling his injured arm, and Raven's father assisted Aster onto the horse with Torren before mounting his own.

Raven moved as though in a trance, barely aware of her actions as she moved to her father's horse to join him.

"Hey, Rae." Kanan's voice broke the heavy silence. "Ride with me."

TWENTY-EIGHT

A ir wouldn't come. She couldn't breathe.

She met her father's eyes, her own dread mirrored there.

"Raven..." Helpless despair dripped from the word.

None of them could do anything. They'd just had a firsthand demonstration of what would happen if they refused Kanan.

"Raven," Kanan said again, using her full name instead of the shortened version he'd been favoring. She didn't know which she preferred. "We don't have all day."

She shared a last look with her father before she closed her eyes, swallowed the hard lump in her throat, and turned. She could barely lift her feet or make her legs move.

When she was close enough, Kanan extended a hand toward her. She could only stare at it, the fine lines, old scars. That hand had touched her in ways no other could, had sent thrills of pleasure coursing through her body. Now, the pit of despair inside her opened further.

"Raven."

She looked up into his narrowed eyes, at his raised brow, the impatient expression on his face. Her Kanan was nowhere, she couldn't even find him buried behind his gaze. She swallowed thickly and raised her hand to his.

With barely any effort, he swung her up onto the horse in front of him and she flinched away when he reached around her to grasp the reins. Then with a light kick to the horse, they were moving.

She sat with her back straight, trying to avoid any contact with his chest.

His hand came around to rest on her thigh as he whispered into her ear. "Relax, Rae."

She jumped, her breath stuttering, goosebumps immediately breaking out across her skin.

His hand slid further, his fingers brushing the inside of her thigh as he rested his cheek against her hair. "Then again, maybe you should be scared. I do have orders."

The chill raced up her spine, lifting her hair off her scalp. She stiffened, fighting to keep the trembling at bay.

If Kanan noticed, she didn't know. He continued talking, each word making it more difficult not to break down.

"Make you suffer, that's what I was told. Not just *you*, of course. All of you." As he spoke, his hand continued to move, sliding over her torso, his fingers making idle circles. "Though, given their history, the King may have more interesting things in mind for your father. Sebastian, I mean. I guess your *father* already suffered. Logan, can you believe it? What a surprise twist, it's like a play."

Logan's tortured cries, his bleeding face, his still body. A sudden sob she couldn't contain burst from her throat.

A puff of breath stirred the hair around her ear as Kanan laughed.

His hand moved again, fingers splayed on her stomach, thumb just brushing the underside of her breast as he pulled her flush against him. She froze. Even her breaths ceased.

He must have noticed, but he continued speaking, his voice growing lower. "I've been thinking about how to make you suffer. I know how to make you moan, but this is a whole new area for me to experiment with. I know the best way to make Sebastian suffer would be to hurt you and let him listen, all while knowing he can do nothing." There was such intent and menace in his words she knew this was exactly what he had planned.

He rested his cheek softly against hers, his thumb still moving over her as we went on, "Don't misunderstand, I'm going to hurt him too. You'll just be first."

She bit her lip, squeezing her eyes closed, trying to stop the sob, but her breath hitched anyway as a shudder wracked through her.

The speech would have been awful coming from anyone, but from Kanan... She could tell herself all day long that it wasn't really him, not anymore. She could say the King had changed him into something else. But it was still his voice in her ear, his hands that touched her, the faint scent of lemons that still clung to him.

"Then there's those two." She'd been so lost in her thoughts she startled at the sound of his voice. "Torren needs to toughen up. Do you think killing her would help with that?"

Raven sniffed back the tears as much as she could. With a sigh, Kanan released the reins and dug in his tunic. He pulled a handkerchief from a breast pocket and waved it in front of her face. She didn't want to accept it, though she did need it. He waved it one more time before he dropped it in her lap.

Kanan cleared his throat and raised his voice as he continued, "You didn't answer me, Raven. Do you think killing the girl will toughen Torren up?"

Both Torren and Aster's heads lifted at the comment.

"Please stop." She could only whisper the words.

"You prefer to keep our conversation private?" he mused.

"Please," she breathed out. She would have preferred he stop talking altogether, but she suspected that was too much to ask.

"Alright." Kanan lowered his voice to a intimate tone, as though they were in each other's confidence. "Just between us, I am going to kill her. Maybe tomorrow. Maybe slit her throat. How does that sound?"

"Why are you doing this?"

He let out a deep, overexaggerated sigh. "We've been through this. I have orders."

"You don't have to follow orders," she said. "Two days ago you were—"

"What?" Kanan interrupted. "Touching you? Kissing your neck? Inside you? I can do those things now."

His lips brushed the skin behind her ear. She jolted and he chuckled.

"I have a purpose now. I didn't really before. I mean, I crafted swords, I helped my grandmother, I made you come, but... I didn't really feel like I had a purpose. The King gave me a reason, a goal. I'm here to make you see the error of your ways. I have purpose."

She said nothing, her tears dropping silently, soaking into Kanan's sleeve.

"You want to know what I'm going to do to you?" His voice took on an intimate tone that sent a shiver down her spine. "First, I'm going to take him—" he pointed to where her father sat on his dappled grey horse "—maybe break a couple of his fingers, run a hot iron over his skin, bust his face open... But then I'm going to lock him in the room right next to yours."

Dread coiled deep inside her, nausea churning low in her gut.

"You, I'm going to tie you down and I'm going to use that hot iron." He slid his hand back to her thigh and her body went so stiff she shook.

"I'm going to brand you once for each person you dragged into this mess." As he spoke, he traced invisible lines with his finger. "Torren. Aster. Esrae. Me. Logan. Sebastian."

Kanan moved his hand to the band of her skirt and began pulling at where her shirt was tucked. When he freed the material, she whimpered as his fingers slid just underneath it, brushing the skin there. "Then, I'm going to take my knife, and . . ." He paused, pulling his hand free and returning it to rest on her leg. "Actually, I think I'll keep some mystery."

She hated the way her body betrayed her, but she couldn't stop the way it trembled. His low chuckled vibrated against her back.

"So," Kanan's tone was suddenly conversational again, as though he hadn't just been speaking of torture, "why were you going home?"

She didn't want to share idle small talk with him. She hated the sound of his voice. Every time he spoke, it was like a nightmare that she couldn't wake from.

"Rae? Hello?" He snapped his fingers in front of her face. "Why were you going home? Was it for this?" He reached beside him to where Raven's sword hung from his saddle. The metal hissed as he drew the sword from the sheath. The sound drew the attention of the others and they turned in their saddles.

Kanan brandished the sword before he turned his wrist, bringing the blade around until the point nearly brushed her cheek. Her body went stiff as she leaned away from the blade, simultaneously pressing herself into Kanan's chest.

Her father reined in his horse, turning to face them, eyes wide with fear.

"Don't worry, Sebastian." Kanan wrapped his free arm around Raven's waist, squeezing her to him. "I have much more interesting things planned for your daughter. Keep moving."

Her father turned his horse and gave it a soft kick, urging it on. Raven couldn't tell if her father had moved under his own will or Kanan's.

"It is beautiful." The sword again hovered uncomfortably close to her face. "I imagined you while I made it. Pictured what you would look like holding it, swinging it. I wanted every inch to be just right for you. I think I did well." He slid the sword back into the sheath. "You know I love you, right?"

Raven couldn't stop the sudden scoff. "You used to love me."

"You don't believe I love you now?" He pulled her hair away from her face, tucking it behind her ear. "I do. And I want you to know I'll do my best to keep you from death. When this is over, after the King's anger is sated, I intend to ask for you."

Raven turned her head away from his touch. "I'd rather you kill me."

"Hmm." He ran a knuckle down her cheek. "Yes, you will."

A shiver chased down her spine at the implication.

"But I won't. I love you and I know you love me. Unless I misread all those pleading moans in my bed."

"You're not the same person," Raven said.

"No? I can be." He rested his cheek against her hair and spoke softly. "I could make you love me, you know? You wouldn't even realize what was happening. You would just be happy."

Her throat went dry, spots stirring in her vision at the thought of being trapped like that, of no longer being in control of herself. She tried to breathe, but her breaths were so shallow they did nothing.

"How?"

"How what?" he asked.

"How can you do that? The things the King does—make people do things?"

He shrugged. "Honestly, I don't know. But whatever the King did to me, I'm grateful. It's an extremely useful trick. Watch."

For a moment, she didn't know what she was supposed to watch. But then it became clear. In front of them, Torren shoved Aster from the horse. She yelped as her body thudded into the dirt and she rolled, cradling her arm.

Torren jerked the horse to a sudden stop and jumped off, dropping to the ground beside her. "I'm so sorry. It wasn't me. Aster, I promise, are you alright?"

"She's fine," Kanan called. "*Tell him you're fine.*"

Raven watched in horror as Aster looked from Torren to Kanan and back. The pained expression on her face morphed to one of amusement as a smile lit her features. "I'm great."

"Now *thank him*," Kanan said.

"Thank you so much!" She reached out to touch his arm and left a streak of blood from the large scratch she was cradling.

Kanan chuckled and Raven bit down so hard on her lip she tasted blood. "Must you be so cruel?"

"What are you talking about? That was funny."

"Hurting people?"

"Does it matter? She'll be dead tomorrow," Kanan stated the words as fact.

Torren shot Kanan a hateful look as he helped Aster back onto their horse. "You don't have to kill her."

"I don't *have* to, but it'll teach you a lesson." Kanan shrugged. "Stop pulling innocent people into your murderous schemes. Her death will be on you. Consider it punishment."

Raven couldn't pull her eyes from Aster. It *was* her fault Aster was in this situation, and if Kanan did kill her, that would be on Raven. Yes, Aster chose to come on her own, but if Raven hadn't been at the palace, carrying out their foolish plans, Aster wouldn't be in danger.

"What about you? You were part of this too."

Kanan hummed low and his voice grew quiet, a bitter edge creeping into his words. "You don't think I've suffered? You stood there and watched. You saw what the King did to me. You don't think that was suffering? Do you want a taste?"

He didn't give her an opportunity to answer. She barely had a chance to take a breath before the pain started.

Searing, pounding, stabbing, white hot pain began behind her eyes and spread. She clutched at her head, holding on, desperately trying to keep it from breaking into pieces. A shrill screeching sound rang out in her head, intensifying the already nearly unbearable pain. Then it stopped just as quickly as it began, leaving behind only ebbing tendrils that seemed to go out like a tide as she pulled in great gulps of air.

Kanan's voice was low and deadly in her ear. "I suffered."

TWENTY-NINE

Raven was still gasping for breath when she looked up to find every eye trained on her, horror etched into their expressions. Her father's eyes were wet with tears and he seemed to be straining against some invisible force. She swallowed, willing her breaths to settle as she tried to give him a reassuring nod.

"Shows over, *turn around*," Kanan's sudden command caused her to jump.

When her father turned his horse and kicked it forward, Raven knew it was not under his own volition.

The silence as they rode was thick, and dread coiled tighter and tighter inside her, anxiety growing with each step closer to the palace. She watched her friends, her family, riding ahead of her. There was a feeling growing deep inside that she didn't want to acknowledge, an awful certainty that they would not all make it out of this alive.

The saddle creaked as Kanan shifted behind her with a groan. "I think we should find a place to stop for the night. I'll be glad to be off this horse, what about you? We should find somewhere those two can get some time alone." He gestured to Torren and Aster. "At least give them that for their last night together."

"Stop saying that." It was a plea with a small voice.

"Why?" Kanan said. "I told you, now you can tell them. Wouldn't you want to be prepared? I suppose you could choose not to tell them, let them live in blissful ignorance. It's up to you."

Soft splashing drew her attention and she looked up to see the others crossing a narrow stream.

"Perfect." Kanan reined in his horse and called to the others. "We're stopping here for the night. You first." Kanan's hand closed around her arm, gently steadying her as she dismounted.

The heat from his touch crept through her sleeve, warming her arm. All her attention refocused on that one spot where they touched, and for a moment, she could imagine everything was normal.

"You're going to have to get down."

His voice brought reality crashing back on her. She swung her leg over the horse's neck and, still supported by Kanan, slid to the ground, her legs tingling from disuse.

Kanan's heavy boots hit the ground behind her with a thud. When he moved around her to lead the horse to the water, his hand brushed over the small of her back. It was a simple gesture. A Kanan gesture. He often stole small touches as he passed her. A hand on her back, a soft tug on her hair, a bump of his arm or a tap of his foot on hers. She knew it was a muscle memory sort of gesture, and it nearly sent her to her knees as she swallowed down the sob.

She watched as he led the horse away, despair like she'd never known forming a ball in her throat. She'd never, in her entire life, so desperately wished she could just wake up and see that everything was only a terrible nightmare. Fear stole her breath and she gasped to refill her lungs. What if she never got him back? What if this nightmare turned reality was the only future she had before her?

She squeezed her eyes shut, doing her best to slow her heart and regain control of her breathing. Falling apart wouldn't help, it would probably just entertain

Kanan further. Pressing her lips together, she pulled in a few more breaths before she opened her eyes.

Her eyes fell on Torren and Aster crouched together, filling their water skins. She glanced at where Kanan did the same further up the stream. She moved to them, keeling on the cool earth.

"I have to talk to you." She nearly choked on the words, trying to speak without crying.

"What?" Torren was alert, looking from her to Kanan. Beside him, Aster's brow creased, waiting.

She looked between them. How did she even start?

"Raven?" Aster's brows rose.

"Stay together." Her eyes met Torren's pointedly and then shifted to Aster before coming back to rest on Torren, reluctant to speak the next words. "He said he's going to kill her."

Torren's head whipped between the two of them, his eyes going wildly from her to Aster to Kanan and back to her. "What?"

All color drained from Aster's face, her shoulder's dropping, a word formed on her lips and then disappeared with a breath. She tried again. "Why?"

Her father stepped up beside them, brows drawn together, clearly picking up on the tone of the conversation.

"I don't know." Raven bit her lip, fighting the wave of hopelessness that seemed about to take her under. "Because of the King? Because you helped us? I don't know. Just stay together."

"What good is staying together going to do?" Torren's voice was whispered but angry. "He could kill her from over there." He gestured to where Kanan still crouched by the water, splashing the cool liquid over his face, seemingly ignoring them.

"I don't know, alright!" Her voice, pitched high and breathy, did not sound like her own. "I don't know!"

"What exactly did he say?" her father asked.

"He just said he was going to kill her. Maybe tomorrow." Raven glanced at Aster, hating every word that came from her lips.

"How?" Aster's shaking voice was barely audible over the softly flowing stream.

Raven swallowed. "He didn't say," she lied.

Torren rocked back onto his heels and then dropped fully to sit on the damp ground. "How did this happen?"

Raven sat too, crossing her legs in front of her. "I don't know." Her voice was no louder than a whisper.

Behind them, Kanan had returned to the horse where he stood, rummaging through a saddlebag. "You should eat." He pulled the pack of food Raven had purchased from the saddlebag and took a few steps toward her before tossing it at her. She caught it on pure reflex.

He tore a bit off the end of a slice of jerky with his teeth, glancing at the sky. "Doesn't look like rain, but we should build a fire. It'll get colder when the sun goes down. Wood?"

Raven studied him, still feeling the warmth of his hand on the small of her back, trying to find Kanan behind the mask that had been forced on him.

"Aster, want to help me get some wood?" The slight upturn to Kanan's mouth was enough to motivate Raven.

"No. No." She jumped to her feet. "I'll help,"

Surprise lit Kanan's face. "Alright, let's go. The rest of you stay close now, *no running off.*"

Kanan spoke the words lightly, but it was clear they were a command that could not be disobeyed.

Raven moved to his side, though she still kept enough space between them that he couldn't touch her. She couldn't handle another absentminded brush of Kanan's skin on hers.

He nodded behind him. "I guess you chose information over ignorance."

"They'll defend themselves." It was a statement but a warning to him also. She didn't want him dead before they found a way to fix him.

He looked at her like she'd sprouted horns. "No, they won't."

She swallowed. Under normal circumstances, they might try to defend themselves, but Kanan could make them yield. If the incident with Torren and the knife showed them anything, it was that Kanan didn't have to kill anyone. He could make them do it themselves. Something cold and icy snaked down her spine.

Kanan bent gathering together sticks for kindling. "Did you come to help me or just keep me away from the others?"

She didn't reply as she bent to pick up a large branch in her path.

When they returned a fire already blazed, a stack of wood piled beside it.

"Look at this. So helpful." Kanan dropped his armful of wood beside the rest.

The sun had begun to descend, painting pink and orange streaks across the sky. Raven studied the clouds. It wouldn't be long before the remaining light was blocked out completely by the trees.

Alone in the dark with Kanan. Every hair on her body stood as a chill skittered down her spine, stealing her breath.

"Beautiful."

She jumped, scrambling away from Kanan, cursing his ability to move so silently. As she moved, her foot snagged on a root, momentum sending her flailing. She threw her arms out in front of her to brace herself, but instead of hitting the ground, she was caught mid fall as Kanan's arms circled her waist.

Kanan held her close, her back against his chest. "Watch your step." His breath skated across the shell of her ear, sending her hair billowing.

Her breath hitched and she closed her eyes, counting silently backward, trying to regain some sort of control over herself.

"Why are you trembling?" Kanan hummed softly in her ear. "Don't you miss this?" His thumb began to trace circles where he held her.

Her breath shook out of her, a reaction to the way he held her and the memory of his touch. "I do."

He turned her in his arms so she was facing him, his fingers still pressed firmly into her hips. She looked away, unable to meet his eyes, desperately wishing she could seep into the ground, anything to be out of his grasp. Something seemed lodged in her chest and it hurt, making breathing difficult.

His gaze burned into her and suddenly she had to know. She dragged her eyes to meet his, searching. Looking as deep as she could behind the olive irises she loved. He had to be there. Something that was really him, something had to be left from before this nightmare in which they now lived. She could not believe that he might be gone forever, it hurt too much.

He held her gaze for a moment before a smirk turned up the corner of his mouth. "What are you looking for?"

"You."

He dipped his head, his lips brushing her ear. "I'm right here."

Ice dripped down her spine, stopping to lodge in her stomach. She broke his gaze. "No, you're not."

His grip tightened and she stiffened as his voice dropped, taking on a low, seductive quality. "I could be whoever you want me to be tonight."

She closed her eyes, tilting her head away, wishing he would stop talking.

He traced a thumb down her cheek and over her bottom lip. "And you would enjoy it. You would pant and scream my name, right here for everyone to hear."

His mouth hovered a breath from hers, and as much as she wanted to, she couldn't turn away any further. Helplessness enveloped her. He could, he could do all of that and she would be powerless against him.

"P-please..."

Her voice was small and weak and she hated herself for the sound. But she had nothing else. He was completely in control of this situation, they both knew that. Even if she fought back, he would still be in control.

But then to her complete shock, he released her and stepped back. She swayed at the sudden loss of support. "Suit yourself. Maybe Aster's lonely."

Kanan turned to walk back to the fire and Raven followed, urged on by fear of what he might do.

Kanan seated himself in front of the fire, leaning back against a large boulder. "Are those berries?"

Between Aster and Torren sat a large leaf filled with small purple berries.

"Not sharing?" Kanan looked at Aster, his eyebrows raised. Immediately she stood, picking up some of the berries and carrying them to him. He held out a hand and she dropped the berries into his palm. "Thank you, Aster."

"Leave her alone."

Kanan turned his attention on Torren, looking amused at the other's tone. "I didn't touch her. Yet."

Anger sparked in Torren's eyes and he shifted to stand, but Raven's father caught his arm, pulling him back as Aster refilled the berries and moved back toward Kanan.

"Aster..." There was a pleading to Torren's word.

Kanan held Aster's gaze, the only sound was leaves crunching as he repositioned himself.

To Raven's horror, Aster lowered herself onto his lap, facing him, her knees on either side of his thighs.

"You should eat something." Kanan's fingers played across Aster's thigh. "We have another long day tomorrow." He took a long swallow from his water skin. "Saints, I wish I had wine."

Raven couldn't pull her gaze from Kanan and Aster. Would he kill her now? Right here? Her stomach churned. She needed to eat something but everything inside her was tied up in knots.

"Don't you wish there was wine?" Kanan handed the water skin to Aster and she took a long pull from the bottle. "Sebastian, do you remember that wine that we had at last year's harvest gathering? That had to be your best."

"Yes." Raven's father's gaze was wary and attentive and Raven admired the sense of calm that had seemed to settle on him. She wished her own heart would take note.

Kanan took another drink of water and suddenly his eyes lit up. He was planning something. Unease grew and she shifted uncomfortably in her seat, waiting.

"Aster, have a drink." He handed Aster the water skin, and Aster swallowed some of the liquid. "Isn't that good wine?"

Aster's expression turned surprised and she shared an almost conspiratorial look with Kanan. "The best. I usually prefer white wine, but this is amazing."

Every gaze narrowed on Kanan. Kanan gave them a pointed look before he returned his attention to Aster. "*Have another drink.*" He gave her a grin and nudged her elbow, and she brought the water skin to her mouth again.

She swallowed down a long drink.

"*Tell your friends to eat.*" Kanan took the water skin from her and handed her a strip of jerky. He held out the skin to Raven. "Wine?" He winked.

"No, thank you."

"Raven, it's so good!" Aster said. "Have some."

"Listen to her, Rae." Kanan brushed Aster's red curls from her face, his fingers lingering on her neck. He chuckled. "Have some wine."

"If she won't, I will." Aster reached out and took the water skin back from Kanan.

A low chuckle emerged from Kanan. "Careful, you'll get *drunk.*"

"Worth it." Aster swallowed down a gulp.

Raven glanced at Torren. Horror shone in his wide eyes and she thought he might be trembling. Silently she begged him to keep his seat.

"Wine, Sebastian?" Kanan held the water skin out to him and laughed.

"No, thank you." Her father's tone was icy. How could he appear so calm? She longed for that ability. Instead her stomach buzzed like she'd swallowed a beehive, like the insects were under her skin, searching for a way out.

Kanan shrugged and handed it back to Aster. She took another drink and giggled. "I think I'm drunk." She let her head drop back, her shoulders going slack.

Kanan's gaze raked over Aster's exposed throat and down the front of her top before he shifted his eyes and smiled at Raven. She could only describe his expression as wicked.

He looked back at Aster as he raised his hand to brush her hair back again, letting his fingers brush along her temple and down her face. Aster let out a long sigh as Kanan's fingers drifted softly down over her neck, tracing the neckline of her shirt, curving over her breasts.

He turned his attention on Raven as he brought both hands to rest on Aster's hips before working them under her shirt.

She wanted to look away but it was like something prevented her. A burning sensation filled her chest as she watched Kanan's hand rove beneath Aster's shirt. She was so familiar with his touch she could almost feel the way his fingers brushed over skin. A desire to reach out and still his movements hit her, guilt close on it's heels, because the desire didn't come from concern for Aster. No, it was because he wasn't supposed to be touching other women like that. She nearly choked on a bitter laugh at the idea. Did she want him touching *her* like that? Not now. Not like this. *Saints.*

Kanan smiled at her, licking his bottom lip like he knew what she was thinking. His hands moved higher and Aster reacted, her chest rising on a long inhale, as she leaned into his touch. Her eyes fell shut and she shifted her hips on his lap, seating herself lower on him.

Raven swallowed down whatever churned inside her. From the corner of her eye she saw Torren move, and her father again reached out to restrain him.

Aster let out a soft moan as Kanan's hand's moved under her shirt, tracing from her chest to her back and returning to her breast. She shifted her hips again, a more desperate whimpering sound slipping from between her slightly parted lips.

Kanan looked at Torren and smiled. "She ever make these sounds for you?"

Even her father wasn't quick enough to restrain Torren as he leapt from his seat and lunged toward Kanan.

Raven screamed, "Torren!"

In the same instant, Kanan's hand was wrapped around Aster's throat.

Raven's heart thundered in her chest as Kanan leveled his gaze on Torren. "Sit down."

Sebastian looked on, his usual composed expression gone, replaced by wide-eyed fear. He again caught Torren's arm.

Raven pleaded, her eyes darting between Aster and Kanan and Torren. "Sit down, Torren, please."

Aster's face grew a bright shade of red as she struggled for air.

With a wild, panicked look between Raven and Aster, Torren backed off, returning to his place. His chest heaved as he threw his hands in the air. "I'm sitting. I'm sitting."

Kanan withdrew his hand from Aster's neck and she gasped, inhaling deep, gulping breaths. Raven let out her own breath.

Kanan shifted Aster off his lap. "I'm going to get some sleep. I don't care if you sleep or not, but understand this: *you will not run and you will not attempt to kill me in my sleep.*"

The coercion of his words settled into her, stripping away her free will. It must have been what a bird trapped in a too small cage felt like.

Kanan moved to a kneeling position, looking to where Aster still sat beside him. He reached out to trace his thumb along her jaw. Then, looking directly at Torren across the fire, he leaned down to kiss Aster.

It was a lingering kiss. His mouth worked over hers, their tongues sliding together, as his hand moved down over her neck and over her shirt, cupping around her breast. Aster moaned into his mouth, reaching up to grasp a handful of his tunic in a tight fist.

When Kanan came up for air, he was still watching Torren with a smug smile. "Goodnight."

Raven drew her knees up to her aching chest, resting her head on them. Emotions rioted inside her. When Kanan had kissed Aster, her already broken heart had shattered into so many pieces that she didn't know if it was possible to mend it. She'd never seen him kiss another girl. It had always been her. But the very idea of him pulling her into his arms and kissing her when he was like this exacerbated the churning in her stomach.

Tears slipped silently down her face as a coldness seeped into her, a coldness that went deeper than the temperature of the air around her. Would she ever have him back? She stole a glance in his direction and found him watching her, a small smile on his mouth. She shivered, it was not a smile that spoke of love. Kanan threw her a wink and stretched out on the leaf-covered ground, folding his arms behind his head and closing his eyes.

THIRTY

Torren scrambled to where Aster sat, her attention fixed on Kanan. She had a finger on her lip, a dazed expression on her face.

"Come on, Aster, come over here with me." He placed his hands gently on her shoulders and she allowed him to help her to her feet.

Raven watched Kanan, wary of movement. But beyond cracking an eye open to peer at them as they moved to the other side of the fire, he did nothing.

Torren stumbled slightly as Aster shifted all of her weight onto him, looking up into his face. She giggled. "You have pretty eyes. So brown." She reached up and gave him a soft bop on the nose. "Will you stay with me?"

Torren threw Raven a helpless look. "Of course I will. Just come over here." He led her back to where he sat and she dropped to the ground, resting heavily on him. In moments, she was asleep, and Torren shifted her so her head was in his lap. Raven joined them, trying to get as far from Kanan as she could.

"Can't we just leave?" Torren whispered.

"No." Exhaustion edged Raven's father's words. "I've tried.

He'd tried? "What happened?"

"Nothing." He shook his head. "I couldn't move."

"So what, we just wait to die?" Panic filled Torren's voice. "We'll be back at the palace tomorrow!"

"And then the fun begins." They turned to Kanan. He still lay stretched out on the leaves, eyes closed, arms behind his head. "Also, I'm going to kill her." He lifted a finger, pointing it at Aster.

Torren moved so quickly, Aster's head hit the ground and dirt flew as he stormed to his feet. "You son of—"

Both her father and Raven lunged to catch him, though neither of them was fast enough.

Kanan was. He hadn't even moved, but Torren's words were cut off as he hit the ground, curling into himself, his feet scraping the dirt and leaves as though he could run away. His fingers dug into his scalp as he clutched his head, a groan pushing through his gritted teeth.

"Kanan, please?" Raven's hands shook as she rested them on Torren's back, his muscles tight and rigid. She knew the pain, she had experienced this trick of Kanan's.

As quickly as it had started, it stopped. Torren still trembled, panting, but his hands that had been clenched around his head relaxed and Raven could feel his muscles loosen.

Kanan's head rolled to the side and he fixed Torren and Raven in his icy glare. "You're lucky I'm tired." He closed his eyes again and turned his head back toward the sky.

"It's alright, you'll be okay," Raven tried to reassure Torren.

"Hey, Rae, if you get cold, there's a place by me," Kanan called out.

She held her breath, waiting for the command she wouldn't be able to ignore. Instead, he shrugged and remained quiet. She blew out a quiet breath.

She and Kanan had slept under the stars before, curled around each other for warmth. Looking at him, eyes closed, seemingly asleep, she could almost imagine things were normal. There was nothing outwardly different about him, certainly not when his face was relaxed in sleep. At that moment, he was just

Kanan. She almost wanted to go curl up beside him. She'd never wanted so desperately to wake from a nightmare. She swallowed, forcing the tears back.

Her father slid an arm around Torren and helped him move back to where he had been. When Torren had settled into the spot, he lifted Aster's head and placed it back in his lap. She slept on.

"We should sleep, as well," her father said.

Raven turned an incredulous look on him "How?"

"Try. He doesn't want us dead, he's taking us back to the palace." Her father's brow creased. "And I don't know what's planned for us when we get there, but I expect it would be better dealt with if we get rest."

Raven looked away, she knew exactly what awaited them. Kanan had explained it to her in great detail as they rode together. A shudder rocked through her. How could she sleep?

"If not sleep, rest." Her father moved back to lean against the trunk of a tree. "Just try."

Raven moved to lean against a large tree on the other side of where Torren sat, still brushing Aster's hair back from her face.

Raven's chest tightened, forcing air from her lungs. If she could just go back, back to that day in the wine cellar when she'd overheard her father and Logan talking. If she could just turn around and walk away, ignore the things that were not her business. Go back and not tell Kanan what she'd heard, not draw him into this. Everything that had happened was her fault. Because of her decisions they were doomed, Logan was dead, and Kanan was the villain, taking them back to face the King.

Again her attention turned to Kanan. Asleep, features relaxed, he was the man who'd proposed to her. The man who'd crafted her sword. The one who'd gotten drunk with her on a bottle of her father's wine when they were both far too young. The man who would trace his name across the skin of her back in the wee hours of the night. She could almost feel the tips of his fingers gliding over her. Her breath caught painfully.

"Rae, you're staring." She jumped and looked around. There was no reaction from the others, and she was surprised they slept. "You have something to say or are you just admiring the view?"

She swallowed. "Is the King going to fix you when this is over?"

Kanan heaved a dramatic sigh as he pushed himself to a sitting position. Raven stiffened; she hadn't intended to have a conversation. Then Kanan was on his feet, brushing at his pants. He moved closer to her and her whole body tensed at his presence.

"Relax." He stopped a few feet from her, tossing some sticks into the glowing embers of the campfire. "I have bigger plans for you, don't you remember? You, me, hot iron?"

Was she supposed to be comforted or alarmed by those words? She held her breath when he stepped closer, stooping to gather more sticks.

"I'm not broken, Rae. I don't need to be fixed." He dropped the sticks into the crackling flames and took another step toward her. He stood so close she had to crane her neck back to look at him. "How do you know this isn't the real me?" He kicked her foot softly for emphasis. "That whatever the King did just released my inhibitions?"

She shook her head. "Because I knew you when you were twelve and you helped me care for an injured bird. That's who you are, kind and compassionate, under whatever it is the King did to you." She brushed away the tears that had begun sliding down her cheeks. "Not someone who takes pleasure in hurting people. In hurting me."

He crouched in front of her, holding her gaze for a long moment before he reached out and took a lock of her hair in his hands. He wound it through his fingers. Emotions warred inside her as Kanan gave a soft tug and released the hair, allowing it to spring back into place.

"You keep telling yourself that." He stood and moved back to his spot. "Get some sleep."

She buried her face in her hands as the hollowness inside her seemed to expand, near silent sobs shook her body. The only other sound was the crackling of the fire.

"Up. We have an appointment." Kanan punctuated his command with a kick to her foot.

She jumped as her eyes snapped open. The brightness of the sun, sitting high above the clearing where they'd slept, left her blinking. She'd actually fallen asleep? Kanan stood by his horse, cleaning her sword. Something dark covered the long cloth. She blinked again, trying to focus.

"This'll never come out now." Kanan sounded annoyed as he swiped again at her blade.

Her vision cleared. Blood, the cloth was covered in blood. She whipped her head to where the others slept and terror seized her. They lay lined up in a neat row, a dagger protruding from each one of their chests, blood soaking the ground around them. She clapped a hand over her mouth as a scream worked it's way up her throat. Then the word came, one word, over and over, crescendoing with each breath: "No. No! No!"

"Raven, wake up!"

She opened her eyes to find her father kneeling beside her, shaking her. Her eyes shot to where Torren sat, watching her with wide eyes, Aster still asleep in his lap. Alive.

She twisted her neck to find Kanan watching her with an amused expression. "You alright over there?"

She sagged back against the tree trunk, her breath leaving her in a whoosh. A dream. How had she even fallen asleep?

"It's alright." Her father ran a hand over her back, the gesture reminiscent of her childhood. "You're alright."

"No," she spoke quietly. "None of us are alright."

He remained quiet. He'd never cared for lying.

"You can come lay with me." There was almost a playfulness to Kanan's words. "I'll keep you safe for the night. I promise. I'll have you nice and relaxed in no time, I can even keep the dreams away."

She looked at him sitting on the ground, an arm propped on one knee, the other leg stretched out in front of him. Beside him was the empty spot where she fit so perfectly. It was easy to imagine settling in beside him and resting her head on his chest, because she'd done it so often. She swallowed.

Kanan shrugged. "You should go back to sleep. You'll probably wish you would have tomorrow."

She met her father's and Torren's eyes, neither of them looking like they wanted to sleep.

"Let me help," Kanan spoke. "Raven, *look at me.*"

The compulsion weighed on her, tugging at her. She had no control as she turned her head to meet his olive eyes. He stood and moved toward her. She had a vague sense of her father protesting, but Kanan waved him away, and from the corner of her eye she saw him stumble backward to the ground.

Alarm blazed inside her head, her body telling her to run, but she couldn't tear her gaze from Kanan's. When he was in front of her, he dropped into a crouch and reached out to run a warm finger over her cheek before placing it under her chin and tipping her head back. His eyes held hers for a long moment and she thought they looked like her Kanan's. Then he whispered one word: "*Sleep.*"

She had only seconds to panic before darkness crowded in.

She was being softly shaken. She pried her eyes open to find Kanan beside her, his hand on her arm. "Rise and shine, love."

She sat up; the others, including Aster, were already awake. Aster sat by the edge of the small stream, filling the water skins while her father doused the campfire, extinguishing any remaining embers.

Raven walked over to the stream and dropped down beside Aster, splashing water on her face. "Are you ok?"

Aster squinted at her. "My head is pounding, I feel like I have the worst hangover ever."

"Do you remember anything?"

"Not really." Aster shrugged. "Did we have wine?"

Raven shook her head, feeling sympathy for the other girl. "All you drank was water, but he told you it was wine and you acted like it was."

Aster's eyes went wide with alarm. "What did I do?"

Raven opened her mouth to answer, but Torren appeared on Aster's other side, giving Raven a pointed glance.

"What? Tell me," Aster demanded, her gaze shifting between the two of them.

Raven ignored Torren's warning look, instead facing Aster. "You kissed Kanan."

Aster's head turned in Torren's direction, her mouth falling open. "Not really?" She looked back at Raven.

Raven closed her mouth. There was nothing she could say to make it better.

"Up!" Kanan ordered. "Grab your packs, let's go. It's only a few hours to the palace."

Raven choked on the breath she was inhaling, her stomach churned. The pictures Kanan had painted so clearly about what would happen at the palace reformed in her mind.

"Unless you want to bathe?" Kanan looked at Raven and gestured to the stream.

"No, thank you," Raven answered.

"Shy?" He smiled. "It's not like I haven't seen it all before." His eyes did a slow perusal of her body, down and then up. "I know every inch of you."

Her cheeks blazed and she hated herself for giving him the satisfaction.

His smile widened, but then he shrugged and walked back to the horses. "Let's go."

They stood and Aster groaned. "How can I have a hangover from water?"

Torren shot an unpleasant look in Kanan's direction. "You can't. He's still doing it."

"He's still in my head?" A look of distress crossed Aster's face, and she wiped her brow as though she could wipe him away.

Raven glanced between them. She didn't expect Kanan to care, but they couldn't be worse off than they were. She moved to where he stood buckling his bag on his horse.

His hands ceased their movements but he didn't look at her. "Something I can do for you?"

She swallowed. "Make Aster better." Even Raven wasn't sure if it was a question or not.

He began again to work the buckle. "What makes you think I'm doing anything to her?"

"She drank water, not wine." Annoyance crept into her tone. "You don't get a hangover from water."

Kanan turned his head toward her before he glanced at where Aster and Torren were readying their horse, her father doing the same beside them. Then he leveled his full attention on her.

She inhaled and, with effort, held his gaze. He scared her, everything about him scared her now, but she had no desire to give him the satisfaction of seeing that in that moment. She did her best to keep her breathing steady.

He took a small step toward her and then another until there wasn't even room for air between them. She had to tilt her head back to hold his gaze.

He cocked his head to the side. "What'll you give me?" He waited, but she didn't answer. He bent his head toward her and lowered his voice to a conspiratorial level. "A kiss? A real kiss."

No. No, no, no. Her mind screamed the word. She couldn't. Her resolve slipped.

Kanan continued, his voice dropping again to a seductive level. He reached out and trailed a finger lightly up her arm, from her wrist, past her shoulder, until his hand came to rest on her neck, his thumb moving softly under her jaw. "Long and slow and deep? Let me taste you? Run my hands over you while you moan into my mouth?"

She couldn't. She couldn't do it. She tore her eyes away from his. Something inside clawed, calling her a coward. He wouldn't help Aster without this cost, and she couldn't pay it. It was only a hangover, no one died from hangovers. Aster would have a headache, maybe a queasy stomach, but she would be fine. Guilt roiled in her gut.

A low chuckle rumbled from Kanan and he dipped his head. "It's okay, Rae. I won't tell. She'll be dead by the end of the day anyway."

Her head snapped up to meet his eyes, but he had already turned back to the horse. "Mount up. I have things to do." He swung up onto his horse.

Torren met her gaze with a question in his eyes. Another churn of guilt in her stomach caused her to drop her attention to the ground, and she shook her head. Kanan huffed a small laugh.

Kanan turned an amused expression on Aster. "Don't worry, it won't last long."

Raven stiffened at his words. To anyone else, it would sound like an encouragement that this would pass, but she knew it for what it was. A threat.

Kanan spoke again, "Aster, why don't you ride with me today?"

Aster's head whipped toward him from where she was just about to climb onto the horse with Torren, fear shining in her eyes.

"No." Raven's voice was barely above a whisper, but Kanan heard her anyway. He looked down to where she stood beside his horse.

"No?" He raised an eyebrow.

"No," she repeated only slightly louder. "I'll ride with you."

He studied her face for a moment. "Fine. You're always welcome in my lap." He reached a hand down toward her and she took it.

"Did you miss me?" Kanan whispered in her ear as he nudged his horse to begin walking.

Tears sprang to her eyes. She did miss him. The last time they'd been on a horse together, before their Saints forsaken assassination plan, they'd gone to their favorite place along the river and shared lunch. Neither of them had made other plans that day, only to be with each other. She'd told him about the broken barrel in the wine cellar and he'd told her about the new anvil he ordered.

They didn't discuss mad kings or changing the world. They discussed nothing, for hours, and it was perfect. And she longed for it. She would give anything to go back and start again even from that day. To make different choices.

"Yes," she whispered the answer to his question on an exhale.

"Yes?" Kanan echoed her word back to her. "So where's my kiss?"

"Not you." She knew he already knew, but she said it anyway.

"I'm still me."

"No, you're not." Deep sadness spread through her, giving her limbs a numb quality. "Do you remember the bird?"

"What bird?"

"When you took me to see the lemon trees at your house and we found the bird on the ground." Her voice broke. "It was dying, we couldn't help it. I was so upset, I cried and you hugged me." She sniffed but didn't bother to wipe her tears. "I thought you were perfect, I was eight but I still knew." She allowed the sob to burst out before sniffing again. "That's the Kanan I miss, the one I hope is still inside. The one who held an eight year old girl when she cried. The one who would never do the things you're doing, certainly wouldn't threaten to kill Aster or anyone."

The saddle creaked as he leaned closer, his words and his tone both showing her story had had no effect on him. "It wasn't a threat."

The blood in her veins ran cold at his deadly tone and she squeezed her eyes shut.

He leaned back. "If it bothers you so much for me to kill her, I could just have Torren do it."

"No." The word was a plea. She wanted to scrub away the images that formed in her mind.

"You prefer I do it then?"

She shook her head. "I prefer no one dies. Why do you think you have to kill her?"

"Treason." His tone brooked no argument. "Your fault. She wouldn't be in this mess without you."

"Because she's my friend," Raven said. "Not because I made her do anything. She wanted to help me and Torren. They're close. Don't you remember what it's like to care about someone?" She couldn't say, *'Me. Care about me.'* "You used to."

"Raven."

He spoke her name softly, quietly, the way he had so many times. A dull ache formed in the back of her throat and she tried to swallow it down as she braced for whatever his next words would be.

"I don't care." His voice was still quiet, but it held an edge as sharp as any knife. She stiffened in her seat.

For a long time they rode in silence as Raven's mind wandered ahead, down the dirt road, past the trees that were beginning to grow orange and red, to the palace and what awaited them. It was like the trees were closing in on her, stealing the air around her.

"Hey, hey, we need a break." Torren's panic edged voice pulled Raven from her thoughts. "I think she's sick."

"Are you doing this?" Raven turned her head to speak to Kanan.

He shrugged. "Hangovers."

"Why don't you just stop it then?"

He leaned in and his breath tickled her ear. "Kiss me."

She pulled her head as far away as she could manage on the horse. He laughed quietly.

Torren had reined in his horse and jumped down, pulling Aster along. As soon as her feet hit the packed ground, she doubled over and vomited up her breakfast.

Torren shot an angry look at Kanan from where he knelt beside Aster. "What are you doing?"

"Why is everyone assuming this is me? When you drink like she did, you get sick."

"It was water!" Torren shouted.

Raven's father had dismounted and come to stand beside Aster. "You'll be alright, it'll pass. Drink." He handed Aster the water skin and she gave it a wary look. "It's water, I promise." He took a drink himself and offered it back to her.

She took a long drink and immediately spit it back on the ground. Kanan laughed.

"Stop!" Raven surprised herself as she brought an elbow back into Kanan's ribs causing him to grunt.

Kanan caught her arm and she flinched at the pain as his fingers dug into her flesh. He stared hard at her as he spoke to the others. "Fine. Drink."

Aster brought the water skin to her lips and tasted it tentatively. When she was satisfied it was water, she took a longer pull. Raven exhaled.

Kanan suddenly yanked her close to him, close enough to put his face an inch from hers. His words were slow and vicious. "If you ever hit me again, you will regret it, instantly." She gulped down the air in her throat as his fingers dug harder into her arm. "Do you understand me?"

He continued to apply pressure until her fingers began to tingle. "Yes," she said through teeth clenched so tightly it hurt.

Immediately he released her. "Good." He raised his voice to be heard by the others. "We've stopped long enough, let's go."

"She's not well." Raven's father stood beside Aster.

"She can get back on the horse or I can kill her here," Kanan replied. "Either way, we're leaving."

Raven didn't want to believe that Kanan would kill Aster, but she also didn't want to test him. "Come on, Tor, get her back on the horse."

"I'd listen to her if I were you." The warning in Kanan's voice was clear.

Neither her father nor Torren hid their glare as they helped Aster stand.

"I'm fine," she said, waving them off. "I just needed some water."

Even Aster threw a look of hatred in Kanan's direction. Torren mounted the horse and Raven's father helped Aster on, as well, before climbing onto his own horse.

Kanan inhaled deeply behind her. "If we stop again because of her, she's dead." He left no space for protests as he pulled at his horse's reins and urged him back onto the road. "We should be at the palace before noon. If there are no more interruptions."

THIRTY-ONE

"Beautiful."

Kanan spoke the word like a prayer, drawing her attention upward even as her heart plummeted to her feet.

The palace was indeed beautiful. When she'd first arrived with the King all those weeks before, they'd entered through a rear servant's entrance, directly to the stables. But now Kanan led them to the front door.

"There were times when I was a boy and my grandmother had business in the area. I always begged her to bring me along just so I could see the palace."

For the first time in a long time, he sounded like the Kanan she knew. Then she remembered his dark promises.

"Keep up," Kanan said to the others as he urged his horse to go faster. Raven bounced against him as they sped on. "Hang on, darling."

"I'm not your darling." Raven's voice was choppy, matching the horse's hoofbeats.

They passed through the outer wall that ran the length of the grounds and the palace came into full view. There were no obstructions to block out the dark grey granite walls or the mighty towers that rose to scrape along the clouds.

Her eyes drifted to a tower far to the right where ivy climbed its way up to the crenulations.

Would Kanan lock her in a tower? Or would it be the dungeons for them? The beauty of the palace dulled as she imagined what would happen once they were inside the walls.

Kanan slowed his horse, allowing it to walk toward the ivy-covered tower, then passing it and continuing until servants wearing mostly yellow sashes greeted them. Kanan stopped the horse and tossed the reins to one of the servants.

"Everybody down." Kanan swung off the horse, his boots thudding on the ground. Then he reached up to lift Raven down, as well. His hand lingered on her hip, as he bent his head toward her, meeting her eyes. "You stay right here." She didn't feel any command in his words, though there was nowhere she could go anyway.

Her father dismounted, handed his horse's reins to one of the servants, and moved to her side.

Torren and Aster both remained on their horse and Kanan heaved an annoyed sigh. "I'm waiting." Aster still looked a bit green and it was obvious she still didn't feel well.

Slowly, Torren climbed off the horse and reached up to help Aster down. As soon as he placed her on the ground, her knees buckled beneath her.

A breath puffed from Kanan's nose, as though he were a dragon and could breathe fire. His eyes flicked to Raven and then back to Torren and Aster.

Raven saw the moment he made the decision. Her breath seized, actually stopped like there was no more air around her to draw in.

"I've had enough." He closed the distance to Torren and Aster in a few long strides.

Her breaths resumed with the thudding of her heart as raw terror hit Raven. She knew what was coming. He'd been telling them since yesterday.

"No! Kanan, no! Please?" She launched herself at him, catching his arm in both of her hands, pulling at him with all her strength.

He stopped and looked down at her, unamused. "You going to kiss me now?"

"Yes!" Yes, she'd do anything to keep him from killing Aster. Saints, anything.

His eyes met hers, and they held no surprise or amusement. "Too late."

Torren had moved, placing himself between Kanan and Aster. His eyes were wide, mirroring the terror inside Raven. Her father had also moved, standing close and looking helpless

Kanan shook Raven off hard enough that she nearly lost her footing. He continued moving toward Torren.

"Leave her alone." Torren's words were more pleas than statement. His hands were clenched into fists at his sides, but they still shook.

Kanan shoved Torren with one arm, sending him crashing into Raven's father, both of them sprawling far off to the right of Aster. Raven moved to run, to place herself between Aster and Kanan, but Kanan turned to her.

"I said: *stay there.*" With one look from Kanan, she was rooted where she stood, unable to move. Unable to do anything but look on in horror and beg him to stop.

Everyone else in the courtyard, guards, servants, everyone had stopped to watch the scene unfolding before them.

Kanan approached Aster and bent down, pulling his dagger from where it had been concealed in his boot. He latched onto her shoulder, pulling her to her feet. "Sorry, Aster. It's really not personal."

In a blink Kanan pulled his arm back and drove the dagger forward. It slipped easily into Aster's chest and her eyes went wide, her mouth opening into a silent gasp. Her body slumped forward, falling against Kanan.

Raven screamed and screamed.

The world seemed to stop around her, everything going silent and narrowing to that place where Kanan—*Kanan*—stood. One hand on Aster's shoulder, the other, turning a shiny crimson, on the handle of the blade in her chest.

How could he come back from this? If they found a way to bring him back, this is what he would have to live with. That red stain would forever be on his hands.

The world resumed. Her screaming, Torren sobbing and calling Aster's name again and again from his place on the ground, Raven's father by his side, shock streaked across his features. And the sound of Aster's body as it dropped to the dirt at Kanan's feet.

Kanan leaned forward and took a handful of Aster's skirt to wipe his blade. The hold on Raven's mind released and she crumbled to her knees, shaking, screaming, gasping, "No. Kanan, Kanan, how could you?" The words a gasping lament as the tears ran, unchecked, down her face. Her chest ached and her body shook with sobs she couldn't control as she stared at Aster's lifeless body. A pool of blood had begun to seep around her, soaking into the dusty ground, turning it to a sickening mud.

Red. It was so red and there was so much and she couldn't help and Aster was dead and Kanan had killed her and the world was crumbling. She coughed, choking on her cries as she vomited into the dirt. Her father was next to her, kneeling in the dirt, his hand on her back. When had he moved there?

Raven was vaguely aware of Torren rising. She looked at him, his face wet with tears. He drew his focus from Aster's body and turned a furious look on Kanan. With a sound that resembled an animal in pain, Torren charged at Kanan.

Kanan didn't move, didn't so much as flinch, as he turned his head toward Torren, and Torren dropped to the ground like a sack of grain. "Unless you care to join her, I suggest you stay where you are."

Raven couldn't move but Kanan had nothing to do with it. She simply could not make herself move. He'd killed her. Kanan killed Aster. Raven began to shake. Not trembling—full body tremors that she couldn't stop shook her. Her father gathered her into his arms and held her.

Kanan called two yellow sashed servants over from where they had been looking on, their job of tending to horses forgotten. "Take care of this." He indicated Aster's lifeless body at his feet. "And these three, I have rooms ready for them, please show them there. I need to see the King."

Kanan's long strides carried him away from them.

"He killed her. He killed her." She clung to her father, sobs now joining the quaking of her body.

"I know." Her father's hands smoothed the hair on her head, his voice steady and calm.

He was trying so hard to be strong for her, but she could feel his quick short inhales and exhales where she was cradled against his chest. Servants murmured around them, but Torren's cries rose above all other sounds. She turned her head. He was on the ground on his hands and elbows, sobbing as his fist pounded the dirt beneath him.

A pang of guilt hit her. She had been so focused on Kanan, on what he had done and how she didn't know if he could come back from it, how it would haunt him forever, that Torren's pain at losing Aster had been pushed to the side. Her heart broke for him as she took in the despair in his form.

"What are we going to do?" She fought to gain control of her breaths and emotions but her words were still clipped.

"I don't know." Her father's words were clearer, more solemn, and she pulled away enough to look at him. His face, wet with tears, held a note of resigned finality. She knew where his thoughts had wandered. If they couldn't fix Kanan, there would be only one other way to stop him. Another sob escaped her lips. She loved Kanan, but this wasn't him. Was he even in there? And what if he was? What if he *knew* what was happening, aware but unable to do anything to stop it? It might be a mercy to end him. Her cries quieted but the tears still ran in unending rivulets down her face as her stomach twisted painfully.

They joined Torren who now knelt beside Aster's body, Kanan's command finally gone. His shoulders shook violently as he gasped for air between sobs.

A thought struck her, a foolish one, but it was the only idea she had. Kanan was still nowhere to be seen. Doing her best to avoid looking at Aster, she reached out and placed a hand softly on Torren's back. He started at the contact, turning to face her. She swallowed. She'd never seen him like this. Torren was always the one who could be counted on for a joke or a smile, but he knelt in front of her now, utterly broken. His eyes were red, his face wet with tears and snot, and he had a look of helplessness that might have broken her heart if she let it. She willed herself to push those emotions down; she needed to be firm and clear and couldn't afford grief right now.

"Torren." She cast another glance around the yard, at guards and soldiers who'd gone back to work. "You have to get out of here."

On Torren's opposite side, her father placed a hand on his shoulder, pulling him off the ground. To any observer, it would look like they were just trying to pull him away from Aster's body. "You can't do anything else for her."

Raven was infinitely grateful that her father seemed to understand her plan.

"She's gone, but you can still help us." Her father's voice was quiet but demanding. "Raven's right, you need to leave. Go, Torren."

"Go?"

Raven froze, her heart plummeting to her feet. She knew the voice that spoke behind her, recognized it instantly. All hopes of escape dissolved into wisps of smoke as she turned. Her neck craned up and up to meet the gaze of the broad-shouldered, blonde soldier. Holden.

Holden reached down and clamped a hand around Torren's arm, the dust scratching beneath his shoes as he was dragged to his feet. Raven and her father stood as well.

Behind them, two servants finally came, picking up Aster's body and carrying it away.

The four of them stood, staring at each other. Holden's gaze surveyed the area before he met Raven's eyes. She bit down on her lip as he held her gaze for a long moment, then turned his attention on Torren. "Hit me."

"What?" the word hissed from Raven's lips as shock and confusion roiled inside her. Was it a trap? Another game?

"Hit me. Now," Holden insisted, begged. "Hit me and run. If you make it behind the stables, you can find the servants' tunnels."

Torren's expression cleared, understanding, and he blinked back the tears in his red-rimmed eyes, sniffing, before he gave a quick nod of his head.

"Now!" the word ground out from between Holden's clenched teeth.

Raven jumped as Torren pulled his leg back and let it fly at Holden's groin. The large guard cried out and dropped to the ground. Torren didn't look back as he exploded into action, running for the woods behind the stables.

In moments, more soldiers swarmed them, catching Raven and her father in vice-like grips. Others helped Holden to his feet while still others pursued Torren into the woods. Raven prayed to any Saint that would listen that Torren would be able to get away.

Her eyes found Holden's, blue and still pinched in pain and holding her gaze. He had helped them. Why?

THIRTY-TWO

Inside the palace, the guards led Sebastian and Raven through a labyrinth of staircases and hallways until they came to a pair of rooms. Raven didn't recognize this part of the palace. It was nowhere near the King or his rooms. At least she was glad for that. Malakai was certainly one of the last people she wanted to see. Not to mention Esrae.

One of the guards opened the door to the first room. "You, in here." He shoved her father inside and closed the door.

The guards pulled Raven to the next door and pushed her inside. "Kanan will be back soon," one of them said before pulling the door closed, the lock clicking into place.

She pressed her ear to the door and listened to their retreating footsteps. When she couldn't hear them anymore, she tried the handle. As she had expected, it didn't budge at all. She turned, taking in the room. It was large, much larger than the room she'd slept in as a servant. But dark wooden floors and stone walls made it feel tight. A large fireplace was set off to the left of the door and behind her was an ornately carved, four-poster bed. A mustard-colored coverlet was spread across it as though it was awaiting guests.

"Raven?"

She turned toward the sound of her father's voice. It was so clear, like he was standing in the room with her. She rushed to the wall and pressed her ear against the cold surface. "Papa?"

"Raven, are you alright?" he asked.

"I'm fine." She stepped back, scanning the surface of the stone. How was it possible she could hear him so clearly? Her eyes snagged on the vents near the ceiling. Three of them were cut into the wall between the two rooms.

"I'm going to lock him in a room next to you."

She swallowed hard, panic pushing in as she recalled Kanan's words.

The sound of voices sent her heart into a gallop. "Someone's coming," she hissed through the vent.

"I hear them," her father replied. "Be safe, Raven."

She stepped away from the wall and moved closer to the door. Be safe? She strained to hear what was being said outside, the conversation sounding tense.

The door opened and Kanan stepped inside, his eyes glinting with controlled anger. When he spoke, his voice remained calm but sharp with a deadly edge. "Where is he?"

Raven took a deep breath. "Who?"

Kanan cocked his head to the side, and at the same moment, a searing pain hit Raven. *Saints,* her head was going to explode! She clutched at her head, trying not to fall to the ground. It only lasted seconds and then she was gasping for air.

"I said: where is he?" Kanan repeated.

She heaved in deep breaths through teeth gritted tight, still holding her head. "Who?" she huffed out, her voice shaking.

Kanan nodded. "Alright."

He strode to her, stopping only inches in front of her. Instantly, the pain returned, though this time it was so much worse. Her head was going to crack in half. Her hands fisted in her hair and her knees buckled. She hit the ground, her knees cracking off the hardwood. The pain grew worse and she could no longer keep silent. A high pitched keening sound escaped her teeth.

Distantly she though she heard her father calling out, but she couldn't tell what he was saying. Instead, the pain in her head was so intense it seemed to come with with a sort of deafening nothingness.

Once again, the pain stopped. Kanan dropped into a crouch in front of her, his hand closing around a fistful of her hair, pulling her head up, forcing her to look at him. "Where is he?"

"Gone," she said between large gulping breaths.

Kanan smiled. "He won't get far. We'll find him."

He released her hair and she slumped back to the ground, her palms slapping the floor as she panted on her hands and knees.

"He's long gone," Raven said with effort. "You won't find him."

"It's just a matter of time," Kanan said. "Until then, we'll just have to find a way to occupy our time."

He studied her before standing again. "But, I think, him first." Kanan cocked his head in the direction of her father's room.

Any defiance she had dredged up against him evaporated. She rocked back to sit on her heels, trying to shake her head but stilling when the movement caused too much pain. "Kanan, please. Please don't do this?"

Kanan reached down and placed a finger on her lips. "Shhh. You should save your energy. You're going to need it."

He pulled back and there was no time to react before he let the back of his hand fly at her face. The pain was momentary before her vision swam and blackness poured in.

He caressed her face and goosebumps prickled her skin as his fingers danced softly down her arms, along the side of her breast and stomach, until his hand came to rest gently on the curve of her hip, his skin warm on hers. "I love you." His whispered words tickled her cheek as he placed a soft kiss on the corner of her mouth. She smiled into the kiss.

Raven opened her eyes, blinking away the fog in her head. She didn't know where she was at first, the remnants of the dream still on the edge of her consciousness.

A series of deep, groaning cries from the next room put everything back into stark focus.

"Papa!" She tried to leap to her feet, but unexpected resistance held her back. Her heart began to pound as she tugged and pulled frantic to be free of the ropes binding her hands and feet, but they were secure.

How long had she been out? Hours? Days? How long had Kanan been in there with her father?

Sebastian's cries continued. "Papa!" she screamed for him, straining at the ties, tears streaming down her face. "Papa!"

The cries quieted and then stopped completely. And suddenly she was back in the throne room when Logan's cries had ceased. Her heart sped and missed, and her vision swam, threatening to pull her back under.

The door to her room opened and Kanan strolled in ."Good morning. I was just visiting your father. He says 'hi'. He's having a nap right now."

Relief hit her. Not dead, he wasn't dead. "You never loved to hear yourself talk this much before," Raven said.

"What can I say?" Kanan said, as he walked over and the bed dipped when he sat down next to her. "I'm a new man."

She turned her head away from him.

"Look at me," Kanan ordered. She did not comply. "I could make you, you know."

She flinched away when Kanan reached up and brushed the hair from her forehead. Still she looked away, though fear gnawed at her.

The thought of him controlling her, of that power that he had over her... Her breath hitched.

"How long was I asleep?" she forced the words through her gritted teeth to keep her voice from shaking.

"All night. It's a new day, Rae. Did you miss me?" Kanan asked, his fingers still dancing lightly across her forehead and across her face and jawline, trailing down over her dress. She stiffened at the touch.

"Don't you miss me? Conversations in the middle of the night? Sword fighting in the vineyard? Walks along the river? Making love under the stars? Tea and wine and muffins and secret betrothals?"

His voice was soft and sweet, like his touch, but Raven knew better. The mention of his proposal was like a knife twisting into her heart.

"I miss Kanan. You're not him. You're just a monster wearing his face."

He fisted a handful of her hair, pulling, forcing her to face him. "You're wrong about that, you know? I'm still the same man that asked you to marry me. I have the same memories, the same desires." His eyes drifted to her lips. "I still want to do this."

He leaned down, covering her mouth with his. The kiss was gentle at first but soon grew more demanding, and then the pain started. Knives of torment lancing through her head. The pain grew and she wanted to scream, but Kanan's mouth still covered hers. She could only squeak into his mouth as her back arched. She pulled at the restraints, needing to hold her head. It would come apart if she couldn't hold it together.

Finally, Kanan released both her lips and her mind. She fought desperately to catch her breath.

Kanan's thumb slid under the hem of her shirt, lifting it to expose her ribcage. "Do you remember the last night we were together in the palace? You told me I didn't need an invitation." He bent and placed a featherlight kiss just above her naval. Her breath caught and she froze under his touch. He hummed as he ran an open palm across the skin. "You are mine, Rae, and I'm going to make sure everyone knows."

A soft hiss drew her attention. She sucked in a stuttering breath as her eyes came to rest on the small knife he held in his hands. Instinctively she pulled away, but the ropes that held her would not relent.

A smirk turned up the corner of his mouth as he laid the blade softly against her cheek and slid it down her jaw and over her collarbone. With his free hand he held the collar of her shirt as he drew the knife across the fabric, slicing her clothing open. A low hum of approval issued from his lips.

She held her breath as he rested the blade below her neck and drew it down slowly over her sternum, then along the underswell of her breast until the cold metal of the blade came to rest on her bare ribs.

Kanan glanced at her and then back down to the knife. "Something so you'll always remember me. As if you could forget."

She squeaked, panic clawing at her insides as she strained hard against the ropes.

Kanan stood, turning to look her in the eye. "Hold still, now. I don't want to mess this up. Feel free to scream, though. I don't mind, and you won't bother anyone else, either. Trust me, we're quite alone in this part of the palace. Except for your father."

Her body seized at his words, at the blade of the knife resting on her skin. She was unable to control the way her body shook, panic buzzing in her chest, her heart thudding against her ribs.

He ran the blade along her stomach again and suddenly the sensation of cold metal was replaced by white-hot pain as the knife dug into the flesh just to the side of her hip.

Her entire body went taut, fingernails digging into her palms, the shaking resuming as the blade cut into her. She could feel warm blood running over her skin. But the sensation was nearly eclipsed by agony of the blade carving into her. A scream built in the back of her throat before it burst from her lips in a loud keening groan.

It seemed to last for hours, hours of cutting and screaming and tears. It couldn't have been hours, but it seemed that way. When he finally stopped, Raven's whole body trembled against the ropes, and she couldn't get air to make a difference. Every inhale seemed to do nothing.

Kanan's hand was on her again, around where he had cut. "Perfect." He leaned over her so he could look her in the eyes. "Now, it's no question. You're mine. My initial, right there, in the flesh."

He looked back down at his handiwork and then back at her. "It really turned out better than I expected." He paused, examining the K he had carved into her flesh just beside her hip bone. He reached down and ran a finger along the edge of one of the cuts. Another jolt of pain rocked her body, blurring her vision, and she cried out, spasming against the ropes.

He stepped back and studied it for a few long moments before he leaned over and met her gaze. "And we're only just getting started."

Raven's breathing was finally starting to come at regular intervals, but she turned her head away from him. Tears ran out of the corners of her eyes. She couldn't look at him. She couldn't see the face of the man she loved and associate him with this pain.

A thought reared in her mind: Was the Kanan she knew in there somewhere? Was he aware of what was happening, of the things he was doing? She hoped for his sake he wasn't aware of anything.

Kanan stood. "Enough. For today."

Raven released a breath, wanting to cry in relief.

Kanan pulled at the tendrils of her hair that sweat had plastered to her forehead. "Get your strength back. I'll have food brought for you both and I'll be back tomorrow,"

He brought the knife close to her again. Red stained the edges of the blade and she jerked again at her bonds, her heart palpitating wildly.

"Relax, Rae." He moved the knife lower and suddenly the resistance on her hands and feet was gone as he sliced through the ropes that held her. "See you tomorrow."

Raven refused to watch him leave, to look at him at all. But she breathed a heavy, stuttering sigh of relief when the door closed and the lock clicked into place. She tried to lift her arms and a sensation like being pricked by a thousand tiny pins coursed through them. Her muscles and joints ached from being held fast for so long. When she tried to sit up, a new wave of pain hit her from the wound Kanan had left.

With effort, she hoisted herself onto her sore elbows and peered down at the bloody mess on her lower stomach. Just as he had said, a perfectly cut letter K now marred her flesh. Would mar it forever; even when it healed, if she lived that long, she would have a scar.

She considered pulling her shirt off but the thought of the effort it would take made her nauseous. Instead, she pulled the ends that Kanan had cut together and secured them in a knot beneath her breasts, far from the angry wound.

Every movement was an effort. Her fatigue reminded her of the day after you were sick in bed. Bone deep weakness. Careful not to twist or bend or stretch any more than she had to, she slid from the bed. She turned toward where a small table sat with a pitcher and a basin and stopped. A mirror stood along the wall and in its reflection stood a bruised and bloodied girl. Her lips parted on a small gasp as she took in the sight. Blood smeared across her stomach where Kanan had wiped it away, and still more blood traced trails from the slices in her skin to soak and stain the waistband of her skirts. A large purple bruise had formed on the side of her face where Kanan had struck her.

She tore her eyes from the grim sight and continued to the basin. As best she could, she cleaned herself up, washing away the stains of blood. And then carefully, gingerly, with trembling hands, she cleaned the wound. Every drop stung and an aching soreness was beginning to settle into the cuts. She had no way to bind the wound. She'd considered the bed sheet, but the thought of the effort it would take to tear the cloth caused her hands to shake even more.

She turned to move back to the bed and was once again greeted by the sight of the girl in the mirror. Now, with the majority of the blood washed away, the angry red letter on her hip stood out even more.

She swallowed as it settled on her. This is what she would look like from now on. Forever branded by her intended, but not her intended. She squeezed her eyes shut and tears flowed down her cheeks. With her eyes closed, so she didn't have to see the reflection. She turned toward the bed. She wanted to curl into a ball on its soft mustard blanket and sob, but that was impossible. She couldn't even sit without causing the edges of her wound to pucker and pull. Instead, as carefully as she could, she lay back on the bed where she brought her hands to her face and sobbed.

"Raven?" Her father's voice filtered through the grate, thick as though he was just waking up.

"Yes?" she choked out. It came out too quietly. She took a deep, lancing breath and called out louder. "Yes?"

"Are you alright?" There was pain in his words, as though it hurt him to speak.

"I'll be fine." What use was there to worry him further?

His voice shook. "What did he do to you?"

Nothing would make her answer that question. "I'll be fine," she repeated. "I just need rest."

Exhaustion pulled her under and her dreams were filled with Kanan's mocking smile and whispers of all he would do to her.

THIRTY-THREE

Raven jolted awake at the sound of someone moving about in the room. Before she could think, she'd jumped and scrambled backward. The pain was white-hot as it lanced through her, and the high-pitched sound that tore from her throat startled her. It had been two days. Despite what Kanan had promised, he hadn't been back the previous day. It was just another form of torture. Let them wait and anticipate and expect the horrible things that were coming, and then wait some more.

"I'm sorry. I'm so sorry. I brought you breakfast," a small shaking voice said from the foot of the bed.

The girl's eyes were wide and terrified as they rested on the cuts on the lower portion of Raven's stomach. They'd begun bleeding freely again with the sudden movements.

She was young and wore the blue belt of a kitchen servant. The tray in the girl's hands trembled, the sounds of cups and saucers clinking against each other filling the space.

"Put the tray down," Raven encouraged through gritted teeth.

The girl seemed to come to her senses and quickly placed the tray on the table. She backed away, eyes wide and unblinking. Was she even breathing? She raised a trembling hand and pointed it at Raven. "You're bleeding," she stammered.

If Raven had the energy, she might have rolled her eyes at the obvious statement. As it was, she glanced down at where she could already feel the blood trailing. "Yes. Thank you."

The girl's eyes snapped up to Raven's, wide as though she had just remembered something extremely important. "I can't talk to you. I have to go."

"Wait—" But it was too late, the girl had already disappeared out the door. The lock clicked into place.

Raven moved to slide from the bed and winced, letting out a whimper. She cursed as she shifted, each movement causing the edges of her wound that had begun to mend together to pull apart again.

She needed food, even though she really didn't have much of an appetite. She pulled in a careful deep breath and blew it out in a slow steady stream, focusing on that instead of the pain as she made her way to the table where the girl had left the tray.

Eggs, bacon, juice, and water. Raven took a bite of the bacon, but her stomach revolted almost instantly. She clamped her lips together as she placed it back on the plate. Instead, she picked up the glass of water and the white cloth napkin and moved back to the bed. She used the napkin and the water to try to clean the cut better. She hissed, squeezing her eyes shut at the burn as the water washed away the fresh blood. She hoped keeping the wound clean would lessen the scarring, but didn't expect it.

She had just finished when a door, not her own, banged closed.

"Sebastian."

Raven froze. She dropped the napkin and slowly slid from the bed. Through sheer force of will, she moved to the wall, pausing beneath the vent.

"-pitiful father," Kanan was saying. "Is it easier to justify it all now? It's not your fault she's mixed up in this, it's Logan. She's his blood, not yours. Maybe she's even a little disposable. Not really your daughter."

Her father interrupted, "She is no such thing. Raven is my daughter. She will always be my daughter."

Emotion bubbled inside her, forming a lump in her throat.

"Always, until I kill you. Then instead of two fathers, she won't have any." Kanan's voice was cold.

"Kill me then," her father taunted. Raven wanted to scream "*No!*", but she couldn't make a sound. "Get it over with. You're a lot of talk, Kanan. You never talked this much before."

"Am I?" Kanan did not sound amused.

Then she heard the sound that was now too familiar. It started as a low rumbling groan that quickly escalated into agonizing screams.

She began pounding on the wall that separated her from her father, her palms slapping against the rough stone. "Kanan! Stop! Please, stop!" Sweat beaded on her brow as desperation filled her.

Kanan's voice came through the vent loud and clear. "Don't get excited, love. I'll be there in a minute."

Her father had stopped screaming. He spoke, his words coming out between panting breaths, "Leave her alone, Kanan, please? Me. Not her."

"I have orders to make you both pay," Kanan spoke the words as though he'd already explained this a thousand times. "I find it appealing that I can kill two birds with one stone."

"But you've already done it," her father huffed.

"Stop begging, Sebastian, it's not becoming,"

The door opened and closed. She jumped back, moving as far across the room as she could. Instincts told her to hide, but what good would that do? She could only move to the back wall, pain slicing her with every step.

The door opened and Kanan stepped inside. "Good morning, Rae." He stepped up to the table and helped himself to a piece of bacon. "That's good. Did you have some?"

Raven made no sound as her emotions warred with each other. Kanan stood before her, eating a piece of bacon. A completely normal act, but she didn't feel normal. Instead, his presence brought with it a bone deep chill. She was afraid of him, and that was not supposed to be normal. Yet in the past days it had become so, and that left her feeling heartbroken.

"You're bleeding." Kanan gestured toward her with another piece of bacon. "I'll have a physician come take a look at that. Wouldn't want an infection."

He studied her for a few moments. She wanted so desperately to see some of the old Kanan in his eyes, but there was nothing. No light, no dancing mischief, no affection, only scrutiny and cruelty.

"I'll send the physician now and come back later." He glanced at the fire. "That'll need to be stoked. I'll send someone for that too."

He took one last piece of bacon and pulled open the door. "Oh, I almost forgot. Torren said 'hi', or 'agh', or something like that. He probably would have said 'bye,' too, if he'd had the chance, but sadly, he wasn't thinking clearly." With one last smile, he exited the room, pulling the door closed behind him.

Torren? A sob punched from her as he chin dropped to her chest. They'd caught Torren and killed him. Grief ripped a gash inside her.

She had stopped crying and now sat on the bed, staring at the floor but seeing nothing. How had they ended up here? Only weeks ago they were gathered, happy and laughing around the table at her house. Now their group of six had been shattered and torn apart. Logan was dead. Aster was dead. Torren was dead. Esrae had betrayed them. She and her father had been dragged to the palace. And Kanan—Kanan's mind had been remade into the King's monster.

Raven longed for Logan's wisdom. She missed Kanan so much it made her chest ache. And she was afraid. Not only physically, but of the future. If somehow they managed to escape all of this, she was afraid that everything that had happened between them had ruined their relationship forever. She didn't want a life without Kanan, but how could they have any hope now?

Once she used to dream of Kanan and his smile and the life they had and would have. Now when she slept, she still saw his face, but it was only in nightmares. She dropped her head into her hands and allowed herself the luxury of tears; real, flowing, unquenchable tears.

Her door opened sometime later and an older, rather kind-looking man entered the room. The physician.

"I was sent to tend to your wound. Please lie down." His voice sounded stiff and unnatural.

"Are you alright?" Raven asked.

"I am not to speak with you beyond the necessity of tending to your wounds. Please lie down here," the man answered.

A sigh pushed through her teeth. She'd been holding on to a hope that maybe when the physician came, he might be able to help her beyond only tending to her wounds. Clearly, Kanan had the same thoughts and had taken preventative measures.

"He was afraid you might help me so he told you not to talk to me."

Carefully, Raven lay back on the bed. The physician had no reaction at all when he saw the mark. She let her head fall to the side so she could look at the man, "In case you're in there, I just want to let you know that I'm not angry with you for not helping me."

The physician did not speak but went straight to his task, checking and prodding and cleaning the cut that now took up space on her hip. He pulled a roll of white cloth from his bag and she nearly sighed with relief. Carefully, after covering the wound with a pale yellow salve, he wrapped the cloth around her waist. She was glad to have something covering it finally.

"I will return tomorrow to check this again and care for your other wounds," he spoke the words with no emotion as he repacked his bag.

"I have no other wounds."

"Not now." Ominous words. A spike of fear stabbed at her, leaving her hands trembling. The physician exited the room, and Raven was left staring at the door, dread coiling into a tight knot inside her.

THIRTY-FOUR

"Raven?" her father called from the other side of the wall.

Though it still hurt, it was much easier to move with the bandage wrapping her wound. She moved to the vent. "Yes?"

"Are you alright?" he asked.

"I am." She didn't want to talk about what happened wtih Kanan. It was done and there was nothing he could do about it.

"Raven, he told me what he was going to do to you." He stumbled over the words, his voice laced with pain.

She swallowed. He knew? Did he know everything? Nausea rolled through her. She didn't reply to his statement, instead she changed the subject. "Are you alright? I heard you."

"He was only in my head," he said it as though it were nothing.

"Only?" Kanan had been in her head too. It certainly was not nothing.

"Raven."

"I'm alright. Really." She tried to sound convincing. "He said he would be back later. I don't know when." She paused for a moment. "They killed Torren."

The silence stretched for a long time before her father spoke again. "You should rest."

"I hardly think that's a possibility." There was no way she could rest knowing that Kanan could walk in anytime to make good on his promises.

Raven's door opened and she jumped, eliciting a sharp pain.

"I'm sorry, miss." *Maci.* It was the girl who tended the fires. "I was told to come stoke the fire."

Raven's stomach leapt to her throat, dread filling the space it had vacated.

"I have bigger plans for you, don't you remember? You, me, hot iron?"

The girl didn't notice Raven's reaction as she grabbed the iron and prodded at the embers. "It seems warm enough in here. Were you cold?"

Raven could barely inhale enough air to breathe out a shaky "no," in response to the girl.

Maci's eyes passed over Raven. "Are you sure? You're shivering."

Raven swallowed. "I'm not cold."

The door swung open again and Kanan's large form filled the space. His gaze cut to Maci, where she stood next to the fireplace. "Leave."

"Of course, sir." Maci replaced the poker and poured the shovel of coals that she held into the flames before she quickly gathered her things and moved to the door. "You shouldn't need that, it's burning quite well."

Raven followed Maci's gaze to Kanan's hand. A long shudder shook her body as her throat closed up. In his hand, Kanan's perfect hand, he held a long iron poker.

Kanan lifted the iron, his eyes running the length of the metal before he focused beyond the poker to Raven. "It's not for the fire."

The girl glanced between Kanan and Raven, fear filling her eyes at the implication.

"I said: leave." Kanan still looked at Raven.

"But, sir, I—" she began.

Kanan turned his attention to the girl, pointing the end of the iron at her slim figure. "I said: leave."

She didn't speak again. She didn't even look at Raven. She turned and fled the room, taking her bucket with her.

Kanan turned to the fire and buried the iron deep into the dancing flames. Her heart began to thump in her chest, pounding so hard she wondered if she would pass out. She wished she would. Her shoulders heaved as her instinct to flee crushed her. But there was nowhere to go. She backed away from him until she hit the wall behind her, her whole body trembling.

Kanan continued to advance on her until he was directly in front of her, towering over her. His eyes searched hers. He looked at her like he was trying to work something out.

"What?" She spoke with more confidence than she felt.

He reached up and ran his thumb over her bottom lip. "I'm just thinking about kissing you."

"Is it a nice memory?" She barely managed to speak the words without her voice cracking.

He tilted his head to the side, his look softening just a bit. "You know it is."

"I can fix that." She brought her knee up, hard, into his groin.

He lurched forward, letting out a loud grunt through gritted teeth. He caught himself with both hands on the wall behind her, caging her in place. Any softness in his gaze was gone. He glared at her, panting hard, and the vile word he spat at her using Kanan's voice was so awful she flinched.

He slid his hands off the wall enough to clamp them around her arms, painfully. He spoke through gritted teeth, "Let's make new memories."

His hands tightened around her arms until she knew it would leave bruises. She squeaked. Kanan pulled her away from the wall and then slammed her body backward again, causing her head to connect violently with the stone. Blackness swam at the edge of her vision before it enveloped her altogether.

THIRTY-FIVE

Raven woke with a start, pulling at the ropes that, once again, held her. The back of her head throbbed like a pulse. She was sure that if she had been able to reach up and touch her head, she would find a knot.

"Welcome back."

She turned her head in the direction of his voice and found him standing over the fire.

"You know..." He turned, taking slow steps toward her.

From where she lay it was hard to see, but every few seconds she caught sight of the glowing tip of the fire iron as he swung it.

"I was thinking about before, how I would have felt if someone hurt you and I couldn't do anything about it."

Before. As though now he didn't care. And of course he didn't.

He stopped beside her but continued speaking. "How I would have felt if I had to listen to your screams, knowing you were in that much pain and I was helpless to do anything about it. Devastated. I would have been broken."

Kanan brought the glowing poker down to her forearm and a soft hiss filled the air as it left a two inch brand. The action had been so sudden she hadn't had time to prepare, not even to take a breath. A strangled scream wrenched it's way free from her at the searing, white hot, pain.

"Just the thought of someone torturing someone I love, really, I can't imagine." He moved the iron, bringing it down again.

The pain. She couldn't think around the pain. It shot through her arm and up into her neck. She screamed again but had no time to recover before he was branding another mark next to the first two. Her body jerked and shook involuntarily, pulling at her bonds. Her stomach threatened to revolt at the smell of burnt flesh.

He lifted the iron to examine the tip. "Time to reheat."

She clamped her teeth together but it wasn't enough to hold in the sound that was part scream, part groan. She lifted her head to look at her arm but couldn't see it clearly; her vision was blurred and it felt like her whole arm was on fire. The pain was worse than when Kanan had cut her. She fought to pull in a full breath, but it felt like the air was no help.

Kanan was speaking again, as he stirred the flames. "Remember what we talked about? Just a little record to keep track of all the people you pulled into this mess? Of all the people you got hurt, or killed." He pulled the iron from the fire and moved back to her side. With the glowing orange tip he pointed to the marks on her arm, each in turn. "Me, Torren..." He met her eyes, giving her a disappointed look. "Esrae." He moved and this time Raven had enough time to pull in a breath, though it was no help when the tip came down on her skin, tracing another tick mark.

"Aster... What a waste there." Another mark. "Your father."

She screamed. Saints, it hurt so bad, her body shook against the restraints. Why? Why wouldn't he stop?

He raised his voice, turning his head toward the wall. "Did you hear that, Sebastian? That one was for you."

Tears ran down Raven's face as she tried to catch her breath. Kanan crouched down beside her, leveling his gaze on her tear stained face. "And Logan."

Raven tensed, holding her breath, squeezing her eyes closed, waiting for the last burn. But it didn't come, not right away.

Kanan reached up with his free hand and brushed her hair off her neck where it was plastered with her sweat. "I have a secret."

She didn't care, he could keep all his secrets. She just wished he would knock her out again so she didn't have to deal with the pain, at least for a while.

He leaned in close enough for his whispered words to tickle her neck. "He's alive."

Raven's eyes flew open and Kanan met her gaze, smiling. At the same moment, he brought the poker down one last time on her arm, leaving it just a bit longer than before. He gave a quick raise of his brows as she screamed.

When Kanan removed the hot iron, Raven fought yet again to catch her breath. She flinched when he pulled out his knife. Not again.

"Relax." He said as he brought the knife down to saw through the ropes that held her. "I'll send the physician and then I think I'll go see Sebastian." He picked up the fire iron and moved to the door.

"Wait!" Raven panted.

He turned, holding the door open, a questioning look of surprise on his face. "You want me to stay?"

She ignored the question. "Is Logan really alive?" Her words came out with a high choppy sound that surprised even her.

"Yup." Kanan pulled the door open but stopped. "Don't worry, I visit him all the time too. I'll tell him you said 'hi'." He stepped out of the room and pulled the door closed behind him.

She struggled with each breath as pain sparked up and down her arm. Her fingers twitched in response. The feeling of Kanan's whispered words in her ear lingered as a chill raced over her, cooling her.

Alive. A sudden sob burst from her lips, her injuries throbbing with the movement. Truth? Lies? She didn't know. She had no way of knowing if this was just another game he was playing. But if it wasn't... Logan was alive. Logan was alive and Kanan was hurting him too.

A thought slipped into her mind and the hole that had been growing steadily inside her opened wider. Maybe it would be better if he were dead. Maybe it would be better if they were all dead.

THIRTY-SIX

Kanan had left Raven and gone immediately to amuse himself with her father. Her father hadn't cried out, but the noises he had made through clenched teeth had been enough to make Raven press her hands over her ears.

The first thing her father had said when Kanan entered the room was, "You will regret ever having touched my daughter." Kanan's only response was to laugh.

Hours later, the door opened. Raven held her breath at the sound of the lock turning, but it was only the physician. She let out a small sigh of relief. The burns were large and angry on her arm and she hoped the physician had something to prevent infection. The pain was strange to her. The immediate area of the brands was not the problem. She assumed the nerves had been damaged there. It was the area around the marks. Her whole arm had turned red and the entire area seemed to radiate shooting pain that came in bursts. At times she had to close her eyes and force herself to breathe through the pulsing spasms.

The physician had the same glazed look he'd carried the day before. There was no reaction when he saw the burns on her arm, none besides general medical treatment. He did provide her with a salve to keep infection at bay, for which she was extremely grateful. He also changed the dressing on the wound on her stomach, which looked better as well.

When the doctor left, she lay down, hoping for sleep. Kanan did not return.

She woke to voices, not in her room, but her father's.

"Why her?" Her father sounded tired and so sad.

"She was part of your foolish plan."

The voice did not belong to Kanan. Indeed, in the last few weeks Raven had come to easily recognize the deep rasping tone. Malakai. The King was in the room with her father. She stood, trying to keep her groans of pain quiet as she moved closer to the vent where she could hear better.

"She's suffered enough." Sebastian's tone held a pleading note. "I don't know what he's done to her, but I know she's suffered."

"And you? Have you suffered enough?" Malakai asked.

"Do what you want with me, Malakai." The resignation in his voice squeezed something in Raven's chest. "Just let Raven go."

There was silence before her father spoke again. "If Serene knew what you were doing to her daughter—"

"Serene—" Malakai spit the word out, cutting him off "—would not have allowed this to go so far. She would never have entertained any talk of killing me. You know that."

More silence. "You're probably right. She always was better than us. Please, Malakai? Raven is still her daughter."

"I'm doing nothing to her daughter. I have done nothing to her daughter," Malakai answered.

"Saints! No, you're letting *him* do it because you wouldn't be able to. He's hurting her, Malakai. It would kill Serene. She loved her so much."

There was another long pause, and Raven swallowed the knot of emotion that formed in her throat.

Her father continued, "I know you cared for her. She cared for you too. She loved you."

"Not enough, apparently," Malakai said.

"Not like you wanted, but she did love you," her father said. "Please stop this? Do what you want to me. Be angry with me for trying to kill you. Be angry with me for marrying Serene. But please, for Serene's sake, stop what you're doing to Raven."

"Have a good night, Sebastian," Malakai said, and the door opened and closed.

Raven rushed back to the bed, afraid the King would stop at her room next. Each movement sent waves of pain through her as she climbed into the bed and pulled the blankets up to her chin.

Her breath caught when the door opened, but she quickly forced herself to breathe normally. It was an effort not to squeeze her eyes shut or burrow further under the blanket. As if that would protect her from Malakai.

She concentrated on breathing normally, praying that Malakai would think she was asleep and not wake her. Praying that he would leave.

She felt his presence looming as he drew nearer to the bed. Oh, Saints. Her heart began to pound. Could he hear it? She could tell, without looking, that he was standing beside her, could feel his gaze heavy on her.

Then his fingers were on her forehead, gently, brushing her hair back from her face. She tried not to flinch at the contact.

Malakai released a long, soft breath. Then, without saying a word, he turned and left. When the door opened and closed again, Raven's shoulders heaved as she released the tension.

She tried not to move for the rest of the night to give her wounds time to heal.

A loud clattering sound woke Raven.

"I'm sorry!" A young blonde girl with a blue belt stood wide-eyed next to the table. "I dropped the cup. I didn't intend to wake you."

Raven relaxed, exhaling a shaking breath, grateful she was not Kanan or Malakai. "It's fine, really. What time is it?"

"After noon, miss. You've slept for a long time," the kitchen servant answered as her eyes drifted to the bandages that encircled Raven's forearm.

"After noon? I slept that long? No one came by?" Raven said as she very slowly and carefully moved to a semi seated position.

"Well, they came to bring food, but you were asleep so they left."

Raven nodded slowly. No Kanan, no Malakai, no one. Was this another break before Kanan came for another round? What was left? A vague memory of him mentioning broken fingers popped into her head and she shuddered. Alternately, why were they still alive? She had a sinking feeling she would have an answer to that sooner than she'd like.

The young girl stepped toward Raven, but she seemed apprehensive. Raven was the last person, literally the last person, that any of the servants should be afraid of.

"What is it?"

"I'm sorry, miss," the girl began, her brow furrowing deeply. "I can't help you. I would if I could, but he said I can't."

"I understand." Kanan was certainly careful with those he sent into her room.

"But, I was wondering... I mean, we were told that Aster betrayed the King and left, and that she's dead now. Is it true?" The girl's voice was small, as though she was afraid to hear the answer.

A deep sadness settled in Raven's chest as the scene played out, yet again, in her head. Sadness for both Aster and Kanan. Aster's lifeless form on the packed dirt, Kanan's hands covered in blood. She closed her eyes, hoping to banish the memory, but it did nothing.

"Yes, it's true."

The girl's lip quivered. "I liked Aster. She was nice to me."

Raven forced a small smile. "She was nice to me too."

"How did she die?" The girl did not meet Raven's eyes.

Raven couldn't bring herself to say that Kanan did it. She could still barely believe it herself. "She was stabbed, with a dagger."

"My..." The girl's voice was only just above a whisper and she'd gone slightly pale.

"Are you alright? Do you need to sit?" Raven shifted to make room beside her, the action sending pain through her stomach and arm. She did her best to hide her cringe.

"I'm fine." The girl's eyes widened. Apparently she hadn't hidden her reaction very well. "I brought you food."

Raven looked to where the girl indicated. A plate of eggs and sausage sat on the table. "Thank you." Then Raven realized she didn't know the girl's name. She stood, gritting her teeth. "What's your name?"

"Mara, miss," the girl's voice came out as a whisper as she watched Raven move.

Raven swallowed and held up a hand, forcing the best smile she could. "Please, don't call me 'miss'. Call me Raven."

The door opened and both she and Mara turned toward the sound. Raven's stomach dropped.

"Leave us."

Mara's eyes grew wide as she dropped into a low curtsey. "Yes, Your Majesty."

THIRTY-SEVEN

Raven pushed to her feet though she did not curtsey. It wasn't out of any act of rebellion. She was simply frozen, fear twisting inside her as she watched Mara leave, leaving her alone with the King. As though the girl provided any protection. Still, she wanted to call out to her and beg her not to go. Whatever Kanan had done to her was sure to pale in comparison to what Malakai would do. The door closed behind Mara, and Raven blew out slow steady breaths, trying to stay calm.

Malakai noticed, his head cocked slightly to the side. "Have you forgotten what I told you? Slow your breathing, take deeper breaths, count backward."

"Counting, sure. What order did the numbers go in again?"

"You should relax," Malakai said. "I'm not here to hurt you, and Kanan will leave you alone today. You and Sebastian both."

Raven swallowed. She hadn't expected a reprieve. There must be a reason.

Malakai studied her. "I prefer you both to have your strength tomorrow."

There it was. "Tomorrow?" Raven managed to ask.

"When I will call the palace together and inform them of yours and Sebastian's betrayal." He sounded sad. "Then you will pay for your crimes."

It was a final statement and it would be a final act. A chill crawled up her spine, raising the hairs at the back of her neck. "And Esrae?"

Had she seen an actual spark in Malakai's eye at the mention of Esrae's name? When he spoke, his voice was wistful. "She is remarkable. I've never met anyone like her."

Raven furrowed her brow at the King's comments. "What will happen to her?"

"Nothing," Malakai spoke with confidence. "She will stand with me and support whatever I choose to do."

"You're so certain." She wasn't questioning him. It was just surprising to her that he had no doubt Esrae would stand with him. "You're so certain that if you bring her friends into your throne room and execute them in front of her, she'll just stand by you?"

"You forget," Malakai said, "if she hadn't told me of your plan, if she hadn't turned you over to me, then not only would I not have known of your treason, but I might also be dead now. She saved my life."

"That doesn't mean she'll be okay to sit by and watch while you kill her friends." Raven found her words coming easier.

"Esrae understands that justice must be paid," Malakai said.

"What did you do to her?" Raven couldn't understand what it was that had turned Esrae against them.

Malakai smiled, his eyes widening slightly, as though he was surprised by her question. "I did nothing to her. I'm not the monster you and your friends believe me to be. I simply listened when she spoke. Gave credit to her words, gave her a safe place to sleep. Treated her as an equal and not a slave. I showed her her worth. I complimented her, praised her, built her self-esteem. I gave her pleasure. I was kind to her. All things she seemed to be severely deprived of. I listened when she spoke and she listened when I spoke and she answered back. She's not afraid of me, not afraid to share her thoughts. It's quite refreshing.

And she understands that I can't let these things go. She didn't argue about Logan."

At the mention of Logan, all thoughts of Esrae dissipated. "Is he really alive?" Raven's voice came out much quieter than she had intended, desperate to hear the answer but afraid of the same.

"Kanan told you then," Malakai said. "He's physically alive. I can't speak to his mind. Kanan has been visiting him, as well."

A painful knot formed in Raven's stomach and tried to work its way up her throat. "And Esrae's okay with all of this? Just sitting by while you torture Logan and my father? While you torture me?"

"I haven't harmed you."

Something inside her snapped. She forgot her fear and moved in front of him, ignoring the sudden pain the action caused. Anger permeated her words. "Stop saying that! You turned Kanan into a monster! He would never have done any of the things he's doing now. You did this!"

Raven held out her arm, hissing in pain as she tore at the bandages, exposing the raised red welts. "If my mother were alive, she would kill you herself."

Malakai took a step toward her and dipped his head, his voice low and deadly. "If your mother were alive, we would not be here. Serene always chose to see the best in people. If Sebastian and Logan had told her of their plan, she would have put a stop to it. Your mother was kind. Always kind. To everyone."

"You think she still would have been kind to you if she'd known what you're really like? How you rip people away from their families? How you torture and kill people for the smallest offenses? For entertainment?" Raven's voice grew quieter. "How you take over people's minds and change who they are and make them do terrible things to the people they love?" Her voice broke. "How you turn people into monsters so the people that love them are afraid of them?" Tears fell down Raven's cheek.

Malakai pulled his gaze from hers to peer over her head at the room around them, though it seemed he was seeing something far beyond the four walls.

When he spoke, it was quieter. "If your mother were alive, we would not be here."

The words were the same, but it felt like they held a different meaning this time. She inhaled deeply, the breath shaking as she swiped at the tears. "Is there something else you wanted? Or did you just come to torment me some more?"

Malakai's gaze returned to hers. "You speak rather freely with me, no?"

Raven shrugged. "I've been tortured, mentally, physically, emotionally. You've already told me you're going to kill me tomorrow. I have nothing to lose."

Something almost like admiration sparked in Malakai's eyes. "Well, as I've also already told you, you have today. You won't be bothered again. Good day, Raven." He turned and exited the room.

THIRTY-EIGHT

Raven slumped into the chair beside the table, wincing at the pain. What did someone who was slated to die the next day typically do with their last hours? She reached across the table and picked up the fork and hurled it at the wall.

After the painful, emotional ride of the last few days, she could almost welcome the thought that it would be over soon. Her thoughts drifted to Esrae and her anger revived.

During the weeks leading up to putting their plan into action, and even after they'd made it to the palace, she'd imagined a lot of ways things could turn out. Esrae turning on them was not one of them.

"Raven?" her father's voice filtered through the vent.

"Yes?" she called back, standing and moving closer to the wall.

"It was quiet," he said.

"I'm alive." Raven let out a bitter laugh. "For now."

There was silence from the next room.

"Are you alright?" she called.

"I'm also alive." Something inside her twinged and she realized he must have felt the same when she'd spoken the words. She could readily admit that she was almost glad it was going to be over soon. But the thought of her father dying as well left a sick feeling in her stomach.

"He said we get the day off." She rolled her eyes. "No torture today."

"I heard."

"How does one spend their last day alive?" Raven mused.

"Sleeping?" he offered.

"I'm going to spend my last day alive sleeping?"

"Read a book?"

"Plot a way out of this?" If only that was an option.

"There's that," her father said.

"Do you think there's a way?" Raven didn't actually expect an answer. There was no way out.

There was silence for some time on the other side of the wall. "I don't know, Raven. I can't imagine how there could be."

"That's what I thought." Raven shrugged, even though he couldn't see. "We could just bust the doors down and leave. I could take the guards." She sighed again. She probably could take the guards if she wasn't in so much pain she could barely move.

"I don't doubt you could."

She leaned back, resting her head against the wall.

"Every last one of them," he continued.

Raven smiled slightly at his words but then it faltered. "Do you think Logan is really alive?"

For a long time there was no response. When he spoke, his voice was quiet and Raven had to turn her ear to the wall to hear. "I don't know. And I don't know if it would be better for him to be alive or dead."

Something tightened around Raven's heart. What kind of shape was Logan in? Both Kanan and Malakai had said Kanan had been visiting him. She knew what he'd been doing to her, could guess at what he was doing to her father. But Logan had already been beaten and tortured when she thought he'd died. What would more torture on top of that do to a person? How could someone, even someone as strong as Logan, endure that?

Before she could respond, the door to her room opened and Raven turned, expecting to see that Malakai had returned, or Kanan. But she had not expected to see the person who entered the room.

"What are you doing here?" Venom dripped from her words.

"I came to see you." Esrae's voice shook slightly.

Good, she should feel bad. Raven swallowed the lump in her throat and allowed the anger she felt to permeate her words. "Well, now you've seen me and you can leave."

"We were friends," Esrae said.

"Were we?" Raven's hands tightened into fists. "Because I don't think a friend would do what you've done."

"You don't understand." Esrae's voice rose as if she felt as though she could defend her actions to Raven.

"I understand." Raven gritted her teeth. "I understand so many things I never understood before. I understand what it's like to find out someone is your true parent, only to watch them die in front of you. I understand what it's like to look into the face of the man I loved and watch as he cuts into me and burns me for pleasure. I understand what it's like to hear my father in pain in the next room and know there is nothing I can do." Angry tears fell down her cheeks. "And I understand what it's like to watch the kindest man I've ever known bury a knife in my friend's chest. I understand, Esrae. Do you understand that all of these things are your fault?"

"Malakai didn't deserve to die..." Esrae's voice was still quiet, but an edge of anger seemed to have crept in.

"And we all do? Because now we will." Raven drew in a deep, seething breath. "I hope you're okay with that too. Aster, who had nothing to do with this, is dead. Torren, Esrae—Torren, your friend, is dead. Tomorrow you get to watch your precious Malakai kill me and my father and probably Logan, for real this time. Why? Why would you stand up for him? How could you?"

"He was only ever kind to me," Esrae blurted out. "Only kind. The first night I spent with him, we didn't do anything. He didn't force me or threaten me. He asked me questions. Asked me about me." Esrae planted a fist against her chest, above her heart. "Do you know how long it's been since someone took an interest in me?"

"I did, Es!" Raven's voice rose. "I was interested in you."

"Not like this." Esrae's voice was thick with tears. "You were my friend, but it wasn't the same as this. I don't know. I can't explain it. He made me feel special, like what I said mattered. Like *I* mattered. Like I should be something besides a servant who's abused. Like it was just me that he was interested in. He hasn't taken another woman to his bed since I came here."

"Well, congratulations. I hope it's all worth it," Raven bit out.

Esrae ignored her. "He's given me gifts. He's comforted me. He tells me I'm beautiful and remarkable. Raven, no one has ever said those things to me. No one ever thought I was worth anything. Certainly not a king. He didn't deserve what you all were going to do to him. You don't know him. You just need to know him."

Raven stared, disbelief drowning her. "And those nights where he pulled us all into his throne room and made us watch while he tortured and killed innocent people?"

"They weren't innocent, Raven," Esrae snapped, her voice laced with venom. "They were guilty, too, of betraying him. He's the King! He can't let these things go. If he does, everyone will turn against him." She flung a hand toward the walls as though she believed everyone was out to get the King.

"They should!" Raven was nearly shouting now. "He's a monster!"

"Don't say that!" Esrae spit the words at Raven. "You don't know him!"

"What about when he told you he wouldn't hurt us and then he did what he did to Logan anyway?" Raven countered.

"Logan was going to kill him! I told you. He can't just let those things go."

"And what about the rest of us? What about me?" Raven did her best to calm her words and lower her voice. She needed Esrae to hear her next words. "When he takes us into his throne room tomorrow and kills us. Will you justify that too?"

"He won't." Esrae shook her head. "Not if you change. Tell him you're sorry. Beg for his forgiveness. He may let you live, maybe even still let you serve here. Not in the kitchen or as his servant, of course. But he may let you clean, or something. You may yet live."

"I would rather die."

"And what about Kanan?" Esrae said. "You'll lose him."

"Kanan?" Raven asked, shock permeating her voice. She pulled at the sleeve of her shirt, flinching, exposing the marks and bandages. "I've already lost Kanan."

Esrae looked but didn't speak.

"Get out, Esrae," she whispered the words. "If this is my last day to be alive, I don't want to spend it with you."

Esrae inhaled deeply, squaring her shoulders and smoothing a hand over her dress. She didn't speak again, and after a moment she turned and left.

Raven moved to her bed and dropped onto the soft blanket. The marks Kanan had left on her stomach pulled with the motion, and she was vaguely aware she might be bleeding again. She ignored it. She hadn't wanted to cry, but she was being pulled under in a riptide of emotions. Her tears drenched the blankets around her, and she finally fell asleep, too exhausted to fight it anymore.

THIRTY-NINE

Raven's eyes flew open as a hand clamped down over her mouth. Her scream emerged as a squeak, and she blinked hard, willing away the sleep induced blur.

"Shhh, Raven, it's me," her assailant spoke, before removing his hand from her mouth.

Raven blinked, sure she was still asleep and dreaming. "Torren?"

"It's me," Torren assured her. "Can you sit up?"

Raven tried not to wince as she propped herself up into a sitting position. She was stiff, the cut to the side of her hip and along her stomach pulled, and arm ached. But she pushed it all aside. Torren was in her room.

"Torren, what are you doing here? They'll kill you. How did you even get in here?" She kept her voice low so anyone guarding her door wouldn't hear.

Torren gave her a sad smile. "I worked as a servant here too, remember?"

Raven wanted to slap herself for not thinking of it sooner. "The passages!" Could this really be their way out? She sat up straighter, feeling the cut on her stomach pulling again. "But why are you here? It's suicide to come back."

Torren reached into his tunic and withdrew a small leather pouch. "This is why I'm here."

Raven looked at the pouch, her brows drawing together. "What is it?"

A corner of Torren's mouth quirked up. "Wait here, I'm going to get Sebastian so I only have to explain this once."

Go get her father? Again she wanted to kick herself for not even considering the passages, and that they might exist in her room.

Torren disappeared behind a large, heavy tapestry that hung on the wall. In moments, she could hear Torren and her father speaking. And then, as though stepping through the wall itself, Torren reappeared, her father behind him.

Her father's appearance sapped the breath from her body. Tears sprang to her eyes. He was bruised and swollen, and walked with a limp as he moved to her side and folded her in his arms, tears in his eyes. She'd never needed a hug so badly in her life, though the sudden movement sent ripples of pain through her. She clamped her teeth shut, refusing to cry out. But as hard as she tried she couldn't stop a sharp hiss from escaping through her teeth.

Her father backed off. "I'm sorry."

"No, I don't care," she breathed. "I'm so glad to see you."

"You too," he agreed. He took her in for a moment before turning toward Torren, though his arm remained around Raven's shoulder. "How did you get here?"

Torren's eyes moved between them. "When you told me to leave, I had no idea where to go. I just ran. Then I remembered. Do you remember the story Aster told us? About the woman with the tea?"

At the mention of Aster, her mind replayed, in vivid detail, Kanan driving his knife into Aster's chest. Her stomach threatened to revolt as she blinked, trying to clear her head and focus on Torren's words.

The tea. Aster had told them the story of a woman who drank tea to suppress the ability to control people. Raven's stomach did another flip. "Yes."

"So did I, and I thought someone should tell Aster's family..." His voice faltered, and he swallowed before he continued, "Tell them what happened. So I went back to Kancar."

"I'm so sorry, Torren." Raven reached out and placed a hand on his arm.

He shook his head and his eyes dropped to her arm, snagging on the bandages. His gaze moved from her arm to her face, and then to her father's face, littered with bruises. Torren stood straighter, his eyes widening slightly. She could see the gears turning in his look as he put together the source of the cuts and bruises.

His eyes traveled between them again before he continued, "Anyway, I went back."

"I knew she said she had family there. But she didn't even try to see them."

"No." Torren shook his head. "She was trying to protect them. She thought if she didn't tell anyone they were related, then they wouldn't be counted with the traitors."

"Us," Raven clarified.

"Us," Torren echoed. "They didn't even know she'd been in town. When I found them, when I told them..." He pulled in a deep breath, shaking his head. "It was terrible."

Raven wanted to say something, to be of comfort to him but, "*Sorry my intended killed your girlfriend,*" didn't seem right.

"I told them everything. I thought they deserved to know," Torren said.

"And by 'everything' you mean...?" her father asked.

"Everything," Torren repeated. "I told them about the plan to end the King and how things went wrong. I told them about Logan and Esrae and Kanan. How Kanan has the King's ability now. And then I asked about this other person with these abilities, and Aster's grandmother told me the story."

Her heart, desperate for good news, skipped at Torren's excitement.

Torren shrugged. "She told us what Aster told us, about a girl with the same ability. She said she tried everything she could to find a way to get rid of it. She even went to people who claimed to have magic. When that didn't work, she tried a more natural route. She started to experiment with different plants and herbs. She said she tried for years until one day it worked."

"She found a way to turn it off." Her father's voice was wistful.

Torren nodded.

"Well?" Raven threw her palms out in front of her, desperate for more. "What? How?"

"Aster's grandmother said she thought it was just a simple blend of herbs," Torren said.

"But if we don't have the herbs, then this information does us no good." Her father sat back in the seat he had found as Torren spoke.

Torren smiled as he held up the small pouch that he had shown Raven earlier.

Raven held her breath and leaned forward. "Torren?"

"I found her." Torren's eyes widened, brow raising in emphasis. "She's old now, lucky to be alive kind of old, but I found her. She said no one should have those powers."

He placed the pouch, almost reverently, on the table. "She was more than happy to help. She said she brewed it and drank it as tea."

Raven fell back against her seat and squeaked as the movement sent bursts of pain through her. "How can that help us? They're not going to drink anything we give them."

"No, but she said they can be dried and crushed and inhaled too."

Raven sat up, something foreign blooming in her chest. She'd almost forgotten what hope felt like. "It won't be easy, but we have more chance with that than them drinking anything."

Torren pulled two more identical pouches from inside his tunic and placed them beside the first one. Every eye turned toward them. "Let's do it."

FORTY

Her father looked from the pouch to Raven and Torren. "Now we only have to decide what to do and how to do it."

Raven shook her head, her eyes on the small pouches. They had a chance. It was an extremely long shot, but they had a chance. "What and how, and when. There's no more time. Tomorrow is it. Tomorrow he drags us into the throne room and executes us. There are no more chances."

"No." Torren shook his head, then repeated the word louder, "No. We've been through too much for it to end like this." He stabbed his finger into the table, making a small thumping sound. "Especially when we have a weapon."

"We would have to get to both Kanan and Malakai at exactly the same time. If we don't, the other one will just…" She rubbed at her temple with her uninjured arm, her hope fizzling out as quickly as a flame doused with water. "And even then, that room will be full of guards. This is impossible."

"What if the guards aren't loyal to Malakai?" Torren asked. "I mean, he did kill Logan for just that reason."

Raven sat up straighter in her chair, this time feeling the edges of the cut on her stomach separate. "Tor! Logan! He's not dead."

Torren's eyes widened to the size of saucers . "What?"

"He's alive. Malakai and Kanan both said it. Though, by now, he may wish he was dead," Raven's father added the last part quietly.

"Which leaves us with one more problem," Raven said. "We can't leave him here. We have to get him out."

"Raven, I don't—"

"No." Raven cut Torren off with a tone that dared him to question her. "I will not leave him here."

Torren threw up his hands. "So between the guards and Logan, I tracked this down for nothing." Then he planted his hands on his hips and studied the ground, drawing in a deep breath. "What if I could get the guards away?"

"All of the guards? Everyone is called to the throne room for an execution," Raven said. "It's not like there'll only be five or six of them."

"There are people here who aren't loyal to the King."

The image of Luc dead on the floor flashed in Raven's mind.

Torren continued, "If I went to them and explained, they might be willing to help cause a distraction."

"Enough to get the guards away?" Disbelief coated her father's words.

"Some of them. I don't know." Torren shrugged. "We could attack the palace."

"Attack the palace?" Raven repeated. "You and the kitchen servants?"

Her heart sank. Torren had gone to all that trouble for nothing. She could see no way to get to the King and Kanan at the same time and not be taken prisoner once again.

"Look, I know it needs work. But do you have a better idea?" Torren asked. "Maybe I can get enough people together—" Torren stopped speaking mid sentence, his head popping up and his eyes leaving her, fixating on nothing.

"Torren?"

He looked back to her. "Leave the guards to me. I'll take care of it."

"But how?"

He gave her a quick nod. "Trust me."

She had no choice but to trust him, but that didn't stop the nerves that continued to squirm inside her. "Okay."

"Torren, did she say if she could feel the effects of the herb right away?" her father, who had been mostly quiet, spoke up. "Or if there was any outward evidence?"

They both looked at him and Torren nodded. "Yeah, she said she didn't know it had worked until later in the day when she spoke to her husband. She tried to use her influence on him, and it didn't work."

"So if she didn't know it had worked, maybe we could give it to them somehow without them knowing?" Raven was willing to latch on to any possibility, especially since this was their last option.

"Until they try to use their powers and it doesn't work," her father added.

Raven continued, "What if we could get them both here before tomorrow? Torren, did she say how long it lasts?"

Torren gave a slight one shouldered shrug. "About a day between doses."

"So if we can get them here, one to you and one to me," she indicated Sebastian, "make sure they inhale the powder, then maybe by the time we get to the throne room, their abilities won't work."

Even as she spoke them the words rang hollow. There was no way they could get them both there and coordinate something like that through the walls. A frustrated puff of air left her as she scrubbed at her face.

The sound of a key in the door lock drew Raven from her thoughts. Torren's reflexes worked first. He sprang into action, latching on to her father and hauling him back behind the tapestry. Raven scrambled to get back into the bed, grimacing at the spasm that lanced into her stomach. She felt the wetness under her shirt as the blood began to flow again.

The door opened and Raven was grateful for the dimness of the room so she could peek discreetly at the person who entered. Maci, the girl who tended the fires.

She moved to the fireplace and stoked it with the iron Kanan had left. Then the girl walked to Raven's table and dropped something there before leaving the room.

She glanced toward the wall and hoped desperately that her father was back in his room, and Torren well hidden, in case the girl went there next.

When she was sure Maci was gone and not coming back, Raven climbed, carefully, out of the bed and moved to the table. A folded paper lay there. Raven picked it up and moved toward the fireplace so she could read what was written there.

You will be given one final chance to acquiesce to the King. Should you agree, you will become a servant at the palace permanently. Should you refuse, you will be taken to the throne room and executed. Sebastian will be given the same option. Take time to consider your choice.

Raven read and reread the note. She was still reading when a noise behind her startled her and she spun toward it. Torren stood there, holding a note identical to hers, a familiar smile on his face.

"I have a plan."

Her heart kicked up at the confidence in his expression. "And?"

"You get a private audience with the King tomorrow." He pointed the note at her. "That's perfect."

"Okay..." She wasn't following. "What if Kanan isn't there, though?"

"He doesn't have to be, it might even be easier if he isn't." Torren shrugged again. "Though, I think he will be. I expect everyone will be there. Kanan, Esrae, Logan..."

"You're probably right." Surely the King would bring them all there together for this final judgement. "Now, how?"

Torren nodded. "You and Sebastian each take some of the powder. You'll need to work out some sort of signal between the both of you so you can act at the same time. One of you take Kanan and the other, the King. Then, if you can get a weapon, you can take Malakai out right there."

Torren's confidence was contagious, but there was still that note of finality. This was their last chance.

Her shoulders drooped. "How are we supposed to get a weapon?"

"I imagine Kanan will have a sword for sure," Torren said. "Raven, you can take him. Hand-to-hand, you're better than he is. You can get it from him."

"Then we'll need to get out." Her father appeared from behind the tapestry, joining them in the room. "Immediately. The guards will be right there."

She appreciated their confidence but, as if in reminder, a lance of pain shot through her arm. Under normal conditions she could only just barely beat Kanan. But she was injured. Very injured.

She pulled in a breath. She would fight through the pain. There would be plenty of time to heal later. She gritted her teeth and said nothing.

"I'll be waiting for you," Torren said. "There are passages all over this place. We can get out through one of those."

Another thought pushed its way into her head. She spoke quietly, barely able to get the words out. "If we kill Malakai, what's going to happen to Kanan?"

Sebastian and Torren both looked at her almost as though she was mentioning something they hadn't thought of.

"I want to say that Malakai's death would break the hold over Kanan," her father began, "but, truthfully, we've never faced this before. Raven, I don't know what will happen. There's no experience to back up the theory."

"If the hold doesn't break, we kill him."

The words hit her like a blow. Torren spoke such coldness. "Torren..."

"What?" Torren bit the word out. "We can't just let him go. He's a monster like that, Raven. He killed Aster. He's been torturing you. If he isn't released from whatever hold Malakai has on him, we have to end him."

A wave of dizziness washed over her and she moved to grasp the back of a chair. He was right. Saints, he was right. If the power on Kanan wasn't broken, then he would be too dangerous to have around. She found it hard to catch her breath.

"He should die anyway." Torren spoke the last words so low it was nearly to himself, but Raven heard him.

"Torren, Kanan has no control over what's happening. You know that, right?" Raven said. "You know him, he's not like that. It's all Malakai and what he's done to him. Kanan would never do those things."

Torren gave her a look, his brows lowered, but said nothing.

"And Esrae?" her father said.

Hot anger bubbled inside Raven. "She's made her choices on her own. She can stay here, for all I care."

Her father nodded once. "That's everything then. If we assume Logan will be there too."

"Surely Malakai wouldn't let him miss it." Too many emotions pressed in on her and, as though in defense of her sanity, a numbness settled in on her.

He nodded. "Then we can do no more until Malakai calls us. We should rest."

Raven offered a nod, though she knew she would get no rest. She looked at Torren. "Where will you go?"

"I'll find a place to stay, I won't be far. And when they come to get you, I won't be far then either."

Her father nodded. "The next time we see you, hopefully, it will be to put this place behind us."

Torren reached out and her father took his hand, shaking it once. Torren pulled one of the leather pouches from his tunic and handed it to him.

"Thank you, Torren," her father said sincerely.

Torren nodded. "See you tomorrow."

"Night," Raven said quietly as her fingers closed tightly around their freedom.

Her father pulled Raven, carefully, into another hug and placed a kiss on the top of her head. Then, he and Torren disappeared behind the heavy tapestry that hung on the wall.

Raven sat on the bed before moving further onto the soft blanket. She lay, staring at the ceiling for a long time, before finally drifting off into sleep.

Raven opened her eyes, her lids heavy with sleep. Kanan sat on the edge of her bed, watching her.

Wide awake, she scrambled backward, crying out at all the ways it caused her pain.

"Careful, Rae." He looked amused. "You don't want to hurt yourself."

"What are you doing here?" Raven moved as far away from him as the bed would allow, her back coming to rest on the carved headboard. "The King said he told you to leave me alone."

"That was yesterday. It's a new day." He slid his hand toward her ankle and she recoiled, pulling her leg away from him.

Kanan laughed. "Relax, Rae. I'm not here to hurt you." She lifted her brow. As if she believed that. "I promise." He held his hands up in front of him.

"Then what are you doing here?"

"I came to talk," Kanan said, leaning back against the post of the bed and bringing one knee up to his chest, letting the other rest on the floor. He looked very relaxed, surveying the room around them.

Raven waited.

"We were good together, you and I," Kanan said, letting his head fall to the side so he could see her. "We still could be."

Raven scowled. "What are you talking about?"

He studied her, letting his eyes travel over her. "I'd hate to break our engagement. You don't have to die today."

"No?" Her voice was hoarse.

"No," Kanan repeated. "You say the word and you can join us. You and me. Together. Working for the King. Can you imagine?"

"No." She did not have to think about his offer.

His face grew more serious. He leaned forward slightly. "Killing you is a waste, Rae. You're talented. You can use a sword. You fight hand-to-hand better than anyone I know. Except maybe for Logan. But probably better than him now. Better than me, for sure. You're just going to throw that all away?"

"If my only other option is becoming a monster like you, then yes. I will gladly throw it all away." She had to put all her concentration into keeping her voice steady.

Kanan's jaw twitched in what appeared to be irritation. He considered her for a few moments, narrowing his gaze. "I could make you, you know?"

Raven's breath hitched and she bit her lip. He could. Saints, he could make her do anything. Kanan had the power to make her do whatever he wanted, and she wouldn't put it past him to use it. And then what? With her out of the fight, worse, on the enemy's side, they had no hope of fulfilling their plan. Her father would die. Logan would die. For all she knew, she would be the one to do it. She had no response for him. She didn't know what to say.

"Please..."

"Please, what?"

"Please don't." Raven whispered the words. She didn't know what else to say. She didn't really expect him to care, but she was desperate.

"You're begging," Kanan said. It was an observation, not a question.

"What else do I have?" Raven answered. "If you care at all, please don't."

He leaned closer to her again, the conversational air gone from his voice. "I don't care."

He stood and moved to the door, but before he left, he turned back to her. "I'll be back to get you. Then you'll wish you would have taken me up on my offer."

Raven flinched at the sound of the door closing and the note of finality it brought. Today was the day she was supposed to die. Either their plan would work, or they wouldn't have to worry about it anymore.

FORTY-ONE

Raven lay on the bed, staring at the dark beams crisscrossing the ceiling as she mentally ran through the plan they had put together. Silently, she pleaded with the Saints to show them favor in this ridiculous endeavor.

At the sound of the key in the door, she dumped the contents of the small pouch into her palm and squeezed her fist closed until her nails dug into her palm. At that moment, her prayer changed. She prayed with all her might that the powder would not all slip through her fingers before she needed it.

Raven stood and clasped her trembling hands in front of her and waited. The door opened and Kanan waited on the other side. He stepped to the side and fixed her with his beautiful, terrifying olive eyes as he inclined his head toward the hallway, inviting her to join him.

She was struck again by a bone deep sadness. This was the man she loved, the man that loved her. She inhaled deeply, trying to tame her racing heart as she stepped toward the door. Kanan moved, allowing her enough space to exit the room.

Raven looked around. "No guards?"

"What could you do to me, Raven?"

He hadn't used her full name in so long, it sounded foreign to her ears. He was right though. He could stop anything she planned with only a thought.

They stopped and Kanan opened the door to the next room. Her father joined them in the hallway, offering Raven a weak smile as they began moving down the halls.

"Have you reconsidered what I offered?" Kanan asked quietly over his shoulder. "We could be great together."

She let her eyes travel over his large form, his broad shoulders, they way the muscles in his back moved, the hair that curled at the back of his neck, and a pain settled deep in her chest. "We *were* great together."

As they walked on, Raven was aware of nothing so much as of each and every tiny spec of herb that escaped through her clenched fingers. Her attention was so focused on keeping just the right amount of pressure on her grasp she almost ran into Kanan when he stopped.

"This is it." Kanan pulled the door open. Her father entered and Raven followed, Kanan behind her.

There was no one else there, not even guards. Either Torren had managed to get them away or Malakai was confident in his ability to control them should they attempt to revolt. She assumed it was the latter. He had nothing to fear from them. Just the three of them stood alone in the room. Or so she thought. When she turned, she saw him sitting on a lone chair.

"Logan!"

She rushed to his side and her breathing faltered as she registered his appearance. There were bruises everywhere; both dried and fresh blood covered his face from various cuts. His lip was split in two places, and one eye wouldn't even open it was so swollen. The other seemed to be staring off into nothing.

She dropped to the floor in front of him, afraid to touch any part of his body, not knowing where other bruises might be hidden.

"Logan? Logan?" Tears fell down her face. "Please answer me. Are you alright?"

Behind her, Kanan spoke, "He is most definitely not alright."

She did her best to ignore him. "Logan?"

"Raven." The word was so quiet, she thought she might have imagined it. But then he said it again, and this time, one edge of his bruised mouth ticked up ever so slightly.

The sound that escaped Raven was part sob, part laugh. She wanted to fling her arms around him but refrained, sure that would hurt him. Instead, she dropped her head into her own hand and cried. Relief that he was alive, horror for what had been done to him, sadness for what would come next.

Kanan's hand wrapped around her arm and hauled her to her feet. "That's enough,"

When he pulled her up, she saw there was a throne in the room, though Malakai had not yet appeared. Beside them, her father slowly inched a bit toward the throne. Her breath caught. With him moving to where Malakai would be, she could only hope Kanan would stay by her side.

"Remember that I tried to help," Kanan spoke into her ear, sending a shiver dancing down her spine.

"You've done nothing to help me." Raven did not look at him.

The door opened and Raven's heart began thudding out an erratic rhythm, her skin prickling, as Malakai entered. If she passed out they would all be lost, and with the spots dancing at the edge of her vision, that was a distinct possibility. There was no longer space for mistakes or missteps. They were out of chances.

Esrae entered behind Malakai and Raven wondered if Torren was there somewhere, hiding.

Malakai stopped in front of her father. "Look how far we've come. After all we've been through together, this is where it ends."

Her father didn't respond, only glared back at Malakai.

Malakai moved in front of Raven. "And you. So much potential put to waste." He glanced at Logan, who was still seated, too weak to stand. "Like father, like daughter."

He turned, taking a seat on the lone throne as Esrae moved to stand just over his shoulder. Raven glared. She didn't even seem to care at all that this was her fault.

Malakai let his gaze slide over them as he ran a thumb across his bottom lip. "Well, here we are. I'm giving you this final chance. Join your friends, swear your fealty to me, or you will be executed."

Something that sounded very much like a scoff escaped Logan's lips. Malakai looked unimpressed.

Kanan spoke up from where he still stood behind her. "Come on, Rae. You're too talented to waste."

Raven swallowed hard and remained silent along with her father, even as her chest ached.

"Please, Raven?" Esrae pleaded. "Please.

Fury flashed in Raven's chest and she shot a piercing gaze at Esrae. "You just remember: this is all your fault."

"Raven, please," Esrae said again.

Kanan leaned forward, his warm breath coasting over her neck. "Listen to her, Raven."

He had called her Raven again, and it sent a pang through her. She turned to look at him, their faces inches apart. "You are—all of you—monsters." She turned back to Malakai. "Just kill me."

Logan lifted his head just enough to look at her. She met his gaze and she thought he might have smiled, or maybe it was a wince.

"Raven," her father breathed her name and her heart faltered. She turned to look at him.

It was time. No more planning, no more thinking, no more dreading what would happen. *Saints.*

He gave her the most subtle nod, and she nodded back.

Moving in unison, as though they had practiced it, he turned toward Malakai and Raven spun on Kanan.

Kanan caught Raven's arm, but she'd already raised her closed fist to her mouth. She opened it, alarmed at how little of the powder remained. With one last silent prayer, she blew as hard as she could across her palm.

The breeze sent thousands of tiny dust-like particles directly into Kanan's face. He released her and stumbled backward, coughing, his eyes blinking rapidly against the onslaught.

"Raven!" her father shouted, and Raven turned in time to see Malakai also coughing. "The sword!"

Her eyes fell on the wine colored hilt of her sword where it hung at Kanan's side. She lunged, latching onto it and heaving. His expression held absolute shock, but he didn't try to stop her. She raised her leg and kicked him in the gut, sending pain through her and him sprawling backward. The sword withdrew on its own as Kanan fell. She turned and tossed it to her father, who snatched it easily out of the air. Malakai blinked wildly, his hand going instinctively for his own sword. She couldn't afford to watch as she spun back to help Logan.

Raven slid her arm around Logan, helping him stand. He grunted and she cringed, aware she was causing him pain with her sudden movements.

"Raven, what's going on?" Logan's voice was low and raspy, the voice of someone who had been screaming. Raven ignored it, refused to let herself think about it.

"We're getting out of here."

They turned back and she watched as her father advanced on Malakai. The King swiped at his eyes, confusion written all over his face. He held his sword but it was obvious he couldn't see clearly to wield it. "What have you done?"

"This is for my family!" her father grunted loudly as he drove Raven's sword home. It slid halfway into Malakai's chest and stopped.

Malakai's eyes flew open in shock as Esrae's screams filled the marble walled room.

"Malakai!" He slumped to the ground as Esrae dropped on top of him.

"We have to get out of here. Let's go!" her father called to where Raven and Logan stood. But as he turned to leave he was met with Esrae, who now held Malakai's fallen sword.

Raven whirled toward her father's voice, still bracing Logan. She froze, terror gripping her chest like a fist at the sight before her.

Something visceral flashed in Esrae's wide blue eyes, her expression taking on the look of a crazed, wild beast. Raven had never seen anyone look like that. Esrae looked like a madwoman.

"You killed him!" her screech tore through the air, ricocheting off the high stone ceiling.

Before Raven had time to react, before she even realized what was happening, Esrae shrieked again, the sound slicing the air as she drove the steel into Raven's father.

"No!" Raven's knees buckled beneath her and she crumbled to the floor, taking Logan with her.

Pain lanced her chest. Close, they had been so close. About to walk out and be done with all of this. She could not pull in enough air. She could only sit, staring, her lungs burning for oxygen.

Before them Esrae seemed to regain her senses all at once. She released the hilt of the sword as though it burned and stumbled back. Her hands shook as she rubbed them against each other, like she was trying to clean them. She turned away from where Raven's father had slumped to the ground and moved back to Malakai, resting her head on his barely moving chest.

Weakly, Malakai raised a shaking hand to Esrae's head. At the movement, Esrae looked up, but when Malakai touched her the effect was instantaneous, and her head dropped back to his chest, her arms going slack beside her, unconscious.

Raven's attention turned to Malakai and she watched as the life drained away, leaving his eyes vacant. His hand fell back to the floor with a slap.

He was finally gone, but the cost was so much more than Raven had wanted to pay. She looked back to where her father lay, the sword embedded in his chest, the life gone from his chestnut eyes. She would never hear his voice again, never see his smile.

A hand rested lightly on her back and she remembered Logan, she turned to look at him. Even broken there was pain in his expression.

Tears fell down her face, she tried to get them in check but it was too much. It was too much.

"Raven! Come on!" Torren's voice rang out from a corner of the room.

"Torren," Raven sobbed, looking from Torren to where her father lay on the floor.

Torren's eyes widened in shock as he shook his head. "I'm sorry, but we have to go or we'll all be dead. Please." He held out a desperate, shaking hand to her.

"Go, Raven," Logan's raspy voice sounded in her ear.

With another sob, Raven stood and did her best to haul Logan up with her. She moved toward Torren, her grip on the much larger man slipping.

A hand closed around her arm. "Raven?"

She pulled out of his grasp, pulling Logan with her. Her head was swimming. "Kanan?"

Sheer confusion etched his features. "What's going on?"

"We have to go, Raven," Torren called again.

Kanan's eyes moved from Torren to Raven. He had the look of someone who was waking from a long sleep. "What hap—" He reached a hand toward her shirt, now stained red where the wound had opened. Concern bloomed on his features. "You're bleeding. Are you alright?"

Again, she recoiled from his grasp. Was he being serious?

Kanan's confusion deepened. "What happened?"

"We have to go, Raven!" Logan rasped.

"Yes, come on." Torren rushed to their side, taking Logan in his arms, freeing Raven. They began moving quickly.

Raven turned to Kanan. He looked completely lost. She wiped at the tears on her face and blew out all her breath as she made a decision. She reached out, latching onto his wrist. "Come on."

Raven, pulling Kanan along behind her, followed Torren and Logan away from the dais. She only stopped briefly to retrieve her sword. Torren rushed to a place where the wall opened into another passageway leading into darkness.

"Close it," Torren said over his shoulder as they shuffled through.

Kanan pushed the door closed, cutting off Raven's view of where her father lay on the floor.

"Follow me." Torren's voice brought Raven back to the present. "Stay close."

They followed Torren through a series of twists and dark hallways until they emerged into the twilight colored forest.

"We have horses," Torren called, and Raven was greeted with another shock as Holden stepped quickly from a dark shadow, the reins of two horses held in his hands.

"Holden," she breathed his name. "Why are you doing this?"

Holden's mouth set in a grim line. "Not everyone here is a blind follower of the King, Raven."

Raven gave him a confused scowl. "But you, you're awful."

His brows rose and his head tilted to the side. "I do what I can from my position. If I'm awful, there's less reason to suspect me."

Beside them, Torren began to aid Logan in mounting his horse and Holden moved to help him.

"But, Laurise, that man..." Raven continued speaking as images of Holden and the guards hauling the woman away from her family played in her mind.

Something like a shadow crossed Holden's face and his hands stilled where they worked to further secure the saddle Logan sat on. His voice was quiet and hoarse. "I can only do so much. But, I promise, they didn't suffer."

The implication settled like a stone in Raven's stomach. But before she could dwell on it for too long, she was pulled from her thoughts by Torren's voice.

"We could only get two horses."

She turned to him, the meaning behind his words was clear. Someone was going to have to get on a horse with Kanan. She looked at him, biting down on her lip.

Kanan's brow creased as he looked at her. "Raven?" He reached out a hand toward her and she jerked back, away from his touch. Kanan pulled his hand in, his eyes going wide, panic appearing there. "Raven, what's wrong?"

She couldn't breathe around the ache in her throat. With effort, she swallowed, tears filling her eyes. Did he really not know? Could he not remember? That was probably for the best, but it didn't make anything any easier for her.

"I'll ride with Kanan," Logan said through a coughing fit.

Raven met Logan's eyes and she hoped he understood how grateful she was. She didn't think she would have been able to share a horse with Kanan. She wasn't prepared to be that close to him again. Not so soon.

"I'm sorry, I could only get two." Holden's words were rushed as he glanced between Raven and Kanan.

Raven turned her gaze, blurry with tears, fully on Holden. Without him getting them horses, they wouldn't have stood a chance at escape. "Thank you." She hoped, in their haste, she was conveying the deep level of appreciation she felt.

He nodded as he moved quickly to the side, jerking his chin from Kanan to the horse Logan sat on. "You can ride here."

She could sense Kanan's hesitation beside her. "Raven?" The confusion in his voice was too much. She couldn't face it, she turned away, hurrying to the other horse that Torren had mounted.

Out of the corner of her eye she saw Kanan take a step but any further movement was blocked by Holden's large frame. She remembered the day on the street when Holden had approached her and Kanan had stepped into his path. Everything was so wrong now. She swallowed back the tears, it was not the time to fall apart, they had to get away.

Torren reached down from where he sat on the horse. "Give me the sword."

She handed the weapon to him and he held it in one hand as she took his other hand, climbing up to join him on the horse. He handed the sword back to her and she held it with one hand, grateful it wasn't too heavy as she wrapped her other arm around Torren's waist. She could no longer see what was happening behind them, but she heard the creak of the leather and assumed Kanan had climbed onto the horse with Logan.

"Wait…" Kanan's voice was quiet, and Raven heard the sound of leather and buckles.

When Holden appeared again at her side, he handed a sheath and belt to her. "Here." It was still warm from where it had been strapped around Kanan's waist. She accepted it and slid her sword into the leather sheath. The belt, however, was far too large for her. Instead of buckling it on her waist, she buckled it and pulled it over her head to lay across her back.

Then there was no more time as Holden glanced over his shoulder, his eyes growing wide, reacting to a sound she didn't hear. "Go. Be safe."

With a nod and a kick, Torren launched the horse into a gallop, Raven holding tight to his waist. The hooves of the other horse pounded the ground behind them. She squeezed her eyes shut, resting her head against Torren's back.

They were once again fleeing from the palace, but this time it was over. For real. They'd succeeded in their plan, the King was gone, but so was her father. The price was too great. He hadn't even wanted them to do this. It wasn't fair. She swallowed down the ache in her throat. She could fall apart some other time.

FORTY-TWO

They rode hard at first until common sense told them to let their horses relax. Riding over hills, through streams, over rocks and rugged terrain was daunting for both rider and horse, especially when they were doubled up. Though nothing was sufficient enough distraction to tear Raven's eyes from Logan and Kanan.

She kept a constant vigil. At the palace, it had appeared that Kanan was free from Malakai's grip; as though the King's death really did sever the hold on Kanan's mind. But she'd been fooled by Kanan in the past, and if he was indeed still acting, Logan was in very real danger.

Raven lurched to the side as the horse under her and Torren stumbled again. "Should we stop?"

"I think that would be a very bad idea." It was the first thing Kanan had said since they left the palace. His voice, it had always been Kanan's voice, but something seemed softer now. Different.

"I don't want to say it, but I'm going to," Torren began. "I agree with Kanan. We haven't put nearly enough distance between us and the palace. I'm sure as soon as they discovered the King's body, they sent soldiers after us. I'm surprised they haven't caught up yet."

"But what if the guards were all under Malakai's control?" She wanted to believe the words, but she didn't really.

Kanan spoke again, "It doesn't matter if every soldier in the palace was under his control. The Queen wasn't. She'll send people after us."

Torren reined in their horse and Raven gripped him tighter at the sudden top as he turned them. Every eye was on Kanan. The air left Raven's lungs. "Did you say 'Queen'?"

Logan and Kanan stopped beside them.

Kanan met Raven's eyes. "You didn't know?" His voice was soft but held genuine surprise.

Raven looked away, finding it hard to meet his gaze. "I wasn't exactly in the loop."

"Queen?" Torren repeated.

Raven forced herself to look at Kanan again. He looked exhausted, like he hadn't slept in a week. He nodded and when he spoke, he sounded as tired as he appeared. "He married her. Last week sometime, I think."

"She married him." Raven's voice broke.

Even after all that had happened, it still felt like a betrayal. Why she was still surprised at Esrae's betrayal, she didn't understand. Her mind played it out again, the wild look in Esrae's eye as she drove the sword into her father. Could this emptiness inside her grow any further?

Kanan turned to her, his eyes full of sympathy. "I'm sorry, Raven."

It was so strange to see him looking at her like that again. He spoke as though nothing had transpired between them in the last week.

She looked away from him and swiped at the tears on her face. "Just go," she said to Torren.

He spurred the horse on, but they didn't get very far before Logan's weak voice broke the silence. "I think it's too dark to go on tonight."

When had it grown so dark? She hadn't even noticed.

"We can rest here. Try to sleep. No fire. We can get back on the road at daybreak," Logan rasped.

Torren's sigh sounded resigned. "Fine."

They dismounted and led the horses deeper into the woods off the path. Maybe the Saints were watching out for them, because a tiny stream, barely the width of a hand, ran near the path. Both the horses and riders drank eagerly.

There was barely enough light from the moon to find a patch of ground large enough to accommodate all four of them. When they did, Raven sat down next to a large tree trunk and let her head fall back against the rough bark. She closed her eyes and blew out a long breath. But then her father lay before her. She snapped her eyes open to find Kanan beside her.

With a loud gasp that was almost a yelp she jumped, scrambling away, pain shooting across her abdomen.

Alarm shone in Kanan's eyes and he reached out as though to steady her and she moved away again. His brows dipped together and he drew his hands back in alarm. "I'm sorry."

She clenched her teeth at the waves of pain that ran over her. Would this never heal? Not if she kept tearing it open.

"Raven, are you alright?" The panic was still in his eyes and he held a hand out toward her shirt. "You're bleeding."

She looked down. Indeed, blood was seeping into the cloth of her shirt. She looked up at him again. He didn't know why she was bleeding. He didn't remember?

His gaze was so intent on her that she had to look away again. It held no malice, but still she couldn't stand the weight of it.

"Raven," his voice was soft, pleading. "What happened?"

She was vaguely aware of Torren and Logan watching their exchange. Logan limped to where she was and slowly lowered himself down beside her, the movement eliciting a series of groans and grunts.

She met his eyes, though his face was blurred by the tears that were building in her vision.

Logan took a shallow breath, as though anything deeper pained him before he looked at Kanan. "Kanan, Raven needs a moment, would you mind sitting over there?" He glanced at a tree a number of feet away.

She could feel Kanan's eyes on her. "I need someone to tell me what happened. I can barely remember anything. Raven, are you alright?"

"We will tell you," Logan promised. "Just please, give us a moment?"

She allowed herself a glance at him and something inside cracked at the hurt in his eyes. But she couldn't, she just couldn't. She wanted to to be able to forget everything that had happened. Hadn't that been what so much of their fight was about? Getting Kanan back? And now that he was here with her again, she couldn't bear to be close to him. Nothing would ever be right again.

After another moment, he exhaled. "Okay, I'll be right over here." His voice was so quiet. To lose a week of memories must be extremely confusing. Her throat ached. Boots scuffed on dirt and she looked up to see him moving to lean against a tree across the small space they'd found.

"Are you alright?" Logan asked.

She looked at him but no words would come, she let her head fall into her hands, her shoulders shaking with the force of her cries.

Logan's warm palm rested on her back. "I'm so sorry, Raven."

She didn't allow herself to cry for long. Swiping at the tears on her face she turned to him, taking in his swollen face. He'd washed most of the blood off in the small stream. "Are you alright?"

His voice was strong when he answered. "I'm fine. I just wish this would have turned out differently."

Yes, no doubt they all wished that. Again, she saw her father on the ground. It was like Logan again, only this time he wouldn't be coming back. She'd left him, just left him there, dead, beside Malakai.

"He didn't even want us to do this." After everything, all his protestations regarding their plan, he was the one to end up victim to it. She scrubbed at her face, clamping down on her lip. Aware of Kanan watching them. She had to change the subject or she would come apart again.

She turned to Logan and studied his face, his eyes. "Is it true?"

He pressed his swollen lips together and blew out through his nose. She hadn't clarified what she meant, but he seemed to understand. "I think so, yes. I'm sorry."

He was sorry? Sorry that she was his daughter? "Why are you sorry?" She was almost afraid of the answer. Did he not want her to be his?

"To learn of something like that under those circumstances..." he began. "It's cruel."

"It was a shock," she started. Guilt hit her. She'd just lost her father; was this being unfaithful to his memory? She pushed past it. Logan was all she had left now, and she wouldn't waste their time. "But I'm not sorry. Logan, if I had to choose someone else to be my father, it would have been you." Tears came again, would they never end? "I'm so glad you're here." She wanted to hug him but his injuries looked painful, and she didn't know what hid beneath his clothes. Instead, she took his hand in hers.

"Raven..." He ignored all his injuries as he reached out and pulled her against him. He said nothing else.

When he released her, they sat in silence for a few moments. Logan reached out and gently brushed the tears on her face. A half smile, that she didn't have to force, came to her lips.

But then her eyes found Kanan again. He'd stopped watching them, instead studying the ground at his feet. Still she looked away quickly. Would she never be able to look at him again? Pain, actual pain, stabbed at her with that thought. Was all they had gone, just like that? With a few thoughts from a mad king, her life was turned upside down and ruined.

"I think he's back," Logan said softly. "Kanan, I mean. Our Kanan, your Kanan." Logan nodded toward the other man, but kept his eyes on Raven. She glanced at Kanan. "That's him."

Kanan heard his name and looked up at the same time she looked at him. Quickly she diverted her gaze to the leaves on the ground beneath her. "I know."

"I'll stay awake if you'd like," Logan offered. "Keep watch."

She knew he didn't mean to keep watch for the King's guard, but to keep watch over Kanan. Even though he expected Kanan was no longer under the King's control, he knew Raven still needed that assurance.

Warmth spread through her at his consideration. She offered him as much of a grateful smile as she could. "You don't have to do that, but thank you."

He nodded. "Try to sleep."

"I will." It was a lie. Even if she did try, she knew sleep wouldn't come. Every time she closed her eyes she saw her father or Aster, dead, or Kanan standing over her with a bloody knife. And she would have to open her eyes again to make sure he was still sitting across from her at their little camp.

It grew late and still she watched him. Eventually, the sounds of soft, even breathing met her ears and she knew both Logan and Torren had fallen asleep. From Kanan, she heard nothing.

After a long time, Kanan's soft voice broke the silence. He hadn't moved; he still sat with his arms crossed over his chest, his head down. "If you keep looking at me like that, you're going to burn a hole in me."

"Interesting choice of words." Raven had intended to speak louder but all the words emerged as a whisper.

He exhaled. "Raven, I—"

"What?" she interrupted, her voice breaking.

"Raven, I can't remember a lot of what happened." He shook his head, confusion playing on his features, lit only by moonlight. "My memories are coming back but in pieces. And you're all acting like I did something awful." He paused, "If I hurt—"

"If?" Raven's voice came out higher than she intended.

She heard his sharp breath. "Raven, it wasn't me. You have to know that? Whatever happened, whatever I did, whatever the King *made* me do, it wasn't me. I would never hurt you." His voice faltered on the last words.

"I know. But you did."

She captured her lip in her teeth, trying to keep it from trembling, trying to keep the tears at bay. He was right, she knew he was right. Hadn't she been the one saying it so many times? It wasn't Kanan who was doing those things. But now, having him back, her common sense was pushing against her memories, and her insides churned.

"You really don't remember?"

"No." The word was only an exhale of breath. "Only pieces. I remember that the King married Esrae. I remember being in the dungeon with Logan, standing over him. I remember talking to you in a bedroom and tending the fire."

Raven stiffened at his words. She swallowed. "You should probably hold on for when you do remember."

Kanan was silent for a few moments, but when he spoke, fear coated his words. "It's very bad, isn't it?"

"I can't believe you can't remember." Raven's voice was a whisper.

"Tell me?" There was a tremor in his voice.

She shook her head and her breath caught in her throat. "I can't. I– I can't."

"I'm so sorry, Raven." His voice was thick with tears. "Whatever he did to me, it's over. I promise."

She shook her head, forcing herself to speak through her tears. "I want to believe you, but I've been here before. I've heard this before. You promised me it was over and then h-hurt me again. How can I know?"

His breath left him in a shaking stream and she knew he was crying. "Raven, I love you."

She inhaled sharply at his words and a sob worked its way out. She wasn't ready to hear those words. Not yet. Tears burned her eyes and another sob escaped before she could stop it. "I can't— you should sleep."

It wasn't fair, none of it was fair. Not to him, not to her. She cried then, her shoulders shaking. It wasn't fair.

Kanan didn't say anything else but she thought she heard him sniffling. The sound only broke her heart further.

She leaned back against the tree, not looking at him again, trying to quell her own tears. She didn't expect to sleep, though she closed her eyes.

Raven's eyes flew open at the sound of the snapping of a twig. "Kanan!"

He was right there. She jumped, recoiling away from him, but she wasn't quick enough. His hand shot out, catching a fistful of her hair, stopping her with a painful jerk of her head.

"Where are you going, Rae?" Kanan said. "I was enjoying our conversation. Don't run now. You must know that you can't get away from me."

She glanced around the camp. Logan and Torren both lay where they had been asleep, though something seemed off.

Kanan followed her gaze and shrugged. "They're dead, Rae. No help there."

"What?" A sob escaped her lips as utter devastation hit her square in the chest.

"Dead," Kanan repeated the word, slower, with emphasis. He stretched an arm out beside him and pulled an iron rod from out of the campfire, bringing it around in front of her face.

She tried to recoil, but Kanan's hand was still tangled in her hair. He brought the iron down across her cheek and she shrieked.

FORTY-THREE

"Raven!"

Raven's eyes snapped open to find Logan shaking her.

"It's alright, you're alright. You were dreaming."

Indeed, light had begun to brighten the overcast sky.

She heaved, trying to catch her breaths as she looked across their fireless camp to where Kanan sat, his eyes red rimmed and wide, watching her. Torren was still in his spot as well, though also wide awake.

She brought her hand to her cheek. There was no sign of a burn. Of course there wouldn't be, she'd been dreaming. She willed her breathing to slow. Her eyes found Kanan again. Malakai's Kanan, her Kanan. Fear twisted inside her. But not fear of Kanan. Fear of herself. Fear that she would never again be able to separate the two in her mind.

Kanan met her gaze. His brow was furrowed and she could see the pain and tears in his eyes. He looked at her as though he was looking at a ghost. When he spoke, his voice was low and barely loud enough to be heard. "I'm so sorry, Raven."

Raven dropped her eyes back to the ground. Her chest ached with emotions she couldn't name, and she just couldn't look at him.

"Are you alright?" Logan's voice was soft in her ear.

She inhaled deeply, blew it out slowly, and nodded.

"Good." Logan rested his hand on her back. Warmth seeped through her shirt at the contact, and she was suddenly aware of the chill. "Are you ready to ride?"

She shivered. "Already?"

"Sorry. The sooner the better."

She nodded and stood, brushing away the twigs and dirt that clung to her. She reached a hand toward Logan, who accepted her help and stood. Torren and Kanan also stood.

Raven glanced at Kanan and then turned to Logan. She hugged her arms around herself and lowered her voice. "I'm sorry you have to spend so much time riding with him after what he did. It must be hard."

Logan gave her an almost sad smile. "Raven, I knew Malakai for a very long time. I wasn't a stranger to his whims or his tricks. I've seen him control many people. What happened to Kanan, Malakai did that to him. I know it's hard for you to see it right now, but Kanan is just as much a victim as you and I. He was forced to do those things. Can you imagine what that must be like? Kanan now has to live with the consequences of a madman. When his memories return fully, and I expect they will, he will have to live with that knowledge, knowing the things he did to you. I know it's hard, but it's something to remember."

Raven studied the ground before nodding once and moving to join Torren.

"Are you alright?" Torren nodded at the place where the blood was visible on her shirt. "Do you need to clean it?"

She didn't reply as she turned and made her way to the small stream of water. Placing her back to the others she moved the shirt and cupped her hands, filling them with water before letting it spill over the wound. She had no other means to clean it. This would have to do. This and prayers to the Saints that infection would stay away.

When she rejoined the others at the horses, she was met with so many expressions. Torren's brow dipped deeply as he eyed the bloody place covered by her shirt. Kanan had gone pale but she looked away before she could read anymore into his expression. Logan's mouth was set in a line but he said nothing. Thankfully, none of them questioned her because she had no answers she was willing to share.

They rode for hours through the chill. Thanks to the clouds covering most of the sky, the day never warmed up. Raven was grateful to be able to lean into Torren; at least they helped keep each other warm.

There were no signs of pursuit, which Raven found odd. Perhaps they'd just managed to choose a way the soldiers hadn't. But it was still odd. Though she was grateful.

Finally, they stopped near a brook to allow the horses some rest and all of them some water.

Raven walked away from the men to find some privacy. She lowered herself onto a fallen tree and exhaled deeply, rubbing at her stiffening neck. She allowed herself the luxury of closing her eyes for just a few moments, of shutting everything out and taking some deep breaths.

When she opened her eyes, she was looking directly at a pair of dark boots. A gasp ripped from her throat and she recoiled, the sudden motion sending her tumbling over the back of the log.

He moved to the log, reaching out toward her.

She'd recovered her foot quickly but lunged further back at his proximity, tripping again with the momentum. She ignored the stabs of fresh pain, simply needing to be away from him, out of reach of his grasp.

His eyes went wide and he stopped, throwing his hands up in front of him. He took two steps backward, speaking quickly, "I won't touch you, I promise. Are you alright?"

Pain shone in his gaze. Her heart thundered, her breaths coming too quickly as spots swam at the edge of her vision. "What are you doing?" she gasped.

"I'm sorry," Kanan said, still holding up his hands. "I'm sorry. I just wanted to talk to you. I—" He swallowed, pulling in a few quick breaths. "I remember."

Raven flinched, shaking her head. "Talk? About what?"

More pain creased his face. "Nothing." He shook his head, pain turning to despair. "Not really." His voice broke and his eyes filled with tears. "I'm just sorry. I could never hurt you like that. What he made me do . . ." He stopped for a moment and placed a hand over his mouth, closing his eyes and breathing deeply, like he was trying not to be sick. "I wish I'd had the power of will to fight him. To keep him from getting control over me. I wish I could have done that for you. I'm just so sorry."

Tears streamed down her face as Logan's words came back to her. "*Kanan is just as much a victim as you and me.*" And she knew that, she knew it was true, but the fact warred with the memories of Kanan's hands on her as he dug his knife into her.

Everything inside her was tangled and knotted and she wanted to scream. He couldn't help what he did, had no control over any of it. Yet, when she looked at him, she saw the knife in his hand and the glint in his eyes.

She said the only thing she could think, the words squeaking through her clenched teeth, followed by a sob: "I'm sorry."

"You should go."

Raven whirled, Logan leaned heavily on a tree behind her. She moved to his side and slid herself under his arm, offering support.

She looked back at Kanan. His brows were knit together and his face was wet with tears, but he sniffed and nodded before he turned, walking away.

When Kanan was gone, Raven met Logan's eyes and there was a weariness there she hadn't seen before.

"Are you alright?"

Raven wanted to speak, to answer him, but she truly didn't know if she was alright. She swallowed and tears spilled from her eyes as her jaw began to quiver. Logan pulled her closer and she leaned into him, burying her face in his chest.

He didn't say anything as he stroked the back of her head and allowed her to cry.

Raven found that once she let herself cry, she couldn't turn it off. Everything she'd been holding in came pouring out. Tears for her father and Logan, for Kanan, for Aster, for Esrae's betrayal. Tears upon tears. She knew that Logan must be using every ounce of his energy to stand there, but he still said nothing; he only held her until her tears were finally spent.

When Logan and Raven returned, it was to tense silence. Torren sat staring at the ground in front of him and Kanan sat with his knees drawn up, his elbows on his knees and his head on his arms. Raven looked anywhere but at Kanan.

"Ready to go?" Logan asked.

"Yes." Torren stood quickly. "Let's go."

Raven glanced in Kanan's direction and found him watching her with red-rimmed eyes. Quickly she averted her gaze. She knew he noticed, but it was just too much.

As Raven waited for Torren to mount their horse, she watched as Kanan helped Logan onto theirs. He was so careful with him, making sure the other man was steady before joining him. She saw him ask a question she couldn't hear and Logan nod in return, a *thank you* on his lips.

That was her Kanan. She saw him there in his kindness toward Logan. And Logan's attitude toward Kanan surprised her just as much. How could he just go back to the way things were? She wanted so badly to be that person, but her wounds were far too fresh and raw. She hadn't faced these kinds of things for years like Logan. Hadn't developed the ability to separate Malakai's victim from his influence.

For another day and night, they pushed on. Every time they slowed or stopped Raven expected to hear the hoofbeats of approaching soldiers, but no sounds pursued them. They hadn't set out with a destination in mind. When they came to a crossroads, they chose based on nothing but a whim.

In the early evening of their second full day of riding, when it became clear they needed to let their horses rest for more than an hour, they stopped at the next town they came to. It was small and the sign on the road said, *"Welcome to Jakanter, You'll be Plum happy you stopped."* On either side of the well-man-icured sign was painted a large purple plum. Raven's mouth began to water as she thought of biting into the juicy fruit.

Their first stop was a stable. Kanan bartered the sale of their horses and Raven, Logan, and Torren waited, praying their questionable appearances didn't draw too much attention.

"They're not exactly in pristine health." Kanan dropped a bag of coins into Logan's hand. "But I persuaded him. Managed a decent price, considering."

"Antyhing is better than nothing." Logan tucked the bag into a pocket. "Let's find a place to stay."

They stopped at the first inn they came to. The sign above the door swung in the breeze, but it wasn't damaged or weather beaten. Hopefully the inside of the inn reflected the same care. The words were clear: "Plum Place."

Torren held the door open as they entered. "Is everything named after a plum?"

Behind a long bar stood a tall woman wiping down the surface. Her straw colored hair was in the sloppiest bun Raven had ever seen. When she saw them, a warm smile spread across her thin face. "Good evening, I'm Myra Plum. Call me Myra. Can I help ya?"

"Your name is Plum?" Torren sounded as amused as Raven felt.

"Aye, it is." The woman's accent was almost melodic as she spoke. "My great-great-grandfather founded the town. He was a witty one. Thought he could capitalize on his name, so he planted the plum trees and here we are."

Raven couldn't help but smile at the woman. It felt good.

"We're looking for a room," Logan said. "Two, actually."

"Well, that's why I'm here." Myra smiled, though her eyes widened slightly as she focused on Logan. "Are you alright? We do have a physician in town."

"I'm fine." Logan offered a half-smile that was still charming even on his bruised face. "I fell off my horse."

"Into a thicket?" She was obviously skeptical as her eyes scanned his face.

"Yes." Logan's tone, while still polite, clearly implied he was done speaking about the subject. "Rooms?"

The woman shook her head, named the price for the two rooms, and Logan dropped the coins onto the counter.

"Follow me."

Myra pushed open the door to the first room. "This one and the other one next door. Do you need anything to eat?"

Food. *Saints, yes*, Raven wanted to shout.

"Please?" Kanan spoke the word with such kindness her heart squeezed.

She'd wished so hard to hear that voice again but feared she never would. She watched him as he spoke to Myra, his smile, the way he set people at ease. Why couldn't she just let go of the past weeks?

The four of them entered the room to wait for the food and Logan carefully lowered himself into a chair by the window. He looked out through the thin curtain, surveying the street below.

His still scratchy voice broke the silence. "We can't ride forever. We should consider what our futures hold." He moved his gaze from the window and found each one of them in turn. "We can't go back to our homes."

Raven dropped her gaze to the floor. He was right, but still, the pain was real when she thought about never being able to return to her father's winery. She had nothing of his, and now she couldn't even go home. She swallowed down the tears past the ache in her throat. She couldn't allow herself to cry again. Last time she almost didn't stop.

Logan continued, "Our old lives are over. All we can do is look ahead." He looked out the window again. "I'm staying here."

Raven looked up, surprised. Here?

"Here?" Torren did not look impressed as he echoed her thoughts. "In Plumville?"

Logan shrugged, a small smile tugging at his mouth. "It's as good a place as any. I like plums. You're all free to do as you'd like, of course. I'm not suggesting you stay here. I'm only saying you should begin to think about what you'll do." Logan spoke to all of them, but his eyes rested on Raven.

"Why here?" Every eye turned to where Kanan stood, arms crossed over his chest, leaning back against the wall.

Logan shook his head. "No one knows us here, for one. There won't be judgement for what we've done. It's a fresh start. And I'm tired."

"Until the palace guards show up," Kanan pointed out.

"If that happens, I'll face it then," Logan answered.

"I'm not staying here." Torren shook his head.

Logan nodded once.

"Where will you go?" Raven asked.

She'd lost so much and there'd been so much change. She didn't want to be selfish, but she didn't want to think about Torren leaving and losing him too. All of them—Kanan, Torren, and Esrae—had been together, inseparable, for so many years.

Torren looked at her. "Back to Aster's family."

She didn't miss when Kanan's held fell, chin dipping to his chest.

Torren continued, "They're good people. I liked them."

Raven nodded slowly in acknowledgement.

"I hope you find happiness," Logan said.

Torren nodded, a sad expression on his face. "Maybe one day."

There was silence for a long moment until Kanan spoke. "I won't stay either."

A frown tugged at the corner of Logan's mouth, the loss clearly visible in his eyes, but he nodded.

Raven couldn't pull her gaze from the floor as she tried to remember how to breathe. A knot had formed in her throat and her chest constricted as conflict warred inside her.

She couldn't lie, certainly not to herself. She was glad he was leaving. She wasn't sure if she could bear to see him everyday. But at the same time, it felt very much like a hole was opening up inside her that she knew would be there forever.

She'd loved Kanan. Fiercely. She'd loved him with everything she'd had. Once he'd been her safe space and the place she ran for comfort. She thought of the times they'd spent together, talking, loving, or just staring at the stars in silence. She was going to marry him. Now, she could only wonder if her life would ever make sense again.

She swallowed back a sob as her lip trembled, but she didn't look at him.

Finally, when she trusted her voice again, she faced Logan. "I'm staying. I like plums too."

Logan smiled. "I'm glad."

She'd forced the joke out, not feeling it at all. But Logan's smile made it worth the effort. A tear fell down her face and she quickly brushed it away. She could feel Kanan's eyes on her, but she'd returned her attention to the floor

The next morning, Raven stood with Logan and watched as both Torren and Kanan loaded fresh supplies on new horses.

Torren hugged both Logan and Raven before he mounted his horse and rode off, ignoring Kanan.

For long moments Kanan, Logan, and Raven stood in silence. Raven watched the way the dust of the road swirled around her shoes in the soft breeze. Beside her, Logan shook Kanan's hand and wished him well.

"Raven?"

Her heart splintered and cracked into a thousand pieces at the sound of his voice; the uncertainty and apprehension in his tone. She closed her eyes and allowed the shudder to work its way through her body, shaking her from her head to her toes. Finally, she lifted her head.

Kanan stood beside his horse, reins in hand, watching her. He looked at her with the saddest expression she'd ever seen. His olive eyes were wet with the promise of tears. It took her breath away and she bit down on her bottom lip, trying to quell her own tears.

He opened his mouth and then closed it, swallowing thickly. Finally, he opened it again. "Take care. Be safe."

She dropped her chin again, trying to hide the way it trembled and how the tears had started falling freely down her cheeks.

The saddle creaked as Kanan mounted the horse and then the soft clopping of hooves on dirt began, the sound growing quieter until it was nothing but a whisper on the breeze.

Shops lining the way were just beginning to open, proprietors brushing off stoops and propping open doors, oblivious to the events that had transpired in the lives of the new people standing along the road.

A deep desperate sense of loss and emptiness filled her. Her friends, even her father, were all gone. A cavern of loneliness opened in her chest and she reached beside her and threaded an arm through Logan's, leaning her head on his shoulder, reminding herself that she wasn't alone.

He placed a kiss on the top of her head. "It'll get better. I promise."

She sniffed and nodded. "Do you think we'll see them again?"

"I think we will," Logan said. "Would you mind?"

She inhaled deeply and blew the breath out slowly. "Maybe not, eventually."

He draped an arm over her shoulder and they stood in silence for what seemed like a long time. She looked up. "We need a place to live."

"Well then." Logan smiled. "Let's go find one."

EPILOGUE

He sat at the bar, his brow furrowed, his gaze intent on the amber liquid in the glass in front of him. He should just go to bed. Sitting at a bar wasn't going to help anything.

"Hey, stranger," a female voice said, coming up beside him, placing herself squarely into his space. A playful smile curved her full lips, her soft brown curls falling lightly around her face.

He acknowledged her with a glance out of the corner of his eye.

She ran a finger over the back of his hand. "What's your name, handsome?"

"Kallen," he answered, not meeting her eyes.

Finding a new name for himself was harder than he'd expected, and when he spoke it aloud, he immediately decided he would try again.

"Kal, I like it." Her eyes brightened. "I'm Nola. Where ya from, Kal?"

"Kallen," he corrected. Yes, he definitely needed another name. "Far away from here."

He still didn't look directly at her, taking another sip from the glass dwindling contents. The last thing he wanted was to flirt.

"Well, I hope you stick around for a bit." Her finger continued to trace a line from his shoulder to his elbow as she pushed further into his space.

He picked up his glass again and drained the contents. "I'm only staying the night. Leaving in the morning." Would she not take the hint?

"If you need some company tonight, I can definitely be of some assistance." Her hand moved to rest on his thigh.

He turned to look her in the eyes and she smiled brightly at him, candlelight shimmering in her grey-green eyes. He lifted her wandering hand from his thigh. "Look, miss, I'm not interested in company."

"You got a girl already?" Her hand found his leg once more.

That despair that he tried so hard to ignore, to drown with liquor, rose with her question. "No." He lifted his glass again before he realized it was empty. He set it back on the counter with a thunk.

"In that case..." Nola squeezed his thigh under her hand.

He'd had enough. He didn't want to hurt her feelings, but he'd tried subtlety and it hadn't worked. He looked her in the eye. "You need to go away."

Instantly she pulled her hand from his thigh with a shrug and a smile. "Okay. Bye."

His lips parted in surprise, his eyes widening. "No," he breathed, as she sauntered away, hips swinging. The alcohol he'd consumed churned in his stomach and he inhaled slowly, focusing on not vomiting.

"Get your hands off me, Oren." The voice was female and sharp.

He turned, the commotion behind momentarily drawing him from his thoughts. Another patron, Oren, he assumed, a large bald man, had his arms wrapped around the waist of a serving girl. In vain she shoved at him, trying to free herself from the bald man's grasp while he laughed.

He stood and walked to the table. He needed to test a theory, and this was as good an opportunity as any. He placed a hand on Oren's arm.

The man turned to him, anger flaring in his eyes as he stood, and he found himself looking up to meet the bald man's eyes. No turning back now. "I think it's time for you to apologize and leave."

In an instant, the anger left the other man's eyes. Immediately he turned to the serving girl. "Sorry, Pol."

The serving girl's mouth fell open as she looked between the two men.

Oren began to move toward the door.

"Tip," he called out, and the large man stopped to dig in his pocket before he turned and dropped some money on the table while glaring. "More." More coins rattled onto the wooden surface.

Oren left and he turned to the serving girl, Pol. "You won't have to worry about him anymore."

A hole had opened inside him and it was quickly filling in with despair. He'd had dreams like this, though from them he'd always woken up.

Pol's mouth still hung open slightly. "How did you do that?"

He blew out a defeated breath. "I can be persuasive." He turned to walk away. He'd planned to go to his room but instead exited the inn, following Oren.

"Excuse me."

The large bald man turned, anger flaring in his eyes again, his hands rolled into fists. "What did you do to me?"

"Call it a curse," he answered. "You leave that girl alone from now on. In fact, leave them all alone. And always tip double."

He turned to walk back to the inn. Oren called after him, but he ignored him. He had far more pressing things on his mind just then.

Continue reading for a
preview of the next book:

PERSUASION

OF

DESTINY

KANAN

He brought the hammer down one last time, the clang of metal-on-metal reverberating around the space as it connected with the still-glowing blade. He picked up the sword, and the blade hissed as he plunged it into a waiting bucket of water. Steam billowed over the edge, and Kanan pulled a cloth from his belt to mop at the perspiration beading along his brow. He didn't mind summer, but the heat was not forgiving to smiths.

"Excuse me? Hello?"

Kanan turned his head toward the voices at the front of his shop. He pulled the sword from the bucket and placed it on the table, then dipped his hands in the bucket and rinsed them quickly in the warm water.

Grabbing a towel from the bench beside him, he dried off as he moved through an open doorway separating the workshop from the rest of the building. At the front of the shop stood a man and a young boy, perhaps ten years. From the look of their clothes, they neither lacked wealth nor the knowledge of how to spend it.

"Good morning, how can I help you?" He tossed the towel to the side where it landed on a long table.

The older man spoke, "Sir, do you do repairs?" His accent told Kanan he was from somewhere near the coast, perhaps Kankadre.

"I do." Kanan nodded. "Are you looking for something specific?"

"As a matter of fact, I am." The man held up a scabbard, a knife sheathed snuggly inside.

Kanan accepted the scabbard and slid the knife free, studying it. The smallest portion of the tip of the blade had chipped off. He twisted his wrist to examine it from the other side.

"Can it be repaired?" the man asked.

"It can. I can do it." Kanan slid the knife back into the sheath. "When do you need it?"

"As soon as possible," the man answered. He gestured toward the boy, who had turned to examine a pile of horseshoes. "My son and I are on our way to Doronall, and I don't want to delay our journey for longer than necessary."

Kannan nodded once and glanced toward the boy at the same moment as the boy turned, revealing the sword hanging at his hip.

Kanan's breath hitched, his heart skidding to a stop in his chest.

"It's yours."

"I can't." Her hair bounced lightly with the soft shake of her head.

He smiled, shaking his head and laughing softly. He knew she'd try to refuse it. "Yes you can. I made it for you."

"Are you all right?" There was concern in the man's voice as he glanced between Kanan and his son.

Kanan shook off the memory and swallowed. "Your son's sword."

The man looked at the sword that hung at his son's waist and his eyes lit up with his smile. "It's lovely, isn't it? You'd never believe where we got it. A peddler."

Kanan turned his head toward the man as his heart again missed several beats. "A peddler?"

"Amazing, isn't it?" The man had clearly misread Kanan's shock as awe. "Why anyone would part with it, I don't understand. Cohen, come here, let me see your sword."

The boy came to stand by his father and drew the long silver blade from the sheath. He handed it to his father, and his father held it out to Kanan.

Kanan stopped breathing as he reached out and wrapped his fingers around the swirled wine-colored hilt. His hands began to shake. The weight was so familiar to him, even after so long. He pulled it in to examine it more closely. The zirconia caught the light and sparkled, casting dancing reflections on the ceiling. An empty socket sat near the edge of the hilt and he ran a finger over the hollow space feeling the small nick. Someone had pried one of the gems out, no doubt to check if they were real diamonds. They must have been disappointed.

"How much would you take for this sword?" He kept his eyes on the blade in his hands, fear that they would refuse settling deep in his chest.

"Sir, it's not for sale."

Kanan's heart stuttered at the boy's words. He needed this sword. He studied the boy, who had turned a confused look on his father.

Kanan's eyes moved from the boy to his father, back to the sword, and back to the boy as an idea struck him. "What's your favorite color?"

The boy's brow knitted, clearly not following Kanan's sudden change of subject. "Black, sir."

Kanan leveled his gaze on the boy, willing him to understand and agree with his next words. "What if I could remake this sword, specifically for you, in black?" He held his breath and did his best to control his expression, not wanting to appear too hopeful. He stilled further when something sparked in the boy's eyes as he turned to his father. Inside his chest was rioting.

"Father, black." The boy's words were soft, almost reverent, hopefulness shining in his eyes. "And gold? Not silver?"

Kanan allowed himself a small exhale and a smile. "Absolutely."

The father's expression was less hopeful. "Sir, we don't really have the time to—"

"One week," Kanan offered, cutting the man off. "In one week, I'll replicate this sword in black and gold, and I'll repair your knife at no charge."

The boy turned pleading eyes on the man. "Father, please?" Uncertainty filled the man's face as Kanan once again held his breath.

The man glanced between Kanan and his son, looking almost helpless. "One week?"

Both Kanan and the boy released their breath. "One week," Kanan promised.

"And you'll take that sword as payment?" The man nodded at the sword Kanan still held in his hands.

"Yes," Kanan breathed the word, hoping he put enough volume behind it for the man to hear. "Absolutely."

"Fine." The man looked at the boy who had let out a small gasp as he bounced once on his toes. "But only because it's almost your birthday."

Excitement flashed across the boy's face as he looked at his father and then at Kanan. "Can you make the small stones black as well?"

Relief poured through Kanan as he returned the boy's grin. "Black and gold, consider it done."

"You're certain you only need one week?" The man eyed Kanan as though he expected to be swindled.

"I don't enjoy boasting, sir," Kanan began, "but I am proficient."

"Very well, one week."

"You will not be disappointed." Kanan nodded once to the man and then threw a wink at the boy, who beamed back.

He sat, staring, his chair pulled so close to the side of the bed his knees touched the blanket. The sword lay unsheathed; the wine-colored pommel and stone with its shining silver guard stood out in stark contrast to the deep green of the quilt.

A peddler. They bought it from a peddler. What else should he have expected, really? Of course she wouldn't have kept it. Not when every time she looked at it, she thought of him. Not when every memory of him was laced with horror.

He dropped his head into his hands and blew out a long breath. A peddler.

His attention was drawn away from the sword by a knock on his door. He turned his head and watched the wood pulse with each thump. "Kade? You in there?"

Marcus. With a sigh, he stood. "Yeah." He reached the door and pulled it open.

A tall, thin man with close-cropped black hair and dark skin stood on the opposite side of the door, hand poised to knock again.

The man lowered his arm and grinned. "You promised you'd have a drink with me. I've listened to enough of your refusals, and—" The man paused, seeming to notice Kanan's expression. He took in the room as though he expected to find another person there. His eyes settled on the sword before he returned his gaze to Kanan, his grin slipping. "Are you all right?"

Kanan glanced over his shoulder at the sword where it lay mocking him. He huffed out a long breath. "Let's drink."

Marcus' brows rose toward his hairline, his eyes finding the sword again and then Kanan. "Right then, let's drink."

He moved to the side as Kanan stepped through the door and pulled it closed behind him, shutting the sword inside. If only it were that easy to shut his memories away as well. He stalked past the other man and down the stairs, eager to pour a pint or two or three of dark alcohol over his sick heart.

"Kade," Marcus called from behind him, picking up his pace to match Kanan's who was already on the street, his shoes kicking up dust clouds. "Kade? What's up with you?"

Kanan didn't slow his strides. "I don't want to talk about it, Marcus." He hadn't intended for his words to come out quite as resigned as they did.

"It's just that you seem a little upset, and I saw the sword— I just wanted to make sure you're not going to hurt yourself or anything."

Kanan twisted his head toward Marcus, his brows creased together. "Saints, Marcus!"

Marcus lifted his hands in front of him, giving a defensive shrug. His eyes darted around at the few people on the street. "No need to swear. I just don't see you like this very often. "

As if he would hurt himself. Kanan wanted to roll his eyes. He did lower his voice slightly. "I'm not going to hurt myself. I just— I do have a past, and today it reared up in an unexpected way."

"A girl?" Marcus raised a brow. "A guy?"

Kanan exhaled deeply again. Marcus was not going to let this go. "A girl, yes."

Her face filled his mind. The soft, secretive smile she reserved only for him when they were buried in each other sat on her mouth, and his chest tightened to the point that he had to remind himself to breathe.

Saints, he missed her so much it was nearly a tangible thing. As was the grief and regret and utter despair that weighed on him when he thought of the monstrous things Malakai had made him do.

"Kade?" The insistent way Marcus said his name told Kanan that it wasn't the first time he'd called it.

"What?" He hadn't meant for the word to come out like a bark, but he knew it did.

To his credit, Marcus didn't flinch. "Are you sure you're all right?" There was genuine concern in Marcus' question.

Kanan stopped walking in the middle of the street so he could look his friend in the eye. "Are you here as a physician or as a friend looking to have a few drinks?"

Marcus' mouth opened, but he closed it quickly and sighed. "A friend. But sometimes the physician just comes out, you know?"

"I know," Kanan conceded. "But can we keep him at bay, at least for the night? I really don't want to talk about it, and I really do want a drink."

The concern didn't leave Marcus' eyes, but he nodded anyway. "I'll do my best."

"Thank you." He really did just want to have a few drinks and attempt to drown out the past, if only for a few hours.

They walked in silence the rest of the way to the Iron Pony, their preferred tavern. Once they ordered their drinks and had them in hand, they found a seat at a table in the corner of the half-filled room.

Marcus still watched him warily but remained quiet, and for that Kanan was grateful. The only sounds were the low din of patrons conversing and silverware clinking.

He took a long drink from his foamy tankard, savoring the feel of the cool liquid as it slid down his throat. Just four or five more mugs of the dark ale and he didn't expect he would have to worry about anything else until the next day.

Marcus' tankard clanked against the wooden table, a bit of the dark liquid sloshing over the edge. He mopped at the spill. "I almost forgot. Did you hear the news?"

Kanan was eager to hear anything from Marcus that didn't involve himself. "What news?"

"I had a patient come in today, broken toe, you wouldn't believe how he did it. He was standing—"

"Marcus? What news?" Kanan interrupted, knowing Marcus could get off on a tangent and he might never find out.

"Right, sorry." Marcus took another drink. "He was traveling, originally from Doronall."

Kanan's eyes snapped to his friend's. While before he had only been giving Marcus half his attention, the mention of Doronall brought his full focus back to the man.

"He said the Queen is touring the towns. I guess she wants to see her constituency up close." Marcus shrugged. "Maybe we'll make the list."

There was a reason Kanan had chosen Carobas to live. It was small, too small for anyone to notice. Certainly too small for the *Queen* to notice. There was no chance she would show up there.

"Kade? Kade?"

He looked up. Again, Kanan could tell from his tone that Marcus had called his name more than twice.

"What in the Cursed Land is wrong with you tonight?" Marcus' brows were drawn together, and he was clearly the physician once more.

Kanan opened his mouth and drew in a breath to speak, but didn't know what he could say. He gave a small shake of his head. "It's been a long day. And you know the Queen isn't coming here, right?"

"Don't ruin my fun." Kanan knew Marcus was trying to tease, but there was also still concern in the other man's eyes.

"Fun." He knew that derision seeped from his words, but he made no attempt to hide it. "Be careful what you wish for."

Marcus let out a soft laugh. "Did you and the Queen have a bad date or something?"

"Marcus." Kanan let the slight warning edge creep into his voice.

Marcus raised his hands in mock defense. "All right, all right. Maybe you should go home to bed?"

Bed. His bed was occupied by a sword and a sheath and about 90,000 memories. "All the effort you put into getting me out with you and now you're telling me to go home?"

"Well, when I invited you out, I actually thought you might be here."

Kanan drained his tankard. "No, you're right, I'm sorry. I'm just distracted tonight." He suddenly needed air. "I think I am going to go. I'm sorry, Marcus. We'll do this again, I promise." He stood and dug into his pocket, coming up with a handful of coins. They thunked dully as he dropped them on the wooden surface of the table. "It's on me. Goodnight."

Marcus' brows crowded into each other. "Kade—"

"I'll be fine, Marcus, really." Kanan placed a hand on his friend's shoulder as he passed him on his way to the exit. "Goodnight."

"Goodnight," Marcus responded, and it was clear from his voice that he didn't actually believe Kanan would be fine.

Did you enjoy Persuasion of Deceit?

I f you enjoyed this book, please consider leaving a review on Amazon and Goodreads and anywhere else you can think of!

As an indie author, word of mouth is vital. I would be forever grateful. Thank you!

Also, if you would like to keep up with my shenanigans, please feel free to subscribe to my newsletter or find me around the web:

Newsletter: www.antoniakane.com/newsletter

Instagram: www.instagram.com/antoniakaneauthor

Website: www.antoniakane.com

Other books by Antonia Kane

Blood and Fate

Acknowledgements

For as long as I can remember, it's been my dream to be a published author. Over the years, I've written a lot of words. Some original stories and some fanfiction. One day, while reading one of the fanfictions I'd written and thinking about how much I enjoyed the story, I thought, "I wish I could just publish this." And that's where it all started.

I began thinking of ways to turn that fiction into an original work. It went through many draft ideas, one even involved fae, but I finally landed on an idea I thought might work. I began the task of rewriting. Basically, nothing remains of that original fanfiction. And to be honest, not much remains of that original draft. (Kanan and Esrae were a couple in that one, and Logan didn't even exist. What?!) But I'm pretty happy with how it turned out.

I have so many people to thank. Because without them, I wouldn't be where I am, and you wouldn't be holding my life's dream in your hands.

First, I'm so thankful to the Lord for salvation, for His many blessings, and for being an ever-present help in times of trouble. I'm grateful that He gave me a mind full of stories, one that never ever shuts off, and is always working overtime. I've been accused of thinking too much, but I prefer it to not enough. I like the way God made me.

Thanks to my husband for putting up with my craziness. For dealing with my early morning alarms and for taking care of the kids when I disappeared for hours to write. I couldn't have done this without you! I like you.

Thank you to my kids for being awesome. For putting up with me talking about my book when I'm sure you didn't care. For being the inspiration for the names of countries and towns all through the story and for helping me settle on which name mashups to use and which to toss. And for just generally being around to squish and snuggle. I love you to the moon and back, to infinity and beyond!

Thanks to my parents, I am who I am today because of you. I *hope* you see that as a good thing. I'm so thankful for your thoughts and your wisdom. For keeping me alive when I was small. For helping to keep my kids alive while I wrote. For letting me bounce ideas off of you or for just listening when I rambled excitedly about my story.

Thanks to my first editor, Savanna Roberts. Girl, you made this book what it is, absolutely and unquestionably. I can probably blame a good 50,000 words of this thing on your notes. And they're definitely the better words. Thank you!

Thanks to my extra editors, Mariella Taylor and Hanah Stevens. I appreciate the extra sets of eyes and thoughts when I, like a crazy person, decided to revise this story. You made it better and I appreciate it!

Thanks to my cover designer, Mulan Jiang. You are AMAZING! I was blown away by this cover and the level of detail you went into. You literally created Raven's sword! I mean, you made it, it's right there! Thank you so much for your work. You're my favorite cover designer and I can't wait to work with you again!

Thank you, Sarah Montanari. Thank you for being the first person besides me to read this story and tell me what you thought. It took a lot for me to share that tiny, sad, first(ish) draft with anyone and I appreciated your positive response. It gave me the courage to push on with this book and find an editor.

Thanks to my Yoda! Carol Beth Anderson, you have been sooo much help, you just don't even know! I so appreciate you letting me come to you with random questions, and you taking the time to answer them all so very well. Admit it, I'm the reason you wrote *Early Readers Catch the Worms: How Alpha, Beta & ARC Readers Can Help You Publish a Better Novel*? *Wink* Ugh, here comes Toni again, I'm just going to write this girl a book. Haha. But seriously, your advice has been so helpful and so was your book! Also, for your notes on my blurb! Blurbs are hard and you made mine better!

Thanks to my beta team, Brittany Bateman, Marilyn Bordelon, Ruby J. Gay, Caroline Hannam, Cassie Hicks, Hope Moore, Donna Wall and Oana Zanfir.

You were all so helpful and encouraging! Thank you so much for taking the time to read and for helping to make this book better. I am in your debt.

Finally, thanks so much to you, the reader! Thank you for taking a chance on my little book. For picking it up off the shelf, or dropping it into your online cart, and cracking open the pages. You are holding my dream in your hands, and by reading, you're participating in that dream! This story is so deep in my heart, and I adore that you're sharing it with me. I hope you're entertained, and shocked, and fall in love with the characters like I did. It's pretty wild to me to think that your mind has brought this story to life by creating pictures and images that I'll never even see. The magic of books!

I'm wildly grateful to everyone who has had a hand in helping to create, to promote, and to encourage this work of fiction. On to the next!

About the Author

Antonia began writing fan fiction at a very early age and has never looked back.

She loves writing fiction, escaping into new worlds, and getting to know new characters. Writing is a form of therapy for Antonia, and she thrives on it, even when it's difficult.

Along with writing, she's an avid reader and is always on the hunt for her next book boyfriend. Of which she has a finely curated collection.

When she's not writing or reading, she's Mom to three boys and two dogs. She's also active in her church. For obvious reasons, coffee is her best friend.

Antonia and her family live happily nestled in the center of Oklahoma.

Kanan and Raven
Art by:
Incendiosketches

Torren and Aster
Art by:
Oblivionsdream

PERSUASION OF DECEIT

ANTONIA KANE